the disenchanted

By Budd Schulberg

What Makes Sammy Run?

The Harder They Fall

Random House · New York

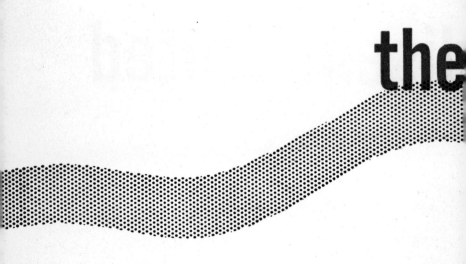
the

disenchanted

Budd Schulberg

Fifth Printing

The quotation on page 86 is from T. S. Eliot's "The Hollow Men," and the one on page 108 is from "The Waste Land." Both quotations are from Mr. Eliot's *Collected Poems 1909–1935*, copyright, 1936, by Harcourt, Brace and Company, Inc., and are used with their permission.

The lyric on page 230 is from "Nagasaki" by Harry Warren and Mort Dixon. Copyright, 1928, by Remick Music Corporation. Reprinted by permission.

Published in New York by Random House, Inc., and simultaneously in Toronto, Canada, by Random House of Canada, Limited.

Manufactured in the United States of America by H. Wolff

Designer: Ernst Reichl

For Arthur and Rosemary

"The wondrous figure of that genius had long haunted me, and circumstances into which I needn't here enter had within a few years contributed much to making it vivid . . . . More interesting still than the man—for the dramatist at any rate—is the S. T. Coleridge TYPE; *so what I was to do was merely to recognise the type, to borrow it, to re-embody and freshly place it; an ideal under the law of which I could but cultivate a free hand. I proceeded to do so; I reconstructed the scene and the figures—I had my own idea, which required, to express itself, a new set of relations—though, when all is said, it had assuredly taken the recorded, transmitted person, the image embalmed in literary history, to fertilise my fancy . . . . Therefore let us have here as little as possible about its 'being' Mr. This or Mrs. That. If it adjusts itself with the least truth to its new life it can't possibly be either. . . ."*—HENRY JAMES; from his preface to "The Lesson of the Master and Other Tales."

the disenchanted

1

It's the waiting, Shep was thinking. You wait to get inside the gate, you wait outside the great man's office, you wait for your agent to make the deal, you wait for the assignment, you wait for instructions on how to write what they want you to write, and then, when you finish your treatment and turn it in, you wait for that unique contribution to art, the story conference.

Older Hollywood writers knew how to get the most out of this three- or four-week lag. They caught up on their mail or did a little proselytizing for the Guild or wrote an original against the rainy season or went in for matinees or worked out the bugs in their tennis game (with secretaries trained to page them promptly at the Club if *the call* should come).

Shep just waited. At first he had brought in a couple of books, *Red Star Over China*, Malraux' *Man's Hope*, but it was no use. Not with that phone at his elbow about to ring any moment. For over three weeks now Shep had arrived at his cubicle on the top floor of the Writers' Building at nine-thirty and departed at six: 105 hours. He had kept track of them with the desperate patience of a prisoner in solitary—with nothing to do but await the verdict of Victor Milgrim, known on the lot as "The Czar of All the Rushes."

Six months before, young Shep had come home to Hollywood from the hills of New England and the ivy-covered walls of Webster with a summa cum laude in English and the conviction that movies, as the great new folk art, needed young men with his combination of talent and ideals.

But nobody had been deceived. As his agent had explained, somewhat petulantly, "Look, kid, they won't even make *It Can't Happen Here* when they bought it already and that's got a name behind it. So if you wanna put yourself in a selling position, go write yourself a hunk a pure entertainment."

Shep had a girl he was interested in marrying and his old man had a studio car-rental business he was interested in avoiding. So, for the moment, he had knocked out a slick little trick called *Love on Ice*. It was not exactly what Professor Crofts had predicted for him when presenting him with the Senior Prize for Literary Composition, but it was, in Shep's young and optimistic mind, that most convenient of apologetics: the means to an end.

Hired to develop his story for a brief trial period as a "junior writer" (Shep found sardonic pleasure in his official title) at a sub-respectable hundred dollars a week, he had been encouraged when word filtered through to him that "the Boss is hot on the idea" and wanted to know how rapidly Shep could "do a treatment." Shep had received five calls from the front office in the last ten days to learn how soon Mr. Milgrim could have it. He had staggered across the finish line at ten-thirty one Saturday night under pressure of a Red Arrow messenger who had arrived at seven to rush the scenario to Mr. Milgrim in Palm Springs by motorcycle. Then this feverish tempo had abruptly slow-timed into three weeks without any reaction, three weeks of maddening silence. This was what oldtimers had learned to accept as they accepted the great man's eccentric hours and his erratic outbursts of good taste.

Now another fruitless day had passed and Shep was on his way to the little self-operating elevator when he heard his phone ringing. One minute to six. Just time to meet his girl, grab a bite and go on to the rally for the Lincoln Brigade. That damn phone. Should he go back? It was just possible that it *could* be—

At last. Miss Dillon herself, the great man's secretary. "Well, young man, congratulations. HE just mentioned your name. He wants you to . . ."

"Don't say it—*stand by*."

"Lucky you. He says he definitely wants to get with you tonight."

"Any idea what time I'll get in?"

"*Oh*. You *naughty boy*." It was Joe Penner now. Miss Dillon liked her conversations to brush lightly here and there the electrified fencing of sex. It was a form of corruption, Shep recognized, these little verbal sops to His secretary's inclinations. "Now be a stout fella and stand by."

4

So Shep was to keep himself available for a conference that might take place in ten minutes or ten hours. The best Milgrim could do was to promise "to work you in" some time during office hours that always lasted until midnight and frequently extended until daybreak.

Shep felt a twinge of disgust at the sense of panic that fluttered in his stomach, the sense of impending crisis. He had pretended to laugh at the "option jitters" that almost always seized the writers as they went into conference with the head man. Shep and his girl even had a phrase for it: "The final degradation of the artist." Children of depression, guided by hearsay knowledge of Marx and Freud, they were always having to sum things up and fit them neatly into cubby holes.

Now that *word* had come at last, Shep tried to fight down over-anxiousness. He wanted Miss Dillon to hear the little shrug in his voice. "Okay, dig me at the pub across the street."

At the curb outside the studio entrance, Shep glanced at the headlines:

COWBOY ACTOR RUNS AMUCK

———

SMASH REDS IN BARCELONA

Another republic was going down in blood; the whole precarious structure of peaceful living was threatened now. Shep wondered at himself for clinging to *Love on Ice,* this flimsy raft that would float or sink at the *word* of a very big man in a rather small pond.

Uneasily, he entered "Stage One," hangout for Hollywood's version of the hewers of wood and drawers of water, the vital but anonymous cogs whose names never win mention in the celebrated columns, whose romances or indiscretions are never set forth between mischievous dots. These were assistant directors, cutters, bit players, second cameramen, sound men, juicers, grips, special effects men, Hollywood's exclusive proletariat, earning three to ten thousand a year, whose hands literally *make* pictures.

Shep had his usual Scotch with a finger of soda and listened idly to the chatter along the bar. It was all solid shop-talk from technicians who could never quite relax from the pressure of their jobs, a blowing off of steam against superiors with whom they dared not publicly disagree. But here in the privacy of their own place, with two-drink confidence, it was:

—"That lucky bastard, if he's a director I'm Shirley Temple!"

—"So I says, listen you bitch, I says, I don't give a flop if you are Box Office Queen for 1938—you'll be Queen of my S-list if you don't move your keester out of that dressing room and take your place for the next scene."

—"Three times I try to tell him about the mike shadow but the stubborn Lymie nipplehead just goes ahead and shoots it anyway."

Shep looked up over the bar at that stock embellishment of all studio bistros, the collection of publicity stills autographed by stars present and past. Together on the top row were Phyllis Haver, Sue Carol and Sally O'Neill. He leaned forward and squinted to make out the name of a fourth beauty with the bangs and spit-curls that were glamour in the Twenties. Marie Astaire. The old names, the old styles in feminine lure never lost their fascination for Shep. At Hollywood High back in Twenty-nine he had momentarily caught the coat-tails of an era. Like the college boys, some of whom already had given up these hi-jinks, he had waited impatiently for each new issue of *College Humor* and had felt the compulsion to inscribe those witty sayings of the period on his slicker, his cords and his second-hand Chevvy. His first faint flush of adolescent desire had been aroused by Jacqueline Logan in *The Bachelor Girl* and *Midnight Madness*. *Midnight Madness*. Ah, there was a film to stir the blood of awakening high-school freshmen.

In the corner, quietly scoring Shep's mood, an unobtrusive little man played a portable organ that the customers acknowledged only by raising their voices to drown it out. This instrument, like its musician, Lew Luria, had been salvaged from the silent days when the organ, accompanied by a soft violin, was indispensable for summoning from the actors the emotions de-

manded by the script and the director. If you bought Lew a drink
he would tell you how he used to get Clara Bow ready for her
crying scenes by playing "Rockabye Baby." But just as Lew's real
profession had died with silent pictures, so had his repertoire. His
favorites were "Mary Lou" and "Avalon Town." When he
wanted to play something more up to date, it was usually "The
Wedding of the Painted Doll" or "Broadway Melody."

Shep had another drink and went to call his girl, working late
at another studio farther up the boulevard. "Damn it, Shep"
(never darling or sweetheart or honey because she said the
movies had worn the shine off the sweet words), "I'll be a little
late, at three o'clock, a whole stinking magazine novel to read
and synopsize—of course they *had* to have it tonight, wouldn't
you know?—Faith Baldwin—*Four Daughters* all over again
without the Epstein dialogue—God, I hate women writers—
Parker and Hellman of course, they don't count, they're just
writers—won't it be awful when my grandchildren ask me what
I was doing the day Barcelona fell and I have to say I was synop-
sizing Faith Baldwin!"

All of this took less time to say than most people would need
for Hello, how are you. She talked her own kind of shorthand.
There was never quite enough time to fit in all the different
ideas.

Snap judgments, damning criticisms, whopping generalizations were part of her charm, signs of the form youthful
vitality had taken in a year when crisis was everybody's breakfast
food.

"Listen, Sara, I can't make it at all. Milgrim called. I've got to
stand by."

"Hooray. You mean he's actually read it?"

"I suppose so. But Christ knows what time he'll see me. Let's
just hope he likes it."

"Now don't be a worrier. Milgrim will love it. Why shouldn't
he? He's made the same story at least twice before."

"Nice talk," Shep said, half aware of the increasing influence
of the studio idiom. "Think I'll trade you in for a woman who
looks up to me."

"That'd be dull," she said. "Gotta go now. Faith Baldwin's leaning over my shoulder. Call me after you've had your audience, no matter how late."

Shep wandered back to the bar. He sent a highball over to Lew Luria and Lew played some old Rodgers and Hart things he had always admired: "I took one *look* at you . . ."

There was a call for Shep from Milgrim's office. He showed his youth in his effort at nonchalance.

"The Great White Father is looking at rushes now."

He smiled at Miss Dillon's familiar mockery. There was always that air of amused boredom in her voice from having to white-lie and alibi and brush off so many suitors for Milgrim's attention.

"Peggy, I'm pining for you. How long would you say it'll be?"

Studio life prescribed set patterns of behavior. Stylized flirtation was the rule of the game. Miss Dillon was so accustomed to flattery and elaborate sweettalk that she would think she were being insulted if addressed with ordinary courtesy.

"Shep, for you, darling, I'll try my best to get you in by 10.30."

"I love you," he said automatically, as, six months ago, he would have said "Thanks."

At the bar familiar faces were saying familiar things. "So I said . . . I went right up and told him . . . I'm the kind of person who . . ." The atmosphere vibrated with the first person singular. Egos, like corks submerged by studio routine and held down by stronger personalities, were bobbing up all over the place now that the pressure had been removed.

Half an hour later Miss Dillon was on the phone again.

"Can you stand a small shock, darling? The boss-man has just started running *Hurricane*. He wants to make sure his sand storm is bigger, louder and more destructive than the Goldwyn blow. So stand by, honey-chile."

"My God, he's going to run the whole thing? Couldn't he just see the last reel?"

"You know my Boss. Celluloid-happy. He just loves to watch them moom-pitchurs . . . Hello, are you there old boy?"

"I didn't say anything. I just sighed."

"Want me to send you over some bennies?"

"Had two already. I'm vibrating like a hopped-up Ford."

"Relax, relax. Who's Victor Milgrim? What's he got that God ain't got except three Academy Awards?"

"May the Lord—I mean Milgrim—bless you, Peggy. You're God's gift to a persecuted minority—the junior writer."

"Pul-lease," Miss Dillon hammed it. "Do not take the name of my Boss in vain."

Peggy Dillon was a good kid, Shep conceded. Just too many late nights, too many benzedrines and too many witty or would-be witty gentleman callers who practiced their art of seduction on her to sharpen their technique for their real quarry, Victor Milgrim.

This time the bartender, who picked up bit parts in pictures, said "What can I do you for?" It made Shep conscious of how much Hollywood talk fell into familiar speech patterns. It disturbed him when he caught the Hollywoodisms in his own speech. "How do you LIKE that?" "Good—it's but terrific!" The social and financial extravagance was reflected in verbal extravagance. People were forever calling pictures *sensational* that were just all right; men called each other *honey* and *sweetheart* when they weren't lovers or even friends. It's a world fenced in with exclamation points, Shep thought, a world where hyperbole is the mother-tongue.

We haven't made men out of celluloid, we screen writers —we've made celluloid out of men. We're both Prometheus and the vulture who feeds on his liver.

Shep was indulging a young man's dream of rescuing this captive giant when the phone called him back once more to studio reality.

"Shep darling, I hope you're in an awfully good mood."

It was a little late in the evening for Miss Dillon's whimsies but Shep played along. "You mean . . . as they say in the movies."

"The boss-man was just about to have me buzz you when Yvonne Darré called. Seems she's all in a tizzy over the Empress Eugenie script and she can't get her beauty sleep until she comes down and cries on his shoulder. My poor boss. Sometimes I almost feel sorry for him."

9

"I feel a helluva lot sorrier for me. When do I get in? Some time in July, 1945?"

"Just stand by, Buster. He'll probably get to you around midnight."

"A junior writer," Shep said, "is such a low form of animal life that it reproduces by mitosis."

"I don't know what that means but I doubt if you could get it by the Hays Office."

"Mitosis, my dear Miss Dillon, is the least pleasurable method of reproducing oneself. You just swell up and split in two."

"Is that what you learn in college?"

"You learn all kinds of reproductive methods in college."

"You go right home and wash your mind out with soap."

"Suppose I try Scotch?" he said.

Taking his place at the bar, he drank strategically, trying to reach just that right peak of confidence without sliding down the other side into self-delusion. The waiting, his mind groaned, the interminable waiting. He sent another drink over to Lew Luria and the little, almost-forgotten man smiled formally and began to play "Sweeter Than Sweet."

Shep was chasing his Scotch with coffee to keep awake when, a little before one, just seven hours after the initial call, Miss Dillon phoned him to hurry over.

2

Shep had been in the Victor Milgrim office only twice before, for two minutes of routine charm when he was first hired, and for a ten-minute monologue by Milgrim on his ideas for developing *Love on Ice* when Shep was assigned to screenplay. The proportions of the room met the generous standards of Hollywood's inner circle, but Victor Milgrim had proud confidence in the superiority of taste that marked his furnishings. It was all authentic Chippendale personally purchased for Mr. Milgrim by Lord Ronald Acworth, World-Wide's British representative. As in his film productions and his racing stable, Milgrim had demanded the very best. Not even previously imported Chippendale would satisfy him, lest he should be inadvertently duped by reproduction. The possibility that a copy could be rung in on him from the British Isles did not suggest itself to him. Although his knowledge of England was limited to a few ceremonial tours, Milgrim had an abiding, almost mystical devotion to the Empire. Several people had seen him cry unabashedly, even ostentatiously, at Edward's abdication speech.

The mellowed mahogany was set off by rich wine-red carpeting, eighteenth-century brass and royal blue draperies selected by one of Hollywood's more discriminating decorators, Fanny Brice. One entire wall was lined with books in fine leather bindings, mostly sets, Shakespeare, Thackeray, Hardy, Galsworthy, Kipling, Shaw, with a few of the American bestsellers that had inspired Milgrim films. One of the sets elegantly bound in full morocco consisted of all the scenarios of Milgrim productions, some thirty-seven of them, all with the name of Victor Milgrim stamped across the backbone, the embossed gold letters seeming to add the name of Milgrim to the immortals among whom it stood. On the walls behind the great mahogany desk were handsomely framed 11″ × 16″ autographed photographs of President Roosevelt, Herbert Hoover, Ambassador Kennedy, the Duke of

Windsor, Bernard Baruch, Winston Churchill, James B. Conant, Thomas Lamont and Governor Merriam of California. Mussolini, on whom Milgrim had made an official call in 1935 when his film *Moll Flanders* had won the Italian cinema award, had recently been removed. Now that Merriam had at last gone down in defeat to make way for the candidate who inherited the following of Upton Sinclair, the big bald head with the dull political face would probably be removed too. Milgrim was nominally a Republican, just as he was nominally a monogamist, but his first loyalty was to success, contemporaneous success. Even last week's would not do. Having fought his way up from borderline illiteracy to the point where he could discuss literature with Somerset Maugham in an accent that had more in common with Maugham than with his childhood neighbors, it was only natural that he should identify himself with and cultivate the main line of prestige. Archbishop Cantwell, Henry Luce, young Vittorio Mussolini, fresh from aerial triumphs over naked Abyssinians, whoever held, for almost any reason at all, positions of prominence, were honored guests of the studio.

The wide expanse of the Milgrim desk supported hundreds of items, pieces in an endless game played between Milgrim and Miss Dillon. He was always snatching things up and laying them down on the wrong pile; she was forever rearranging so that the huge desk should not appear cluttered. At the moment Miss Dillon had gained the upper hand. In fifteen or twenty neat piles were scenarios to read; multiple note-pads to catch the happier results of "thinking out loud"; the schedule of appointments for the week, professional, social and the large category in which these intermingled; regret-letters to sign, letters to schools and institutions, flattering letters to people who in large ways or small could be of service to World-Wide Productions; a letter to an old friend refusing a loan of five thousand dollars; a check for $7800 lost to Val Steffany, the agent, at the last Saturday-night poker game; several advertising lay-outs for *Desired* from which he was to pick the one he liked best; the stills of a dozen undiscovered ingenues from whose ranks Milgrim hoped to select the ideal *Heather* for his next five-million-dollar epic; a file of B.O. returns on his last picture and the week's reviews; the evening papers with those parts marked by Miss Miller that would be of special interest to him (Miss Miller, waiting for her chance to be promoted to assistant producer, even red-penciled story possibilities in topics of the day).

On one corner of the desk was a framed title page of the scenario of his first triumph, *Orphans of the Night,* autographed by the entire company. The director of *Orphans* was a charity case at the Motion Picture Relief Home now and the female star, Betty Grant (about whom people would say occasionally now *What ever happened* to Betty Grant?), had just been told by Miss Dillon that Mr. Milgrim was engaged in finishing one picture and planning another and could not say when he would be free to give her an appointment. On the other corner of the desk was a color photograph of a creamy full-length Alexander Brook painting of Mrs. Milgrim, the former English beauty Maud Leslie, painted some years ago, though not so many as the glossy youthfulness of the face would indicate.

Milgrim was tilted back in his chair with his hands to his eyes in a gesture of weariness when Shep approached. "Hello, Shep," he said (last time it had been "Stearns"), rising to extend a limp hand that had been for too many hours making notes, turning synopsis pages, picking up phones, shaking other hands and emphasizing decisions or suggesting emotional nuances. *Who's Who* had Milgrim down for not quite forty, though his hair was thinning rapidly and what remained had long been prematurely gray. He was not a handsome man but he dressed in such excellent taste and had such an abundance of personal magnetism that he would have been immensely attractive to women even without the glamour of his office.

"How about a cup of coffee?" He buzzed for Miss Dillon. "My doctor tells me to cut out coffee, but how the hell can I stand this grind if I don't take something to keep me going?"

He smiled the smile that melted hard-trading agents and headstrong directors, softened bitchy stars, warmed cynical playwrights, and charmed beautiful women.

Shep just sat there waiting. There was nothing to say. Milgrim had seemed to make it clear that he did not really consider this a two-way conversation between equals. Milgrim was being the good guy, the rare creature of success who manages to remain a regular fellow, who somehow achieves high office without the usual medieval maneuvering. Shep was conscious of admiring a performance rather than responding to his appeal. He merely wondered when Milgrim would work the conversation around to *Love on Ice.* He wished he could come right out, lay it on the line, *Well, Milgrim, am I in or out?*

Milgrim sipped his coffee slowly, and Shep could see that he even drew satisfaction from these periods of let-down, as the cross-country runner measures his achievements by the muscle aches and the painful breathing. "The trouble with me, Shep," Milgrim began a confession the young man was sure he had recited many times before, "is that I put too much of myself into every picture. Too many details, too many responsibilities, it's what killed Thalberg. But I'm not just trying to make another Box Office Champion. I've got to make sure every picture with my name on it"—

—"Five or six times," Shep thought irreverently.

—"has the Milgrim *feel* to it."

"*Playboy* was a marvelous job," Shep put in for punctuation. "I honestly didn't think you could change so much of what Synge wrote and still come so close to the original flavor."

Shep heard himself say this as if he were sitting on his own lap, both dummy and ventriloquist. Why, he wondered, are we left no area between outright rebellion and groveling sycophancy?

"I dreamt of doing *Playboy* ever since I saw the Abbey Players do it on Broadway when I was only an assistant producer." Milgrim rewarded Shep with another smile for having introduced one of his favorite subjects. "I knew I could lick it, even if it did take me twenty-three writers, and I wound up having to write most of it myself. You don't make pictures like *Playboy* for money. No, that was a labor of love, just like *I Die But Once.*" *Die* was last year's historical fiction bonanza, which had just been released. "Naturally I'm not in business to lose money. But something Irving told me when I was a kid I've never forgotten—" the voice lowered in reverence as the local saint was invoked—

14

" 'Pictures are more than a great business, Victor. They're a social responsibility.' "

While Milgrim paused dramatically, Shep tried to imagine what possible connection there could be between social responsibility and *Love on Ice*.

Love on Ice seemed to be completely sidetracked in the teeming depot of the Milgrim mind. "Shep, the trouble with this business is that there's too many people in it who have no real loyalty to it. All they're doing is selling their minds to the highest bidder. They have the same sort of contempt for pictures that whores have for the act of two-dollar passion. They just don't have the foresight to see that our medium is going to begin where the other arts leave off."

Like all first-line salesmen, Milgrim was his own best customer. The coffee and the benzedrine, brewed together on the inextinguishable blue flame of his ego, were producing a characteristic regeneration. Throwing off the weight of fourteen hectic hours in this office, he rose from his chair and began his famous pacing. Although Shep knew he was saying whatever came into his head, his words had the timbre of brilliance. Since the death of Thalberg, so many people had turned to him in their need for a substitute genius that he had answered the call.

"Twenty years from now, if we can keep improving our product as much as we have since the War, the Hemingways, Fitzgeralds, the Wolfes and the Hallidays will start out as screenplay writers instead of novelists. Wait and see if I'm not right, Shep. The great American writing of the future will be done directly for the screen."

Shep, waiting for Milgrim to come to the point, wondered how much this heady alchemist knew about "the great American writing." It was studio-writer talk that the only form of writing with which Milgrim was acquainted was the synopsis. Perhaps his knowledge of modern American literature had come to him in that same easy-to-swallow capsule form. But he had the chameleon talent for taking on the intellectual coloration of whatever idea he happened to fasten onto. An accomplished rustler of the mind, he could sneak into other people's intellectual pastures, ride herd on their ideas and quickly brand and market them as his own.

"*The Sun Also Rises* reads like a screenplay . . ." Milgrim had this bone in his mouth, Shep conceded. But where was he running with it? "Almost all dialogue, dramatic climaxes, description stripped to bare essentials. And *Farewell to Arms*—that was pure pictures. And wasn't Fitzgerald writing movies when he had Gatsby staring across the Sound to the green light at the end of Daisy's dock? And look at Halliday—God knows he wrote like an angel—you could never get on film the marvelous style, but the characters, the *scenes*—the party in the Nogent hospital in *Friends and Foes,* and that drunken ticker-tape dream in *The Night's High Noon* . . . I'd make that in a flash—if I could only lick the Hays Office angle . . ."

Only Shep's outer ear was listening to Milgrim now. Withdrawing from this room, from the self-hypnotic music of the Milgrim profundities, from the momentary anxieties of his own film career, he was with his own thoughts of Manley Halliday. That assignment in American Lit—*The Night's High Noon.* He had taken it back to the dorm to skim through for a quiz next day, found himself reading and marveling at every line, and had hurried to the library as soon as it was open to get more of Halliday.

Whenever Shep thought about the Twenties after that—and he thought about them often, drawn toward them with an incomprehensible nostalgia for a world he never knew—he was really thinking about *The Night's High Noon, Friends and Foes, The Light Fantastic* and even the lesser novels and short story and essay collections.

As a child of his time, Shep belonged with the school of social significance, but at odd moments, like the clandestine cigarette smokers behind the school-yard wall, he would sneak off to his admiration for Halliday, the grace of the prose, the interest in people rather than programs, manners rather than class doctrine.

"By the way, have you ever read Halliday?" Milgrim was asking. "Do you like his stuff?"

For a moment Shep just looked at him. "Do I like his stuff? I think he was up there with the best we had."

16

The Milgrim smile was a little smug and possessive. He always smiled for things he had or for impressions he wished to make.

"Think you'd like to work with Halliday?"

"Work with Halliday! Are you kidding? He's dead, isn't he?"

Milgrim looked at the young man and smiled the smile of superior knowledge. "He's in the next room reading your script."

The rest of what Milgrim said was lost on Shep. Manley Halliday *in the next room*. (*Manley Halliday* in the next room.)

"If he likes the set-up he's going to work on it. I thought I'd keep you on with him. The scene is your college, so you should be able to help out a good deal with the background. And I'd like you to check over his dialogue. Probably a lot of new expressions you can drop in to make the kids sound right. Like this word *meatball* you use, and *wet*. Manley" (the chilling effect of this casual use of the great name drew Shep back to the conversation) "may be a little out of date. Come on in and meet him."

For the second time that day Shep felt himself going through the motions of simulated casualness. Shaken, mystified, he followed Milgrim through the doorway.

3

Manley Halliday was reading the scenario when Shep entered. He did not look up until they came half way across the room to him, and when he did Shep saw an old young face with ashen complexion. Could this be Manley Halliday?

Halliday lifted himself out of the deep red leather chair with stiff good manners. Shep was surprised to see that the author was several inches shorter than the image in his mind, not much over five six, a slender, delicately made man with the beginning of a small paunch.

"Glad to meet you, sir," Shep heard him say under his breath. But the soft hand hurriedly withdrawn, the disinterested flick of the eyes drew the meaning of the words.

Shep's own response embarrassed him even though he was helpless to temper it. "It's a great pleasure to meet *you*, Mr. Halliday."

"Manley, it turns out he's one of your fans," Milgrim said with a laugh.

Shep felt he was being offered up to Manley Halliday. He wished Milgrim had waited for him to tell Halliday in his own way.

Halliday acknowledged the compliment with an almost imperceptible bow and the faintest suggestion of a smile, reflecting disbelief rather than pleasure.

"Manley, I thought I'd keep young Stearns on to collaborate with you—if that's all right with you, of course . . ."

Shep had never seen Milgrim hide his own positiveness under so much deference. Even the way he said *Manley* seemed to imply not a casual familiarity but a respectful request for permission to call him Manley. The first time Shep heard it, he thought Milgrim had gone out of character. But then he realized that Manley Halliday was a celebrity from another world, to be admired like Baruch and Lamont and Einstein. Crawford and Hitchcock and Cary Grant were the everyday commodities of Milgrim's world. But Manley Halliday, even ten years late, even on the skids, was a self-made businessman-artist's ideal of eloquence, of literacy raised to the level of Pulitzer Prizes and Modern Library editions.

Manley Halliday's *collaborator*. When Milgrim made the suggestion, Shep tried to meet the author's eyes and smile to signal his realization of the preposterousness of the idea. But Halliday was polite, in that mannered way associated with capes and walking sticks, in that way which leaves one totally incapable of perceiving the intention behind the social mask.

"I haven't collaborated with anybody since—Lord, since my roommate and I wrote the Hasty Pudding show of Fifteen."

He paused, and then added, with what Shep feared was reluctance, "But I'll be glad to try it with Mr. Stearns."

Shep noticed for the first time how Halliday talked. The words came up out of a face that paid no attention to them. Only what had to be said was said. It was said nicely, with a care for amenities, yet accompanied by the unspoken hope that what had just been said would suffice.

In a delayed take—as Milgrim would have said—the producer seemed to realize the incongruity of teaming Halliday with young Stearns, for he hastened to explain, "You may find writing for the movies a little different from your novels, Manley. Most of our writers, even some of the big playwrights, find it easier to have someone for a sounding board." Sensitive to the possible effect of this on Shep's morale, Milgrim added, "And then if there's anything I don't like I can always blame young Stearns here."

Milgrim placed his hand on Shep's shoulder and squeezed it gently to emphasize the good nature of the little joke. But Shep was still too overcome at finding a dead god transformed into a live colleague to care whether he was called collaborator, copy boy or male stenographer. He had even forgotten to worry about the suspended sentence his script apparently had received. All he could think of just then was that he was to have an opportunity

19

to know Manley Halliday, talk to him about his work and discuss the Twenties toward which he felt this incomprehensible nostalgia.

"Well, if everything's all right with you, Manley, I'll leave you two geniuses to work out how you want to get started," Milgrim said, cheerfully managing to pay homage to Halliday on one knee while having his fun at Shep's expense with the other. "Manley, we'd like you to come for dinner soon. Maud will call you. And by the way she's dying to have you autograph your books for her. She's a great collector of autographed books. And she's always said you and Louie Bromfield are her favorite American authors."

Halliday had answered Milgrim with another little dip of his head and a muttered something about being delighted of course.

When Milgrim left them alone they looked at each other—a little guiltily, Shep thought. Why did scenarists so often get that feeling of fellow conspirators?

"I'm afraid I haven't quite finished your script. I'm a very slow reader."

Shep wanted to tell Halliday that the script wasn't really worth his time, that it was just a routine college musical written on order. But then he remembered, almost with a start, that Halliday was being hired to work on *Love on Ice*. Halliday was being paid to read *Love on Ice*. Shep wondered why. He wondered what could have happened to Halliday that would bring him down to this.

He watched Halliday's face as the author supported his head with his thumb to his cheek and two fingers pressed against his forehead. A familiar pose, Shep thought, and then he remembered the jacket of *The Night's High Noon,* when Halliday was the wonder boy of the Twenties, the triple-threat Merriwell of American letters, less real than the most romantic of his heroes, the only writer who could win the approval of Mencken and Stein and make fifty thousand a year doing it and look like Wally Reid. From the rear flap of that book, Shep remembered the exquisite chiseling of the face, the theatrically perfect features, the straight, classical nose, the mouth so beautiful as to suggest effeminacy, the fine forehead, the slicked-down hair parted in the middle. Only an extra delicacy, a refined quality of sensitivity (was it the faint look of amusement uncorrupted by self-satisfaction about the eyes?) marked the difference between that face on the flap and the favorite face of the period. Strange, Shep thought, how faces pass in and out of style like fashions in clothes. The style to which Halliday belonged was the magazine illustration's, the matinee idol's and the movie star's in 1925, the sleek, shiny, Arrow-Collar perfection, finely etched, sharp-featured, a prettyboy face drawn with the symmetry of second-rate art, pear-shaped, with a straight nose, cleft chin, dark hair parted smartly down the middle, combed back and plastered down with vaseline or sta-comb, the face of someone who has just stepped out of a Turkish bath miraculously recovered from the night before, the clean-cut face of the American sheik, the smoothie, the face of the young sophisticate who has gone places and done things, yet a face curiously unlived in, the face of Neil Hamilton, the face Doug Fairbanks could never quite conceal behind his gay moustaches and Robin Hood's cap, the face Harold Lloyd parodied, that Ramon Navarro and Valentino gave slinky, south-of-the-border imitations of; this was the face of the Twenties, turned in now on a newer, more durable model as befitted more spartan times, but still worn by Manley Halliday like a favorite suit that has not only passed out of style but has worn too thin even for a tailor to patch. The bone structure was still there to remind you of the days when women admirers pasted rotogravure pictures of him inside their copies of his books as others prized photos of John Gilbert and Antonio Moreno. But the hair, still combed back though parted on the side now, was gray and thinning; the famous turquoise eyes had washed out to a milky nondescript; the skin had lost color and tone; the face that Stieglitz had photographed, Davidson had sculptured and Derain painted with such flattering verisimilitude had lost its luster. The association pained Shep but he suddenly thought of the famous juvenile of the Twenties he had seen on the lot the day before, whose receding hairline and expanding waist-line could not alter the fact that he would be a juvenile, irreprievably, until he died.

Reading very slowly, as though reading were a physical effort, the turning of a page a challenge to his strength, Halliday finished the script. Then he read the last page again, stalling for time.

"Well, Stearns, I don't suppose you expect to win any Academy Awards with this but" (Shep saw the attempt at a smile) "I suppose it could be worse. I think we may be able to make a nice little valentine out of it."

But this was the last thing Shep wanted to talk about with Manley Halliday.

"Mr. Halliday, if we stay here and talk, Milgrim'll think we're standing by and grab us for a conference. He seems to be queer for these early-morning conferences. So what do you say we go catch a drink somewhere?"

That was as casual as he could make it; he was eager for the answer.

"I'm not drinking any more."

Halliday wished he had put it less revealingly. To correct the impression, he added hurriedly: "Diabetes. Doctor's orders."

"Then how about a spot of coffee?"

Halliday saw the interest in the young man's eyes.

"Well, I should have been in bed hours ago—more doctor's orders, but maybe one cup of coffee—a quick cup of coffee," he amended. He took a childish—or was it an author's—pride in being able to talk the language of this new generation.

"Swell. How about the Derby?"

"Don't they close at two?"

"Just the bar. I think we can still get in if we move fast."

Shep reached the Derby entrance at least five minutes before Halliday. Two newsboys, a legless veteran and a paralytic, guarded the entrance like deformed sentries. Halliday drove up in an ancient Lincoln roadster. Vintage '33 or '34, Shep pegged it. What's he doing with that beat-up old wreck? The paint had faded, one fender was crumpled and the motor obviously labored under difficulties.

Halliday came toward him out of the darkness of the parking lot and Shep saw why he seemed so out of place here in Beverly Hills; his appearance made no concessions to local fashions. He wore a dark wool overcoat, much too heavy even for the brisk

California nights, and a gray homburg. He looked like Fifth Avenue, around the Plaza, on a snappy Sunday afternoon. The image of a ghost came back to Shep as he watched Halliday approach in the pale blur of the street lamps. The ghost goes west, he thought irreverently. Then eagerness hurried him forward.

"Well, did you think I wasn't going to make it? The Smithsonian's been trying to get that bus away from me for years."

It was forced gaiety, delivered with that forced smile that was beginning to make Shep feel uncomfortable.

The Derby was almost empty. Just a few stragglers, a middle-aged man whose face was no match for his sporty clothes, with a very young showgirl, and two men in their middle thirties whom Shep recognized as a successful writing team.

They couldn't help watching their waitress' legs as she strode toward the kitchen. With those Derby get-ups, you had no choice. They wore brown starched hooped skirts that fell short of the knee. It wasn't graceful or becoming and it certainly wasn't practical—just a little public exhibition thrown in with the service. The costumes always bothered Shep. It wasn't like these places he had heard about on the Rue Pigalle where they didn't wear anything at all. At least that was out in the open. This was American sex, awkward and self-conscious and cautiously obscene.

Shep was wondering what Halliday was thinking about.

"Have you worked out here a long time, Stearns? You seem to know your way around."

"This is my first writing job. But I've lived here all my life."

"You mean Hollywood's your home town?" Halliday was mildly interested. "That must have been quite an experience."

Halliday had the typical outsider's view of Hollywood. Though now that Shep thought about it, that wasn't too surprising. One of the weaknesses of *Shadow Ball*—for all its brilliance—had been the inaccuracy of its atmosphere. Not that any single reference had been mistaken—Halliday was too thorough a craftsman for that—it was just that there had been too much atmosphere, too much *Hollywood,* the way one sees it when he's just come in and makes a point of recording all the special things about it, the palm trees, the flamboyancy of the architecture, the jazzed-up mortuaries, the earthquakes, the floods, the pretties on Hollywood

23

Boulevard in their slacks and furs, the million-dollar estates of immigrants who never completely mastered the language of the country they entertain—all these things could be found in Hollywood, but not all run together like that.

"Hollywood was just the name of my home town when I was a kid," Shep tried to explain. "I raised pigeons, we had gang fights in vacant lots, I ran the 660 for the class B track team at Hollywood High, I sold magazines at Hollywood and Highland, the good-looking girls I knew in school tried to get into the studios the way girls in Lawrence, Mass., tried to get into the textile mills."

"Is your father in the picture business?"

"In a way. He rents cars to studios, all kinds, museum pieces, trucks, break-aways . . . See, that's what I mean, Mr. Halliday. I never thought of Hollywood as anything special at all until I went away to Webster."

"Webster—I used to go up there for football games and parties."

"You did a honey of a job on that flashback to a Webster houseparty in *Friends and Foes,* Mr. Halliday."

So the young man did know something about his books. At least he said he did. Even that was something, these days. "I used to know Webster pretty well. I went up there for a houseparty one fall and stayed until Christmas vacation."

For the first time in years Halliday thought of Hank Osborne, in whose room in the Psi U house he had spent those six crazy weeks. It had been in Hank's room at three o'clock in the morning that they had both decided to quit school and join the Canadian Air Force. Hank had become one of the first celebrated American flyers. After he was shot down and grounded, they had had some high times together in Paris. Hank had written the first sensitive account of a flyer's experiences, done a little painting, married Mignon, contributed to *transition* and helped edit it for a while—then had come that horrendous night—it almost seemed in his life the inevitable night—of the fight: my God, he couldn't even remember *touching* Minnie . . . Years later he had heard that Hank was back at Webster teaching European literature or something.

"You didn't happen to know an instructor called Osborne up there? Hank Osborne?"

"Professor Osborne! Sure, I had him in Modern French Literature. A swell Joe. And terrific on Zola and Balzac. He was head of our chapter of the League Against War and Fascism when I was up there."

Yes, Halliday remembered Hank's going left. Back from Paris in Thirty-one, out of a job, out of money and, even more serious, out of a way of life, there probably hadn't seemed any other place for Hank to go.

"Professor Osborne's a great admirer of yours, Mr. Halliday."

So Hank hadn't let these years—Lord, was it more than ten!—of bad feeling influence his opinion of Manley's work. Well, that was pretty decent of Hank, more than he might have expected. After all, in those good years on the continent, Hank had been mighty jealous of his success. The time he accepted Hank's invitation to tell him *exactly* what he thought of his novel, for instance, the one that never got published—*that's* what it had really been about, not the silly drunken business of Mignon.

"Well, I'm glad to hear I still have a few boosters."

Halliday had meant it to pass for modesty. He was a little dismayed himself at the tone of self-pity that accompanied it. This had happened several times recently and he must guard against it. There must be no more of this going around to the back door begging complimentary handouts.

"Mr. Halliday, I might as well jump in with both feet. I've read all your books. *High Noon* was the closest thing to a Bible I had in college. There used to be a group of us at Webster who'd sit around quoting Halliday to each other."

"Is that so?"

Shep saw a flicker of interest in Halliday's eyes.

"I know it sounds kind of—grandiose, but our whole intellectual attitude toward the war and the Twenties was based more than anything else on *Friends and Foes* and *The Night's High Noon*. Gee, Keith Winters, Ted Bentley and those other characters of yours, we knew them so well they were almost like roommates."

Halliday was listening intently. Shep hurried on.

"I really felt I was living through the Twenties with Ted Bentley. He was such a terrific symbol of the conflicting values of the times, the corrosive materialism. And yet he wasn't a symbol. Not a theory dressed up as a man like Charley Anderson in *U. S. A.* Bentley lives in your book. Sometimes in school I'd find myself arguing about various attitudes typical of the Twenties as if I had actually been around in those days and experienced them myself. And then I'd realize it was actually Ted Bentley's experiences, Ted's attitudes I had lived my way into."

This kind of enthusiasm could not be fabricated. Halliday's ego was warmed as surprisingly as if one were to go out for a night's stroll and discover the sun. He often found himself slipping into the vain third-person: nobody reads Halliday any more. The year before last he had written his publisher suggesting a one-volume collected Halliday to reintroduce him to the new readers of the Thirties. And Burt Seixas, his old friend, his discoverer, had given him that old run-around: "Now doesn't seem to be quite the right time" . . . Maybe after they published that "new" novel Manley had been promising ever since *Shadow Ball* . . . But here, from a most unexpected source, was what he was hungering for—proof of the lasting value of his work.

"I'm honestly surprised my books stay with you this way. They were written so long ago, in such a different time. I had the idea your generation went in more for Steinbeck and Farrell and Tom Wolfe. The holy trinity!"

Though the remark was dusted with sarcasm, Shep's earnestness brushed it off. "I think Steinbeck's the kind of writer we've needed in the Thirties, maybe the best we've got who's producing at the moment . . ."

Shep was too wound up to notice the slur or its effect on Halliday.

"—at least he tries to deal honestly with the depression. With people, I mean working people. You know what Ralph Fox says —the only class that can still produce heroes."

Because each was willing to accept the other as representative of his time, they stepped gingerly over the lines of disagreement into the area of common understanding.

"How long has it been since you've read *High Noon*, Stearns?"

"I know this sounds phony, but I read it again just a couple of weeks ago. That girl you've got in there, Lenore Woodbury, she fascinates me. That's a great scene, really a terrific scene, when she calls Ted up at the Club after he's left her and tells him what a wise move she thinks this is for him, how she realizes she can't help making a mess of everything she touches because she's sick inside with the incurable sickness of the times—and all the while Ted has his bag packed ready to come back to her. And then it almost drives him nuts trying to figure out whether she called him to get him back or to strengthen his will to stay away."

"Poor Lenore didn't know herself."

"That's the way you make us feel about your characters—that no one is forcing them to do anything—that they're living, trying to make up their own minds from page to page."

"I guess that's the hardest part, trying to keep your long arm out of your characters' way."

"I suppose everybody asks you this, Mr. Halliday, but was Lenore a real person—someone you actually knew?"

As if awakening from a long sleep, the loneliness in him stirred to find her again—Jere . . . Jere . . . Calling into a void, into nothing, nothingness, and the only answer was the muffled echo jeering *ree-ree-ree* . . . It was a buzzing in his ears, a familiar symptom.

"Mr. Halliday, are you all right?"

"Yes—yes—these late hours. Better get our check."

While they waited for their change, Halliday braced himself. He had a strong sense of pattern, and since this had been a good evening he did not want to let it down. "Well, we didn't accomplish too much with *Love on Ice*—except to break the ice a little bit ourselves. But, this has been rather pleasant. When I think of some of the collaborators I might have drawn . . ."

"I've still got a million things to ask you about your work. I hope you don't mind."

"Not at all, not at all. I'm delighted to find a young man seriously interested in literature—especially my own."

Shep grinned when he saw the quick light that brightened Halliday's face—his first spontaneous smile of the evening.

Halliday was in his car now. "Well, Stearns, I'd better get

home and start catching up on my sleep. I've read somewhere that the secret of screen-writing is a sound mind in a sound body."

The smile was meant to be as genuine as the one that preceded it, but something began to go wrong with it. It proved to be a dud and fizzled out.

What time should they meet next morning? Say around ten, Shep suggested. Halliday's creative juices weren't used to flowing much before noon, but he'd try. Anything to please a gentleman and a collaborator, and, most important of all, Halliday added with a little flourish, "a loyal reader."

He touched the homburg in a dignified—and to Shep strangely old-fashioned—gesture of farewell.

Shep stood there watching while the old Lincoln moved slowly down the wide boulevard. When it was almost out of sight a hopped-up Ford with a gaga passenger list of three high-school couples came up fast on the outside and let the Lincoln have it with one of those comical horns that play *My-dog-has-fleas*. Halliday cut sharply to the curb and proceeded at an even slower pace until Shep lost him in the fog of the street lights.

4

Halliday followed the winding path through the tropical landscaping, through, he thought wryly to himself, the Garden of Allah. This outlandish name for an apartment-hotel was a stale joke at which he still smiled from force of habit. Thirteen years ago, when he had stayed here on his first trip to Hollywood, architecture had seemed to be an extension of the studio backlot with private homes disguised as Norman castles or Oriental mosques, with gas stations built to resemble medieval towers, and movie houses that took the form of Egyptian temples and Chinese pagodas. In that lavish heyday of the parvenu, when everything was built to look like something it wasn't, a bungalow court with accommodations indistinguishable from a hundred other bungalow courts came to be called the Garden of Allah.

In the moonlight the row of two-room bungalows looked remarkably like mausoleums. It was uncanny, Halliday thought, how many talented men of his generation had chosen these stucco tombs. Were they unconsciously laying their talents to rest? Bob Benchley, Sam Hoffenstein, Scott Fitzgerald—they and many more had all lain here. Some of the bodies, he thought bitterly, had not yet been removed. As he approached his bungalow he could hear the infectious early-morning laughter of Mr. Benchley, sitting up with his friends Johnny Walker, Johnny McClain and Charley Butterworth.

Benchley's laughter mounted up and up, a great roar of mirth from within the sealed tomb, sent up by an indefatigable spirit which could still laugh at those who had buried him alive.

For a moment Manley was almost tempted to join the laughter. He had known Bob for—it was going on twenty years. But with his present program of austerity he was no longer a fit companion for Uncle Bob. To drop in on Bob and refuse a drink was to put to sea with a Gloucester fisherman and then inform him that you had scruples against dropping a line over the side. You would be no longer in his world. There had been a time when the festive sounds of early morning, the laughter and the tinkling music of ice stirring in a sparkling highball, had been a standing invitation he could never resist. But he had had too many good nights with Bob to impose himself on his old friend now.

The realization that he and Bob and Dotty Parker and Eddie Mayer and Sammy Hoffenstein and perhaps half a dozen others of the old gang had all been brought into the Hollywood fold suddenly oppressed him. There had been so many luncheons and cocktails and all-night sessions when Hollywood had been only a term of derision, when they had vied with each other in witty denunciations of this Capital of the Philistines. No one with any self-respect, he remembered saying, would ever go to Hollywood, except possibly to pursue Billie Dove.

And fifteen years later here they were, all lured to the Garden of Allah, all on weekly pay rolls or, worse yet, trying to get on. Were they men of inadequate wills who had acquired the authors' cancer—expensive tastes? Or could they, like Manley himself, persuade themselves that this was merely a stop-over on the way back to positive work?

Manley was glad to reach the door of his bungalow. Perhaps he could leave those questions outside, slam the door on them as he had done so many times before. They would rattle the door and scratch on the window-pane (squeech squeech on glass scratch scratch on nerve-ends) but he would not let them in. He would hide away for a few hours in that dark closet of oblivion. Nembutal would see to that (if one doesn't work I'll try two and if two won't knock me out . . .).

"Hello, dear . . ."

Ann had been stretched out on the couch reading, Manley noticed, that new book for the layman by Einstein and somebody else on the evolution of physics. She read almost no contemporary fiction. One of her hobbies, of all things, for a companion of his, was mathematics. When she talked about films it was nearly always in terms of photographic composition and the way emotion is aroused through a creative linking together of separate shots. Even her politics, left of center, avoided the usual abstractions. She didn't want to talk; she wanted to get things done, things she could see and feel. Manley interpreted this pragmatism as part of Ann's rebellion against her Hollywood background. Her father, Sam Loeb, had been one of those fabulous soldiers-of-fortune who could sell you the Brooklyn Bridge and then when you came back to complain about being stung, sell you the Bear Mountain Bridge. As a child (so he worked it out) she must have been smothered in hyperbole—run-of-the-mill films sold as the greatest ever made, mediocre talents passing themselves off as geniuses. Hers must have been a world of brag and bombast and heady exaggeration. Probably that was what had attracted her to cutting. She could take the film in her own hands, cut it with scissors and splice the loose ends together again. Sometimes you got a good idea and you put it together to see if it would work. But it had to *work*. You had to be able to see that it worked with your own eyes.

One of the things that had made their arrangement possible was Ann's rational, almost inhuman control of emotions. Manley had reached a point where his own emotions—or was it his nerves —had worn so thin that he had little patience with anyone else's.

Ann rose to meet him and he kissed her perfunctorily. He had forgotten he had asked her to stay tonight. But now he remembered having thought he would need the company to break the loneliness he had expected to carry away with him from his first big studio conference. But the surprising qualities of that young man had served the purpose quite adequately. In his mood of self-pity (which he had called "being realistic") he had been gloomily positive of meeting studio people who would not even recognize his name. But now, after this evening of unexpected adulation, he felt tired, wretchedly tired, too tired even for Ann.

"You poor guy. I was beginning to worry. You must be exhausted."

"I've gone into the lion's den and come back alive." He smiled for her. He was exhausted. This was exactly what Dr. Rubin (why had he always felt more secure in the hands of Jewish physicians?) had told him not to do. He sank down in his favorite chair (he noticed with a faint sense of self-ridicule that he was reaching the age when he had favorite chairs, favorite corners, etc.), loosening his bow tie and removing his coat. Ann hung it up with a rapid, automatic gesture. Nothing had surprised her more than her discovery that she liked to wait on him. None of the studio wolves who found her such a cool one, who had even mistaken her aloofness for some variant of abnormality, would have believed her capable of so much feminine solicitude.

Ann had worried about herself sometimes; maybe there was emotional inadequacy in a woman who reaches the age of twenty-seven without having once gone down the chute called "falling in love." At twenty-seven she had been—only a trifle unhappily—resigned to the life of a bachelor girl. Maybe it had been only a barrier in her mind against her stereotype of the Hollywood male. She wasn't sure. All she knew was that her first talk with Manley Halliday, a chance meeting on the beach at Topanga, had seemed to change her chemistry. All the inadequacies and blocks she had once even considered passing on to an analyst removed themselves as suddenly and mysteriously as juvenile warts. She was surprised, really shocked at the way she had gone out to Manley. Almost from that first day, she had been ready to follow him, to share his anxieties, to marry him if he should ever ask her but not to withhold herself from him if he should not.

"I'll make you some hot Ovaltine," she said. "It will help you sleep."

Manley glanced wearily at the morning headlines—*Mussolini Hails Victory in Spain—FDR Ok's Planes For France—GOP Asks New WPA Cut—New Violence in Palestine*. It was the kind of news that would provoke a violent reaction from young Stearns, but it left him with a terrible sense of resignation. Another war was coming. How calmly they floated toward the falls. He turned to the movie column with relief. There was his name! How could they have managed it so fast? "Our enterprising Victor Milgrim, who has brought so many famous writers to Hollywood from Somerset Maugham to William Faulkner, now does himself proud once more. He's just signed the illustrious Manley Halliday, author of one of the most famous bestsellers of the 1920's, *High Noon at Midnight*, which won the Pulitzer Prize. Manley, who once gave one of those parties we oldtimers still remember, hasn't come back to see us in y'ars 'n' y'ars. Welcome back, Manley, and happy screen credits!"

Manley dropped the paper with a faint groan.

"Here you are, dear." The Ovaltine was in his hands. "How did it go tonight?"

"Oh, all right."

Ann's fingers rubbed the back of his neck. He closed his eyes. It felt good. He was very tired.

"Did you read the script?"

He nodded without opening his eyes.

"Bad?"

"Bad."

Her fingers traced the fine line of his nose up to the base of his forehead, easing the throbbing nerves. "I hope I didn't get you into something you'll be unhappy about."

Something in him stirred resentfully, not against Ann, though he knew it sounded that way. "Oh, what's being unhappy got to do with it? I'm unhappy about a lot of things. I'm unhappy about not having enough money to go on with my book. I'm unhappy about having to borrow money from you for Douglas' tuition. I've been unhappy for months about not being able to get a job. So now I really shouldn't complain about being unhappy for ten weeks—at two thousand a week. Incidentally, I want to pay you back out of this first check."

"Oh, for God's sake will you stop worrying about that?"

But he did worry about it. In all his years of borrowing— Lord, the friendships it had undermined—he had never taken money from a woman before. He was old-fashioned enough to feel this placed him in an equivocal position. Not that it meant anything to Ann. Money wasn't any sort of symbol to her. But the combination of taking her money (the increasingly insulting tone of Douglas' letters had driven him to desperate lengths) and staying home while Ann hurried off to her factory job identified her much too explicitly as the breadwinner. Despite Manley's reputation as one of the least restrained flambeaux of his age, he had a deep streak of bourgeois conventionality that was offended by the inverted economics of their relationship.

"I'm not worrying about it, Ann. But I do intend to pay it back immediately."

She saw the look on his face, the strain, portent of storm clouds gathering in his mind. Much as a trained nurse would, she wondered how he could be made more comfortable.

By diversion, perhaps: "I had kind of an interesting problem tonight. We decided to end the second sequence with Tommy Mitchell staring after the girl. The audience knows what he's thinking, so it can run long, ten feet maybe. We need a good long pause there before coming in on the fast action of sequence three. But the director hadn't protected himself with enough footage on Tommy. So I tried a little sleight-of-hand. We cut from the medium shot in which Carole walks out on Tommy to a closeup of Tommy from an earlier scene. Reverse printing it he's looking off camera left, which works out fine with our action. And I don't think the audience will ever know it's the same shot they've seen before . . ."

Usually Manley welcomed Ann's discussion of film technique. His sense of craftsmanship was excited by this new form. His mind was speculative, imaginative, sensitized, maybe that was why he was attracted to the medium. He had the poet's admiration for the surveyor. Only in Ann's profession—and this is what interested him—the poet had to be a surveyor as well. But tonight she wasn't getting through to him. He was turning his head to the wall in some tortured corner of his own.

"*Love on Ice*," he interrupted bitterly. "May the Lord have mercy on my soul."

"Bad as all that?"

"I didn't have the heart to tell the kid who wrote it—he seems like a nice lad by the way—but it's about on a par with these *College Humor* serials—the bad ones. Not even the Katherine Brush ones. The Dorothy Dow ones."

"*College Humor* and I just seemed to pass each other without meeting," Ann said. "All I remember are those two-line jokes they used to reprint in the *Chaparral*."

34

"Oh, yes, we were very funny."

"Manley, you're getting those deep circles under your eyes again. You ought to come to bed."

Come to bed. Is that what she had been waiting for? He looked at her carefully. She was a good-looking woman. Her body was strong and firm, not fashioned along the sleek, narrow-hipped lines currently in favor; there was too much European peasant stock behind her for that. And she had a good, strong face, a striking face, almost beautiful when you got to know it well. But, thank goodness, it wasn't one of those Hollywood pretty-pretties; strength was the main attraction for him now. And she had that, not only had it but gave of it generously. Sometimes he wished he could give more of himself in return, or rather, that there was more of him left to give. But it was all so much effort now. He wondered if she knew how much of an effort even their occasional nights together had become. All his emotions, he was convinced, had to be strictly rationed if he were to survive.

"I'm not an invalid. I know when to go to bed."

Stung for a moment, she quickly remembered her resolve not to let his flurries of irritability offend her. "Of course you do, Manley. There's a little more Ovaltine left."

"Tonight I think I'd like a drink."

Ann frowned. "Manley, that's the one thing—you know what Dr. Rubin says."

Ovaltine and nembutal and Dr. Rubin and insulin and ten hours' sleep and a mistress who was becoming each day more of a mother and a nurse. It maddened him. A random invitation from long ago suddenly returned to torment him: "Please try to come. You know what everybody says here, the party hasn't really started until the Manley Hallidays arrive."

"I said I'd like to have a drink."

"Darling . . ." She was a little frightened now, "you've been so sensible. And if you could keep it up for seven months, it seems a shame to . . ."

"And maybe after this one drink I'll go on being sensible for another seven months. For God's sake, Ann, don't treat me like a dipsomaniac. Take off that white attendant's uniform.

All I said was I feel like a drink. It's been an unnerving day. One small drink isn't going to kill me."

"Manley, I wish you wouldn't."

Her face was coming up to his, in that instinctive way women have of offering themselves as an end to argument. But he turned his head impatiently. He wasn't up to Ann tonight. The nerves in his face threatened to twitch in the weak place where it always started, at the left-hand corner of his mouth. The weakness exasperated him. Decline and Fall of Manley Halliday . . . the silly phrase beat in his brain. Self-pity, self-pity, he fought back. You have nothing to fear but (ah, the President's useful sedative) your debts, nothing to fear but the possibility that you've lost your touch, nothing to fear but Victor Milgrim and (he couldn't help groaning every time his mind phrased the title) *Love on Ice,* nothing to fear but the love-hate he felt for Jere, nothing to fear but himself.

"For God's sake, Ann, will you stop pestering me? Stop smothering me!"

Ann subsided obediently. "All right, dear. Call me in the afternoon if you want me to have dinner with you."

After she was gone he went over to the cabinet where the liquor was locked. But he didn't bother to open it. Ann and Dr. Rubin were right. It would be foolish to risk a drink after seven months. Now that he was alone, he wasn't even sure he had wanted that drink. Had it been merely a device, a diversion to draw her away from his incapabilities? But what a needless scene! After all, he could be frank with Ann. He had never known a woman so ruthful. She was the harem, summoned when he desired, rejected when he wished to be alone. Only it had seemed easier to provoke this stupid little quarrel tonight. Was it because his talk with the young man had shaken the dust off his memory of Jere? Damn Jere! The last time he had been with Ann, at the very moment when he should have devoted all his strength and feeling and mind to her, his thoughts had suddenly strayed back to Jere. Home to Jere. Oh, Jere, you were lovely. Jesus, it was lovely with you, Jere . . . After the breakup there had been a period when he had looked for other Jeres, settled for lesser Jeres, but that had been worse. Jere had been the experience. Trying to use others who were almost as attractive or almost as quick or almost as much fun was as bad as no Jere at all.

That's where Ann had helped. He would hardly have expected to find a woman who had so little in common with Jere. Ann was intelligent, Jere intuitive; Ann was self-disciplined, Jere impulsive; Ann was essentially independent but accepted her place; Jere was hopelessly dependent on him but resented it; Ann was dependable; Jere was the most irresponsible human being he had ever known.

For these antipodal characteristics he had loved Jere and had learned to appreciate Ann. They were not in competition. And Ann was sensible enough not to try to tip the balance in her favor. Sometimes—when he was sure he had emotion to spare —he worried about Ann. Marvelously convenient for him, their relationship was mined with danger for her. She had driven up a narrow dead-end street and some day if she wanted to get out on a main thoroughfare she might find it impossible to turn around and difficult even to back out. But she was almost thirty years old and she knew her own mind. He accepted her love as a patient receives a necessary injection from his private nurse. His conscience was clear. He had made it a rule never, even in release, to speak the three mysterious words proscribed by the conventions of romance. Instead he had always said, "I'm fond of you, Ann," or "I feel close to you." And from the beginning Ann had been wise enough to understand just how much of Manley's emotions she commanded. Characteristically, she had even reduced it to a mathematical proportion, summed up in the half-joke, "I'm as bad as your agent, willing to settle for ten percent."

With a sudden warmth for her that often came to him when he was alone, he went to the phone. She should be home by now. She only lived a few blocks down the Sunset Strip.

"Hello, Annie?" That was what he always called her when he felt this way.

"What timing! I was just opening the door."

"Our timing is all right once in a while."

37

"I'm glad you're feeling better."

"Annie, sometimes I wonder how you can put up so long with a crotchety old man."

"Listen, do you plan to stay up all night? You'll be a wreck in the morning."

I'm a wreck now, he thought. You can pound out the dents and get the motors running again, but they're never the same after a smashup. "All right, mother. But I just wanted to let you know —that little outburst I had—I'm not fit company for anyone these days. Not even myself."

"Manley," she said, "will you please get some sleep and stop all this nonsense?"

"What's so special about sleep? It never knitted up my raveled sleave of care. Recognize that, Annie? That's by Odets out of Shakespeare."

He was coming out of it.

"Well, anyway *I'm* going to bed," Ann insisted. "I've got to be back in the cutting room in less than five hours."

"See you tomorrow evening then."

"Tomorrow evening is less than twelve hours away, dear. Even if you have trouble falling asleep, don't take over two pills."

"Miss Loeb—" he tried to wing it in with his old flippancy— "what would I do without you?"

Something that was either a yawn or a sigh whispered across the wires. "Sometimes I really wonder."

He did too, but he laughed it off. After that, Ann cut the conversation short. Her manner was always dry and efficient on the phone. For her it was just an instrument for confirming appointments and setting times to meet.

Manley was a long time in the bathroom, where the medicine chest was full of pills and variously colored liquids for real and imagined ills. With a repugnance he had never been able to overcome, he punctured the skin for the insulin. Then he took the two nembutals (Ann's warning having succeeded in heading off a third) and stretched out on the bed to read until sleep should overcome him.

He glanced impatiently at the first few pages of the script again. So this was all there was to it. If he had deceived Milgrim in telling him he saw enough possibilities in the story to take the job, it was not a dark lie. In return for two thousand dollars a week he would do his best, his best second-best. He would, as they liked to say out here, make with the talent. Yes, his talent was an old firehorse which may have seen its best days but was still in there ready to run its heart out when it heard the alarm. Here talent, nice talent, there's a good talent, here's a little sugar, two thousand bucks' worth of sugar, now run to this little fire, and maybe poppa will let you run to one more big one, a whole block on fire, a city, a world. . .

Halliday caught himself just as he was about to sneak out over the fence that bounded this assignment. This was an old trick of his, escaping, but he was forty-three now (yes, yes, he knew he looked fifty-three) and he liked to think he was disciplined. At least he had learned it was time to start learning discipline. No good thinking about the big fire that his big talent was going to make a final run for before it died. First there was this little one of Victor Milgrim's to worry about, this sparkler with its little false tongues of flame that sizzle but do not sear.

Strewn on the floor around the bed were a dozen books, current novels, mysteries from the lending library (which he hardly ever remembered to return) and some things he had been re-reading, Shaw's Prefaces and Euripides. He reached down for the first book that came to his hand. Evelyn Waugh's latest, *Scoop*. In the first ten or fifteen pages, he always said, he could get the feel of any book and this one was a faint, fifth carbon of those triumphs of cynicism that had seemed so hilarious ten years earlier. The book cackled with a hollow, imitative laugh and the fact that the author was obviously only imitating himself made it all the more depressing. Brittle jokes about the Abyssinian war. Good God, what was Waugh after all but a Rudyard Kipling with a shrill sense of humor and an inverted class consciousness? *Scoop* slipped back onto the floor as he picked up *Monday Night*. Kay Boyle. She had been near the top of his list of young hopefuls ten years ago. But the first few pages of her new novel gave him the jitters. It was such nervous writing about such nervous people. The effect was brilliant but nerve-racking. His patience hardly survived the opening chapter. What had happened

39

to these people? Or was it that nothing had happened to them and the times had changed? Or again, was it his own tastes that had changed? Perhaps he should reread *Vile Bodies* and see if it still struck him as a limited masterpiece. Was there any tragedy greater than a writer's outliving his gift, petering out like so many he had known? Well, he supposed a good many of his old admirers thought this had happened to him. His novelettes in the women's magazines. But he knew better. He'd show them better. He may have been a poor judge of his own life but he mustn't fool himself about his own work. He didn't think he was deceiving himself about *Folly and Farewell*. He was pretty sure that opening chapter was the most artful beginning he had ever made.

Monday Night was back on the floor now and he was dipping into *Orestes*. These ten weeks on the movie must simply be taken in stride, that's all. He must plane down the rough surfaces and hammer in the nails like a good little carpenter. His was not to reason why, his was simply to earn twenty thousand dollars. (Now Euripides was on the floor.)

When the close text of Euripides had begun to slide out of focus, he had mistaken this for drowsiness. But the moment he plunged the room into darkness it seemed as if the lights had flashed on in his head. (He should have taken that third nembutal after all.) The lights were flashing numbers in his brain. Two thousand for ten weeks is twenty thousand minus the agent's ten percent leaves eighteen thousand after paying back Ann it's sixteen five as they say out here and payments on his back taxes brings it down to eleven thousand (still twenty-six thousand short of squaring himself with Uncle Sam) another eight hundred due Jere on back alimony and five hundred a month on the new settlement and the thousand he had borrowed on his insurance and the allowance for Douglas (so he didn't see how he could get by on less than the other boys, did he?) damn it, he had lost track of what the balance was now, and by the first there's three months due here at the Garden another six hundred that was one thing he had kept from Ann because she would have paid it and that would have been the topper the crusher as they say here—now let me try to get this straight

2000 and
1500 and
800 and
500 and
600 and

he tried to count back in his head, lost track, began again and then, feverishly awake he switched on the light and began to add the figures on a scrap of paper from the nightstand, $14,666 from $20,000 would leave him $5,334. How long could $5,334 last him? Not five months with the load he had to carry. Time enough to finish the book? Maybe, with a couple of slick stories thrown in, and maybe one more advance from Dorset House, though he mustn't count on that any more. He was already into them for ten thousand. That's what had kept him going the past two years. And he still owed them seventy-five hundred on that Aimee Semple MacPherson novel he had put aside after two chapters. (How could he have gotten so far off his track?) Debts kept buzzing inside his head. He had had ninety-seven thousand dollars once. 97,000 dollars. $97,000. He and Jere had thought of it as bottomless wealth, providing fast cars and good Scotch and villas at Florence and Neuilly and now ninety-seven thousand wouldn't pay his debts, not if he actually set out to pay everybody back. By God, he'd square himself yet. Nobody would ever know how much he had hated to ask for that money. So much so that he could never feel completely friendly with his benefactors again. But the old debts would have to wait another year or two when (the dream promised) the new book would sweep the country like *High Noon,* only bigger with the book clubs now, $50,000, maybe even a movie offer, they were buying all kinds of things now. Ah, for another of those double successes. The Sunday book sections would offer up their front pages in a rush to get on the bandwagon, making up for their years of neglect by bringing out all the fancy literary adjectives *definitive, searching, majestic, masterful* to hail the return of a major novelist. . . .

A sudden, involuntary twitch made him realize he must have fallen asleep for a moment. The sheet of paper had slipped from his hands. Picking it up he noticed for the first time what

41

he had been scribbling his figures on. A brief correspondence from the Garden of Allah management:

My dear Mr. Halliday,

We beg to remind you that we have not yet received your remittance for rental covering the months of November, December. No doubt this is a mere oversight on your part. But now that we again call it to your attention, would you be good enough to . . .

Was business the last refuge of courtesy, or of hypocrisy? He studied the letterhead: Garden of Allah. He remembered a friend of his—had it been Van Vechten?—had once written him from the Garden of Allah in the early Twenties and he thought Carl had been indulging his supercilious sense of humor. The Garden of Allah. There could be no such place. Well, there was no such place, really, but he was here. Was it possible, if there were no such place, that he was here?

He felt rotten. He felt as if he were sinking, sinking . . . But not into sleep. How obscene to be reported to have died in the Garden of Allah. How would you ever live a thing like that down? What was he thinking about, live it down? He was dead. Daid. I'll be glad when you're daid you rascal you. All right, try it with the lights out again. But there they go those damn lights in the head again. He was counting thousand-dollar bills jumping over the fence, getting away from him, twenty, eighteen, sixteen, fourteen. CHRIST LET ME SLEEP I'VE GOT TO GET SOME SLEEP. Headache, coming on fast. Lights on again. Bathroom. To hell with Ann, one more little yellow capsule and a couple of aspirins. Now back to bed. Slide down into sleep, to sleep the death of each day's life, the balm for mind's pain—no that wasn't quite it. Did Shakespeare have debts? Did Shakespeare have troubles like this, did you, Bill? Can't hear you, Bill, speak louder louder LOUDER. My God he'd been snoring then he was sleeping but it didn't seem like sleeping the lights were all different colors now and they were flashing on and off and going around and around peg in a square hole idea for a story if he could write it down quickly enough but he

42

couldn't find the light only there was a soft blue light in the corner Jere must have put it there Jere and her lights those love lights pastels for the different moods of love. Who else but Jere would have thought of that? *I feel pale green* or *I feel bright red tonight* and there were her colored lights to match and afterwards reading Verlaine to him in that soft accent. Where was that pale blue light coming from? And the distant laughter? Oh that was Bob in his stucco tomb. But the light? Hardly blue any more diaphanous diaphanous dawn hadn't he written that in a book once . . .

Suddenly he jerked to a half-sitting position. Dawn. That explained the blue light in the corner. Fumbling for his watch, he saw it was six thirty-five. He closed his eyes again as if to outwit himself with the deception that he really had not been awake. But it was too late. A minute of tossing and the light was on once more. Another book from the floor, this time Rex Stout. Whodunits were the opium of the people and the movies were the opium of the people. But *Love on Ice* wasn't opium. There wasn't enough fantasy there. It knocked you out like chloroform. Artists in chloroform. At two thousand a week you have to be good. You have to deliver the goods. He had to pack up his troubles in his old kit bag and—something shot by his window with a loud clanging. A fire. His fire-horse? Calling all talent, calling all talent, come to the aid of Manley Halliday at World-Wide Studio. . .

At seven o'clock nembutal and aspirin dull the sharp edge of anxiety, smother growing uncertainty and fear in the soft-pillow euphoria of oblivion . . .

5

Shep had breakfast as usual at Armstrong-Shroeder's. The waitress—a pinch-faced little woman not nearly so sour as she looked —brought him the customary grapefruit juice, Danish pastry and coffee. In the headlines Il Duce was hailing the achievements of his Blackshirts in Spain. It was all over. Three do-nothing years of sophistry and hypocrisy. Shep wondered, with a mouth full of coffee-cake, whether this meant bankruptcy for the Western world. Non-intervention, "neutrality," Munich—once more the clocks of the world seemed to be striking 1914. Everyone who came back from over there read the same signs in the darkening sky: war, this year or next. Suddenly Shep was overwhelmed with a sense of his own non-intervention. What was there to show for all his political passion (or was it merely political irritability?) —some meetings, some money, a few half-convinced friends brought around to the Government side, a telegram to Roosevelt urging an end to the embargo? Yet, Hollywood as a whole had done its share. If every community in the country had responded as well. . .

"Say, you're coming up in the world, Shep. Got your name in Parsons' column. Lemme show ya."

The waitress lifted the paper from the counter and pointed out the item linking him with Halliday.

"Will ya still come in for breakfast when ya get two thousand a week?" she mocked him cheerfully. "Betcha won't be able to get up so early in the morning then. Prob'bly stay in bed till noon with some glamorous movie star."

"Oh, sure," Shep said, uninterested, but going on with it to humor her. "With a couple of shiny Ethiopians bare to the waist fanning us with palm fronds."

Seeing Halliday's name in print, in the same line with his own, Shep's optimism leapt high. He had been writing down on *Love on Ice,* shamelessly, or was it shamefully. But now, with Manley

Halliday leading the way, they'd turn this into a real sleeper. Milgrim had wanted a moderately priced, conventional success to balance some of the extravagant prestige pictures he liked to make. But surely Milgrim couldn't expect routine competence from Manley Halliday. Shep drove on through the bright winter morning to the studio with his mind full of day-dreams.

The top floor of the Writers' Building was a kind of attic, an architectural after-thought where junior-writers, technical advisers and other semi-entities were assigned to cubby-holes partitioned by beaver board. Through pull with the janitor, Shep had managed to promote a decrepit couch, though possession of a couch was usually a sign of scenarist affluence, or at least respectability.

But the second floor presented an impressive row of offices, spacious, with new Venetian blinds, and lamps and furnishings as tasteful as those in a good, second-class hotel. These were appropriate domiciles for creative personnel enjoying honorariums of from five hundred dollars a week up.

As Shep approached Halliday's office, he passed an adjoining door on which a desperate humorist had written:

SCRIPTS

Cleaned, Pressed, or Written

While You Wait!

Nice clean work done here or your money back

(if you can run fast enough)

H. Kurtz

Shep announced himself to Halliday's secretary, observing that even the stenographers on this floor seemed younger and prettier. Had Mr. Halliday come in yet? No—well, he guessed it would be all right for him to go in and wait in his office. They were going to work together. "Oh, you're Mr. Halliday's collaborator." The girl took this as a matter of course. After all, Manley Halliday had no important screen credits like John Lee Mahin or James Kevin McGuiness.

On the desk Shep saw every preparation had been made for the immediate application of genius. There were the long, yellow, ruled writing pads. There were the dozens of gleaming pencils carefully sharpened to pin points. There were the scratch pads on which genius could doodle and experiment. There were the erasers, with which genius could rub out that rare mistake. On the typewriter stand waited a resplendent machine, freshly oiled, with a new ribbon. Everything, Shep thought, was marvelously virginal. The bridal suite awaited only the arrival of the groom who would apply his pencil to the germinal conception.

Shep sank into an easy chair to scan *The Hollywood Reporter*. In a few minutes he knew almost everything there was to know about what had happened in Hollywood in the past twenty-four hours. He knew whose preview was SMASH B.O. and whose was just OKAY. He knew who had been penciled in for the lead opposite Gable and who had been planted at Warners'. He guessed the name of the *what* director whose car was reported to have been parked all night outside the Bel Air home of *what g.g.* (the abbreviation automatically recognized for glamour girl) and he knew what famous couple it was, mistakenly reputed *phtting* by a rival columnist, who were actually more *thatway* than ever.

When the girl in the outer office said she was going down to the commissary for coffee, Shep realized it must be 10:30, time for the mid-morning break. Halliday was yet to make an appearance. He had noticed that the time at which a writer began his working day corresponded roughly to his socio-economic standing—junior writers in at 9, $350 writers at 9:30, $500–$1500 writers at 10, and from two thousand a week up, 10:30 or 11, when they did not enjoy the privilege of working at home.

When Shep heard Halliday coming in, shortly after eleven, his sense of exhilaration was so intense he wondered self-consciously whether he should rise. Halliday came in coolly self-possessed. If this was Shep's idea of how a great man of letters should enter a film studio, it was no less Halliday's. For he had thought it out quite deliberately. It was not a putting on of airs but an arming for the fray.

They said good morning quite formally. Shep put his hand out and Halliday touched it and gave it back to him. Neither of them seemed to know how to begin. They were both shy men, really, and the process of creating anything in pair, even so public a document as a screenplay, was embarrassingly intimate.

Halliday looked up and studied Shep. The boy smiled at him nervously, ill at ease. He seemed like a nice boy. Big-boned, husky, good-natured, easy-going. Twenty-two or -three. That wonderful age. He had been twenty-three when he finished *Friends and Foes,* twenty-four when it came out. That was the way to be twenty-four. God, how *right* he had felt when he was twenty-four. These writers today didn't seem to click that young any more. They had to develop, and they didn't do much of that. They weren't *naturals*.

But the boy was waiting, with his brown mooncalf eyes . . . oh, hell, this was the trouble with pictures; it wasn't writing, it was diplomacy. He would have been wonderful at it once when he wasn't so tired. But in those days, of course, he hadn't needed pictures. He had been able to indulge himself in a lofty contempt for movies.

Halliday sat down at the desk.

"All these writing supplies inhibit me. When I was writing my books I was always trying to find a pencil. And my portable was forever getting stuck."

It was Shep's cue to tell him some of those stories of writers' Hollywood debuts. A writer is applying for a job. The producer hands him a pencil. "You're a writer—go ahead and write something."

"Yes, they were telling that one fifteen years ago," Halliday smiled. "And the one about Maeterlinck. Goldwyn—I suppose it's always Goldwyn—handing him a big pencil and saying, 'Now I want to see this worn down to here by five o'clock.' "

Shep had a few new ones. At least they helped postpone the question of just how you go about starting to write a nonsensical musical with a Manley Halliday. Dorothy Parker leaning out the window of the Writers' Building screaming, "Let me out of here—I'm just as sane as you are!"

Halliday smiled thoughtfully. "Yes, that's a good one. Those are really anxiety stories. The age-old protest of the weak against the all-powerful."

Shep felt flattered.

"Of course we have our Guild," he said. "We've gained some concessions for screenwriters—a little more dignity."

Halliday looked at him. Yes, he was perfectly sincere, perfectly sincere and fairly intelligent. So he would not tell this young man how much he disagreed.

"A screenwriter, in fact no kind of writer has any dignity unless he can control his own material," was all Halliday said.

"Maybe that will come some day," Shep said.

"In a major industry like this one—with a bigger market every day? I don't see how."

"I thought *I* was supposed to be the materialist." Shep grinned.

"I'm not completely opposed to dialectical materialism" (with a kind of inverted snobbery Shep was surprised that Halliday even knew the term). "I think it's an interesting theory. It only becomes eye-wash when it's used to explain everything. Then it seems to me to become cant."

"I don't know," Shep said. "When you try to understand the dynamics of civilizations the main idea still makes sense to me— the kind of society we have at any particular time is decided by the methods of production."

Halliday looked at him, faintly interested, faintly amused. "I'm not sure you aren't right." And then he added, "But I'm not sure you *are,* either."

To Shep, this was an almost incomprehensible statement. Quick to read this in his eyes, Halliday said, "That's probably the biggest difference there is between our ways of thinking."

The scream of the noon siren brought a violent punctuation to their exchange of definitions.

"Good thing Milgrim hasn't got a dictaphone in here, Mr. Halliday. We'd be arrested for taking money under false pretenses."

"Yes, how did we get so far from what we're being paid to talk about?"

"I'm afraid it's my fault. There are too many things I want to ask you."

"Don't worry. We'll give Milgrim his money's worth. We need

48

half a day to get to know each other well enough to work to-gether."

He picked up the little four-page trade paper and began to examine it. This two thousand a week was easy money. But his mind kept throwing up barricades to keep that college musical at safe distance. Running down the Rambling Reporter column, Halliday read out an item describing a spectacular rhumba danced the night before by a pudgy, elderly producer and a new Latin starlet called Conchita.

The dark, youthful grace of that girl in the arms of an aging fat man aroused in Shep an unsophisticated bitterness. "These pretty little girls in the arms of those ugly old men—I should think there wouldn't be enough money in the world to make them do that."

Halliday put the trade sheet down and looked at Shep tolerantly. "If you'll forgive me, that's your youth talking. These old men have more in common with those young girls than you'd have. The same sort of people, inside. They're both interested in money."

Halliday's thinking was full of surprising little turns and twists. It was difficult to label and Shep always felt a little lost away from his cubby holes. He couldn't even be sure if Halliday were conservative, liberal or radical. He simply seemed to be standing off and observing his world with an indefinable blend of romanticism and cynicism.

Halliday was making a few tentative scratches on one of the pads. Shep was tempted to bring up some of the questions he still wanted to ask about Halliday's books. But when he saw that Halliday apparently had no intention of settling down to their story conference, he wondered if his role in the collaboration shouldn't be as a kind of sergeant-of-arms who calls the meeting to order.

"Mr. Halliday, I'd a hell of a lot rather talk about your work than this script of mine, but, well, if you could tell me more of what your objections were, maybe that'd help get us started on a new line."

Halliday rubbed his fingers over his eyes and tried to concentrate. "Well, even in a light romantic comedy like this, I'd like to see an authentic background. The campus in your story is the familiar Alma Mammy, complete with cheerleaders and coeds from Central Casting. You and I ought to be able to do something a little better than that. Even if we can't do anything revolutionary, maybe we can make it look as if we've been inside an American college."

"I started out to make it my own school." Shep was a little shamefaced. "But then I began to make concessions to what I thought Milgrim's idea of college would be. By the time I got through I guess it was a casting director's dream."

"I believe in starting from a real base, Stearns. Even fantasy has to have a keel. Where is our college? Is it U.C.L.A.—so much like a movie campus that it's another of those cases where art and reality begin to overlap? Is it one of the big Mid-Western State campuses? Or a middle-size school like Oberlin? Or is it Yale or Princeton, or Amherst or Williams, or Dartmouth, Colgate or Webster? The quality of our campus is bound to influence the kind of story we tell."

"Okay. That's a good start. I picked Webster because I thought an Ivy League college would give us more contrast. A short-order waitress coming to a big U.C.L.A. or Ann Arbor dance is much less of a story."

"Webster . . ." Halliday was trying to give it serious thought. "No place for scholars or snobs. None of your Yale or Princeton aristocracy, except a few who wander in by mistake. Couldn't pass their college boards or something. When you think of the undergraduate body of men, unimaginative, rather wholesome, future solid-citizens, high-class Babbitts, from middle-class families that are well-fixed rather than wealthy in the traditional sense. Not much artistic life—maybe a few outdoor poets who also ski very well . . ."

Shep had to grin at this snapshot of his college.

"That's a little hard on us, but pretty much true. Of course Webster was shaken up a good deal by the depression. The depression was our World War. Only we reacted to it almost exactly the opposite from the way you did. From everything I've read—here I go talking about your books again—the young intellectuals staggered away from the War as they would from a terrible accident. All they wanted to do was forget the whole dirty business. And if Wilson and his Fourteen Points was Democracy, you could have that too. Just leave me alone, you all seemed to be saying. Let me have my fun and let me have my thoughts but don't give me any petitions to sign and from now on keep your goddam causes to yourself."

Halliday was listening carefully now.

"Yes," he nodded encouragement to Shep with a smile so gentle it seemed to belie the words that accompanied it. "Guilty as charged."

Shep was on his feet, popping his ideas with an enthusiasm that Halliday found rather attractive, if somewhat silly.

"Our machine had been in a smash-up too. But we wanted to remain on the scene of the accident and see if we could fix it. We thought we could save it. Instead of a *lost* generation, I guess you might call us a *found* generation. We found out what was wrong. We were pretty damn sure we'd have something new out of all this mess that would be better than anything you had before."

"We had our tinkerers, too, our socialists, anarchists, Tolstoyans. . ."

"No, Mr. Halliday, those were freaks. When I was at Webster, nearly all the intellectuals thought this way. In your day I probably would have been a young snob who wrote bad sonnets for my friends. But at Webster in '35, my chief inspiration was the strike in the nearby marble quarries. And the big worry was, how to find a job when we got out."

"In my day," Halliday said, "the world was waiting with open arms—all the better to crush you with, my dear. Anyone from one of *the* colleges who had a fairly respectable record—hadn't raped the Dean's wife, at least not publicly—could step right into a good New York job. At least—and maybe this is what gives any period its character—he thought he could. Our problem was, as you say, the other way 'round—were we offering ourselves to a system that rolled us flat and stamped us out like sheet metal?"

"The question Ted Bentley kept asking himself."

"Exactly. *High Noon* was important because it ran head-on into the central moral dilemma of our day. Wealth was supposed to be everybody's goal, yet Ted Bentley only began to feel like a failure when he gave up the small salary of a faculty member for the big money on the Street. He had a foot in either world and satisfaction in neither."

"God, it is striking how completely opposite your problem was. Yours was such a world of material success. But the world we found was a world of material failure. When the pump runs too fast you say, 'There must be something in this world more precious than water.' But when the pump doesn't run at all, all you can think of is to try and get a couple of drops on your tongue."

"Yes, that's true," Halliday said. "We talked of Rimbaud and Baudelaire and Pater. You talked about strikes and fascism and Public Works. But, Stearns, from an artistic point of view, I can't help thinking we had a little the better of it. Our age forced moral decisions on us that seem to me to make for better art. In this decade of yours, a playwright like Odets yells STRIKE and everybody puts him up with Chekov and Ibsen. You can talk about your Depression Renaissance, these Writers and Artists Projects and all the rest. But just think of what we had: *The Waste Land* and Pound and Cummings—your poets are midgets compared to them—and our novelists. Why, in one year, 1925, we published *An American Tragedy, Arrowsmith,* Dos Passos' *Manhattan Transfer,* and *The Great Gatsby.* And books by Ellen Glasgow, Willa Cather, Tom Boyd, Edith Wharton, Elinor Wylie and some I've forgotten. Yes, and our stage was alive. We had O'Neill of course, and the Theater Guild really stood for something and there were intelligent plays by George Kelly, Max Anderson and Elmer Rice, Don Stewart—Eddie Mayer. And we had actresses, Cornell and Helen Hayes, Judith Anderson and Laurette Taylor, and Pauline Lord, Jane Cowl and Ina Claire. Oh, sure, they're still around but believe me, they aren't the same. We were all in love with our stars—maybe that made the difference. There was something special about those days. People were wittier and they did things better. And we knew how to give them that feeling that they were better than anyone had ever been before. Look at our athletes, Bobby Jones and Johnny Weismuller, Red Grange, Babe Ruth, Tommy Hitchcock, Hobey Baker and Dempsey and Tilden—they weren't only champions, they had a grace, a spirit, they knew how to be champions. I don't know, maybe I'm just getting to be a crotchety old man, but it seems to me our magazines were better, the *Mercury* and *Vanity Fair,* and the *New Yorker* was even fresher and more alive. And the songs, why were our songs so much better, *Embraceable You* and *My Man* and *Who*—I'll never forget the first time I heard Marilyn Miller sing it—and the Garrick Gaieties, *Now tell me what street compares with Mott Street in July* . . . you don't have anyone who twinkled like Marilyn Miller, haunted you like Jeanne Eagels—I even think our movie stars were better, Valentino was so much more what he was than any of yours today, and Doug had more energy and Pickford and Gish were more wistful, and Barbara La Marr and Swanson were more stunning and Carmel Myers was wickeder and Colleen Moore was cuter and Alice Joyce and Billie Dove had that breath-taking beauty you don't see any more. And we had Lindy. God how we loved Lindy. Maybe that's what's gone—that capacity for abstract love. Anyway, it seems rather symbolic, doesn't it, your Charles A. Lindbergh, the appeaser and our Lindy, the blue-eyed boy, the Lone Eagle, Horatio Alger in an airship conquering space."

Shep noticed patches of color faintly flushing Halliday's cheeks. Shep had seen men proudly possessive of a college or a club, able to enjoy the achievements of classmates or fellow-members as if they were their own. But he had never been confronted by vicarious pride extending over an entire decade.

Even while an inner voice cautioned Shep not to be carried away, that borrowed nostalgia seized him again. Damn it, it *had* been more fun in those days—at least there were no wars or breadlines to threaten them—they had enjoyed that exhilarating sense of kicking over traces—and there was a special glow around a Marilyn Miller, a Helen Morgan. And there was some special happy-go-lucky *zing* to *Sweet Sue* and *The Girlfriend*. Yes, and the writers were all originals, from Eliot and Pound to Hemingway, Lewis, Dos and Halliday. Sometimes you despaired of your own decade-on-a-hotseat. These Troubled Thirties that had smothered all those bright candles cheerfully burning at both ends. Sometimes you wearied of the voice of crisis forever simpering at you through the inexhaustive vocal cords of H. V. Kaltenborn, always there to explain away the inexplicable. What a jolly, irresponsible year 1925 must have been, with stocks going up, gin going down and nothing more serious to worry about than this morning's hangover. And yet, as Halliday had pointed out, it wasn't all glitter, jitter and right-off-the-boat. There was that serious work, damned hard work and damned good work; strange how the decade that had made a virtue of irresponsibility produced more responsible artists than any American decade before or since. The big writers had been producing in those days, with books appearing regularly in healthy flow. There was nothing like it now.

It was painful and disorienting: Halliday standing up for *his* heroes—*his* beauties—*his* songs. For here was tacit acceptance of the morbid arithmetic that he had ceased to live beyond 1929. Actually, Halliday had been—was still—a young man in the Thirties. Yet he seemed to see nothing strange in regarding the Thirties as an age in which he was only an interloper, if not a phantom, a man who spoke of himself as ten years dead.

A momentary silence had fallen over the conversation after Halliday's backward flight. Hold on to yourself, Manley. He had not meant to give way like this. Trying to pick a locale for the story, discussing Stearns' college days, 1925, Marilyn Miller and Jeanne Eagels—Lord, what a hopeless meander. Damned unprofessional, this wandering off from the starting line. Probably would have been healthier to draw a collaborator who never heard of my books—who didn't give a damn for the Twenties . . . Funny, when I think of home, I don't think of Kansas City, I think of those years, a gracefully swinging cantilever bridge gaily illuminated by twinkling evening lights. Now I know the Twenties were just a ten-year stretch to be followed by another ten-year stretch—and another, and another . . .

"It must have been a fascinating period all right," Shep was saying. "I wish to hell I had seen it. But from the point of view of economic morality, it was bankrupt as hell, wasn't it? All that crazy speculation, people buying stuff they didn't need, with money they didn't have. And all the fat cats repeating 'Business is fundamentally sound.' That's what fell on us like a ton of bricks —and we're still trying to dig ourselves out from under."

Shep let his bitterness grow now because he felt a little ashamed of his yearning for an era so irresponsible and economically false. This must be some flaw in him, this longing to go back to a ball to which he had not been invited, in a ballroom which had been torn down years before he had even learned to dance. After all, what better proof of those ten years' sickness than the way they had crippled Halliday?

Now that he had absorbed the initial shock of meeting Halliday, he had made his adjustment by considering Halliday as a relic somewhat miraculously brought back to life. For Shep, an enthusiastic collector of symbols, Halliday was a most satisfactory personification of the Twenties—his brilliant success in 1920— his youthful fame, so perfectly in step with the Myth of Success and the Cult of Being Young—his personal crash in 1929 that coincided so neatly with the Wall Street debacle—then the backwash after the wave has broken: the sorry end of the "perfect marriage," the "posthumous" novel in 1930, a failure that seemed to indicate a spiritual dead end, and which the critics attacked with a ferocity that suggested that they were sitting in judgment on an era rather than a book—and then the twilight years; Halliday a wandering wreck, occasionally appearing in mass circulation magazines with stories increasingly ordinary—and then finally, darkness—Hollywood. Oh, it was perfect. It could not have jibed more neatly with Shep's theories if he had made it all up himself. It was really most obliging of Manley Halliday to have his first success in the first year of the Twenties and crack up in the last.

"I suppose it's natural for you to turn on our generation," Halliday said. "It's one of the eternal cruelties that a son can only gain his independence by kicking his father in the teeth. But we did quite a lot, really. We cleared the landscape of all that rotten Victorian architecture—even if we had nothing to put in its place." He attempted to smile. "I suppose we could go on comparing notes this way for days, maybe months. But after lunch

55

we'll get down to business." Halliday glanced at his watch. "Good Lord, almost one o'clock! I'm supposed to be at the Vendome. I'll try to get back by two-thirty. And this afternoon let's say the first one who gets off the subject pays the other one five dollars."

"Okay, Mr. Halliday, we'll make like honest scriptwriters who never read a book in our lives."

"Right. Only synopses of bestsellers." In Halliday's voice was unexpected warmth. Boy had met Author, the first hurdle of self-consciousness was cleared, and now it seemed as if they would be able to work together. "Till later then, Stearns."

From the window Shep could see Halliday emerging onto the studio lot. The Eastern cut of his clothes and the old homburg set very straight on his head advertised his failure to come to terms with this casual environment.

6

The Vendome's parking lot attendant, a pimply-faced car expert
and confirmed snob, made no effort to conceal his contempt for
Halliday's old-fashioned Lincoln that towered anachronistically
above the sleek Caddy V16's the new Buick 8's, the resplendent
Chrysler Imperials and the new foreign star Rosa Risa's chromium Mercedes-Benz, his special love. Now what kind of a jerk,
he wondered, would be driving up to the Vendome in a wreck
like that? That was the nice thing about this job, you drove nothing but the best. That and the tips. But what sort of a tip would
a Lincoln '32 be good for? A '32—he pushed it into second with a
disrespectful grinding of gears—what a piece of junk! Like driving a cement-mixer. *Scratch* went the old Lincoln fender against
another fender alongside. Oh, well, it could have been worse. The
jerk had gone in already, the fender was scuffed up anyway and
the other car was only a Pontiac 6, a '37 at that.

Halliday passed the glamorous delicatessen counter—which
looked as if it had been moved intact from an exaggerated studio
set—and paused at the entrance to the dining room, his eyes pan-
ning the tables for sight of Al Harper. From the room rose the
blended aroma of expensive perfume—but it wasn't only the
Guerlain and the Caron. Halliday had often sensed that peculiar
bouquet emanating from the exceedingly prosperous. Yes, Halliday felt sure, were he to come into such a room blindfold, he
would know where he was, and in what company.

Looking in at all the beautiful women and men who were
either handsome of face or of position or of sartorial finesse, Halliday hesitated. In a moment he would have to join them, but for
these few seconds he indulged his reluctance. Did he fear these
chic traps now for their own sake, after mature judgment, or
merely because he had slipped down the scale to an unnoticed
background figure, a Vendome dress-extra, like those ghost-stars
of the silent screen now grateful for ten-dollar calls?

"Hello, sweetheart." Halliday felt a solicitous hand at his elbow, guiding him confidently into the room.

"Oh, hello, Harper."

Al Harper, in Halliday's mind, was *my little man*. Actually he was not much shorter than Halliday. He was a bundle of acquisitive energy carefully and expensively attired, in somewhat better taste than Halliday would have expected from a Hollywood agent. His way of dressing, Halliday decided, was a successful hybrid between an elegant Wall Streeter's and a musical comedy star's. The suit was sharkskin from Schmidt, the tie hand-painted from Alexander & Oviatt, the white silk handkerchief artfully hung over the pocket suggested flamboyance. And the shoes, the shoes, Halliday thought, were the give-away, imported brown loafers that, like the tie and the handkerchief, lent a sportive note somewhat incongruous with the shrewd, quick look of the face.

With an insistent familiarity from which Halliday flinched, Harper did not relinquish his arm until they were at the table. There, with a mumbled *back-in-a-sec,* Halliday found himself abandoned while Harper crossed the aisle for a left-handed handshake with Claudette Colbert and her husband, the nice doctor whose name no one ever seemed to remember. On the way back Harper paused for a moment of homage to Louella Parsons. What is the exact word for that false smile they bestow on each other? Halliday mused. Hollywood table-hopping always opened cysts of irritability within him. Smirk? Almost, but not quite. Simper—that was the word.

A cloud of laughter at a witty exit line trailed Harper back to his table. Halliday watched him coldly. Most of his life he had been able to afford to be quite rude to people for whom he felt no particular attraction; the obligation to be polite to *everybody* on the theory that sooner or later he might be of some material service to you was a serious infringement on pure freedom, Halliday thought. Only aristocrats and hoboes enjoyed the luxury of being rude on impulse.

"Sorry, sweetheart."

Impervious to Halliday's troubled silence, Harper bustled into his chair. The waiter hovered with a waiter's mirthless smile. Perhaps a cocktail before lunch, gentlemen?

Glancing at Halliday, Harper barely hesitated before saying, "No, I think we'll go ahead and order, Carlos."

Halliday fought his temper. The little hustler might allow me the privilege of rejecting my own drink. He listened drily while Harper ordered Eggs Benedict, a chef's green salad ("easy on the garlic, Carlos"); he said he would have the same.

"Well, Manley," the pitch began, "got the script all finished?"

This was a standard opener to his writers the first day of any assignment. Halliday tried to oblige with a smile.

"You'll enjoy working for Milgrim," Harper assured him. "That's why I was so happy about getting you this job." (—But it was really Ann who got me this job, Halliday was thinking.) "I could of had you at National weeks ago. But after all you're an important writer. I realize that. Some of these agents out here, just because you haven't got any credits and you're a little hard to sell, they'd of grabbed that National thing and Harry Nochel would of beaten your brains out. Punch in at nine, so many pages a day, you know, the same way he treats those dogs who get three-fifty a week. But you—even if you don't have any credits—you're a highly sensitive personality. You need a producer who's a gentleman, a personality with some background. That's why I think working with Victor is such a sweet set-up for you. Victor has a brilliant mind. And did you get a load of that library? Why, you take that Harry Nochel, he has all he can do to read a synopsis, how Harry Nochel ever got where he is I'll never . . ."

Harper's words hung in mid air, then suddenly fell away into a pocket of silence. Approaching the table with a beautiful, dime-a-dozen blonde was a bald-headed man with the body of a gorilla wrapped in a richly tailored double-breasted suit, an ugly man who dressed and carried himself as if he were irresistibly handsome.

"Harry! sweetheart!" Harper half rose and tried to embrace Nochel across the table.

"Hello, Al," Nochel said. There was a disagreeable line to his mouth, Halliday noticed, even when he was smiling. "When do I get that check for last Friday night?"

"It's in the mail already, Harry. So tomorrow you don't have to worry where the next meal is coming from." He winked at the girl. Nochel and the blonde laughed. They knew where everything was coming from.

"How about a little golfie this Saturday?"

"Gonna be in Palm Springs."

"Yeah? Maybe I'll be down too. I'll look for you, sweetheart." Then, in a quieter tone, the proper vessel for sincerity: "Say, Harry I caught *I Married Your Wife* at the sneak Monday." Here words failed Harper. He merely blew a little kiss of appreciation.

"Darling, I'm but starved," the blonde said.

"What a girl," Nochel said admiringly. "Eats more than Seabiscuit."

The couple moved on to other tables, other left-handshakes, other lies.

Halliday watched Harper's face assume the mood of their previous conversation. Harper's was a chameleon face, Halliday decided, adjustable to whatever type Harper found himself addressing. A moment ago it had been the kind of face that went with Nochel's poker games and his blondes in Palm Springs. But now Harper's face wore a sober look, the expression of a man who does not live by bread and smart deals alone, who appreciates "better things." Harper had never read a Halliday novel. But he identified this client with a vague upper reach. "Better things" were also associated in Harper's mind with impractical things, poems, censorable plays and books that couldn't get past the Hays Office, things studios didn't want. Manley Halliday was very nearly something the studios didn't want, and as a trim little weather-vane on a Hollywood roof-top, Al Harper inclined toward condescension when facing Halliday. But Al was one of those shrewdly ignorant men who knew enough to know how much more there is to know, and he had the semi-illiterate's respect for books he would never read. So braided through his condescension for Halliday's lowly status in the industry there was admiration for Halliday's literary reputation. A Pulitzer

Prize winner, he kept saying to himself, look at his suit, I can buy and sell him a thousand times over, but still, a Pulitzer Prize winner. "Now let's see, where was I, Manley, what was I telling you?"

"I think you were telling me how lucky I was to be working for such a brilliant man as Victor Milgrim."

"Oh, yeah—Manley, the reason I wanted to have lunch with you the first day on the job is this: I'm not the kind of agent that just collects his ten percent and kisses you off. I worry about you, sweetheart. I want to see you make good. Now let's face it, Manley, just between ourselves, you need a credit."

"How about my books? Aren't they *credits*?"

Halliday felt absurdly proud of this little demonstration of twilight courage.

"Sure, sure, in a way." Harper could afford to be magnanimous. "But you know what I mean, a *picture* credit. That's why I'm so happy about placing you with Victor Milgrim." (Halliday noticed the solemnity with which nearly everyone pronounced the full name, as if it were already a symbol like Patrick Henry or Mahatma Gandhi). "I'll tell you, Manley, I'm looking ahead. This should be the beginning of a highly profitable connection for you. Despite what's happened to you, Victor Milgrim still has a lot of faith in you. He tells everybody he meets that you're one of his favorite American authors, and you know, sweetheart, that kind of word of mouth ain't bad. Say, by the way, Manley, I promised Victor I'd get him a whole set of your books autographed. He's got books autographed by all the authors who've worked for him, Aldous Huxley, Vicki Baum, Jesse Lasky, Jr . . . but all your books except that one in Modern Library are out of print."

Harper made this statement of fact sound rather like an accusation, Halliday thought. He tried to listen to what Harper was saying. Harper talked rapidly, with nervous assurance and Halliday heard the words running together, faintly, still fainter, as if he were moving away from Harper, through a long tunnel, tunneling back through time, a year, two years, back to the inside room in the kind of Hollywood hotel never mentioned in columns or featured on the air, with a guest-list that ran to cockroaches, extras, has-beens, the blonde, Georgette whatshername, who had been almost a star in Thirty-one, who was always on her way into or out of one of those terrible laughing-crying drunks and who paid her rent by making available to the manager her tarnished favors . . . Where were all the notes he had made on that place the Hollywood Arms, *into whose scabious arms,* he remembered writing somewhere, *floated the flotsam and jetsam of industrial turnover—in an industry that turned over more frequently than the average restless sleeper.* He himself had floated into the Hollywood Arms from the Plaza, and before that, one step up, the Roosevelt—"one more week, if you could only wait one more week, my agent assures me there's something coming up at Paramount"—oh God, the cliché of the empty-pocket clamping down on your tongue like a leaden bit. And he had come back to Hollywood for money, because Hollywood was money. An agent absurdly named Phil Coyne as in morality plays had promised money and Manley had pulled himself up out of that bender. *Help me Help me I am lost I lift up mine eyes to the hills but there are no hills only this world of darkness, this dark world honey-combed with narrow hotel rooms where a million Manley Hallidays lay with damp towels on their throbbing foreheads.* Benders cost money. You go on a bender because you have no money, so having no money costs money . . . Jere cost money. He had known it would cost money to have Jere. What he had not known is that it would cost more money not to have Jere. Jere and her poems privately printed to make her happy. But they had not made her happy. All they had made was another subject for her analyst, another hour, another fifty dollars, fifty after fifty after fifty, down the drain of introspection-made-easy, down down down down dropped Jere *Doctor I adore Manley . . . only man I ever really loved really really loved . . . but I can't stand for him to touch me, Doctor . . . I love him I miss him and yet . . . I hate to be drunk I hate it I try not to but I need one so badly and then I can't stop always was my trouble they built me with sleek lines and a high-powered motor but no brakes I never could stop I drive through railings and I'm falling falling falling as in a dream only Doctor that isn't true about never hitting bottom I do hit bottom oh I do I do and I splatter all over the place thou-*

sands of little pieces of me strewn over the world and only
Manley can pick them up and put me together and Manley
won't come oh why won't he come he wants me to stay in little
pieces. The Farm one hundred dollars a day Manley darling I
ran away I couldn't stand those horrible guards All they want to
do is try and get you into bed No darling it's true I swear it's
true $50 $100 $50 $100—"I believe she's cured of the physical desire for alcohol, Mr. Halliday. Of course she still requires" $50
$100 $50 $100 and the letters from Douglas, righteous and ac-
cusing My allowance failed to arrive for the second straight
week. You don't seem to realize how embarrassing it is not to
be able to pay my roommate back the day I promised. Marylou
is coming up for the Christmas Dance and I can't very well explain to her that I haven't money enough to buy her a corsage.
Money money a detail a flyspeck enlarged to the size of an elephant.

And in his room at the hotel waiting for the phone to ring
like a hungry extra . . .

Years back he had written just such a story for *Red Book*
called *The Telephone Slave* and everyone had thought it was
quite brilliant. There he was, Manley Halliday, the victim of his
own brilliant plot, answering each ring with half-muffled hope,
borrowing on insurance, selling first editions against that just-
around-the-corner day when Phil Coyne would talk someone
into giving him a job. There was that inevitable afternoon when
he realized he had called Coyne five times without a return, when
he was told once too often that "Mr. Coyne's just stepped out" and
"Mr. Coyne's out of the city until some time next week." That's
when he had sat down in his dark cubicle at the Hollywood Arms
and written identical letters on Hotel Roosevelt stationery to
every important producer in town. " . . . although I have been
back in Hollywood for some months, it is only this week that I
find myself in sufficiently good health to accept a studio assignment. I assume that you have some acquaintance with my
written works but in the event that you have not, I trust you will
permit me a moment of immodesty in which to remind you
that critics have been kind enough to consider only Hemingway
my equal as a master of modern dialogue. I am so bold as to

write you directly because I have come to have a genuine regard for the motion picture medium and I believe I could make a significant contribution to its . . ." *Oh Christ,* he had wanted to cry out *I am hungry. I need work.* But after many drafts the letter had gone off.

Every day for three weeks Manley had called Coyne's secretary to find if there had been an answer. Finally he had stopped calling. And then, the very day he received the bill from Jere's latest sanitarium—that refuge for broken-down socialites on Long Island—for $800 which might just as well have been $8,000,000, Mr. Coyne's secretary called. There was a letter for him, from Joe Munger of Monarch. "Shall I mail it out to you?" asked the sweet voice of unconcern. "No—no—I'll be right down!"

The cab was an extravagant $1.85, plus a quarter tip. Hollywood was a cruel geographical joke on the moneyless, with studios and agencies scattered from Universal City thirty miles across the valley to Culver City. He tore open the letter—he had not mentioned salary but Phil Coyne could settle that now that Munger was interested—and read:

Dear Mr. Halliday,

I was very happy to receive your letter for otherwise I would not have known where to get in touch with you.

Mrs. Munger happens to be one of your most enthusiastic admirers. Her birthday is next month and as an extra little "surprise" I'd love to present her with autographed copies of your books. I would consider it a great personal favor if you would inscribe these "To Mona" with some appropriate personal sentiment.

As to the question of an assignment, frankly we have nothing at the moment suitable to an author of your accomplishments. But I shall certainly keep you in mind, and meanwhile I shall be deeply indebted for your kindness in complying with my request.

With kindest personal regards,
Joseph B. Munger

JBM/ar

Mona. The name was a faint tinkle of a distant bell. Not Mona Moray, who inspired that terrible fight between him and Jere the night of the Neilan party at the Ambassador! By God, he did remember something years ago about Mona's giving up her career to marry some big Hollywood shot . . . the point of this latest joke would have made him laugh if it hadn't drawn blood. Fifteen letters to producers begging a job and his only answer is from Mrs. Munger née Moray, whose husband can have no idea what significance these books—and their author—once had for her.

Well, to hell with Joe Munger and his great personal favors. He knew what that deep indebtedness was worth.

Capitulating to himself, Manley had sent the Modern Library *High Noon* (costing with author's discount 57 cents) to Mona with a restrained, dignified inscription. He had never been sure whether it was venality or vanity or nostalgia or simple generosity that had impelled him.

"—but speaking very frankly . . ." the words sneaked up on Halliday as if they had been stalking him and suddenly cornered him. *Frankly* Halliday brought his mind back to the conversation with a bitter wrench, Hollywood's favorite adverb, "frankly, Manley," Harper was saying, "I wish I hadn't had to ask for this advance."

"But you were able to get it?"

Harper tapped his inside pocket. "Give it to you when we get out. It isn't the wisest thing to do with Victor Milgrim, but since you seem to need it so badly . . . One thing I've learned in my dealings with Victor, he has no patience with any kind of failure, creative, financial or what-have-you. By nature he's a winner himself. He likes front-runners. He'll pay a man anything as long as he's on top. The fact that you have sucl· an immediate need for the money he's paying you may put some doubts about you in the back of his mind. Of course it's nothing serious, nothing a good script won't cure."

"Some of the best writers in America never got out of debt to their publishers," Halliday said quietly. But perhaps he had only said this to reassure himself, for Harper did not seem to hear him.

65

"In getting your two G's in advance, I had to make one little promise to Victor Milgrim, sweetheart. I don't think you'll mind."

"What was that?" Halliday said. He was afraid he knew.

"Well, I—you know this town, Manley, there's bound to be a little talk about your drinking. So Victor wanted you to give him your word you wouldn't touch a drop until the script was finished and okayed."

"Didn't you tell him I haven't had a drink in seven months and twenty-three days?"

"Oh, sure, they know, they know that, Manley. Otherwise they wouldn't of hired you." Harper was uncomfortable. "It's just that—well, you understand, two thousand a week is a lot of money and you can hardly blame Victor for . . ."

"I haven't even wanted a drink in seven months and twenty-three days," Halliday said testily. "In the last three-and-a-half years I have been drunk exactly twice. What does Milgrim want, a signed pledge stamped by a notary public?"

He wanted to say much more. He wanted to say how his flesh was made to crawl. He wanted to say: After twenty years of fame, I will not be talked to by you people like a delinquent schoolboy being considered for his first job. He wanted to say— but, oh hell, there was that nice check in Harper's pocket.

"Manley," Harper was saying, "you've got to pitch in and give this everything you've got. Believe me, sweetheart, it's your big chance. The script has to be only terrific."

Guiltily, Halliday caught himself thinking less of the meaning of Harper's words than of how he said them, the inflection, the phrasing. He could not help running Harper through his character-machine that broke him down into special peculiarities, details of dress, eating habits, idiosyncrasies, distinguishing features of face. For the process of writing (not movie writing but *writing*) had become a reflex and he was forever adding to the notebook in his mind flash impressions, happy phrases, bits of dialogue, give-away traits. Harper's habit of grinning deceptively before saying something particularly threatening, for instance . . .

But he must stop this, he warned himself. He must listen to

his little man and his serious words of local wisdom. For this *was* his big chance and that script did have to be, in their glib jargon, only terrific. Even if Al Harper saw this as the ultimate goal toward which everyone should want to aspire, while Manley Halliday knew it was simply buying time for a second chance.

7

The eyes and ears of Victor Milgrim, it seemed, were in the corridors, the office walls, behind the couches; sometimes the studio itself seemed to be merely an architectural extension of his being. And so, when Peggy's call brought the unexpected information that Victor Milgrim was ready for their conference, Shep wondered if this was the Great Man's way of pointing a finger at Halliday's two-hour lunch on the other side of town. That it could be only coincidence that timed Milgrim's call before Halliday had returned from the Vendome did not even occur to Shep. So saturated with the insistent spirit of Victor Milgrim had this atmosphere become that Shep automatically accepted his call as a rebuke aimed at Halliday's dilatory lunching.

"Peggy, we—can't come right down. Mr. Halliday is—down the hall." In desperation Shep grasped the first euphemistic straw.

"Well, soon as he comes back, get your derrières down here. The conference on now is breaking up and you're next, my sweet."

Shep was too concerned with Halliday's absence to hold up his end of the repartee. Now there was Halliday to worry about. It was 3:05. What if he had quit? Decided life was too short and this stint too gruesome? Could be. A man of Halliday's sensibilities . . . That was it. He had talked it over with his agent at lunch (perhaps some day Shep would rate a top agent like Harper) and decided this ball of damp fluff was not for him. Shep went a little numb with disappointment. He had started so high that morning, borne up in a rush of excitement at the chance to work with Halliday. He had even believed—or was he just kidding himself—a certain tentative bond possible between them.

Halliday came in with soft reluctance. He bowed slightly, with a kind of sarcasm Shep could hardly resent, since it clearly included them both. "Mr. Stearns."

"His Master's Voice calls us," Shep said. The note of badinage was intended to hide his own apprehension.

"Oh, Victor's bothering us already?"

(Damn it, why did he have to play the Great Writer for this boy?) He wished he could feel as aloof as he had made himself sound. He mustn't truckle to Victor Milgrim. What was Milgrim, after all, but a dandy with a flair for success?

But intellectual snobbishness would not exorcise the fear. At least in his old age—he made this jest so often it was coming true—he had become an interchangeable part of the machine. Well, only for a little while, ten weeks—what's ten weeks in a lifetime?—he would play the fool to King Victor. Only he would maintain the fool's delicate line of insubordination.

"I guess he's waiting for us, Mr. Halliday. Seems to want a story conference."

"I can never think in a story conference," Halliday said. "It's too—too public."

"I know a writer who can't write at all," Shep assured him. "But he's a genius when he's talking on his feet."

As they were going out the door the phone began again. "It's Mr. Milgrim," Halliday's secretary said, caught in the web of panic like the rest.

"Tell him—tell him the hook-and-ladder boys have already started sliding down the pole."

But by the time they reached the office, Peggy said (somewhat more formally than if Shep had been alone, in deference to Mr. Halliday's apparent reputation): "It will be just a few minutes. Bill Ross" (that was Milgrim's assistant) "and Blumberg and Marsden" (the writing team scripting *Pursued*) "just sneaked in for a minute."

Twenty minutes passed slowly. Peggy was inside with her shorthand book. It was the waiting, Shep thought, the waiting. Eventually this waiting sawed you off at the base of your self-respect.

As the minute hand crept on, Halliday's spirits drooped. On

his arrival the door should have been flung wide, the carpet un-rolled. The nerve of vanity in him was hopelessly exposed.

Shep Stearns, increasingly responsive to Halliday's susceptibil-ities, but younger and tougher and less reasonable, hated the idea of Milgrim keeping Halliday waiting. For him, whose thinking ran consistently to the grand abstractions, it was a sym-bol of the injustices at loose in the world.

Now the nearest door was opening, releasing the unhappy sounds of obsequious laughter. Julie Blumberg, a sensitive, tal-ented kid when he had come out eight years before, was talented and successful and cautious now, his aesthetic principles sub-limated to the welfare of his family. Lex Marsden was a shrewd man who played golf and cards with the producers and knew the plot of every successful picture turned out in the past ten years. He was useful to Blumberg, who still had to make up in talent what he lacked in push. They had just had a bad time in the conference; Milgrim had thrown out their new line; they'd have to come up with something, but fast. Bill Ross, who had been enthusiastic about their line but had failed to defend it in this conference when he saw which way Victor Milgrim was blowing, Bill Ross whom Milgrim and Blumberg and Mars-den despised, was laughing hardest of all.

Milgrim nodded to Halliday from the threshold and Halliday and Stearns rose. "Boys," Milgrim addressed Blumberg and Mars-den, "have you met Manley Halliday?" The name was too faint an echo for Marsden, but Blumberg reacted as Milgrim had hoped he would.

"I'm one of your great admirers, Mr. Halliday."

Milgrim looked proud. Halliday answered with his slight bow. "Thank you, sir," he said. And Bill Ross, a signal light turned red or green on slightest pressure, now flashed: "It's really a great honor to have you with us, Mr. Halliday."

"Thank you, sir," Halliday said again, and in the way he said this and bowed again, exactly as he had before, Shep felt the mockery.

"Sorry to keep you waiting, Manley." When Milgrim moved in, the charm blew out hot and fast as from the suddenly opened door of a blast furnace. "Come on in."

70

Feeling like an appendage of Halliday which did not need to be individually acknowledged, Shep followed them.

"Be sure to send those flowers to the plane and tell the Markeys I'd love to come if we didn't have a preview," Milgrim called to Peggy as the door closed her out.

"I didn't think that last huddle would take more than five minutes," Milgrim apologized again. "But sometimes I think writers have a genius for confusing simple things. A film story only needs one good problem—will the hero tame the shrew?—will the nice girl win her man back from the bitch? I call it the furnace. Build your fire hot enough in the basement and you'll generate heat right up to the top floor—or, in other words, to your climax. If my writers could only remember that, we'd save a million dollars a year."

He paused to taste his metaphor and finding it good, he sighed luxuriously. "Before we pitch into your story, Manley . . ." the buzzer interrupted. "All right, put her on." Then the change in voice, shamelessly winning: "Jean, have they ever criticized you for anything you wore in one of my pictures? . . . Darling, be a good girl, wear that evening gown. You're the only gal in town with the figure to get away with it."

That seemed to take care of Jean. Milgrim, with a wink to Halliday, picked up exactly where he had left off. ". . . Before we pitch into your story, Manley, are you perfectly comfortable? Office all right? Are you happy with Miss Boylan? Is this guy," acknowledging Shep's presence for the first time "giving you any trouble?"

"On the contrary," Halliday said, "if all of them had Stearns' awareness, I would have to revise my opinion of Hollywood writers."

Everybody was pleased—the Great Man, the Great Author and the Young Man of Promise. At that moment *Love on Ice* had merely to be written and produced to result in an achievement reflecting credit on all three.

"I have a theory about this picture," Milgrim announced. The buzzer signaled another call. This time it was the head of a rival studio from whom Milgrim wanted to borrow a ranking director. "Leo," he fenced, "before you give me a quick answer, what if I should see my way clear to letting Jean Costello do an outside picture?" They decided to get together for lunch one day next week and talk the whole thing over. Once more Milgrim was able to come back to the conference as if he had never been away: "My theory is this, Manley. We've all seen college musicals from *Good News* on. And after a while they all begin to run together. Now I believe in being honest with my writers. I want this picture to be a money-maker. I've made my share of daring subjects and I will again. This time I want to play safe, in subject matter. But I want the quality to be top drawer. That's what I hired you for, Manley. In other words I want to do a story that's—well, let's call it commercially sound—with fresh, believable characters, smart dialogue. I have a hunch we can put together an intelligent college musical without going highbrow. There was nothing sensationally new about *Alexander's Ragtime Band*, for instance. Yet I wouldn't have been ashamed to have my name on it. And you know how high my standards are."

"In other words," Halliday injected quietly, "you believe in teaching old dogs new tricks?"

"You bet I do!" Milgrim took him up enthusiastically. "That's the surest route to profitable pictures I know. Take me, Manley, I'm an old dog. And I'm full of new tricks."

He grinned at his own knack for improvisation. "And then once in a while, for variety's sake, we try a new dog with old tricks. For instance, I'd like to talk with you about doing *High Noon* some time, Manley. Maybe together we could work out an angle."

"I'd rather not have it done than see it made the way the Hays Office would make you do it," Halliday said with a firmness that delighted Shep and even surprised himself.

"I wish my writers out here had that kind of integrity," Milgrim strung along. "I'm sick and tired of you Guild members—" he had suddenly turned on Shep "—complaining about being pushed around, squawking about control of material. Hell, most of you would be lost if we didn't bring you back to sound principles. The ones who get pushed around," he turned back to Manley, speaking less harshly, as if he were explaining all this to a guest touring the studio, "are those who deserve to get pushed around."

"Didn't Sorel say something like that in his *Reflections on Violence?*" Halliday asked.

"I'll come clean with you, Manley. I wouldn't know. I used to be an omnipotent reader when I was in college. But when do I get a chance to read? Scripts to study every night. I think the greatest luxury of my life is to sit down with a good book and not worry about what kind of a picture it's going to make. This year I read *Man's Hope,* by that French writer. Powerful. Simply powerful. But of course it could never make a picture. It's one of those things we just can't touch."

The screenplay Shep hadn't been able to sell had told the story of a young college graduate who goes to fight for the Loyalists.

"Much too controversial," Milgrim answered his look. "See what happened to Wanger's *Blockade*. The Legion of Decency made him cut the script to ribbons and the Knights of Columbus still picketed the picture." Milgrim shook his head wisely. "When will producers ever learn to stay away from politics? I even think the Warners are nuts to make something like *Confessions of a Nazi Spy*. Damn it, no matter what we think of those countries personally, we're still maintaining diplomatic relations, we're still trying to do business with them."

Before you stick your neck out too far, Shep tried to believe, let it grow a little stronger. But now, with Halliday sure to know what he was thinking, it was difficult to hide from himself. "But you can't just lock 'politics' in a little box and throw the key away, Mr. Milgrim. Politics are a lot closer to basic human drives than most people think."

Halliday had been watching the face of the earnest young man. It was a strong face physically, with its irregular, European, unaristocratic attractiveness that was just coming into style with John Garfield. Could it be depression values, Manley wondered, that turned women from the smooth boys with the slicked-down hair to these sturdier, more emotional, non-Anglo-Saxon heroes?

Halliday tried to bring his mind back to the point of discussion. It was all politics now. Just as everything was once reduced to religion, so everything now was forced into the overcrowded corral of politics. And such very simple politics.

The warning buzzer of the dictaphone and the insistent ringing of the phone snapped Milgrim back to the high-strung practicalities of picture-making. "Jimmy, I'll be honest with you," he was telling the agent on the other end (henceforth, Halliday warned himself, when he heard that phrase, *on guard!*) "I want Monica for the part. She's absolutely right for the mother. But I'd shelve the picture before I'd pay her one-twenty-five. Hell, I could get Anderson for seventy-five and she wouldn't be bad either. I'm being honest with you, Jimmy. I'm not trading this time. One hundred thousand for the picture, period. Why don't you talk to Monica and call me back?"

Again he shook his head as he hung up, a man sorely put upon. "These goddam agents are going to put us out of business. Three years ago Monica Dawson was starving to death on Broadway. Now these agents get her so worked up her feelings are hurt if she's only offered a hundred thousand dollars for five weeks' work."

A strange business, Halliday was thinking. These men are in business but they're more emotional than business men. And they're involved with art but they're altogether too business-like for artists.

Milgrim rose and crossed the office into his private bathroom. The moment he was gone they looked at each other conspiringly. "Omnipotent," Shep whispered. They shared the joke with silent satisfaction. It made them feel good: these little things in common that barely needed saying. Milgrim returned to the conference with a clear resolve to dispatch it efficiently. "Well, Manley, you've been thinking about our story for a day or two. Had any hot flashes yet?"

This was what he dreaded, the story conference. Despite everything that had happened he had never, or almost never, lost faith in himself. He had clung to the conviction that he could always lock himself up in his room and lock his mind up in his head, and his characters with it and let them go at it, let them begin to *work*, to catalyze—but that goes on *inside*, not out here, not here in public. And if you talk about them, talk them out of your head they may turn to stone or dust or, worst of all, *words*. So Manley Halliday did not know what to say. Those were only snow girls and boys in *Love on Ice* and the only result Halliday's mind had on them so far was to melt them down to dirty puddles.

"We've dropped a few plumb lines down to try and get our bearings," Halliday said uneasily.

Milgrim wasn't altogether satisfied with that.

"Naturally, I don't want to rush you," Milgrim said, "but we haven't got too much time. Pretty soon you'll want to decide whether to keep Stearns' line and improve on it or throw it all out and start from scratch."

"We've been giving some thought to the two roommates," Shep found himself saying. "We've thrown out the conventional Joe Colleges I started with. We think one of the boys might be the son of the college's richest trustee. And his roommate's a campus radical who has to wash dishes in the school cafeteria and . . ." Shep was ad-libbing shamelessly. In the story conferences he had attended he had watched the talkers with a certain horrified fascination. The man with quick-silver ideas and a quick mouth could work small, tinseled miracles in the early conferences.

"Mmm-hmm, mm-hmm." Milgrim nodded, watching Halliday for corroboration or amplification. "That might work. I'd like to hear it in more detail."

"Victor, we haven't really thought about your story at all yet."

Halliday had been wanting to say that from the beginning.

"Oh?"

As in any game, from bike races to story conferences, the man who jumped off first had the advantage. Milgrim, who usually stayed on top of these conferences, was off balance now and Halliday, speaking with just the right note of dignified reserve, increased his lead.

"So far we've talked about my books, and about contemporary writing; and we've compared a few notes on our respective generations. But I don't think we've been wasting our time."

Not sure whether to be shocked or impressed, Milgrim said,

"Well, Manley, at least I admire your frankness." His tone was purposely ambiguous.

"In other words, Victor, we've been spending our time trying to get acquainted," Halliday went on. "After all, you can hardly expect perfect strangers to shake hands for the first time and just sit right down and start working together. In many ways collaboration is just as complex as marriage—maybe a little more so."

Milgrim chuckled uncertainly.

The Great Author had played his part nicely. After a momentary falter, he had struck an attitude of urbane intelligence that set him apart from the double-talkers who passed through Milgrim's office. This was the difference between artists and hacks, Milgrim obviously had decided, between real authors and clever ad-libbers. This was going to be a great success and Darryl and Dave Selznick and Walter Wanger and the rest of them were going to be saying, "Isn't that a typical Milgrim hunch for you—bringing back a famous has-been like Halliday?" Maybe they'd go on and do *The Night's High Noon*— there were ways to get around the Hays Office. Of course you'd probably have to get the husband and wife together—the end would be a little too sordid otherwise, a little too *down* as Halliday had originally written it . . .

"Boys, could you get ready to take a little trip the day after tomorrow?"

"Catalina?" Halliday had heard from Ann about those trips on Victor's boat. He'd invite his writers for a pleasure cruise and make them talk story all week-end. "A luxurious version of the Bedaux stretch-out," Ann had called it.

"No, we'll do that when we get back, Manley. Next week-end's the Webster Winter Mardi Gras. I'm sending a camera crew up there to get the background stuff. That's why I'll need you along. I'm not expecting a complete shooting script over-night exactly—"—only Milgrim smiled—"but the boys will need a pretty definite outline by the time we arrive."

"But, Victor, couldn't we work that out from here and phone or wire it to you?"

Milgrim shook his head. "After all, the thing that's going to sell this picture is real college types. Your characters 'll have to look like 'em, think like 'em, talk like 'em. I tell you a week-end up there'll give you more fresh ideas than a month in the studio."

The location trip had caught Halliday by surprise and he was vulnerable. The Mardi Gras meant distance and snow and ice and the discomfort of travel and the extra effort of having to be nice to strangers. And the lack of Ann.

"But, Victor, the ink is hardly dry on Stearns' diploma and he seems to be a perceptive young man. I think he knows enough about how they look and talk and think. And since you're in such a hurry for a line, I'm sure we could work faster here."

To travel East with Manley Halliday, come back to Webster with him, show him off to Professor Croft and the other English professors, really get to know him . . . No less than Milgrim, Shep was impatient of Halliday's protest.

"I wasn't thinking so much about Shep," Milgrim persisted. "I thought it would be a sort of refresher course for you, Manley. Those were terrific college scenes in the first part of *Friends and Foes*. But after all that was twenty years ago."

"I remember the Mardi Gras," Halliday said. "I don't imagine it's changed too much."

"Maybe that's one mistake we all make," Milgrim said, obviously including himself for courtesy's sake. "Imagining that things don't change."

Oh Christ, if I could just sit down somewhere and write his old movie for him, Halliday thought peevishly, without all this palaver, without having people constantly rubbing my nose in my own past, without all these additional difficulties, this trip—he'd have to talk Milgrim out of that idea. Travel, like wenching, was a young man's game.

"Victor, do you really think it's necessary for me to go all the way back to Webster? After all, if it's just current collegiana you want me to brush up on, I could wander around U.C.L.A."

"But that's just what I don't want—U.C.L.A. I want the richness, the—fine old atmosphere of the Ivy League."

"You may not remember, but critics used to praise my photographic memory. I don't have to travel three thousand miles to describe Webster." He thought, but decided not to say: And how much of what we really know of a place ever reaches the screen anyway?

"Now stop talking like an old codger, Manley. The trip 'll do you good." Milgrim turned to Shep—using him when he needed him—with a wink. "Wait'll he sees those Mardi Gras babes! It'll make us both feel young, Manley."

Halliday did not like it. He did not like it at all. He was in no mood for other people's parties. He had already gone to too many of his own.

"Seriously, Victor. I'm—at your service, of course—but I hardly think it's necessary for me to make this trip."

"For goodness' sake, Manley"—in Milgrim's voice was the good humor of self-confident authority—"I'm not asking you to go to Tibet. What's New York—fifteen hours—and another few hours to Webster. You'll be back in a week."

What had a week or a month or a continent or a hemisphere meant to him and Jere when the going was good? Hadn't they crossed continents as casually as most people cross streets? Once they had chartered a plane from New York to New Orleans for Toni Michaud's engagement party—and taken off again at 5 A.M. in their evening clothes to keep a date with Mencken in Baltimore. And the time Norman Kerry had called from Hollywood to tell them he wanted to give a party for them, to celebrate his playing Ted Bentley in that silent version of *High Noon*. Kerry had thought he was making a local call to them when actually they were at the Ritz in New York (his secretary having said merely that she had the Hallidays on the line). Instead of telling him they were three thousand miles away they had thought it simpler and more fun just to say they would come. So the next afternoon they went out on the Century. The party had been all right. They had stayed three months. He had even knocked out a magazine serial about the episode, collected in one of those amusing, quickly forgotten books, *Around Hollywood in Ninety Days*. After making over thirty thousand on the trip, it had still cost him money. But the real cost came much later, severe drafts on his spirit when he was already spiritually O.D.

Yes, he had taken enough trains and planes and ships and

78

cable cars and bicycles and ski-lifts to last him several lifetimes, certainly the one he was trying to live now.

"Victor, I . . ." (mightn't be too wise to blame poor health: Harper had warned him of Milgrim's dislike of unsuccessful people: failure to remain healthy might be held against him too.) "I really think the wisest thing is a division of labor. I could be straightening out the line while you and Stearns go East to . . ."

"Manley," Milgrim's tone was growing firmer, "naturally I want you to feel as comfortable as possible on this job. But unless your reason is unanswerable—doctor's orders or something like that—I think you'd better arrange to leave the day after tomorrow."

How could he tell this formidable man, this supremely positive man, this success: I do not want to leave Ann Loeb. I do not want to try to live without her, even for one week. *I can't live without you*—the romantic cliché, essentially false, sometimes furthest from the truth, had gained, in his case, clinical validity. Could he live without Ann Loeb? He hoped to beg the question. He could not bring himself to marry her though. Not while Jere was alive. Maybe not even if he should outlive Jere. Yet in a way they were more married than ever he and Jere had been. After all, from the painful vantage of retrospect he and Jere had never really had a marriage. At its best (and ah how very good that was) it had been a prolonged honeymoon, or a series of honeymoons; suddenly his mind snatched a line from Saroyan's tender vaudeville, "No foundation, all the way down the line . . ."

No, there had been no foundation, neither to his life nor to Jere, symbol of so much of his life. If only divorce could drive a woman out of mind as well as sight. If only she were dead and could be buried in hate or bitterness. If only he could dwell in the golden days. Or if only he could make his peace with the present. Hadn't he the same claim on the present as Victor Milgrim or young Stearns?

"Another reason for going," Milgrim was saying, "is I have to be in New York next week anyway, for a sales convention. So this'll give us a chance to straighten out the story in New York and at Webster. I don't want to tell you how to write your script, of course. But I usually have a few ideas—a few short cuts, call them that," he added modestly. "Manley, I hate to bear down on you so hard, but that's the picture business. I've got to count on you to come up with that line by the time we huddle in New York."

As if to cut off any possible escape, Milgrim called Peggy in and told her to reserve transportation and a suite for them at the Waldorf. Halliday had an impulse to repeat his protest, to insist on remaining behind, flatly to refuse to accompany an expedition in which he could see no possible usefulness, and about which he actually felt a gnawing fear. But he was able to brush the impulse aside as mere neuroticism. All right, he'd go. Halliday, the good soldier. For these few weeks he'd move at Milgrim's command. But then, by God, he'd show them. He'd show the doubters and the scoffers and those who, worst of all, had forgotten him entirely. He would be his own man again, with his own book. And it would be a book. As he sat there in Milgrim's office, resigned to a tedious journey, his confidence grew. There would be ten dark weeks, but he'd get through somehow.

Still another story conference was gathering as Shep and Manley Halliday walked out together. "For a minute there I was afraid you were going to talk him out of it," Shep said. "I hope you don't mind going too much. I think we'll have a swell trip."

There are times, Halliday was thinking, when a young man, any young man, seems repulsively healthy to an old man of forty.

At times, Shep was thinking, his face looks as cold as stone and his eyes look three days dead.

Halliday's voice seemed to escape in thin wisps from a deep hollow: "Son, I never like to dampen enthusiasm. But I made this *swell* trip twenty-three years ago."

8

In the bedroom there was brisk movement between the bureau and the bed; that was Ann Loeb packing Manley's bags. Manley was sprawled on the couch in the other room, surrounded by familiar debris, the evening papers (along with yesterday's as well), magazines, half-read mail, library books. "It's cheaper to buy them than take them out and never return them," Ann was always saying. But buying transitory fiction seemed impractical to Manley. Like most impractical men he made frequent efforts at economy and efficiency.

This clutter was a distraction to him, Manley had claimed at times. On these occasions, preparing himself for work, he felt he could not arrange his thoughts until the mess around him was straightened up. At least once a week Ann devoted an hour to restoring some kind of order to this accumulation. But she accused him of preferring the disarray.

Although his habits inevitably produced the clutter, it really disturbed him, as a tangible expression of his being at loose ends. He was simply unable to extricate himself. He had never learned where to put things. Letters and bills left on his desk to be answered had a way of strewing themselves around the room. Definitely neurotic, he decided. For people like himself, Freud had not succeeded in doing much more than providing a new vocabulary for old faults.

"Manley, maybe you'd better come in and see where I'm putting things. So you'll know where to find them when you want them."

Ann had the large case nearly packed. Two suits had been neatly folded, the way he had never—for all his travels—been able to learn. Everything was in orderly piles, strategically placed. Some people had this gift. They could *do things*. He was sure, watching Ann, that she could rig a sailboat, build a house, kill a chicken.

"This bag we'll check right through for you. I've given you complete changes for six days. There's an extra shirt in the overnight bag in case you're held over anywhere. Now let me show you where the pills are . . ."

There were the nembutals, the insulin, the saccharin, the benzedrine, the empirin, the row of little bottles that sustained him. How had he managed before Ann? She sent his laundry out, submitted his car to periodic inspections, had his income-tax forms completed, took care of those thousand and one little irritations and did them so easily he was never even aware of their being done.

While she briefed him on the layout of his overnight things, he was only faintly conscious of dissatisfaction. Maybe, because Ann was so exactly what he needed, she was not the healthy influence she seemed. Maybe it would be better for him to do his own dirty work, his own packing. Packing had been his job in the old days. The packing and the planning, both of them catch-as-catch-can. There had been no plan to Jere. Strictly a moment-to-moment girl. Even the act of packing a tooth-brush in a toilet case had seemed an impossible demand on her capabilities. "I hate people who drag umbrellas to picnics," she had said once, "just in case it should rain. People who do that deserve to get rained on."

Poor Jere. Only it had never seemed poor Jere then. It had been mad Jere, marvelous Jere, fabulous Jere. Up from Cannes to meet him that time in Paris:

He: Jere, where's all your luggage?

She: Oh, darling, I packed all my bags so efficiently this morning. And then forgot to have them brought down from my room. Aren't you sorry you've got such an idiot wife?

He: I'm crazy about idiot wives. Never going to have anything else but idiot wives.

She comes close to him. It's been three days. The loveliest girl he has ever seen. Three days. To be kissed like that, to be drawn down and down, closer and closer together, deeper and deeper.

April rains rapped lightly at the window but they did not hear. Morning light vaulting over the balcony broke in on them, but for them it was neither morning nor night, nor could there have been for them any greater irrelevancy than the hour of day. Lovers are their own season and their own time.

Then they had gone out to the American Express and since this was one of those days when everything goes right, the royalty check they had been hoping for was there. This called for celebration (though every day together those first years was celebration). By noon (in the new little bar they had discovered and kept to themselves in the hope that it wouldn't be ruined by Americans like them) they were calling Mama to bring them another Grande Fine. And he had sat there wining the afternoon away while Jere went out to replace the wardrobe she had left behind. "Jere," he had told her laughingly then, "the clothes you've left behind in hotel rooms would outfit the entire female population of the Balkans!"

"Manley, are you following me?"

He was staring vacantly into the suitcase, it seemed to Ann.

"Why—" (rocketing back across six thousand miles and fifteen years) "—yes, Ann."

"I just want to be sure you know where your extra bow tie is —so you don't pull everything out trying to find it in the morning."

"Yes, I'll remember, the tie is in . . ."

"Now, anything else?"

"How about the manuscript? I might have a chance to look it over on my way."

"Fine. It'll be right on top. Now, for goodness sake, don't lose it."

He should really concentrate on what she was saying. Good-looking woman, Ann. Large-boned, a big girl but well proportioned. Strong legs, heavy-breasted, but with fine carriage— a statuesque woman, Ann. It was a sign of his development, he liked to think, to find maturer pleasure in her cropped black hair, the fine high forehead, the prominent but at the same time elegant and delicately bridged Semitic nose, the unplucked eyebrows that would have bothered him ordinarily but seemed just right for her and the serious eyes that seemed always to follow you.

He felt a sense of guilt toward Ann. For his infidelity took place in the secret chambers of his mind. But like the husband who sneaks off to actual liaison, Halliday was always shaken by remorse on his way back. In the great tradition of roving husbands, he solemnly avowed, I must not visit that woman again. But his rendezvous were so easily affected. There was no need for elaborate intrigue, surreptitious exit or proficient alibis. He had merely to enter the private passageway spiraling through his mind. There at the bottom of the steps was Jere's door. It was never locked against him.

With the years Halliday had grown increasingly ascetic. Having wallowed in self-indulgence, he had come to identify it with failure and decline. Having achieved his early triumphs with such ease, he had become suspicious of anything too easy. And there was nothing easier than to slip away to his secret door. It was like wearing a magic ring and being your own genie. But what happened in the fable when a greedy benefactor invoked the charm once too often? Manley tried to apply the moral. Self-destruction always had fascinated him. (Remember the dangerous sports he had pushed himself, through fear, to try?) Wasn't it pure self-destruction that lured him onto emotional rocks where Jere beckoned? In fairness to Ann, and for his own peace of mind, there must be no Jere. No Jere.

"Plan to see Jere when you're in New York?"

Guiltily, Manley's eyes turned outward again. The calm directness of her stare almost convinced him that she had eavesdropped on his thoughts.

"Oh, I suppose I'll have to."

A mute of resignation deadened his tone of voice. It was always a bad time, seeing Jere now. He knew being this far away was one of the reasons he had begun to knit a little in California. And perhaps, though he was hardly aware of it (or resisted it), that was one of the reasons that hovered behind his reluctance to make this trip East. The Jere Halliday he would have to see would not even be a ghost of the Jere Halliday in his mind, the Jere of twenty years ago. Had *that* Jere lived merely in his mind too? Now a crippled romantic, a recent convert to skepticism still somewhat unfamiliar with the litany, he wondered if she had ever been all those things his love had credited her with being—the wildest, the brightest, the funniest, the most passionate, the most beautiful, the most talented, the most companionable woman he had ever known.

Now their divorce was five years old, their love was ten years cold. And the last time he had seen her, just before he came West two years ago, they had wrangled about money.

I must stop thinking about Jere.

"Ann, how's Boris? You haven't mentioned him lately."

Boris Beskind, a German refugee director, had made several pictures Ann had edited at World-Wide. He was a moody, insecure man of considerable talent. They had worked closely on the cutting, found they had a good many film ideas in common and had dined together a number of times when Manley had been working on his novel or preferred to be alone. On a few occasions they had all gone out together and Manley, with dog-in-manger keenness, had been quick to detect the look of adoration for Ann that escaped through Beskind's guard of polished manners. Beskind was in his early thirties, rather attractive in an unhealthy, dark-complexioned and melancholy way.

"Boris has been down at Laguna since he finished *Swan Song*. I thought I told you he was taking a month off. He wants us to come down and see him some week-end."

"You should really marry Boris."

She looked up sharply from the suitcase. "What am I going to get now, the I'm-just-a-stone-around-your-neck speech?"

Even when she understood what made him say these things, she was annoyed. It was *messy,* she felt. Her sense of neatness, of pattern, extended to emotions.

"No, seriously, Ann, a woman of your age, with your common sense—he's a young man, with a future, with interests similar to yours. And he obviously wants to marry you . . ."

"For heaven's sake, Manley, what's wrong with you tonight?"

"It's just that—I like to think of myself as a man of honor. You're too much of a person to be—to be . . ."

If he were writing this scene, he was thinking, he wouldn't be having this trouble. The older man would know just how to put it, the delicate phrase for the precise thought. And the girl would say . . .

But she was saying, "Oh, for God's sake, I know you don't want to marry me. I've never asked you, have I? Listen, Halliday, I'll promise never to propose to you—no, not even one of those sly female hints—if you'll promise not to marry me off to the first man who wants to have dinner with me."

The strain of Manley's day showed through his smile. "I know I'm a hopeless egotist, Ann. But now and then I try to think about you."

"I'd rather you didn't." She said it convincingly. "I know you, Manley. Of course you're an egotist. Don't forget I was raised with egotists. You just happen to be the first one who's got something worth being egotistical about. So go on thinking about yourself, doing what's best for you. I'll work out my part of it. I'm not worried."

"Ann, I think you're the only woman I ever knew who was really pulled together. But sometimes I wonder about the contradiction, on one hand so self-reliant, and yet you fasten yourself to me, a tired man who's done most of his living, who . . ."

"Manley, will you let me get this packing done? That's much more important at the moment than trying to analyze me."

He stretched out on the bed, watching idly but with a certain enjoyment the sure movement of Ann's labors. Then he placed his hand lightly on his forehead. Flushed, dampish, perhaps a slight fever. He shut his eyes. A flock of words flew into his mind. When he arranged them he found himself reciting silently:

> This is the dead land
> This is the cactus land
> Here the stone images
> Are raised, here they perceive
> The supplication of a dead man's hand
> Under the twinkle of a fading star.

Dead land, cactus land, stone's image, dead man's hand, fading star—had Eliot been to Hollywood? Ever signed on as a screenwriter? How else could he have written that?

His eyes were still closed and a new flock of remembered

words were soaring down from a great height in his mind when Ann came over to sit beside him.

"I've put the key to the big bag in the right-hand pocket of your overcoat—the key to the little bag will be in the little pocket of the suit you're wearing. Your manuscript's right on top in case you'll want it."

Manley nodded without opening his eyes.

"Not feeling well?"

"I've got a little headache and a funny pain at the back of my neck."

"I think you caught cold staying out so late last night. Get into bed and I'll rub some of that Vicks Vaporub on your neck."

In bed a few minutes later, with Ann's strong fingers working the warm ointment into the muscles of his neck, he felt good enough to say:

"Have you ever rubbed any of this into Boris Beskind's neck?"

"Of course. That's how we spend our evenings. Vicks Vaporub orgies."

"If you did this for any other man I know I'd be violently jealous."

"Idiot."

When she finished he rolled over to face her and she lowered her head to his. "Manley, I wish you weren't going."

"I did my best to talk Victor out of it. But he's like a stone wall that smiles at you."

"Victor doesn't need you back there. I think he just likes to arrive in New York with an entourage. And of course he'd like to show you off at Webster. I wouldn't be surprised if he's bucking for an honorary degree."

"You mean he'll dangle me from his watch chain like a Phi Bete key?"

Her arm slid under his neck. Her face was so close he couldn't see her. "This is a strange feeling for me. I'm really going to miss you this week, darling."

"I will too, Annie."

Her mouth pressed his, tenderly at first.

"You'll catch my cold."

"I don't care."

His arms went around her, dutifully. Her eyes were closed, her mouth was crushing into his. It was overwhelming. He was conscious of the effort he had to make.

Looking down at her and her fine big body waiting, he thought: Nothing I do is spontaneous any more. That's the big difference . . .

"Oh darling, darling, oh my darling." She was covering his face with grateful kisses as he lay resting.

Then she noticed that he had left her again, that his eyes were searching the ceiling as if for some escape.

"What are you thinking about?"

"Oh, about tomorrow. And how I dread flying East again. It's like making a pilgrimage to my own grave."

9

With the abruptness of semi-tropical winter, the weather had suddenly changed an hour before. Now a gray film obscured the sharp dark line of the mountains beyond the airport. Despite the somber lighting and threatening skies, a crowd of perhaps fifty waited hopefully for a glimpse of a new film idol going East for personal appearances. He was a very young, blond boy with soft blue eyes, pink cheeks and a weak chin. When the crowd caught sight of him, conspicuously wrapped in a great camel's hair coat, they became suddenly animated, jostling each other for a better view, waving, laughing and, full of mob courage, calling out his first name familiarly. The young star waved automatically. He had been on top for a good many months already.

Other passengers, carefully inspected by the onlookers for signs of celebrity and then contemptuously rejected, passed gravely through the gate. Shep and his girl Sara, hand-in-hand, smiled at each other, made little jokes about the star, wondered what Tom Mooney was going to do now that he was free, wondered what could be keeping Manley Halliday and anxiously kept watching for him.

"Oh, there he is." Sara recognized him from Shep's careful description.

Gently pushing his way through the knot of people at the gate, Halliday came slowly toward them.

"I was afraid you weren't going to make it," Shep said.

"I almost called to say I couldn't. I was feeling rather badly."

"Well, you can get a good night's sleep on the plane."

Shep was bubbling with so much optimism about their adventure that Halliday could not tell him he had never been able to sleep on a plane.

"Sara's over there—she's dying to meet you."

Halliday made the old courtier's effort to rise to occasions.

His natural curiosity, his interest in Shep and an automatic response to attractive young women helped him shake off lethargy for a moment.

He saw a girl who seemed to have brought her own warm sunlight into this dismal evening. She had a cheerful, puckish, outdoor beauty that suddenly encouraged him. It was as if he had just downed a three-finger whiskey. Despite the drizzle she wore no hat and he liked the way her brown hair, parted simply in the middle, fell softly to her shoulders.

"Mr. Halliday, I suppose you get awfully tired of having people tell you how much they admire your books?"

"On the contrary, young lady. Most authors I've known could live exclusively on such a diet."

"Now you know who she really came down to see off," Shep teased.

"Had I known that I'd have been more prompt."

Halliday punctuated this gallantry with his little bow. But the young couple's vitality and enthusiasm and the play of affection between them was having a reverse effect on him now.

"What I really wanted to tell you, Mr. Halliday—" Sara's words had an accompaniment of laughter "—is that I'm depending on you to keep Shep away from those Wellesley and Bennington girls."

Halliday's effort to join in made his words toneless: "Have no fear. I shall run interference for him against the entire Wellesley-Bennington line."

"But all the polls show they're going for older men these days. I'll probably be running interference for him."

This was enough of a cue to laugh lightly together and Halliday observed carefully how these two were alive to each other. They are "hooked up" together and the juice is on, he thought. For an instant, irresistibly, he compared them to himself and Jere at the same age. This girl was more substantial than Jere, more down-to-earth, less exotic, less dynamic, less driven and self-conscious. Their whole affair, he imagined, was more solid, less romantic, more purposeful, but less exciting.

"I brought this for you as a little going-away present." Sara produced the bottle of Mumm. (Shep already had his.)

"Oh, thank you." He could hardly intrude on Shep and Sara's mood of festivity with the solemn information that he was not drinking. The bottle bulked awkwardly under his arm. He wished he didn't have to drag it along.

"Have a marvelous time, Shep," Sara was saying, offering her bright young mouth to the ritual of farewell.

Halliday moved away discreetly. He turned, tipped his hat to Sara and forced a troubled smile. Then he entered the dark comfort of the plane.

Offering Halliday the seat by the window, Shep sank into the one beside him. The spin of propellers animated this life-like thing; it began to tremble. Shep half-rose to locate Sara. Halliday looked out into the faces of the crowd. It was dinner time; why were they not home? How many would catch colds? It would serve them right. Twenty years from now how many of them would remember their little idol's name? How many to-day remembered John Roche and Eddie Burns?

As the plane began to creep away, Sara was a sturdy, self-possessed little figure enlivening the dusk. Instinctively, Halliday looked from her face to Shep's. The attraction between them suddenly had begun to affect him perversely: would Sara and Shep drift apart or, marrying, grow accustomed to each other? Whatever happened, the edge would dull. The happiest of people were machines running down. As the plane pivoted around toward the main runway, he caught a final glimpse of Sara—she had the face of an old woman and her lovely youth had shriveled. Manley touched his fingers to his lips in a desolate farewell.

"That's my girl!" Shep was waving energetically and grinning. The roar of excitement inside him seemed louder than the roar of the motors. The great metal nose lunged forward in mechanical ecstasy. To avoid conversation with his exhilarated young companion, Halliday laid his head back and closed his eyes.

Gradually the droning in his ears faded to a low, insistent hum. He had slipped off into a choppy, troubled half-sleep. Grotesque fantasies droned in his head. Something that looked like Ann was soaring through the air with arms outstretched like wings and little propellers whirring from her breasts . . .

He seemed to be moving with her in some way he could not quite understand . . . and Milgrim was there too . . . but where was Ann? Milgrim's office was in a toilet and Milgrim was saying, "Your wife has the most beautiful figure in Hollywood . . ." Oh, Christ, this was terrible! Jere was behind that door with Victor Milgrim. Oh, that wench! The thought of what they might be doing filled him with choking rage. He'd murder Milgrim, and Jere too . . . He ran into the room. There were Shep and Sara on a tremendous couch. His mouth was full of apologies as he tried to back out. But his feet seemed glued there. And they did not seem to mind his being there at all. "Have you seen Jere?" he screamed at them. "Oh, we've always wanted to meet her," they said. "Was she really Lenore in *The Night's High Noon?*" Was she really? Was she really was she really . . . A telephone rang. It jangled in Manley's ears. Lingalingalingalingaling . . . "Mr. Milgrim will see you now," a voice said, and then for some inexplicable reason the phone began ringing in his head again lingalingaling-alingalingngn . . .

He could feel himself making a frantic effort to break out of the nightmare's coils.

Shep was watching him nervously. The gray pallor had gone dead white. The head had rolled strangely. Eyeballs had disappeared. He was beginning to chew his lips fitfully. Shep called the stewardess. She took over with crisp efficiency. Her arm propped him up. She was ready with a small cylinder of ammonia. Half-conscious of this, he brushed it aside. He was beginning to know where he was. "Pocket," he whispered, "ri' pocket." In this pocket they found a typed note beginning, "I am a diabetic," with instructions for emergencies. There was also a small bag of lump sugar and the stewardess, following the written instructions, forced several into his mouth. Shep felt a little ill himself as he watched the sick mouth sucking on sugar. But the magic of Halliday's quick recovery fascinated him.

"I'm all right now, thank you," Halliday said. He even managed a smile for the stewardess. He looked at Shep apologetically.

"Are you sure you're all right?"

"I'm fine now. Should have eaten, that's all."

He hated to talk about it. He despised physical infirmities. He felt contemptuous of his own weakness. Regularity, diet, rest, abstinence—this was his program of survival. Right now he should have been home in the Garden, after a quiet supper, talking or playing chess with Ann or perhaps reading over his manuscript . . .

"Do you—have these things often?"

"Just once in a while, if I miss a meal, or forget my shots. Sometimes I just get a sleepy feeling. But I suppose this was almost an insulin faint. I should show you where everything is —even how to operate the damn needle—" he saw the look of dismay on Shep's face "—though the chances are this won't happen again."

Hammering in his head was: I never should have come— never should have come. He wished he didn't have to let this young man in on this diabetic business. Except for medical personnel, no one but Ann had seen these spells before. Once or twice she had had to give him the shots. He was nervous about the needle and never did it well. Ann could do it with a sure hand. But her knowledge of the damned thing was one of the reasons he could never work up any sense of romance toward her. He felt unclean about these injections.

". . . in New York at eight. Let's see, that's eleven our time, that makes sixteen hours . . ." Shep was studying the time-table. He leaned back contentedly. "Gee, I haven't been in New York since I stopped over on my way back from college after graduation. Just by luck I caught the opening of *The Cradle Will Rock*. Now that's my idea of the new idiom for musicals."

"I'm beginning to think I'm old-fashioned about musicals," Halliday said. "I don't like too much art in my musicals. I like 'em rough and ready. Low comics like Ed Wynn and Bobby Clark. Chorus girls. Songs you can whistle." He almost added, "I wish you could have seen Garrick Gaieties," but he was only talking to fill the gap. What could it mean to a boy who couldn't have been over ten years old at the time? The lines rippled in his memory though ". . . our future babies—we'll take to Abie's Irish Rose—I hope they'll live to see—it close . . ." If we had an American poet laureate, I'd vote for Larry Hart, he decided.

The efficient stewardess brought dinner on aseptic metal trays. Her smile was a nice compromise between a cold professional and a warm personal one. It was remarkable how much charm she managed to maintain while performing such menial tasks.

"I suppose your generation will fall in love with airline hostesses the way we did with our nurses," Halliday said.

"This one is a damn good-looking girl."

"They're all damn good-looking girls," Halliday assured him. "And the more you travel on these things the more convinced you'll be that they're all the same damn good-looking girl. I've always wondered how the airlines managed it. Maybe they put them together on assembly lines."

"They should make wonderful wives," Shep caught his mood. "Serving you all your meals right on time. Bringing you reading matter. Asking if there's anything else you want."

"But they're all going to marry their pilots and produce a new race of handsome, airborne mechanics," Halliday insisted.

"Junior, stop following me around the house—go outside and play with your autogyro," Shep offered.

"Can't you see them in bed together?" Halliday went on. "A sign will flash on—'Fasten your seat-belts. Landing in fifteen minutes.'"

Shep went on eating vigorously while they improvised their own little brave new world. Halliday only picked at his tray. He knew he should be eating but he was never hungry any more. Long ago he had resigned from the gourmets. And in the last few years he had begun to take a grim view of food. There had been so many *mustn'ts* that finally he had had to accommodate himself to the sour conception of food as *fuel*.

When the stewardess removed their trays with that same practiced cheerfulness, Halliday came back to their theme with variations. "More likely Miss Heath isn't a model wife at all. When her husband asks her when supper will be ready maybe she snarls, 'Listen, I've been standing over a hot aisle all day. Get your own supper.'"

"And if her old man should wake up and want to assert a husband's privileges in the middle of the night, she probably answers in her sleep, 'I'll get to you just as soon as I can but there are still several passengers ahead of you.'"

Suddenly their nonsense lost Halliday's attention. He was staring gravely at the rain tap dancing on the shiny metallic floor of the plane's wings. He seemed to be crouching down into his own silence. His face was turned away from Shep's as if in search of as much privacy as this public cylinder could provide. Shep found himself conscientiously nibbling around the edges of *Love on Ice*. They had to bear down now. A hell of a lot depended on it. If he and Halliday didn't come through, Milgrim was sure to drop his option. And no credits meant no more Hollywood jobs. They simply had to lick this story before Milgrim joined them in New York. That gave them only twenty-four hours. It probably didn't matter too much to Halliday, but for him it was a turning point. He looked at Halliday speculatively. The author seemed preoccupied. Shep wondered if he was thinking about their story. A new tide of confidence came rolling in. After all, Manley Halliday, even in decline, was bound to come up with something that would solve their problems. Shep had a few little ideas for a new approach, but he hesitated to introduce them. They were ideas which had worn a little shabby with use and Shep feared they would lower him in Halliday's eyes. So he kept on waiting for Halliday to light the dark corners. But perhaps he should prod him again.

"I suppose we should talk about this darn story. The old man is really going to expect something when we hit the Waldorf tomorrow." What he would like to have said: "Let's stop horsing around and do some work for a change."

Shep's challenge filtered through the layers of Halliday's resistance. His mind stretched and yawned. Now let's see, what was this damn story again—two college roommates who ask the same short-order waitress to their houseparty? No, it couldn't be *that*. But if it wasn't, where did he get the idea that—"Let's see," he ventured, "didn't you have some new notion for the girl the other day?"

Shep felt a twinge of disappointment. After all, Halliday was the star. When was he going to start carrying the ball?

"Well, I—I was just sort of thinking off the top of my head, as we say in Hollywood. I thought we might try something like this. Joe, the poor boy, has a kind of grudge against the Mardi Gras. All these rich kids with their Vassar girls. So, sort of in spite, as a kind of social protest, you might call it, he decides to ask a good-looking waitress who catches his eye in a small-town diner. Well, when she's picked as the Queen of the Mardi Gras, it turns out that she's actually a society girl from a Main Line family who's had a hassle with her family and wants to prove she can get by on her own. She's been going to Vassar, but she's dropped out. Her old roommate, who's up with Joe's roommate, recognizes her . . ."

Shep went on building the story conscientiously, cliché on cliché. Halliday listened expressionlessly. Suddenly he asked, "Have you ever known a short-order waitress who turned out to be a Vassar girl?"

"But Mr. Halliday, if you applied that test to every story, ninety-nine and ninety-nine one-hundredths of all the Hollywood movies would never see the light of a projection room."

"What I'm wondering is what would actually make a society girl do a thing like that. I knew a girl on Long Island once who was brought up in a very proper, well-to-do household. Even when she was eighteen her parents had to approve of everyone she went out with and they always waited up to be sure she came in by eleven. If she was as much as five minutes late she'd be restricted to quarters for a week. She was a nice-looking girl, although she was only allowed to use a little lipstick, a fine student, a beautiful pianist. Well, when Elaine broke out it was a real Vesuvius. Her father's private detectives found her in a room somewhere near the East River docks with a French merchant seaman. That was in, let's see, 1916. The last I heard of her, about seven years ago, she was in a private sanitarium."

"We had a case something like that at Webster. Over in Middleboro, the nearest town, there was a sixteen-year-old daughter of the town's Presbyterian minister. She was hot as a pistol and it didn't take long for the campus swordsmen to get the scent. Her name was Polly Ann Dean, but of course all the boys called her Dizzy. One time one of the fellows brought her back to the dorm. She stayed there for nine days and the story was that this fastball who had brought her—a third-string quarterback from Worcester, can't think of his name now—had made himself five hundred dollars setting her up for the boys."

"Dizzy Dean. That's a good story. What finally happened?"

"The campus cops moved in and took Dizzy home. The old man lost his congregation. The quarterback was expelled."

"Well, for the movies we may have to clean it up a little," Halliday said. "Maybe we could get Jeanette MacDonald for the role of Dizzy and give her some songs to sing."

"Jeanette MacDonald will be terrific for the girl," Shep agreed. "And maybe we could get George Raft for the boy."

"With Peter Lorre for his roommate," Halliday put in. "An exchange student from Germany."

"Lorre's date is Fanny Brice," Shep went on. "She's a freshman at Smith. Her mother has warned her about those Webster wolves and she's frightened to death."

"So she decides to room with Dizzy because she'll be safer with a minister's daughter," Halliday continued. He was feeling a little better.

Maybe if we stay up on this cloud a new idea for the story will bubble up, Shep was thinking. Then he remembered the champagne. After all, this ought to be a festive occasion. It wasn't every day that a junior writer reached into the Hollywood pool for a collaborator and drew out a favorite author. Surely that called for a toast. The idea appealed to his sense of romance: drinking champagne with Manley Halliday as they flew East to Webster on this miraculous assignment.

"Mr. Halliday, would you join me if I cracked one of our jugs?"

"Thank you, I really shouldn't." Then seeing Shep's disappointment: "But you go ahead anyway. I wish I could join you."

Shep got some paper cups and brought the bottle down. "Sure you won't have just a drop?"

Halliday studied the bottle. Mumm, 1934. Should be good champagne. The word hummed with pleasant vibrations. His mind toyed with the syllables: cham pagne, sham pain, sham playin' . . . champagne cocktails at Harry's New York Bar at three o'clock in the afternoon . . .

"No, thank you. I don't think so."

Shep filled a paper cup and offered it to him anyway.

"Not even a sip to toast success to our super-colossal epic?"

Well—it almost seemed like tempting fate to reject a few drops of wine on that basis. "Literally a few drops then—mmmnn, that's too much."

They touched paper cups with mock formality. The sound of fizz was a cheerful reminder of brighter days. Manley's tongue met the wine with the warmth of an old friend: Come in—it's been a long time. He let the wine trickle down his throat. It was slow pleasure.

"That's nice wine."

Shep said: "I'm not one of these guys who can inhale the bouquet and tell you the year. I just know it tastes damn good."

"I couldn't always tell the year. But one night in Biarritz we had a blindfold test on Lanson, Moet and Chandon, and Piper Heidsieck. I won a magnum of Lanson. My wife and I lugged it around for years, saving it for special occasion. We really went through hell to save that bottle. We finally opened it in New York for our tenth anniversary. It was completely flat."

The anecdote, Halliday realized, had also lost its sparkle somewhere along the way, but Shep chuckled loyally. "You see, that's what I mean. Don't put off till tomorrow what you can drink tonight."

Halliday nodded appreciatively. He was feeling a good deal better.

"This is extremely nice wine."

He drank it with mounting enjoyment, with increasing suspension of self-censorship. After all, one little cup of wine could hardly hurt him. It might be just the tonic he needed. The very thing to help him forget his cold, the coma and the ordeal of travel.

"Well, just a little more—I said a *little* more."

Shep had refilled the cup. "The bouncing made me do that."

Halliday held up his full cup. He was looking forward to this drink. This would be his last and he would drink it slowly, draining its full enjoyment. "Well," he said, "here's to Dizzy and her Reverend father."

Either his depression was really lifting or he was jacking up his spirits artificially, as if he owed it to the wine to meet it with a happier disposition.

Down the aisle the male starlet had fallen asleep. His mouth was slightly open and he was snoring.

"If the women of America could only see him now," Halliday said, "disillusion would spread like smog over the orange groves."

Oh, he was feeling much, much better.

The wine was fine. The wine was kind. He had always had a happy reaction to champagne. It made him feel a little lighter in his feet, in his head, made the words flow easier, it made him like the sound of his own voice and the devoted way the young man listened—almost like having a disciple. His ego had always craved disciples. Once or twice he had caught one, but they always got away.

" . . . probably the first time a great industry was ever set up to grind out a dream a week . . ."

He punctuated his talk with little sips of wine. He was wound up now. It was good to talk to this listening young man who disagreed with him just enough to give an edge to conversation.

The wine tingled. The wine tempted. From its white paper mouth the wine gave up a golden smile. Wine tickled Halliday's nose and wine tickled his head: the ideal antidote for the poison of old regrets. And he talked and he talked and he talked with the self-intoxication of one only lately used to ideas.

And Shep listened earnestly and refilled his cup and begged to differ. And with the condescension typical of his youth and his point-of-view, he clearly thought Halliday wise in his own outdated way.

" . . . What's wrong with our movies? You say they're too reactionary or escapist, that they shy away from real problems and real people. But I say they lack a soul . . ."

Halliday was beginning to sip his wine more quickly.

" . . . There's one thing we accomplished. We smashed the

icons of gentility and complacency. Your trash is vulgar and sensational. Ours was prissy and pollyanna. But our honest books were more revolutionary than the ones by your so-called revolutionaries. We had a revolution all right, but it was strictly every man for himself."

"But wasn't that kind of romantic? That personal rebellion stuff doesn't get you anywhere."

"It got us some pretty damn good books, baby."

Shep reached for the bottle and was surprised to find it empty. He wondered if Halliday would think him excessive if he opened the other bottle. He had never been more than a social drinker but he found the wine reassuring and—was he imagining it?—felt it drawing them closer together. He was going to ask Halliday if he should go on to the second. Then he obeyed his impulse and pulled the cork.

Halliday was glad. If Stearns had asked him, he would have had to say no. But he welcomed another cupful. It was having a soothing effect on his nerves. Sara was a bright little girl to think of champagne. It was beginning to soften the edges of this ridiculous journey.

The pop of the cork—always a moment of jubilance and festive promise. The cork goes pop and everybody laughs with his own release of pressure. The popping of old corks set up a nostalgic barrage in his head: that New Year's Eve at Davos when he had to bop the Egyptian bey and at Deauville, at Corfu and Rapallo and the Hotel Belvue in Bern, at that villa they rented (and ruined) outside of Rome, at restless back-and-forthing on the *Berengaria,* the *Mauretania* and one particular last night out in Sesue Hayakawa's suite on the *Majestic,* at Ciro's in Paris where he insulted (and was insulted by) Maurice and at Ciro's in Monte Carlo where he flattered (and was flattered by) Julien, at that little place—was it Pharamond's?—near the abattoir where he was so drunk he invited to bloody battle a formidable Parisian butcher, and at the nightstands of a hundred beds where he and Jere delighted each other. He remembered a Veuve Cliquot 1921 in a Hollywood speakeasy that was certainly not 1921 and quite likely not V. C. Why should such a silly little burr of a fact stick to his mind through all these years? And the time they sat on the balcony outside their room at the Ritz sipping a marvelous Pommery and watching the Place Vendôme melt away into purple twilight. Ah, ah, ah that was a good time, a sweet time, a lost time. The staccato popping of corks had been a rhythmic counterpoint as they danced in a champagne haze on the rooftop of the Crillon, in a champagne daze on the rooftop of the world. The days and weeks and months and years had popped and fizzed and poured together in the soft yellow twilight of a champagne haze, the champagne days from the wine-numbed heights of Naples to the Mumm-soaked shores of Santa Monica, from a day in 1927 he managed to remember to a night in 1929 he could not forget. The years of his sleep-walking. Manley Halliday, *homo somnus ambulatus,* Manley Halliday the novel somnambulist, the novel's somnambulist, asleep with his eyes open, asleep at his typewriter, writing the moneytales, asleep at the switch, asleep at tea dances and casual adulteries, asleep on paper, on deck, on the town, on the make, on the *qui vive,* on the rebound, on the pickup, on the skids.

". . . We're two little lambs who have lost our way, baa, baa, baaaa. . ."

Talking their way through the second bottle:

". . . In those days we seemed to be the hub around which parties were always revolving. Wherever we moved our parties always seemed to move with us. Whether we wished it or not. . ."

—now be honest with yourself, Manley. You sought those parties as eagerly as they sought you. Even if they always seemed spontaneous, bumping into an old friend (they were all old friends, those chance acquaintances) in the Ritz Carlton Japanese Garden, on the Blue Train, at Henry's on the Rue Volney, at the Yale game, on the Channel boat . . .

". . . I think I begin to understand what those parties were all about. It was a kind of group rebellion, even if most of us never knew what we were rebelling against."

"But in your books," Shep pointed out, "there certainly seems to be an awareness that there was some explanation, some significance for all the crazy stuff that happened. You certainly feel in *High Noon* that all those parties, all the carousing, the frantic search for oblivion was a symbol of, well, call it group neurosis."

"Tell you the truth, Stearns, I had a big talent and I used it pretty well, in my good years anyway. I put down the things I saw and nobody who looked at the things I was seeing saw more than I did. I didn't worry about proving any points, group neuroses or abortive revolutions. Maybe that's why I was more convincing. Readers want a sharp edge but they don't want to hear the grinding of the ax."

Then Halliday said with an edge of hostility: "I've still got some of my talent left, Stearns, but I've got to channel it, concentrate it."

Halliday stared down into his empty paper cup. He felt quite sure that he was sober. But somewhere in his mind lurked the vague impression that he was talking too much, or too revealingly. He made a hasty recapitulation of what he had been saying—movies, parties, Jere (no, he had been careful not to mention Jere, hadn't he?), writers, himself—it wasn't exactly a jumble, just the informal playing of truth and consequences.

The stewardess was bending over them. "Aren't you two nightowls going to sleep at all?"

Shep held up their half-finished bottle. "Have a drink?"

"Ooh, champagne. Somebody's birthday?"

"No, it's a marriage," Halliday said. "We're eloping."

"I can see you're going to be very happy together."

"And we're going to have a child together and its name is *Love on Ice* and we want you to be its godmother," Halliday said.

"Come on, Miss Heath, a toast to your godchild."

"I wish I could but it's agin regulations. Try me again when I'm on the ground."

"That's the trouble," Halliday said. "Too many regulations. Everybody is so serious. Young girl like you—too many 'sponsibilities."

Shep studied the older man carefully. He felt perfectly sober himself. He hadn't even noticed a change in Halliday.

"Pour me just one more little touch," Halliday said.

Shep poured him a very short one. "Not even one friendly

little drop with us?" he pressed Miss Heath. She smiled a practiced no.

Rain was still falling. The plane plowed through the darkness. The passengers slept. The snoring of the movie star was a gentle satire of the motor's roar. Shep talked with Miss Heath of aerial weather and flight. Halliday leaned his forehead against the window and stared out at the colored riding lights on the wings. Women would be attracted to young Stearns, he imagined. He was that disarming combination of robustness and sensitivity and he spoke with great earnestness and he listened as if he liked you.

—But I was more brilliant and I was more of a natural for women (remember how it used to irk Jere, long before I was unfaithful?) and (losing his way in the dark corridor) the party itself was the thing. Some of those years were lived from one party to the next, with in-between periods used only for recuperation.

He shut his eyes and tried to remember one party in detail, not pop and ha ha ha and who wants gingerale and hey Jere I'm over here but exactly who was there, what was said, why that fight broke out . . . Strange, out of the blur of alcoholic laughter and the more dramatic of the seductions (some not so much seduction as a wandering, lost, into wrong bedrooms) what came back to him most sharply were the casualties: Harry Talbot's suicide the night before they docked in New York, November 19, 1929, the night Ham Cohn, the All-American guard in Manley's class at Harvard, found his wife Bunny with his former roommate and best man Brew Crawford and broke up the party and locked them all out of the house (anything in that he could use on this job?) and the time Jere's friend Mitzi Sedgwick (the one he always hated) got drunk as usual and lost her temper as usual and threw a cocktail glass as usual only this time her aim was better and there was blood all over the white chiffon dress of Betty Lou Vanner, runner-up to the Atlantic City Beauty Contest Winner that year and Manley had rushed her to the hospital and waited in the corridor until the doctor came out and told him she would be all right except for having to lose the eye. They had always seemed to be having so much fun. Yet, looking back, it was the casualties, the trage-dies that stuck up in his mind like telephone poles stretching across the desolate landscape of the past; once the good times had run glistening and taut and wire-fine from pole to pole, but ill winds and the ravages of time had torn them down. Now only the poles remained, giant uncrossed crosses marking the route he had taken.

Miss Heath had removed her trained smiles and her crisp an-swers. A flickering hive of lights behind them was Salt Lake City. The plane floated through the air and they floated through the plane, talking, talking, talking.

—"The wonderful thing about your scenes was the way they not only mirrored but seemed to make a comment on the times. The episode in *High Noon* for instance, where Ted takes Le-nore to the stag party dressed as a boy—I remember writing a theme on that for American Lit. I said that wasn't so much a haphazard stunt as a sign of what modern women wanted in the Twenties. Lenore didn't only want her rights as a woman; she was really an advance scout for the single standard. If men went to stag parties, by God, she'd put on a tuxedo and go along with them. I think that's what real literature should be, entertaining and convincing as contemporary reporting and yet with over-tones of interpretation."

Halliday repressed a giggle. There was a lot of sound poetry in slang. *Oiled* for instance. He was getting a little oiled. There was less friction in him. Ideas slid back and forth across one another more smoothly. Just went to show you, you couldn't always follow the book. The book said stay strictly on the wagon. Only way to feel well and get your work done. But a few squirts of oil took the squeaks out of the old body, made for greater flexibility, easier to face chores like *Love on Ice* . . .

Shep watched Halliday's face crease into a relaxed smile for the first time. ". . . give me more credit than I deserve. Never thought of that stag party as any social symbol. Matter of fact that really happened to Jere and me" (he groped to remember—had he mentioned Jere to this boy before?). "Just after we came back from Europe the first time. We'd decided to do everything together—none o' this Babbitt-husband's-night-out business. She was tall, long-legged, no hips, in my clothes with her hair combed back she could've been Wally Reid's double. Another time we did it at a party and someone asked Jere to come outside and fight for flirting with his wife. We had some wonderful laughs."

Shep was trying to disentangle Jere from the Halliday heroines. Had she finally made a dull marriage for security like Wilma in *Friends and Foes?* Or had she taken an overdose of sleeping pills like Lenore in *High Noon?* Had she been a warmhearted flapper with nympho tendencies like Wilma or a brilliant, self-destroying drinker like Lenore? Hadn't he heard something, somewhere about Jere's having escaped from a home for alcoholics in New York City (had she slid down the side of a building with sheets tied together and had she gone on to the Stork in a nightgown so fancy it passed for an evening dress?) or was that just a snatch of fiction he had read somewhere?

". . . Jere was always crazy about speed. We brought a Daimler back from Europe and Jere used to drive it down Park Avenue sixty miles an hour. If a cop caught up with her she'd listen to the whole *j'accuse* and then produce her honorary captain's badge."

"Then Jere was really the model for Georgette?"

"Oh, you remember that story?"

"I wasn't giving you a Hollywood snow job. I told you I've read everything you've written. Even that little travel book on Hollywood."

"Not the poems. Not the little chapbook I published at Harvard?"

"*Juvenal?* Yup, that too."

"Oh, my God. I was a lousy poet. *Juvenal.* I thought that was so goddam clever. The stage when a young bird leaves its nest and at the same time the name of a satirical Roman poet."

"I remember it well. I even remember it was dedicated to Beatrice."

"You frighten me. Beatrice Vining. I was engaged to her when I went overseas. A real aristocratic beauty. A breathlessly lovely girl." He sounded that familiar philosophic monosyllable: "Hmnn. Beatrice's eldest daughter came out last year. Beatrice is still lovely-looking, with white hair like Billie Dove's, and school-girl complexion. Lady of the old school. Don't seem to breed them so gracious any more."

Vocabulary was running over. He had the feeling that talking, talking, talking would keep the wolf away from his door. No, he didn't mean that, was it the river away from his door. No, no, keep the skeleton in the closet, the nose to the grindstone—oh, he knew what he meant but he couldn't find the words. Must be getting tired when he couldn't find words. Wine made him hazy, made him vague and lazy, but he always said sleep on a plane or a train was no sleep at all, just a brief, uneasy numbing of his consciousness. He'd rather stay awake . . .

" . . . I remember one time" (for some reason he was saying this) "Jere and I tried to see how long we could stay up. It was in the dance-marathon days and we wanted to see if we could stay up that long. On the morning of the fourth day we thought it might revive us if we went swimming. So we drove out of town to the first body of water we could find and got arrested for swimming in a reservoir."

He was traveling along the singing wires, consciously or un-consciously leaving out the poles. His was the generation that discovered it had a sub-conscious. "I know the trouble with you," Jere had turned on a rival, "you're *repressed*." Could one have said anything more crushing then?

"Jere was the most unrepressed creature I ever knew." (For some reason he was telling the young man—must be careful of him, he listened too well.) "She was a one-woman assault on Puritanism. I think she started shocking her parents when she was three. Never really remembered her mother. Her father was strict Episcopalian. Awfully rich. She used to say 'We hated each other on sight. He said I bit his hand before I was a year old.' When she was sixteen she picketed with a bunch of suf-fragettes outside his house on Fifth Avenue. That's when he packed her off to Europe. One time at a cocktail party my pub-lishers gave for me one of those Helen Hokinson literary ladies gushed over Jere. 'It must be simply fascinating to live with a famous author. I'm sure you're a great help to him in his work.' Jere answered in a very ladylike tone, 'All I do is——.' It was a frightful thing to say. I never liked that word myself even if Jere and all my friends did. But I can see how it was irresistible for Jere to use it on that old busybody.

"Jere could always get away with those words, in three or four languages. Somehow they never seemed indecent with her. She was just speaking her mind in a simple and direct way. She could use those words in erotic poetry for instance and make you like it. She was as high-strung and high-spirited as a finely bred show horse. She didn't want anyone to put a bit in her mouth. That's why she kept moving away from me to other—interests."

Inquisitive as Shep was about everything concerning Halliday, he felt for the first time a certain reluctance to listen. It was surprising, after all their years of unrest and separation, to find Halliday's wound at losing Jere still so sensitive. He could not seem to mention her without paying court to her. There was always a silent I-love-you attached to the mention of her name. It was, Shep felt, private talk, of impressions locked away in a vault with fading souvenirs, inadvertently opened with the key Sara had supplied. Shep felt like a trespasser, digging into Halliday's past.

But Shep exaggerated. Actually Halliday was skillfully censoring out all the strain and stress, all the mess and the ugliness. He was sailing along the singing wires:

"Going to a party in the Village one night we got a hansom in front of the Plaza and Jere made the old cabby ride inside so she could sit up on the high jump seat behind. When we got there we took the old driver in with us. It started to rain and Jere burst into tears because the poor old nag was getting wet. She finally took two blankets off one of the beds to wrap around the poor creature. Neglected animals always broke her heart. She was forever picking up stray cats and dogs because they looked so hungry—and half the time forgot to feed them. People thought she was hard and cynical but she was really a sloppy sentimentalist in an age when sentiment was out of fashion . . ."

Listening to the tales of escapade, Shep was thinking: what jerks those people would have been if they tried those stunts in the Thirties. In fact he had once seen a girl take off her clothes as the early morning climax to a fraternity house party and it had seemed to him merely a dizzy blonde hangover from an era of exhibitionists. Not in a million years could he imagine Sara doing any of these things, and if she tried he would have pinned her ears back. But, Shep decided in the words of the old joke, on Jere it looked good. In their own setting, their frivolous little acts of escape took on a romantic glow Shep could not help enjoying vicariously.

There were no hills or valleys or fields or cities or state lines beneath them. In an uncanny vacuum of darkness they roared eastward. For these few hours they were freed from the land-mass that claimed them. The combination of words and wine is an ancient and delicious one. Between them time folds into itself accordion-wise. Somehow, as the first pale shafts began to streak the eastern sky, they were back to Eliot again. Halliday's mind, reeling from topic to topic, had fixed on the point of departure between the writer who succeeds only in catching the moment and the artist who relates the particular moment to the universal "like Eliot. Maybe you'd call him a capitalist lackey, a clerical apologist, a bootlicking Anglophile or worse. But a hundred years from now will people remember that he was a monarchist and that the *New Masses* sneered at him or that he wrote lines like

> April is the cruellest month, breeding
> Lilacs out of the dead land, mixing
> Memory and desire, stirring
> Dull roots with spring rain.

With his eyes closed, remembering in a sort of trance, he did not stop until he had remembered it all, right down to the mysterious coda

> Datta. Dayadhvam. Damyata
> Shantih shantih shantih

For fully half a minute after he had finished his eyes remained closed, though whether in reverence or champagne drowse, Shep could not be sure.

Then Halliday said, "Jere and I used to be able to start anywhere and recite alternate lines to each other. But I haven't tried to go through the whole thing in years. Never thought I'd remember it."

"Datta. Dayadhvam. Damyata. Shantih shantih shantih," he repeated childishly.

Faint grays and pale blues, those anemic heralds of dawn, were gradually lighting the plane's interior.

"What time is it?" Halliday groped for the old-fashioned watch he carried in his vest pocket. "Two-thirty."

"It's five-thirty," Shep said. "You haven't set your watch ahead."

"I seem to be living in the past." Halliday smiled. "Have we been talking all night?"

In the cheerless morning light Halliday looked gray and gaunt. An overnight stubble was beginning to roughen the exceptional smoothness of his face. It was not the kind of face to which a beard is becoming, Shep thought. Essentially boyish and delicately made, it was a face for starched white collars and fresh toilet.

"It's been a wonderful night for me," Shep said. "But I hope it hasn't tired you out too much, Mr. Halliday."

"You might as well start calling me Manley. After all the things I'm afraid I told you, you know me too well to keep up these formalities."

The second bottle of Mumm's had run dry hours ago and the effects were wearing off. As if irritated by an itch that can't be located and has no physical cause, Halliday's sense of guilt made him think he had been more revealing than he had been.

"You know, it's strange, Shep, in this one night I think I've talked to you about more of the things I really think about than I have with my son in his entire life."

Shep glowed with the compliment. His own father had been a devoted parent until Shep began to rebel against the car-rental business. Then had come the years of bitter battles over ways of life and politics, interspersed with periods of uneasy truce.

"Does Douglas show any signs of wanting to write?"

"I'll tell you the truth, Shep—" for some reason, he was confiding in young Stearns "—Douglas has an excellent mind. He's even written a few poems in the *Lawrenceville Lit* I'm rather proud of. But Douglas is an incorrigible snob. He lives for the New York holiday parties and the invitations to Newport. Of course I realize I was just as bad when I came East from Kansas City in 1913. It's only in the last few years I've gotten over brooding about my failure to make the Racquet Club. But at least I sublimated my snobbishness in my work. That scene in the Racquet Club in *High Noon,* for instance. I made my snobbishness pay off, you might say."

"Would you have liked Douglas to become a writer?"

"I'm not sure. Rationally, no. It's really an awful curse to wish on anybody—from the day you begin you never completely relax again. Right this second, to be very, very frank, I'm thinking how I might use you some time, if I want to draw a young, middle-class radical. Even those years I threw away, when the book reviewers were giving me up, I was always worrying about writing, wishing I could find the way to get started again and wanting to push on beyond where I had been. This morning, for instance, when I should be thinking about your story—we'll work that out yet, don't worry—I keep thinking about my new book—how I've got to make it the most thought-out, the most honest piece of work I've done. But to get back to Douglas. Emotionally I've got to admit what a kick it gave me to see those things of his in the Lawrenceville magazine. The whole process of parenthood is completely irrational anyway. Just when you begin to think you're a completely civilized man, you find all kinds of horrid, primitive things popping out of you. You feel an absurd pride when your son turns out to look like you. And another savage shot-in-the-arm when he begins to emulate you. You tell him he should be anything he wants as long as he's happy, but secretly your ego is fattened when he chooses your profession. So I suppose you might say I'm disappointed in Douglas. Even though I know damn well the way he's turning out is mostly my fault. When he was seven I enrolled him at Lawrenceville. I made him feel he could never be a gentleman if he wasn't a graduate of Princeton, Harvard or Yale and didn't date approved daughters of approved Eastern families. I suppose I passed on to him all the shabby insecurity of a Kansas City parvenu. So I should hardly blame him for not finding out what it took me at least thirty-five years and a lot of unhealed wounds to discover."

"Mr. Halli—Manley, if Douglas did turn out to be a writer, what would be the main things you'd want to tell him?"

Halliday spoke seriously, a trifle pompously.

"The first thing I'd talk about would be self-dedication. I'd tell him over and over again that the writing itself, and none of the American by-products, fame, money, adulation, glamorous living, is the only permanent reward. I'd try to teach him not to lose his way."

He paused so long that Shep thought he had finished. But finally he went on, with sudden harshness: "If I had only followed that brilliant advice fifteen years ago, I wouldn't be having to think up the plot for a Hollywood campus musical this morning."

His face, turned to the window again, was silhouetted against the grim morning light. Prompted by Manley's words, Shep saw things in that face he had not seen before. He saw pain pulling it taut. He saw the erosion of anxiety scarring it with deep lines. He saw fatigue, not the natural exhaustion of a day and night without sleep but a profound lassitude of body and mind. And he saw, too, a refusal to surrender.

If it were not quite possible for Shep to read all these things into Halliday's face, it was at least true that these were the thoughts that crossed his mind as he watched the older man.

A moment too late, Halliday seemed to realize how his confessional reference to their movie job might discourage Shep. For now he turned back to him with an unconvincing cheerfulness. "Don't worry, baby, we'll lick this movie. After all, we're still a couple of craftsmen, aren't we?"

Miss Dawson, who had replaced Miss Heath at Kansas City, and who could easily have been her twin sister, came up with orange juice, a too-hearty good morning and the promise of hot coffee.

"Morning, you old stay-ups." Diana at five thousand feet serving canned orange juice in Lily cups. "You can see the New York skyline if you look real hard."

They both turned obediently. There it was, shrouded in winter mist.

"It's always an amazing sight," Shep intruded on Halliday's thoughts. "Right now doesn't it look like a phantom city floating above the clouds?"

Halliday didn't bother to answer. He was staring at the dim turrets of the distant city. Once he had been able to think of it as *his* city. It was all one massive temple built in worship of Success. You brought to its altars your best-sellers, your Wall Street killings, your home-run records, your golden voice, your famous face. And the greedy gods of Success rewarded you, temporarily, with headwaiters who knew your name, with hotel managers who reserved special suites for you, with columnists who recorded your wit, with envious onlookers, with fellow-celebrities for friends. Halliday was remembering the times he had come to New York in triumph.

But commit the unforgivable sin of failure, of letting your batting average or your reputation slump and the temple doors slammed in your face. Headwaiters who guarded them looked the other way. The gods of Manhattan were more ruthless than Jehovah. On his last visit, Halliday had stayed in his third-class hotel room and eaten fig newtons. He could not call his publishers because he had needled them into a half dozen advances without ever delivering his promised manuscript. He could not go to the Algonquin or "21" or the Plaza because he had never answered their requests to pay his bills. He couldn't call his old friend Burt Seixas because he felt self-conscious about owing Burt two thousand he knew Burt could use. At least five other friends had to be ignored for the same reason. He had been afraid to linger in the lobby for fear some enterprising sob-sister would track him down for one of those riches-to-rags human-interest yarns. He even had taken the precaution of registering at a dingy hotel under another name. On that last visit, he had hidden away in a hole in the wall on a nondescript side street. He had not really been in New York at all.

112

Now the early morning mist was lifting. The skyline, still a great many miles away, rose up like a giant battlement.

Somewhere behind that formidable barricade of stone and steel, Jere slept. The roar of propellers sent thunder bowling along into the morning. *Datta. Dayadhvam. Damyata.* Give. Sympathize. Control.

"Boy!" Shep was saying happily, "whatta city!"

10

The white tile of the Holland Tunnel rolled past them as the airline's black limousine raced through the enormous artery feeding the heart of the city.

Finally they burst out into the open, into the swarming labyrinth of downtown Manhattan. There were the trucks, the cops, the bars, the stores, the cabs, the reckless pedestrians picking holes through traffic like shabby Albie Booths. There were fruit, all colors, vegetables, hock shops, Italians, Jews and the global hustle of the water front. Here the bright boys and the smart girls from the provinces come to make their fortunes; here grimy, overcrowded streets offer frantic hospitality to refugees from German bullyboys, Irish famine, Balkan wars, Italian poverty. Bagdad and Rome and Paris and London had had it once, but it was all here now, it was all here, from the Stock Exchange to the pushcart market, from Young and Rubicam and millions of dollars a word to Joe Gould and his millions of words in search of a dollar. It was all here now, the money and the power and the brains they employ and their great army of camp followers catching the crumbs from the tables of Voisin and "21"; and another world that lived richly without wealth at the New School and the New Friends of Music and the old-film programs of the Museum of Modern Art; and another by-far-the-largest world rushing back and forth across the island, punch-in punch-out, spiced-ham sandwich and a cupa coffee, knocking themselves or one another out simply in order to exist in one of the cramped compartments of the Great Hive. As they rushed uptown along the elevated express lane, Shep felt a resurgence of energy. As an eye-opener, this city of New York was a bagful of benzedrine.

But Manley lay with his head back on the seat, his eyes closed. His body felt twitchy with exhaustion and from time to time he slipped into uneasy fits of sleep, some no longer than a few seconds, from which he kept wrenching himself desperately.

He was barely conscious of the tedious stop-go progress through midtown traffic, the screeching stop in front of the Waldorf, the bustling proximity of Shep Stearns, the sense of being piloted around the outer circle of the lobby's vortex. Then a rushing upward through the elevator shaft, an opening of doors and other bits of stylized service from the bellboy, the business of a few coins changing hands; they were deposited in their suite overlooking Park Avenue, each with his own bedroom opening on a central living room.

Shep tossed his coat toward the couch but it slipped off and he let it lie there.

"I'll probably collapse in about five minutes, but I'm feeling great all of a sudden—all hopped up. How you feel, Manley?"

"Like a million dollars," Halliday said slowly, "in old Spanish doubloons buried ten feet underground."

They withdrew to their respective bathrooms. Shep, in an effusion of pent-up vitality, performed some deep knee bends and, a few years out of top condition, was gratified to see he could still touch his toes. His calisthenics were interrupted by a call that warbled uneasily across the suite: "Shep—could you come here a minute?"

Shep found Halliday in the bathroom, sitting on the edge of the tub. He was wearing one-piece BVD's, the old-fashioned kind Shep had never seen in use. His legs looked spindly, his arms were unmuscular and very white and his knees were bony as a small child's whose legs are growing too fast. On his left thigh was a red line where the needle had slipped and scratched his skin. "I hate to ask you, but would you do this damn thing for me?" Halliday's voice went a little strident with self-consciousness. Shep was squeamish about taking the hypodermic needle. He didn't have much heart for these things.

"I've always been lousy at it." Embarrassment kept Halliday talking. "Broke the needle off in my leg once. Been sort of edgy about it ever since."

Feeling a little sick, Shep plunged the needle.

"Too bad we can't trade these old chassis in on new models."

Shep didn't answer. He was still a little faint from the business of the needle. He felt a genuine compassion for Halliday's discomfort, but a more basic reaction resented the older man's flaw. If he wasn't up to the trip why hadn't he said so in Milgrim's office? In Hollywood it had occurred to Halliday: no matter how nice a young man is, inevitably there must be times when an older man will begrudge him his youth. And now Shep was thinking: no matter how much he understands and makes allowances for him, a young man in good health can't help despising, at times, an older man who is ailing.

"You must be tired as hell," Shep said. "We were a couple of dopes to stay up all night."

Damn it, don't patronize me, Halliday thought. It is the one thing I cannot bear.

"I suppose a little sleep wouldn't do either of us any harm," Halliday said. "I think I'll try to nap for an hour or so."

He stretched out on the bed and closed his eyes, but the intense winter light streaming through the ineffectual shades penetrated his twitching eyelids. He rose and drew the curtains. For a moment he thought he had created the atmosphere of sleep. But then, intensified as if by some inner amplifier, he heard the cacophony of the avenue below: the rhythmic a-slosh a-slosh a-slosh of the wheels turning on the melting snow, the clang-acling-aclang-acling of that inevitable loose chain, the constant honking of irritable cab-drivers, the persistent whistle of the doormen. He rose again, groped in his pockets and found some cotton pellets Miss Heath had given him on the plane. Then, with his ears plugged and his head pressed down into the pillow, he tried again. But the elimination of outer distractions only succeeded in intensifying the inner ones. The highlights of this pleasure town pinwheeled in his brain. Where was he now, 50th and Park, once their own special amusement park, their fun house? Every time they threw something, they won a prize. *One was so small you couldn't see it at all but the other had won many prizes.* Jere and her limericks. Jere just a few blocks away. He wanted to see her and he didn't want to see her and—once they had had to be separated for a week when he went home to his mother's deathbed. He had called her from Kansas City three times a day and each time they had said all the same things over again and at the end of every call he had hung up with the same egomaniacal conviction that no two people could have felt *this,* no not *this,* not this exquisite meeting and melting of minds and bodies and dreams. And now, a few years later—he could come to town and not even call her. And there she was, right around the corner. He could be there in five minutes . . . but there was no sleep at the end of that street. Think of something else. Think of Ann. Ann was one of the few people whose judgment of others he trusted. She could make cool judgments without emotional prejudice. Unusual talent. Most people like to think they have it. Funny thing was Jere's transparently subjective judgments. If she didn't like a certain girl it meant the girl had an eye out for him. She was usually right. If she said she didn't like a man, Manley would guess she was physically attracted to him. He was usually right. "The trouble with you, Jere," he remembered saying once, "is that you weren't content just to drink from the Fountain of Youth. You kept leaning over to see your own image in it until you fell in and almost drowned."

"I wasn't leaning in to see myself," he remembered Jere's saying, "I was trying to fish you out."

This is no way to take a nap.

He had to get some rest. That trembling of the eyelids was always a telltale sign. I know how I'll put myself to sleep—he thought of it as a joke—I'll think about our picture. Once upon a time there was a college boy who invited a waitress out of a diner to a Webster house party week-end etcetera and etcetera and somehow or other she becomes the Queen of the Mardi Gras. Could we freshen it up with a little satire on high-pressure advertising? Each of two rival cosmetic companies wants its model to become Queen. They try to rig the election. I know, its rank, but anyway I'm thinking about it. Shep can't look at me with those big brown calf's eyes and beg me to have a try at it. Oh, well, if I'm doing this, I might as well stay up and talk to him, I'm not getting any rest anyway.

He went back to the bathroom, took out a benzedrine tablet and then, with a sense of Ann's restraining hand on his shoulder, broke it in half. It seemed easier to put on the suit he had traveled in than to unpack the ones Ann had folded into the large case. There had been other times in New York when he had felt such devotion to the creases in his pants that he would not have thought of wearing the same suit twice without pressing. But in recent years he had lost nearly all sense of externals. Perhaps the swing of the pendulum had been too extreme in each direction. Unless Ann removed it he would keep putting on the same shirt for days simply because that was less trouble than taking the pins out of a new one.

Entering the sitting room, he found Shep in his bathrobe hunched over the desk, writing in pencil.

"Got our script finished?" He realized he sounded like Al Harper.

Shep grinned. "I thought it might help us get started if we made a list of all the ideas we've had so far."

"Don't forget the one with Jeanette MacDonald as 'Dizzy' Dean."

Shep stood up and stared out the window. He couldn't say this to Halliday directly. But he talked up as if he were by himself, rehearsing lines for a play. "Manley, I know it's easy to kid this thing. Most the time I feel like doing it too. But after all, we accepted the job. Sooner or later we'll have to—roll or give up the dice."

Shep had all the makings of a hack, Halliday thought rebelliously. He had the hack's conscientiousness, the hack's ability to divide his imagination into watertight compartments. And at the same time he thought—that isn't quite fair. The boy is right. It *is* a job of work I'm accepting money for. He himself had been critical of these Hollywood writers who sign long-term contracts and then save their best lines to excoriate the sources of their income. Like any dishonesty pushed to the extremes of logical conclusion, this was a form of insanity. He preferred Shep's attitude. At least the young man professed an honest interest in the medium. Maybe this would be the new attitude, replacing the cynicism and self-contempt of the writers of his generation who had

118

gone out for a soft touch and had developed a taste and finally an insatiable appetite for soft touches.

"Shep, you're right. Let's pitch in and solve this thing."

He sat down as if he meant business. "This is where we'll lick our story. A hotel room. No personality. No associations. The traditional refuge of harassed playwrights, suicides, and other desperate men."

For half an hour or so the room had an atmosphere of righteous labor. As a token of honest effort, Halliday presented his cosmetic advertising idea. It was a small bone to a hungry dog and Shep leapt at it and began to run. The cosmetics model goes up to Webster just to win the Mardi Gras title. Her date, the ski captain, heads the Mardi Gras committee. She vamps him shamelessly all week-end to pull the necessary strings that win the title for her. When he finds out the commercial tie-up he feels like a jerk for having fallen for her. Then, in the finals of the ski-jump, he's injured. The model, who has been falling in love with him all the time, of course, rushes to his side. Somehow all the commercial big city dross has been washed away by the crisp mountain air and the freshly fallen snow . . .

"By God, I think we have it!" The anti-business angle even began to embellish it with "honesty" in Shep's mind.

"Would the boy turn on the girl merely because she was a model for Helena Rubinstein?" Halliday asked. "Maybe we should make that a little stronger. She's not only a model but the mistress of the sales manager. He's the real prince of darkness in the piece. He's come up to Webster as a kind of Iago. He's a typical product of our age, everything reduced to 'public relations' in quotes. He still dreams of retiring to the country club with five million dollars, like Charlie Holt—a classmate of mine who bought a seat on the Exchange when he was twenty-six and shot himself in the men's room of the Exchange when he was thirty-three . . ."

This time Shep's sturdy presence blocked Halliday's trap-door exit to the past. Only a few hours before Shep had been fascinated with Halliday's double sense of time. He did not go back to the past, he carried it with him. But now Shep had begun to be on the lookout for these nostalgic cut-backs. He began to draw a line between the Manley Halliday whose works had so impressed him and the middle-aged collaborator who could not seem to differentiate between plot analysis and reminiscences.

"This sales manager," Shep prompted. "You may have something there. He's a kind of shadow over the week-end. Mmm, how about this? As the climax to his advertising campaign the sales manager wants to stage a mock marriage. You know, just pictures for a full-page magazine lay-out. Well, it's after the ski-jump injury—this would be the tag—the boy and girl are straightened out, slip away and what the sales manager believes to be a mock marriage is actually a real one . . ."

Shep's enthusiasm, self-cranked and back-firing like a hopped-up Ford, struck a rubber wall of silence and bounced back. Halliday gave him a funny look. Then he said:

"Nize baby, et op all de ice."

"What—what's that, Manley?"

"When we didn't like people that's what we always used to do —answer 'em in Nize Baby talk."

For the first time since they met Shep wasn't sure he was going to like Manley Halliday.

"I see," he said. But he didn't. His vision hopelessly normal, he could not see around corners.

As soon as Halliday saw the look on Shep's face he hastened to explain. "Oh, my goodness. I didn't mean that. I like you. I like you very much. In fact, you're the first person I've liked since—since I decided not to like any more people. No, good God, Shep, I didn't mean you. I was talking back to the story, to this ogre of commerce I invented."

"I thought he might put some life into the story," Shep held on.

"He would. But the wrong kind. I suppose you could make a real character out of him if you went ahead and developed him —gave him some shading. So he isn't just a cipher in a morality play. But isn't he really an extraneous element? There's an unwholesome quality about him that leaves an ugly stain on the picture. After all, a college house party is a romantic time. It should be a gay, pretty, frothy picture. There should be a kind of innocence about it, a youthful glow . . ."

Shep sank down into the couch. "Right now I feel about as glowing as a dead fish."

Halliday said: "Was I making sounds like a producer?"

Shep nodded. "I thought it was the Great God Milgrim himself."

"There's something about the movies that brings out these damn generalizations in you. You never think of doing that about a work of fiction. You know who your people are and you track them down specifically one by one."

"Manley, that's what we've got to do, get back to characters, same as if you were writing a book."

"But the trouble is, a book is something that starts inside of you. You work from the inside out. You don't have to sit down and mechanically invent characters and situations. They're all there, ready to be released. A movie is just the opposite. It doesn't start inside anybody. Where was *Love on Ice* conceived, for instance? Certainly not inside Shep Stearns, though I'm sure you could write your own college story. Not even inside Victor Milgrim. It's an orphan child born of artificial insemination on a box-office counter."

At another time Shep might have been amused. But the chances were, Milgrim would be coming in on the next plane. He began to wonder if they were up (or down) to the assignment. He was pretty sure any reliable Hollywood hack would have had it in the bag by now. It was mainly a question of adjusting one's aim. When Halliday wasn't shooting way beyond the target, he was firing right into the ground at his feet.

"Christ, I don't know," Shep said. "This thing's beginning to drive me nuts. Maybe we should go back and take a look at that waitress line again. There is a certain human interest appeal in a waitress—a completely ordinary counter girl—competing against those Wellesley and Vassar debs."

"Completely ordinary except that she's played by Ginger Rogers."

"O.K. Ginger Rogers. Ginger isn't a bad actress. She could play a working-class girl."

"I see. You want a proletarian heroine, Shep. A pretty little union member. None of these café-society fascists. Say, here's an idea—the poor boy has the waitress up, the rich roommate has the Vassar girl, and it's Vassar who turns out to be the Marxist. At least that would be more authentic. So the Vassar girl falls in love with the boy who's working his way through and the waitress, who's a good little opportunist, sets her sights for the rich boy. Why, that rather appeals to me."

Shep had a desperate impulse. It was something he hadn't done since a peerade to Worcester for the big game with Holy Cross. He was going to have a mid-day shot. "I think I could use a drink," he said suddenly. "How about you?"

Use a drink! Yes, he could *use* one all right. Champagne had saved the night. Now he could use something to get him through the day. Christ, if ever a man had a good excuse.

Uh-uh. Self-pity Halliday. Damn it, would he go to pieces the first day away from Ann? He'd be damned if he would.

"No, thanks, Shep. I'd rather not. But you go ahead."

He hoped Shep would decide not to drink alone, but Shep was jittery and at the same time—perhaps still under the stimulus of finding himself with Manley Halliday—expansive. It was still a sort of spree, this being flown across a continent to a great hotel to work on a story with Manley Halliday.

Halliday was pleased with his own moral strength in rejecting the drink. But he was a little dismayed when he heard Shep order a bottle of Ballantine's.

"Might as well have it in the room," Shep had said casually.

Halliday nodded and tried to smile, but he was frightened. "Tell him to bring me a pitcher of ice water." What day was this? Only Friday? And they wouldn't be going back till Tuesday. Tuesday was a precipitous height rising above him. And he would have to climb all the way. The young man would have to exert special effort to pull him along. But supposing he should lose his footing and slip, dragging the young man down? A long way to fall. Mountain-climbing had always seemed to him a tedious and needlessly hazardous excuse for sport. Tobogganing and skiing had been his speed. He and Jere liked to be carried up and to swoosh down.

Together he and Shep made another pedestrian circle around the stubborn walls of the story. The waiter appeared with the

Ballantine's, soda and ice. "Gut morning, chentleman," he greeted them and both of them could feel his obsequiousness filling the room.

Halliday glared at the intruder. "The ice water?"

"Ach! Ice vatter. I haf forgotten zer vatter."

"Yah. Zer vatter," Halliday mocked.

Shep frowned. The waiter looked unhappy. "From zer zink maybe . . ." he began hopefully.

"I want a pitcher of water," Halliday said sharply. "And mach schnell."

More like a rabbit than the walrus he resembled, the waiter scurried off.

Halliday chuckled maliciously. But Shep was appalled and went into action.

"The poor guy. I always feel sorry for waiters."

"I feel sorrier for writers. Waiters in big hotels probably make more money than you do. They're the trickiest people in the world, with the possible exception of Hungarians. And when you get the two together you've got the New Machiavelli. Shep, I'm going to have to get you over this ridiculous notion of sentimentalizing everybody. Most of us are swine. But when it comes to German waiters in big hotels, I tell you there are no exceptions."

Shep poured himself a big one and held up the bottle as an invitation. "I'll get you some water from the bathroom."

"Well . . ." Desire and reason staged a brief, unequal tug-of-war. ". . . a very, *very* short one."

Ah, he had a glass in his hand again. It had happened so easily. He was hardly aware of how it had begun.

It was good though. Even before the touch of the rim to his lips, the fumes whispered *relax* and promised euphoria. He drank thirstily. Shep had taken him too literally. It was good but not strong enough.

The waiter arrived with the pitcher. Manley regarded him slyly.

"How long have you been in this country, Adolph?"

The waiter looked miserable. "Excuse me, pleece. My name iss not Adolph. It is Yoseph."

123

"You wouldn't be ashamed to be called after your leader, though, would you?"

Manley was questioning him with theatrical severity, as if he were playing some official role, an FBI man perhaps.

Watching the waiter redden, Shep felt miserable for all of them.

"He iss not my leader, zer. I am American Zitizen."

"So is Fritz Kuhn. But I know you people. Ein Führer. Ein Volk. Ein Staat."

The waiter's face screwed up as if ready to burst into tears. He had wondered when this would begin.

"No, no, I am gut Zitizen."

Manley poured himself a second drink. He poured it recklessly, without measuring. Shep watched uneasily. It hardly seemed possible that Manley could be in the bag, and yet there was an unfamiliar edge to his voice, a combative look in his eye. And see how his hand trembled when he tried to hold the lip of the bottle to his glass. Of course that could be merely fatigue on top of illness. But these wild things he was saying:

"Tell me the truth, Yoseph, you felt pretty proud of yourself the day your *schöne Knaben* goose-stepped into the Rhineland, didn't you?"

The waiter's eyes rolled toward Shep. "Chentleman, pleece." He was trying to edge his way out. "If you zhould vish somet'ing more . . ."

But Manley would not, perhaps he could not, let go. "Our country's too soft. Like Athens, we've got to be destroyed. When we let suspicious characters like you run around loose, in a big hotel like this, a gold-mine for espionage. . . And who thinks to notice a waiter? They're like part of the furnishings . . ."

This was too much even for Joseph's habitual docility and he broke into an emotional protest, an outburst of anger choked by shrill self-pity.

"Nein, nein, das ist nicht wahr—" In his excitement, after sixteen years he could hardly remember his English. *"Ich bin—*I am not spy. I gut American Zitizen. My zon Hans has four months already in the American Army. You haf no right to say spy of gut American Zitizen."

124

"All right, all right, Joe, he was only kidding. Beat it, forget about it," Shep said.

Joseph retreated behind a rear-guard defense of muttered denial.

Shep looked at Manley carefully. What he saw was deceiving. Manley certainly did not look as far gone as he sounded.

"Manley, I hate to say this, but—that was a silly goddam thing to do."

"Why—what did I do?" He was really bewildered.

"Picking on that poor guy like that. Sure I'm all for the Nazi boycott but we can't start baiting every German we meet. Next thing you know you'll be kicking dachshunds."

"Oh, my God—is that the way it looked?"

It was slightly ludicrous the way he lowered his head. The small boy scolded by his father. "Lord, baby, you're right. I guess that was a wet thing to do."

He jumped to his feet. Shep was still watching him carefully, wondering what he was going to do next. Manley ran across the room to the corridor door.

"Where are you going?"

"Catch the waiter. 'pologize. I'll give him some money."

Shep tossed his drink down and paced the room nervously. In a few moments Manley was back. He was no longer a member of counter-intelligence. "He had gone down already," he said, self-chastised.

Feeling almost too sober, Shep built himself another drink. He hesitated to freshen Manley's. But afraid to patronize him again, he said how about another.

"No, thank you," Manley said. The business of the waiter had frightened him too. Just can't drink any more. Not since I was dealcoholized. Got to be careful now. Damned careful.

Shep was trying to talk story again.

"We've got to bear down now, Manley. Jesus, Milgrim will be on our necks any minute."

The story. The waitress. The roommates. The misunderstanding. The ski finale. The big clinch.

Manley stood at the window, thinking of the city.

"What if the waitress had a baby?"

"What?"

125

He didn't have to look around to see the annoyance in Shep's face.

"I see her on an ice floe with her baby. The ice is beginning to crack. The Webster skier comes by and she throws the baby across the widening chasm into his arms."

Shep couldn't think of anything to say. He stared morosely into his glass.

"I was just trying to get away from all the generalizing," Manley tried to bridge the silence. "Trying to think up a good movie scene."

Is he kidding me? Is he drunk? Is he out of his mind? Shep felt himself being hemmed in by terrible alternatives. For the first time since they left, he saw the gargoyle face of fiasco grinning down at them.

"Maybe we should both go douse our heads under a cold shower, Manley. And try a fresh start in half an hour."

It was the most tactful reprimand he could summon. The willful boy in Halliday seemed to recognize it for what it was. For he answered, "Go ahead, you shower if you like. I think I'll catch a breath of fresh air. Meet you back here in half an hour or so."

"All right—" For the first time, Shep actually welcomed the chance to get away from him. This was the seventeenth consecutive hour without sleep, without rest from each other. "—but don't get lost, Manley. We've got to get our lumps in on this damned story this afternoon."

The homburg seemed to restore Manley's dignity. The crisp "See you anon" was more in key with the famous-author-and-ardent-young-fan relationship of the day before yesterday.

Shep said a dull *s'long*. He hated this feeling of nagging wife. *Get home early, dear*. He noted, with what seemed almost a wife's loving disapproval, how Manley staggered slightly on his way to the elevator.

As soon as Manley reached the sidewalk the winter air took care of that heavy feeling behind his eyes. For the first time all day he felt New York, the rush of cabs, the correct doorman, the Park Avenue wives chic and aging in their furs, the beautiful blue poodle in the arms of the beautiful blonde girl on the arm of a dapper fifty-year-old Park Avenue blade. For just one moment he loved it all again. He felt free, absurdly, boyishly free. Just as on the day he had come down from school to meet Mother and her train had been late. That was one of his first memories of the luxury of time that does not have to be accounted for. Sometimes he wondered if all luxuries could not be reduced to this single formula. For an hour or so he would be free of World-Wide Pictures, of Victor Milgrim, of Shep Stearns, of Hollywood, of responsibility. He took a malicious, vengeful glee in throwing the young man into the pot.

It was only when he turned off Park Avenue toward the East River that he realized where he was going. His need to see her had been compulsive from the moment of arrival. Even though he was quite sure of what was ahead, a vestigial, irremovable romanticism hurried him on. His mind's eye, incurably bifocal, could never stop searching for the fairy-tale maiden who made his young manhood a time of bewitchment, when springtime was the only season and the days revolved on a lovers' spectrum of sunlight, twilight, candlelight and dawn.

Manley's eyes searched along the apartment-house roster: Keyes, Abrahms, Winsch-Barry, de Martino, Wilder-Halliday. There it was, just as in the early days when Jere had clung so desperately to her maiden name. Jere Wilder. She used to love to write it in an exotic flourish over and over again, covering phone books, walls, message pads, tablecloths. Horribly brought up, he'd say jestingly, meaning every word of it. In the white sands of a dozen watering places: Jere Wilder. Sometimes it seemed as if God knew who was going to be named what and then created personalities to fit. Maybe it was because Shakespeare was wrong and Stein was right—once a rose becomes a *rose* never again will it smell as sweet by any other name. Jere Wilder was Jere Wilder was Jere Wilder. This had caused Manley a good deal of futile speculation: one's name is an active factor in conditioning. Could the constant, subconscious association of the given name Jere with the comparative *Wilder* provide abnormal stimulation? It was hardly a scientific theory. And yet—characteristically, Manley's mind was half-serious—to take an even more obvious case, wouldn't there be a special incentive for a man called Strongfort to stand up to danger? Anyway Jere loved her name; it fitted her; she never wanted to let go of it, and, like all impractical people, she had devised a highly practical reason for posting it beside his on apartment doors and hotel registers. In touch with a number of little magazines interested in her translation of French Symbolist poets (would he ever forget that interminable translation of *Une Saison en Enfer?*) she had pointed out that they would continue to address her by her professional name, Jere Wilder. But since the divorce, with a perversity he could well understand, she had published two or three brief translations (*Harper's Bazaar* and *Twice-a-Year*) under the name of Jere Halliday. An over-intense romanticism lent consistency to these seemingly conflicting gestures. Married, she had resisted the merging of her identity in his more

128

famous one. "I can love you better if I'm *me*," she had said one night. "I always want to be the girl you're sneaking into your room past the desk clerk." Now, unmarried, she had grown sentimental. Rarely affected by things as they were, accepting as real the things she made up in her head, she had become increasingly sentimental toward their marriage, imagining them to have been married in a way they never could have been.

Christ, he thought bitterly, turning toward the little self-operating elevator (a conveyance that always mildly alarmed him), it is all so beautifully simple in the beginning. And now look at us, twenty-one years later, tied up in knots like two fish lines snarled together. Flashing across the years came that crazy counterpoint of shrill toy horns, the indiscriminate kissing of strange mouths seeking partners, the brief unprecedented love of Aussie for Tommy, Tommy for Yank, Yank for *poilu,* enlisted man for officer that seemed to be man's way of declaring peace.

He was being carried along with some drunken sergeants from the 301st Tank Battalion and their mademoiselles. One of these girls, an overjoyed lady of fifteen, silly on Calvados like the rest, had thrown herself into Manley's arms, squealing, "My cute little lieutenant, I am going to take him home with me." The sergeant who had been counting on this privilege announced that he had fought his way into Brancourt and was not going to let any swivel-chair hero swipe his piece.

Manley had no wish to interfere with the sergeant's pleasures. On those occasions, twice as an undergraduate and rather more often here in France, when he had accepted women on the basis of availability, even of proximity, he had—what was the phrase? —hated himself in the morning. (Ah, those clichés, our emotional shorthand.) So, interested neither in this worldly child nor the disputatious sergeant intent on celebrating Armistice with her, he had slipped away through the crowd to the first hospitable doorway.

From behind the door, beckoning, came the sound of music, cheerfully sad and sweetly familiar, *Poor Butterfly, in the blossoms waiting, Poor Butterfly* . . . reminding him of the show he and Beatrice Vining had taken in at the Hippodrome his last night in New York. They had made a night of it and when he brought her home at two-thirty, Mr. and Mrs. Vining had been understanding about it in their almost ludicrous efforts to be good sports. After all, Manley was going overseas to defend civilization, that exalted abstraction inseparable in the Vinings' mind from the British Empire. And although he was hardly their first choice (a dear boy, Manley, but from Kansas City and a family not even on the Priest of Pallas Ball invitation list), Beatrice seemed to have her heart set on him. And Beatrice had always been given everything she wanted, within reason.

Out of the crowd's reach for a moment, Manley listened to the saxophone bewailing poor butterfly's solitary fate. Banal songs, he always thought, were the saddest songs of all, having no grandeur to redeem them. Enjoying a sense of pathos he often cultivated, he gave himself completely to the tin-pan condolence. The mood offered him a sense of detachment. Shouting and singing and clowning and kissing anybody was the fool's way of reversing emotions from war to peace. Manley liked parties, but more exclusive ones. Probably he would have stayed there only long enough to catch his breath until the song ended and then plunge into the crowd again to continue fighting his way toward the Café Continental, where Ross, Woollcott, Winterich and the rest of the S & S'ers were supposed to be throwing a memorable brawl. But just as he turned away from the door, it was thrown open violently and two staggering doughboys appeared. They were shouting, exactly as drunken doughboys should, *Finay la guerre!* Then, in a gesture completely baffling to Manley, they turned around, touched their thumbs to their noses and jeered, "Yah, ya still a bunch o' kikes!" Laughing uproariously at their own wit, they threw their arms around each other in mutual admiration and went forth, into the howling sea of faces in the street.

Through the half-open door he had seen a girl so good to look at that he could feel himself smiling. What he noticed first was the contrast of golden skin against white satin. A black satin choker adorned a long slender neck. Another black satin band around her waist accentuated her slenderness. It was the waist of a girl of fifteen. Yet there was nothing fragile or pathetic about her. She was smiling at a tall, Lincolnesque, Jewish-looking soldier of whom Manley was instantly jealous. The smile emphasized the Asiatic cast of her eyes. Her dark hair was cut short (something he hadn't until this minute approved), smartly combed back except for a little fringe of bangs across her forehead. At that moment he also became an enthusiastic supporter of bangs. He was aware of marvelous bones, the fine bridge of her nose, the sweep of the jaw, and the high cheekbones. Must be one of those French Indo-Chinese girls of wealthy parents who come to Paris to be educated, he decided.

He must have been staring rudely. For suddenly his reverie was interrupted by a most unexpected gesture. She was sticking out her tongue at him. Before he could recover, the music had resumed "Oh, Johnny, oh, Johnny, how you can fight . . ." and she was carried off lightly in the arms of the tall Jewish soldier.

Then he became aware of Jewishness all round him, dark, semitic boys in khaki, and a sandy-haired, moon-faced blond-Jew sergeant wearing the proud Red-1 of the Fighting First whom a hostess called Julie. The hostesses, too, with the exception of *his* and one or two others, all had the ancient out-of-style beauty of the Jewess. The saxophone player was a Jew, though the drummer and pianist were Negro SOS privates and apparently the fiddle player was a French civilian. They were surprisingly good.

His mind was on the girl. He took a young man's interest in the long, slim legs, the tiny waist, the youthful promise of exquisite little breasts, the neck unusually long but graceful and oddly becoming. Above all, her smile sparkled. There was a naughtiness about that smile that rushed a young man on. It was not the practiced and slightly cynical smile of the American coquette, the Y or Red Cross girl in Paris with whom he had become so bored.

The dark pianist raised his young face from the keyboard and letting his fingers dance lightly on the melody, sang "Oh, Johnny, oh, Johnny, how you can love, oh Johnny, oh, Johnny, heavens above . . ."

131

Manley was walking toward her. His hand dropped gently on her partner's shoulder. "Sorry, old man." Prom style. The tall Jewish soldier melted away. *"Merci bien, mon chérie,"* her words curled silkily around the head of the departing dancer.

When he touched her, an unfamiliar recklessness possessed him. They moved off, miraculously together . . .

The voice of the pianist filled their silence. Manley was mustering his college French. (He had scolded himself all year for spending too much time with Americans). Something in the yellow-green eyes of this fawn in white satin cued him to put aside the stock openers—What is your name? Do you like American jazz? Do you come here often?

Finally he decided on, "Who are you?"

He had expected the question to catch her off balance, but, behind an elfin smile, her words poured out in such a rapid flow that his college French was soon outdistanced.

"J'ai de mes ancêstres gaulois l'oeil bleu blanc, la cervelle étroite, et la maladresse dans la lutte. Je trouve mon habillement aussi barbare que le leur. Mais je ne beurre pas ma chevelure."

He caught something about the blue-white eye of Gallic ancestors and finding clothes as barbarous as theirs and something that sounded like "I do not butter my hair," but he said *"Je comprends pas. Si vous ne parleriez que plus lentement."*

He translated her deliberate, mock-serious answer. "It is not important that you understand. You are here to dance. And to enjoy holding me."

He was always at his best in conquests that gave his mind a chance to turn a cartwheel or two. He forced his French to its farthest limits. "Perhaps you can tell me what is important."

The quartet had left Johnny for a sing-song classification of smiles.

"Pleasure is important. Not just contentment but *plaisir."* Her emphasis made it sound tantalizingly dangerous. "The enjoyment of beauty. The only truth."

"Ah, mademoiselle," he could almost feel his own charm spraying from his pores, "you are much too beautiful yourself to be worrying about definitions of truth."

"Ho hum," she exaggerated her yawn.

"Oh, I bore you?"

She moved effortlessly in his arms. He wondered what the perfume was; there was a scent of something fresh and growing about her. He was lost in her.

"Being told I am beautiful? Why shouldn't it? Every soldier who wants to use me for a night tells me that. I have eyes. I can see that I am beautiful. In the morning after my bath I love to admire myself in the mirror. I say to myself, 'How much more beautiful you are than those overweight nudes of Renoir.'"

He said, accepting her unconventionality for an invitation, "Perhaps I should be fortunate enough to look into your mirror some time."

She said—he would always remember how out of character it seemed when he still knew her so slightly—"Ish ka bibble."

He: "Oh, I see you've picked up some of our slang."

She: (in English for the first time, with an exaggerated French accent) "Yes, zees slang is—how you say?—very funnee for uz."

He: "Oh, you speak English?"

She: "Just what you call ze bedpillow Engleesh." She gave him an outrageous wink. "You know uz French girls."

That was the only trouble with these girls over here, even the loveliest and highest-born—they did not wait for you to pluck them, they placed their choicest blossoms in your hands.

"Where do you come from? What do you do?"

"I will tell you a secret—if you promise not to be frightened. I am a sorceress."

Manley laughed. "An amateur sorceress, or a sorceress by trade?"

"I have a horror of all trades," she quoted gravely, but with something behind the gravity that was laughing at him. "Masters and workers—base peasants all."

"Haven't I heard that somewhere before?"

"You are not a very well educated young man if you haven't."

"Before I could finish advanced French literature I dropped out of college to do some field work in mass insanity and advanced annihilation."

"At least you recognize French literature. That was written by —my husband."

"Oh."

He would not have believed, five minutes before, that such an admission from the lips of a woman he did not know could do this to him. Of course, over here, it wasn't the obstacle it would have been in America. There might still be room for an *ami*.

The musicians, running out of smiles at last, had momentarily subsided. Two soldiers, on their way out, grinned at her familiarly.

"S'long, Jere. Happy Armistice."

" 'Night, Sid. Come back soon, Leo."

Manley stared.

"You're not French at all!"

Manley thought she looked like a half-grown cat when she smiled. "Were you really fooled? Oh, I love to fool people."

Manley's impressions did a rapid somersault. A moment before she had been a strange French girl. Now she seemed like a young American.

"What sort of place is this anyway? Looks like a reunion of the Twelve Tribes."

"You mean you don't even know where you are? The clubhouse of the Jewish Welfare Board."

He heard another hollow *oh* echoing from him. Then, reluctantly, he asked. "Are you—are you Jewish?"

She answered him gaily. "Of course. My name is Jere Wildberg."

Jere Wildberg. He was afraid the disappointment would show on his face. In these few seconds he had to improvise a new setting. Her father was probably a wealthy clothing manufacturer who could send her to the best schools, well, almost the best. His name was undoubtedly Jerome Wildberg. He really had wanted a boy to take over the business but had thought it would be cute to name her Jere.

"Whatsa matta, you didn't take me for a shicksa, didja?" She was laughing at him. It was waltz time now and the musicians, who seemed to know all the new ones, started up with *Will You Remember?* Jewish, or not, Manley conceded, she was something to look at. And there was a quickness in her, an imaginativeness, a streak of non-conformity, a high-keyed vitality new to him. Wait till he told the boys at Mama's that he spent Armistice

134

night at the Jewish Welfare Board dance, in the arms of an indescribably beautiful Jewess. He was just about to draw her a little closer to him for the waltz when a short, swarthy corporal muttered, "Sorry, Lieutenant," and took her away.

For an hour he was alternately ecstatic and glum as he cut in, yielded, cut in again. In the minutes when he was forced to the sidelines he was startled to find how desperate he became. He had to touch her again, feel her lithe, young body moving with his and marvel at the way her mind whipped unexpected words to her impudent tongue.

"Lieutenant, you mustn't monopolize me."

"You sound like a Bull Mooser."

"You see, it's part of our job to remain in circulation."

"I refuse to have you sound like a lending-library book."

"And anyway, you're much too handsome."

"Why, Miss Wildberg!"

"It's true. You know, you look a little like Byron. You aren't, by any chance?"

"Just call me George Gordon when we're alone."

"I always have to be on my guard against handsome men, men as good-looking as Francis X. Bushman but with something delicate and ethereal about them, something poetic."

"Have you fallen in love with many like that?"

"Oh, hundreds."

"I hate them all."

"So do I—now. I fall out of love even quicker than I fall in. That's why I know I should never be married."

"But—didn't you tell me you were married?"

"Oh, did I?"

A thin-faced private was in the way. "Cutting in, Lieutenant."

Manley retired to the sidelines in frustration. It was like trying to hold a piece of quicksilver, glittering in the palm of his hand but slipping away each time he tried to enclose it.

Before he could cut back, another soldier had taken his place. The little Jewish bitch. She was just playing him the way she did all the others. Look at her smiling up at that Hebe. Well, she wasn't the only girl in Paris, God knows.

Ah, he had her back again.

"Now to get back to this mysterious husband of yours."

"Such a grim look, m'sieur. You aren't an agent of the Sûreté by any chance?"

"Madame, I have been shadowing you for months. Your name is not Jere Wildberg. It is Baroness Hilda Von Fruhling-Spitzel Horsthausenschaft, Operator x2y37 of Imperial German Intelligence."

—"Ach, ausgefundet!" Jere cried. She looked up into his face with her eyes wide open in Theda Bara intrigue.

They were dancing past the musicians. "Play *Madelon* again, Eddie." She smiled at the pianist. Then she looked up at Manley disarmingly. "I like dancing with you. You're romantic."

"How do you know that?"

"The way you put your cheek against mine and close your eyes."

"When I open my eyes, there are yours, your yellow-green cat eyes staring at me. What are you looking at, Jere, when you stare like that?"

"I'm trying to look inside you to see what you really are."

"You told me you were a sorceress, but I didn't take you seriously."

"Never take me completely seriously. But always take me a little seriously."

"I'll remember that."

They took a good look at each other. It was a look of both tenderness and appraisal.

"What is your name—Lord Byron?"

He thought quickly. "Mannie," he answered. "Mannie Hallenstein."

She stopped to execute a little curtsy, playfully but very prettily. "Welcome to our humble chambers, m'lord." He thought her adorable—exquisite—her bright eyes—her quick ways.

An intruder attempting to cut in was rejected rashly. "Come back later, fella."

"Mannie, that isn't nice. It's bad for morale."

"Not for my morale. Now, what's all this nonsense about a husband?"

Her laugh was a little cry of triumph. He didn't see anything to laugh about. Had there ever been a husband, and did he write that stuff she had been spouting before?

Well, in a way.

In what way?

She had quoted from something she was working on. And couldn't a girl be married to her work?

What kind of work?

Translating Rimbaud. She was going to do an English translation of *Une Saison en Enfer*. It was such a magnificent poem, no not magnificent, terrible. She'd say it over to herself at night and feel almost too frightened to be alone. It was that kind of a poem. It wasn't just the words, the meaning, but the *sound,* the *feeling*. But the job of translation drove her to the limits of madness. It was so perfect in French, so passionate, so direct. And when she put it in English it always seemed such a letdown. "Dingy and *blah,*" she said.

"What made you want to do it?"

"Why do people try to climb Mt. Everest?"

The intruder was back and this time he would not be denied. Manley sulked as she was led away. Once, as he waited on the sidelines, she caught his eye over her partner's shoulder and stuck out her tongue again.

When his turn came, he held her closer. The connection was made and the currents of youth poured through them. Shyly his lips pressed through her hair and began to explore the soft warm lobe of her ear. He could feel the involuntary fluttering in her, the quickening. Into the darkness of her ruffled hair he whispered a mysterious incantation, "Jere . . . Jere . . ."

"Mannie . . ." She spoke softly.

"Yes—yes . . ."

He waited for the whispered words of assurance.

"That tickles my ear."

He drew his head away. "Jere, if I weren't an officer and a gentleman, I'd . . ."

"Oui, chéri?"

"I don't know you well enough."

"Oh—foof! Either they tell you you are beautiful, or that they don't know you well enough."

"But I'm ready to devote a major portion of my time—something I've got plenty of—to knowing you well enough."

"Beware, beware my young friend, I warned you, I'm a sorceress."

"And I am already bewitched."

She stopped dancing, placed her palms against his cheeks and puckered her lips in a little mock gesture of commiseration. "Poor Mannie Hallenstein."

He traced the provocative curve of her lips with his fingers. Suddenly she took a little cat-bite. It really stung and she laughed when he pulled his hand away.

The band had reached the final chord for the dancers. The party was officially over but the pianist started fooling around with the keys and he had a nice light touch and a lot of inventiveness. A crowd formed around him and they started singing home songs, *When Johnny Comes Marching Home,* and *East Side, West Side, Beautiful Ohio, My Old Kentucky Home* and *Just Try to Picture Me Down Home in Tennessee,* which soon gave way to the *Tattooed Lady,* with everybody joining in with gusto and a tingling sense of being wicked.

This led inevitably, almost religiously, to a recital of the charms of the busy Mademoiselle from Armentières. The pianist began with the version acceptable even to the Y and slyly worked his way down to the words the boys really sang. Then he grinned around at Jere, "Come on, Miss J.—"

With one foot on the piano bench, Jere sang in a comic, unmusical voice:

> "Oh, Mademoiselle from Armentières,
> Parlez-vous?
> Mademoiselle from Armentières,
> Parlez-vous?
> She met a Y man here in France,
> And showed him what he had in his pants,
> Hinky-dinky parlez-vous."

The soldiers whistled and cheered. But a plump, scandalized matron moved in disapprovingly. *"Miss* Wilder, after all!"

"But Armistice only comes once in a lifetime, Mrs. Levinson."

"You can have a good time without being indecent."

Manley whispered. "How soon can we leave?"

"Meet me in the coat room in ten minutes."

Hidden behind the rows of trench coats, Manley uncorked his bottle of brandy. He needed fool's courage to keep up with this one. What had that goose called her—Wilder? Was it just a nickname? She was wild all right. The brandy felt hot and encouraging. All right, Jere Wildberg, he was up to anything the evening might offer.

Ten . . . fifteen minutes. What if she shouldn't come? Why should he have believed her? She had been full of lies—wil stories rolling off her tongue like—quicksilver again. Would sh be cruel enough to let him waste away out here in this cloakroom Siberia? She had the deviltry for it. He had almost talked himself into the wretched conviction that she had tricked him, just as she had tricked him with the business of being French, and being married, when in she came. He ran to her and grabbed her hands crazily, "Jere, you've come—you've come!"

"Of course I've come, little idiot. Didn't I tell you I would?"

"Yes—yes—but you told me so many things . . ."

She placed her hands against his cheeks again. "My poor Mannie Hallenstein." This time he held her there and came forward to her until he brushed her lips. But at the last moment she turned way and laughed.

"I can't possibly kiss you until I reek of brandy like you do."

"*As* you do. Like is a preposition."

"Oh, *grammar*." She tossed her head. "You know what I mean."

The impulsive way she hurried to catch up with him could have been a forewarning.

"Rimbaud is my first love. But good cognac sneaks up and ravishes me. And I'll tell you a secret—I don't care."

Hopelessly infatuated, even more hopelessly alarmed (hearing faintly the whispered warning from Kansas City and Cambridge *was he letting himself in for more than he bargained*), he took her arm. Together they went out into the swirling night of songs and horns and drunken heralding of the end of a war.

On the corner the deformed little man, who until the day before had been the Emperor, was going up in flames of papier-mâché while revelers in a dozen different uniforms danced around the pyre crazily singing *We'll Hang the Kaiser Under the Linden Tree.* Jere and Manley watched a private and a lieutenant-colonel dancing together wearing each other's caps. A full colonel snatched up a laughing Red Cross girl and kissed her long and passionately while onlookers cheered. Emboldened, Manley reached for Jere. She slapped him.

"Je ne comprends pas," he said.

"I don't want you to kiss me just because everybody is kissing everybody. When you kiss someone I want it to be *me.*"

They went along with the crowd, they sang *La Marseillaise* and *Oh How I Hate to Get Up in the Morning* and endless verses of *Mademoiselle,* they were in and out of packed cafés, they danced, drank champagne on the house, were picked up by a general in an open General Staff car on his way to Maxim's. He insisted on assuming they were married and kept patting Jere's hand and promising he would see to it that her husband was promoted, decorated and sent back to the States. When the general became too interested, they excused themselves to dance and slipped away through the crowd on the floor.

Outside on the Rue Royale they were caught up in a squad of riotous doughboys executing the goose step and shouting in unison *"Ein, zwei, drei, vier—Ach du Himmel!* When they spied Jere they yelled, *"Ein Fräulein!"* and broke ranks to embrace her. One was wearing a Kaiser's mustache of charcoal and several sported Prussian helmets. To Manley's annoyance, Jere kissed each of the boys smilingly on the lips.

Dawn brought them to Les Halles, where they found themselves gorging on pig's feet, washed down with champagne, in the company of a happily drunken French butcher and a giant Senegalese sergeant. Then the four of them, arm-in-arm, walked around the market place together, singing the foulest songs the butcher and the sergeant could think of, which, with a great show of conscientiousness and affection, they were teaching Manley and Jere.

It had been one of those nights when their luck was high. It would have been impossible to find a cab and they were miles from Jere's quarters in the Cité Bergère but suddenly they were embarrassed by too much transportation. The butcher wanted the honor of taking them home in his truck. The Senegalese, for some mysterious reason they preferred not to question, had a motorcycle with a sidecar at his disposal. He would consider himself insulted if they did not avail themselves of its use. The butcher and the Senegalese fell into argument as to who should have the privilege of driving them home. It turned out to be a magnificent match. They were both well over six feet tall and two hundred pounds.

"The first morning of peace in Europe in four-and-a-half years," Manley muttered to Jere as they watched their two friends smash each other's faces.

At last the butcher was overcome. As he lay panting on the sidewalk, his left eye and his nose a bloody mess, Jere addressed him sweetly. "Thank you just the same for your kind offer. Now go straight home and wash your face."

The burly Frenchman, from his sitting position, touched his hand to his sweaty forehead in a casual salute. "Vive la Victoire," he said, and then, with an admiring nod toward his conqueror, "I leave you in good hands."

Except for the fact that their Senegalese seemed to lack either a brake or any interest in slowing down, the ride through the city was uneventful. The Senegalese deposited them at the gate, insisted on kissing them on both cheeks, wished them good luck and a full life, and then, like all good characters in fairy tales and drunken escapades, zoomed off down the street, never to be seen by them again but always to be remembered as a fine figure of a man with a superlative memory for earthy lyrics.

Jere tried the gate. "I was afraid it would be locked," she said.

"Shall I come up for a few minutes?"

He felt sure of himself. The easy way she had handled those blunt verses and how she had laughed at the stories at Les Halles and the little remarks she dropped.

She looked at him playfully. "It's half past five, my lipstick's all smeared, my hair's a mess, I'm two-thirds blotto, I feel older than Elsie Janis' mother—and you still want to come up?"

"I'm a very determined young man."

"Oh, dear, and I'm a very undetermined young woman. That's dangerous."

She turned her lips to him at last, but almost in a taunting way. It made him want to kiss her brutally, to stop this incessant playing. For a moment their kiss was the only reality.

But as suddenly as she had offered her lips she withdrew them again.

"People who close their eyes when they dance always close their eyes when they kiss."

Ready for her to go limp in his arms, he was furious.

"I didn't realize I was dealing with such an expert."

"And your 'Shall I come up for a few minutes?' Oh, handsome Lieutenant Hallenstein, how many Red Cross girls and telephone operators and visiting entertainers have you thrilled with that silken phrase?"

He would have liked to throttle her.

Her hand dropped lightly on his arm. "Mannie, you're forgetting half my warning already. Never take me too seriously." Her hand slipped down into his, and squeezed it consolingly. "Thanks for a swell time."

Managing to mutter something polite, he staggered off in the general direction of the quays. But he had taken only a few steps when he heard a piercing whistle. It was Jere, with two fingers in her mouth like a tomboy. "Don't slouch when you walk," she called. "You'll get round-shouldered."

As he groped his way down to the pont de la Tournelle, he whistled his own flat, who-cares arrangement of *Butterfly*.

All the next day, through a party at the apartment that was less an Armistice celebration than a counter-attack against ennui and let-down, drinking *Big Berthas,* a violent concoction he had named with Hank Osborne, his French nurse Mignon and officers

142

and girls who came passing through, Manley's mind kept wandering off to the Cité Bergère. The problems of the Armistice stirred him less than the riddle of Jere Wildberg. Was she fast? Was she a New World flapper in bright colors? Or was she something strangely un-American, a true eccentric? A self-acknowledged "keen judge of character," this time he had to give himself a failing grade. All he could be sure of was that he was intrigued —no, that word was too mild, and he reached for a more accurate one—*incited*.

Talk curled around him in argumentative smoke-rings. A PRO major from Tours, hopefully Wilsonian, believed in the Armistice as the first step toward a lasting peace and a new world order. But Mignon—Minnie they called her—wasn't sure it wouldn't be better for France and the Allies to crush Germany once and for all while they had the chance. Hank didn't think it mattered too much one way or the other. The Revolution was bound to spread from Russia to Germany and France. "When you keep on using people for cannon fodder, they finally explode in your face." He wasn't a Bolshie, but Christ when you looked at all the raw stuff pulled in the name of Democracy . . . Manley drank his *Big Berthas* and thought of Jere.

"This time the people are gonna be heard from," Hank insisted.

"Aw, in a month you'll be flying against the Bolshies in Siberia and hating 'em worse 'n the Heinies," the PRO prophesied.

"The hell I will," Hank said. "This boy's applying for his discharge as soon as he c'n sober up enough to find his C.O. and make 'im sign the recommendation."

Then they were back on topic A. Provided the war was really over (which no one quite believed yet) how soon would they get back into civvies. And B: what would the States be like? And C: whatinhell were they going to do?

"I know what this boy's gonna do," Hank announced. "I'm goin' out with Minnie to her folk's farm and grow a long beard and sleep till noon and tank up on Burgundy every afternoon and jump into bed with Minnie every evening after supper and sleep until noon again and then get up and eat half a dozen eggs and comb my beard and . . ."

143

"But Henri," Mignon interrupted (they were the only Franco-American arrangement Manley knew that seemed to have a future), "you have an active mind. You cannot do that all your life."

"Who's talking about all my life? I was just thinking of the next forty or fifty years."

Manley was thinking about his plans too. Of course the sensible move was returning to Beatrice. If he could get through law school, Mr. Vining would be obliged to take him into the firm. Why, in twenty years, he and Beatrice—the slide blurred and refused to stay in focus. Damn it, if he was a writer, now was the time to prove it. He had a third of a novel written, and a little money saved up. He should stay in France, where a dollar hadn't lost its prestige, and finish *Friends and Foes*.

He couldn't imagine himself explaining the plan of his novel to Beatrice Vining. Jere was the girl to tell. She had that nice kind of madness. Nothing surprised her. She had a horror of ruts and grubbing.

"Where you goin', Hally?"

"Just remembered. Gotta call Pershing. He's waiting for me to tell him what to do next."

"Tell him I said to get the lead out and let's get the hell home," said a bleary-eyed captain in the Field Artillery.

As Manley flung open the great iron gate, he felt a shortness of breath, a pounding in his heart, a quickening of pulse—familiar symptoms of the psychosomatic affliction called, in the poverty of our vocabulary, love.

Behind the desk a powerfully bosomed concierge wearing a prominent black crucifix was primly knitting an absurdly small pair of socks. "Mademoiselle Wildberg? Ah, Mademoiselle Wildairre. Oui, m'sieur." It was room 37. She would send a message.

"Don't bother. I'll run up," Manley said.

The woman began to protest, then shrugged and returned to her little world of yarn that she could control.

He knocked on the door.

"Come in, Mannie."

The odd yellow-green cat-eyes, peering out from under bangs, regarded him impertinently. "How did I know it was you?

Your knock, m'sieur. No one else bold enough to come up and knock without being invited would knock so shyly."

He looked around at incredible disorder. Old clothes on a pile on the floor. Ends of things hanging out of bureau drawers. Books and magazines scattered on tables, in the windowseat and on the floor. Crumpled papers that had missed the wastebasket. Cigarette butts crushed into damp coffee saucers.

She followed his eyes and grinned. "I suppose you're terribly neat."

"I guess so. I've always had to keep after my roommates."

"Good. Be neat for both of us."

He noticed the steamer trunk in the corner, used as an auxiliary bureau. Stenciled on top was the name W-i-l-d-e-r.

"So your name *is* Wilder?"

"Yes, my lord."

"What made you say Wildberg?"

"Oh, I don't know. Everybody there has a name like that. And sometimes I get tired of being me."

Manley felt as if a sack of stones had just been removed from his shoulder.

"But why in the world do you work for the Jewish Welfare Board?"

"Well, first, Anne Morgan bounced me for being AWOL. Then I found out the JWB let their hostesses wear evening clothes at dances. And I hate uniforms. On women I mean. I wouldn't mind so much if I were plump and homely. But I'm not."

She was wearing an ankle-length green chiffon tea gown that followed her tall, wiry figure.

"That's the main reason I work for the JWB. And then it makes me laugh to think how much it annoys Pate."

"Pate?"

"Papa. Calling him Pate annoys him too. In fact everything annoys him that isn't done exactly the way he orders. Sometimes I think I might marry a Jew—it would serve him right for being so narrow-minded."

"You know, my name really isn't Hallenstein either. It's Halliday. Manley Halliday."

She curtsied prettily again. "Welcome back to the Anglo-Saxon fold, Halliday."

Just the same, and all fooling aside, he was damned relieved.

"For twenty-four hours you were the most beautiful Jewess I've ever seen."

"Are you rich?" she asked. The uniform was expensively tailored and he had the airs that go with money.

He was beginning to get used to her sudden questions.

"You mean permanently? Or tonight?"

"Oh, tonight will do."

"Tonight I've got a month's pay in my pocket—my allowance from Uncle Sam in return for putting in an occasional appearance at the S & S office, where my official job is not to interfere with the journalistic activities of the most ornery assortment of enlisted men to be found this side of a Russian Soviet. But to come to the point, Miss Wilder, my entire wealth is at your disposal."

"In that case you can take me to Prunier's. Did I warn you, I have frightfully expensive tastes? I'm a fiend for caviar and oysters and buckets of champagne."

Even in the crush of diners waiting for tables at Prunier's, they found it easy to talk to each other. And all through dinner and on to the Café de Paris and further on to a little place in the Montmartre that specialized in second-rate champagne and second-hand American jazz they talked the way only young people can when their words glow with the special intensity of romance. Manley liked the way she listened, her head down, her eyes very wide, attentive—somehow she was able to make listening a positive act. (Or was this, he wondered, simply phase one of falling in love?) He told her things he hadn't even revealed to Hank Osborne—his sense of loss, of having missed something vital to his career in not seeing action at the front. His fear, "to be absolutely honest about it," that Hank might crack through with the first great war book ("Hank certainly has it in him") and that his own account of rear-echelon stagnation would seem narrow and tame.

It was probably a silly damnfool notion that he could write a novel. The stuff he had written so far was so much flatter than the way he saw it in his mind. But sometimes he had come right back to the room from evening chow and pounded till daylight and he could feel it coming, pouring out of him in a stream that seemed strangely independent of him. Then he could see it in print, with his name in big letters, hear everybody saying Have you read *Friends and Foes,* why, Halliday has it all over Hergesheimer. Oh, he was a fool, a callow simpleton to have such dreams. There were things he wanted to say but they stayed locked in his head. He would never be a second Wells or Conrad or Compton Mackenzie, he was morosely convinced, jus one more unpublished would-be author.

More than just listening, Jere was going through it with him. He found himself telling her of his visit to a German prison camp some months before, of his revulsion for the profane and ignorant American major who treated all Germans as if they were pigs and of the chance meeting with a prisoner who happened to be a mild but inquisitive philologist.

"It made me wonder," Manley was summing it up for Jere over cognac and coffee, "which was friend and which was foe? Which was the man we've been fighting to defend and which was the tyrant we've been trying to crush? I left the States with a lot of juvenile black-and-white notions about noble and atrocious causes. I would've made a peach of an editorial writer for the *Literary Digest.* Now I just want to write about people, good and bad, some on one side, some on another, caught up in something that carries them all along together, combat men going about their bloody business reluctantly and with no grand heroics, and SOS officers having the time of their lives working the old Army game. I want to get down to the rock-bottom truth of all this, Jere."

A French band straining bravely to render American songs in rag-time had made it impossible for any but the enthralled to concentrate. But now it slipped into something more comfortable. *Poor Butterfly* fluttering from weeping violins.

They looked at each other; they already had quite a repertoire of looks with different meanings.

"Our song," Manley said. This was suddenly much more important than any discussion of literary dreams.

147

"Dance with me."

Tall and thin—*supple* he would have said—she reminded him a little of Irene Castle as they whirled slowly together in a kind of floating somnambulism. He became aware of admiring glances from seated onlookers and other dancers. It gave him a racy sense of appreciation of what a startlingly handsome couple they were. Somehow the tragic death of Vernon Castle lent poignancy to the moment. Just a year or so before, Vernon Castle had lived with the world literally at his feet, with his sweetheart for a partner, his partner for a bride, personifying the triumph of romance over reality. No wonder their place had been called *Castle in the Sky*. But suddenly the castle had become a plane and the plane a junk-pile of twisted metal and torn flesh on a Texas field. Fame, romance, success—these things were so precious that no one could be entrusted with their possession for more than a moment. Here, hold this, it's yours, for an instant! Then it was snatched back and something fell away from under you and you were plummeting to earth—*Crash*.

> *Poor Butterfly,*
> *In the blossoms waiting . . .*

Somehow it was good to feel so sad, to be so young, to have such hope and such vanity, to move with such delicious ease. As they circled slowly in perfect time together she asked, "Why are you so sad, m'sieur?" It was a little coy, but he didn't mind.

"Because while we're enjoying this it's slipping out of our hands. Jere, if we could only stop the big clock and be us tonight the rest of our lives."

"But we can't. We'll grow old and ugly and say *humph* to young people."

He held her very close. She liked the pressure of his hand urging her closer. She was the goddess of fleeting time and if he merged her body with his, prone together like the midnight hands, the works might be stopped, the hour of youth forever suspended.

All this leaped up from a dark fold in Manley's brain as he studied the panel in the entrance of the Sutton Place apartment

house and pushed the button beside the little black letters form-
ing Wilder-Halliday.

What is more painful than the memory of lost pleasures?

As the self-operating elevator moved up the shaft on its creep-
ing journey toward the roof, Manley's mind, in another building
and another time, moved slowly down into the past, level after
level, until he was back at the Cité Bergère.

They were closing the gates for midnight curfew. If he went
up with Jere now he would have to stay until dawn, thanks to
this medieval architectural appendix Paris was too sentimental
to remove. The Rimbaud translation, which Manley now seemed
so anxious to hear, provided a semi-respectable motive for going
back to 37 with her.

Jere poured them each a cognac. Lighting two tall candles, she
turned out the overhead light. It seemed to Manley that the yellow glow of the candles was exactly the color tone of her skin.

"Rimbaud and bright lights just never seem right together. He
lived in his own world of half-light. When you read Rimbaud
—or go into Rimbaud, I should say—you feel sure he must have
written by the light of hell-fire."

Manley realized for the first time what an extremist she was.
She drank her brandy avidly, searched haphazardly among the
helter-skelter of her desk for the work in progress. It was an
atmosphere of dark intensity she created as she began to read,
first from the Rimbaud original and then her own:

"Now let us hear the confession of a companion in hell.
O heavenly bridegroom, do not refuse the confession of
the saddest of your servants. I am lost. I am besotted. I am
impure . . ."

She paused. "The next words are 'Quelle vie!' That's what
drives you crazy. You'd have to say 'What a life!' or even 'What
an existence!' But the thing about Rimbaud is, he's so direct,
blunt. If I could only find two short words that produce the impact of *Quelle vie!* It's a better language, that's the trouble. Much
better for poetry. So the best I can ever do is a dullish paraphrase."

"How about 'Some Life!'"

"Mmm. That's closer to the feeling. But isn't it awfully *American*?" She tossed the scribbled page away impatiently. "Oh, the hell with it. If people want to read Rimbaud, let 'em learn French."

She had drunk her first cognac quickly and now she poured herself another. Manley was still inhaling his luxuriously. He was wondering, should he grab her suddenly, should he lead her gently toward the bed . . . She rose and went to the window. "I think I'll miss the air-raids. When they came over it gave you such a—such a *whole* feeling. All your little worries and fears seemed so futile . . .

"Purification by TNT," Manley said. His voice was low. He had come up behind her at the window.

Lips, open a little in hunger, fed upon each other. His hands were two thieves, one holding her fast while the other made a desperate search, a hurried, clumsy thief pulling at buttons, tearing at openings.

"Mannie, I—I *hate* that feeling."

Fighting him off was passion too.

"Jere, I—I can't help it—you make me . . ."

"Fingers under my clothes . . ."

"Jere, please, *please,* you must . . ."

The words struck him like sharp little stones; "There isn't anything in this world I *must* do, except die, and I'll never forgive God for making me do that."

She drew away. He felt limp, gross, boorish; he loathed himself. All lathered up in a sweat of passion, he thought in disgust.

But she was the one to apologize. "Mannie, I know—it's a compliment. My nose would grow long as Pinocchio's if I told you I didn't want you to want me this way. But—when it happens, there won't be any tugging at buttons. If it happens, we'll both know it's going to happen and we'll come to each other and the clothes will fall away."

Idiotically—or did it only seem so in retrospect—he had taken her hand and kissed her fingertips. "Bien entendu, Mademoiselle Wildberg."

The balance was restored.

150

"I hope you don't think I'm one of those RCV's who's listened to one too many lectures on a Christian mind in a Christian body."

"Now don't forget, we're a couple of JWB kids. When a Hallenstein can't mess around with a Wildberg, what are we Jews coming to?"

At one o'clock in the morning, with nerves still taut, that made them howl with laughter.

"After all," Manley ventured, "it's not your fault if your father slipped an old-fashioned chastity belt on you before you came overseas and locked the key in his safe."

"That's my father—holding all the keys, always—thousands of them—he wears them all on his belly like a fat sommelier."

Conversation and brandy flowed through the night together in a swift, warm stream. Everything one had to tell the other seemed of enormous importance to both. Manley learned that Jere's father was the George Nibely Wilder of Wilder, Spence & Worthington, the Wall Street law firm. Knowing she was a Wilder didn't make her any more attractive. But it did make her attractive in a different way. There were no obstacles to his falling in love, maybe even marrying a Wilder.

He learned that Jere had been packed off to Switzerland when she was fifteen, as a sort of banishment from the Wilder realm. "I was the only one who talked back to Pate. My sisters were broken early like good little colts. Everything he ever asked me to do, I'd do the opposite. He thought he could run our lives by deciding how much money to allow us. He thought money and what he called 'all the advantages' could take the place of—place of . . ." She laughed defiantly. "I showed him. I ran away from that school in Geneva with a French boy called Jean-Jacques. Named after Rousseau. I loved the name. I guess that was the only thing about him I was in love with. As soon as I got on the train with him I couldn't stand him. It had just been one of those school things. When you're with a lot of girls, and you're competing, and you see a boy somebody else likes very much, you can make yourself believe all kinds of things. He had horribly oily hair and was only sixteen years old and had read the complete works of Casanova and he was all *mishy* inside."

Mr. Wilder, using a convenient Government inspection tour, had arrived promptly. He had meant to be patiently firm and severe because, after all, he was a reasonable man and he realized what a handicap it had been for a high-spirited girl to be raised without a mother. But Jere's emotionalism and hateful temper had finally unnerved him. When he placed her in a highly recommended school in Nice, it was with the understanding that they would no longer bother with the conventions of a proper father-daughter relationship. "I will continue to support you and pray that you do no more than you have already done to besmirch the Wilder reputation," he had said stiffly.

"Well," Jere went on, "at Madame Legendre's in Nice, the headmistress was sleeping with the Latin teacher. I found out—oh, in a very sly way—and she hated me like rat poison after that. A bunch of us slipped out through a second-floor window one night and went riding with some French junior officers. We all got caught, because a teacher's pet snitched, but I was the only one Madame expelled. Then I said right out loud in front of teachers and everybody what I knew about her and Monsieur Guillon. It was a terrible thing to do. Because Madame Legendre ran a very respectable school and M. Guillon was married. Sometimes I think I like to hate people. Hurt people, I mean. Always dominating or being dominated. That's why I like Rimbaud. He was such a good hater. I mean, he hated the whole thing—religion, domesticity, business and laws, respectability—'these Occidental swamps.'"

He was beginning to see how her mind worked. It traveled no rational straight line. It was an active but reckless and whimsical mind that rushed to sudden violent conclusions, a mind often struck by brilliance but a brilliance that zigzagged as haphazardly and uselessly as lightning.

While the little cubicle of an elevator crawls up the wall to the penthouse apartment of Jere Wilder Halliday as tediously as a potato bug, the memories slide by with the speed and invisibility of light.

That first post-war winter in Paris, for those who knew their

Army game, foreshadowed the waves of American tourists and expatriates soon to come. More than ever, Manley felt that his uniform was a masquerade, especially since, through a bit of discreet cultivation, he wore the Croix de Guerre.

They mingled with the American crowd busy straightening out the world in the plush corners of the Crillon. The spectacle provided Manley, with a new ending for his book. His last chapter viewed the goings-on at the Crillon as "the crowning absurdity of a generation with a singular talent for embracing absurdities —for rising with earth-shaking enthusiasm to the most absurd of occasions."

Jere, characteristically, expressed her feelings somewhat more directly. At the Crillon bar one evening she and Manley were boasting about their athletic prowess. Manley insisted that he had once sparred with Freddy Welsh and that the champion had told Manley he had the makings of a first-rate lightweight if he ever thought of turning pro. (This fistic myth was to cause Manley considerable difficulty, much climbing through imaginary ropes with six-drink courage.) Jere had boasted of her ability to do cartwheels and backward flips ("I dive fantastically well," she had added). "Look, I'll show you!" she had said suddenly. She executed a perfect cartwheel in front of the bar.

It rated a box in next morning's Paris *Trib* and a few scandalized lines in the *Dyle Myle*. Jere was quoted as saying, "Was it any sillier than some of the things going on in the ballroom?"

Everyone knew Jere Wilder after that. She became a sort of *femme du moment* like Regina Flory.

In March of 1919, to a young man in love, inefficiency, absent-mindedness, lack of regard for money and the ease with which she slipped off the corset of responsibility all seemed to be delightful traits.

People would turn to smile in appreciation when they entered rooms. Manley and Jere saw in their eyes the flattering reflection. They were a kind of double Narcissus.

Spring came to Paris like a big traveling circus. There was music in the streets and the girls were pretty again. Pinched faces filled out, children played round the fountains, Paris wore bright skirts bordered with chestnut blossoms and blue violets. Merry-go-rounds whirled and lovers took to sidewalk tables, parks, little boats, carriages, benches on the Seine, the Eiffel, lacy iron balconies, bridle paths . . .

The first Memorial Day Manley wangled one of the S & S Fords and they drove out to the ceremonies at Suresnes. Jere looked charmingly—deceptively—provincial in her white organdy dress and oval-brimmed straw hat with its little black band running under her chin. They couldn't help laughing as they drove out along the cobblestone streets of the suburbs. Not until they saw the incredible number of little white crosses on the hillside of Suresnes did they remember the mood of the day.

They were able to get quite close to the President. With his top-hat and frockcoat accentuating his height and his angularity, he looked less a popular leader than an undertaker presiding at the burial of a world. They had never seen anyone so severely in earnest. A personification of irony, this dry Scotch Presbyterian scholar who permitted himself to dream, this stern Princetonian aristocrat who, alone of the peacemakers, had captured the imagination of the common people of Europe.

They heard him say:

"These men came . . . to defeat forever . . . arrogant, selfish, dominance . . . and to see to it that there should never be a war like this again.

"It is our duty to see to it . . . that the mothers of America . . . of France and England and Italy and Belgium . . . shall never be called upon for this sacrifice again.

"These men . . . have given their lives that the world might be united . . . in order to secure the freedom of mankind . . . The people . . . are in the saddle . . . this age rejects the standards of national selfishness . . .

"We must have a League of Nations . . . not merely a peace settlement . . . There shall never be a war like this again . . ."

Righteousness, heavy as dew, settled on the brows of the listeners.

Prayers. Taps. Artillery salute. The minute of silence.

In their graves, should dead soldiers lie in a heap as they fell? Or at parade rest?

154

Stiff with virtue, fat with hope, the assembly moved off. Mr. Wilson, the good man gone wrong and/or the wrong man gone good, retired with appropriate solemnity.

"I'm glad you made me come," Jere said. "He makes you feel so positive—and hopeful."

She was easily carried away. Two days later she would be agreeing with all the pronouncements of Wilson's mistakes.

"It sounds good," Manley admitted, "but when you think about the Italian demands, and all this talk about secret deals— Oh, hell, it's too beautiful a day to think. Let's just drive somewhere."

The Ford seemed to lead them back along the Seine through Paris to the Bois de Vincennes. They stopped for *vins blancs* at a funny little place on the corner across from the fortress and then, beyond the suburbs at last, they went rolling on through the soft green countryside, following the Marne in the general direction of Reims.

Manley had never seen her so relaxed. She kept saying how much she loved the sunshine. She stretched and purred in it. All winter she had seemed high-strung and brittle.

They turned up toward Chateau Thierry. Farmers were plowing around shell holes. A country church lay in ruins. A native caretaker was a scarecrow figure of desolation in an orderly garden of white crosses.

For the first time since their meeting half a year before, she talked about the war. He had grown used to the idea of her being so self-centered that the problems of translating Rimbaud would seem more important to her than human suffering and the puzzle of converting Armistice to peace.

"Maybe the little white crosses are better off," she said suddenly when they had been left a kilometer behind. "I did a little aid work at a base hospital at Neuilly—I don't think I ever told you. There were quite a few French *gueules cassés* there. There was one with no arms and no legs and just a mess of burned flesh where his face used to be. He had no mouth at all, just a little charred hole. And yet—this was the scary part—he could talk. He kept pleading with the doctors to kill him. His name was Robert Denise. Before the war he had been a bicycle racer.

One day I had to read him a letter from his fiancée. From the sounds he started making in his throat I could tell he was crying, but there wasn't enough face left to be able to see . . ."

A shadow of silence slipped past them. She took a deep breath, opening her mouth as if the air were something good to eat. "Too nice a day," she said, "too nice a day." She looked over and smiled at him. Her straw hat had fallen back on her shoulders. He had never liked her so much before.

They had passed through a number of partially destroyed villages which were slowly coming back to life. Now they were approaching Vaux. Rising on the left was a gentle slope covered with apple trees in blossom. Just beyond was another small American cemetery where perhaps a company had been wiped out in one of the bitter battles of the last-gasp German counterattack the year before.

"Mmmm, smell the apple blossoms," Jere said. They had seen enough white crosses for one day.

Vaux was the first village of their journey to be totally destroyed. The broken neck of the church steeple drew a harsh line against the sky. Every one of the modest stone houses had collapsed into a pile of rubble. A great city in ruins is a tragic sight. A little village reduced to a junk-lot of broken stones makes one want to cry, the way the crushed body of a little girl side-swiped on a roadside is a more sorrowful sight than thousands of men lying dead on a battlefield. Human emotion has never excelled at higher mathematics.

They had to pick their way carefully along the battered road of the ghost-village. Nothing seemed to live here, not even dogs or rats. Then, in front of the house next to the last, they saw two old people sitting motionlessly on their broken stone steps, staring without watching anything. The roof that shells had ripped away had been replaced by stray boards and tattered tar paper. The torn windows had been boarded up. The only inhabitants of Vaux did not seem to see the Ford as it approached.

"Mannie," Jere said. "Those two old people."

They parked and got out, but the old couple gave no sign of having seen them. Jere said "Bon jour" and "Are you the only ones who have come back?" and "When did you return?" The old man answered in toneless monosyllables. Manley offered them a pack of cigarettes. The old man accepted with a grunt, *merci*. Jere and Manley looked at each other, frowning. They had a common impulse to break through this wall of suspicion, to say, "Look, we're sorry for you. It isn't our fault. We'd like to help you."

"Are you able to manage here all alone?" Manley asked. His heavy American accent hung awkwardly in the silence. For an answer, the old man merely shrugged.

"But why do you stay here? How is it possible to live?"

The hostile silence, infecting them, made Jere sound almost petulant.

The old man shrugged again. The old woman's voice was cracked and she had too much hair on her lip. She was not at all the beautiful silver-haired vision of an old woman young people like to imagine.

"Perhaps if one of our sons is living he will come here."

She glared at Jere.

Jere's lips straightened as if she might cry. Then she quickly slipped off her necklace of amethysts set in tiny heart-shaped frames of gold.

"Here, I want you to have this."

When she closed it into the woman's hand, her own hand recoiled at the boniness. The old woman neither protested nor thanked her.

It was all very unsatisfactory.

There was another awkward silence, and then Jere and Manley got back into their car. They thought they could feel the eyes of the old couple boring into them. These stupid American sightseers touring the battlefields.

They had little to say to each other as they drove on to Epernay. The Marne flowed peacefully, as if it had never seen a war. A red-purple sun was sliding off into the hills behind them when they turned back toward Paris. The world was powder blue when they reached the edge of Belleau Wood. The bare, amputated trees made grotesque silhouettes against the early twilight.

"Look, pussy-willows," Jere said. "I'd love some for my room."

Manley held her hand as they walked to the edge of the ravaged wood. Young pussy-willows had pushed up through the torn trees. One had forced its way up through the loosened root of a fallen beech.

Suddenly, Jere didn't have the heart to pick it. "All these nice trees with their arms and their trunks cut off, this lovely country ripped apart, and then—" She stared at the pussy-willow. Tears came, then she was weeping, and finally she was sobbing in his arms. But in a minute it was over and her voice, still shaky, tried to be smart again. "Don't I deserve the sterling silver spittoon though, bawling over a godamn pussy-willow?"

Manley kissed a shiny spot on her cheek where a tear had passed. She was not wise and self-sufficient and untamably wild after all. The sobbing of her body in his arms had told him all the things she had to cry for that she had been forcing back into herself.

She gave him a funny little grin. "When you take me back to Paris will you make me see a doctor—I'm beginning to babble like a shell-shock case."

"When I take you back to Paris," he heard himself say, "I'm going to marry you."

"Why, Hallenstein," she said, "do you know what you just said? Maybe *you're* the shell-shock case."

Jere cuddled under his arm as they drove back to Paris through the cool Spring night. At Meaux they stopped at an unassuming little restaurant where they had a surprisingly good Potage Crecy and two bottles of St. Emilion. Whenever their eyes met they would smile and everything that was said about the food, the room, the horse-faced waiter seemed uproariously funny.

Then for six hectic weeks the Army of the United States and the Republic of France seemed to be conspiring against the sanctification of their love. They went to sleep and awakened scheming about certificates: birth certificates, death certificates, certificates of residence, marriage certificates, certificates on lost certificates, climaxed by their wheedling a reluctant certificate of permission from Jere's father by a bit of indelicate blackmail fictionizing the urgency of her "condition."

158

Jere, always subject to romantic hallucinations, had wanted to be married in the Cathedral of Notre Dame. "Josephine and Marie Antoinette and Mary Stuart and Joan will be our handmaids." But an Episcopalian and a Scotch-Irish Protestant, little better than heathens from Our Mother's point of view, were not entitled to marriage in the eyes of the true Church. Then Manley had a bright idea. Where should Mannie Hallenstein and Jere Wildberg be hitched? In a Jewish synagogue. They found one near the Etoile. They were just crazy enough to try it. "To make this legal, you'll have to stitch a hem on your dick," Hank Osborne had razzed with a best man's prerogative.

But the Rabbi had rebuffed them with ancient pride. "Children, even if you were serious—which I fear you are not—this is not your father's house. Only if you were to take instruction . . ." Then, to satisfy the whim, Jere remembered the chaplain she had known at the JWB. Capt. Lorwin consented to marry them at the recreation center that had brought them together. Everybody had a good time at the wedding and the party at Hank's place afterward. "To a couple of wonderful kids who deserve each other," Hank had said over the champagne. "May they be as young and as beautiful and as nuts about each other on their golden anniversary as they are tonight."

They drove out toward Barbizon with a case of Pommery 1911 and another case full of dreams, both sparkling, both born in years of bright promise. Forgotten was the bristling cable from Jere's father, still resenting her marriage to "your rash young man from Kansas City," and carrying out his threat to cut her off. Why worry? They had enough money for two months, for Manley was still in the Army, on a sixty-day leave before reporting to Gievres for his discharge. They had borrowed a Dodge staff car from a friend of Hank's who was an officer in the Paris motor pool. And they had been able to get one of the Hotel Cornebiche bungalows in the woods of Arbonne.

Their first dinner had been exquisitely prolonged, though urgent messages kept passing back and forth between their eyes and their fingertips. When they were back in the bungalow, Jere turned out all the lights and lit her candles. He could never forget his first sight of the honey-yellow thighs, the narrow waist, the small, perfect breasts, the slow, serious way she approached him, the surprising shyness of her eyes. But best of all he would remember the sharp pleasure and surprise of finding he had been the first. After all her limericks and bawdy verses and obscene jokes and sly references—the first. He had told himself that it would not matter. After all, he was a man of reason and this was 1919, not 1909. But those had been merely words, merely thoughts. When the moment came, he was buoyed up in an atavistic triumph.

"You silly darling. Why didn't you tell me? I never would have tried."

"I felt like such an old-fashioned ninny. I—I wanted you to think I was wickeder than Theda Bara."

But she was not virginal in mind or heart and she joined him willingly. Those nights at the Cornebiche. In the light of Jere's candles they looked on in wonder at the things young lovers do. It was all new to Jere, but she was eighteen and she had thought about it. In the candlelight, until dawn tapped lightly at the windows, at the Cornebiche, Jere clung to him with a woman's knowledge. She gave herself—as she had given herself to Rimbaud and hatred of her father and adolescent rebellion and a good time—with nothing held in reserve. Jere's moods were changeable, but they never overlapped. Each mood was pushed to its limits, sometimes almost a little beyond. In those weeks at the Cornebiche there was nothing she would not do for love.

Nine years later, retracing their steps in a last desperate search for what they had lost along the way, they had returned to the Cornebiche. But the flicker of candle-light had only irritated them; the champagne had been a fraud and the plumbing in the cottage had been abominable.

11

The door opened into a room that was also a tomb. Jere was standing there surprised, pleased, wishing he had given her time to make up (she had been lying down and looked a fright).

"Well, Mannie, fevensakes, will you please get your ugly puss in here?"

She had always called him ugly-puss, and she tried now to recall the old tone of bantering affection.

He came in stiffly. She had put on weight, even more than last time, around the middle and in the face. He had thought it could no longer matter, but he felt a sharp sorrow for the departed 22-inch waist and the boniness of her face. She still wore the bangs though, exactly the way she had that Armistice night. He wished she wouldn't. It was a senselessly frivolous style for a middle-aged woman. (Only thirty-eight. Could it be possible? She looked ten years older at the very least. Well, he guessed they all did. No one would take him for early forties. At least he no longer wore his hair parted in the middle.) The bangs irritated him. Christ, would the woman never grow up? When she got to be eighty would the needle still be grinding in the twenty-year-old groove? Sure, she had been marvelous at twenty. But you can't go on being marvelously twenty all your life. He had learned that finally. Thirty had seemed so old. The trouble with both of them, he was able to see with such brilliant hindsight now, was they had thought youth was a career instead of a preparation.

She led him through the hallway to the large living room handsomely furnished in modern decor, with an extra-sized window looking out on the river. On the table he noticed the leather-bound set of all his books that had been Jere's birthday present to him ten years before. On a smaller table was a photograph of Manley and Jere when their profiles had been a sight to behold. These things had the same effect on Manley as the bangs. There were too many symbols of the past.

She led him to the couch and pulled up a chair opposite him, crossing her legs. By some corporeal miracle, it was always disconcerting to notice, her legs had remained exactly the same. There was something repulsive about that now, the legs of the marvelously lithe young woman he knew so well supporting the thickening middle-aged body of a stranger.

"In the *Times* this morning I read you were coming on. What in the world are you writing—the *Ice Follies?*"

"Oh, I'm doing a thing for Victor Milgrim I'll be finished with in a month or so, thank God."

"I can't imagine you working for the movies."

He gave a mirthless little laugh. "Neither can I."

She said, "Oh, by the way, I win the fur-lined cuspidor. It looks like New Directions is going to publish my *Saison en Enfer.*"

She had pushed one version through a porthole of Reggie Bankhart's yacht in the Mediterranean and tossed another into the fireplace of a villa near Perpignan. She was forever fiddling with the translation, doubting it, fighting it, until the very mention of Rimbaud had made him a little sick. Something had cracked in her. She could never finish anything she started to do, a translation, a marriage or her own growing up.

"Good. They're doing nice books."

He was careful not to kid with her. He had teased her about this life's work before.

"Laughlin seems to like it. I just have to sharpen *Matin* and *Adieu* and change a few words in *Faim.*"

He tried not to smile. Long ago the second psychiatrist had told him about Jere and her translation. He tried very hard to keep his voice neutral. "Good."

"Oh, I forgot, Mannie—would you like a drink? Isn't it silly, now that I've stopped I forget all about offering it to people."

The last ones were wearing off (or wearing in) and only a drunkard could know the pounding desire.

"No, thanks, Jere, I'm drinking very little these days."

She looked up suspiciously. He didn't act drunk, but he al-

162

ways could carry a lot and his eyes looked fixed and sodden. "Mannie, I know what you're going to say, but we really get the most amazing results with AA."

"Look, Jere, I don't need AA. I didn't have a drink for eight and a half months before I came on this job."

"But, Mannie darling, once you take the step, it's such a satisfaction, such a sense of peace."

"God damn it, I don't want to spend the rest of my life nursing other drunks. I only have another fifteen, twenty years. I've got to *work*."

"Manley, if you could see yourself. You look ghastly." She came over to the couch. "And your clothes." She bent over him. She still smelled of that special perfume. "Your tie's all off to one side."

She touched him to straighten it. He pulled away. "Jere, for God's sake, relax. I don't care about my tie. I don't care how I *look* any more."

"But, Mannie, there's a difference between being informal and being—disheveled."

He was up, spleen angry.

"Jere, I came up here for—well, I certainly didn't come to be picked at."

She softened disarmingly. "All right, Man, I guess I am getting to be an old spinster bitch." She came up to him with a smile he recognized. "But will you just let me straighten your tie like a good fella? There. Now I want no more nonsense out of you."

She sat on the couch beside him. "Who have you seen lately—of the old crowd?"

"I don't see anybody any more."

"Phil?"

"In his second childhood. B scenarios and extra girls."

"Harold?"

"At Romanoff's every night, half-potted, playing gin with his agent until closing time."

"Sic transit . . ." Jere suggested.

"Not gloria. Promises."

"And you've really been working on a book?" Three thousand miles away, writing only to remind him, occasionally, how much he was in arrears, it was remarkable how closely she kept tabs. "Margit told me when she came in for the holidays."

"Yes," he said, "I'm working. When I get rid of this ton of ice I'm lugging, I'm not going to take another movie job until the book is in."

"You'll have enough money to take the rest of the year off?"

"Oh, I'll still be in debt up to here, but at least I'll be able to throw a few dollars to the nearest of the wolves. And I figure the book ought to do a lot for me. After all, I still have a following."

"I hope it's a good book, Man."

"Pray for me, baby. I'm sweating blood."

"I think it's heroic of you to try this way."

"I don't have to try. I've got the call. As bad as you with your AA, I guess."

"Mannie, frankly, I'm surprised to find you so—pulled together."

"Ho ho, I'm pulled together all right. Don't believe everything you hear, Jere, about Halliday coming apart at the seams. They aren't ready to cart me off to the laughing academy yet."

I'm not drunk, he thought, not drunk, just a little wordier than usual, that's all.

At this point Jere decided it was time to say: "Mannie—I hate to bring this up the first time I see you in nearly three years but —well after all we *are* adults, we can talk things over sensibly— you owe me eight hundred and seventy-five dollars. God knows I'd never ask you for it if I didn't need it, but I owe two months rent on this apartment . . ."

"God Almighty, Jere, give me a chance. The main reason I'm in this jam is because of you—the sanitariums, the psychoanalysts, the nutty extravagances . . ." He indicated the apartment with an impatient sweep of his hand. "We can't afford apartments like this any more—you should see what I've been living in these past three years. Lord, Jere, when are you going to realize I'm not made of gold any more? I'll always do my best not to let you starve, but I can't keep you in the style of a—of a . . ."

An elusive figure of speech led him off into the shadows. From the Cornebiche they had gone back to Paris with the manuscript completed. Then began the Hungry Hundred and Seventeen Days. The manuscript went off to Green & Streeter. For a while they lived on severance pay and some money in Jere's private account. The manuscript came back. "Goddam philistines," Hank Osborne had said. "They just don't dare tell the truth." The manuscript went back across the Atlantic, read-dressed to Dorset House. Meanwhile Manley had gone to work for the Paris *Trib*. Jere made the gesture of giving French lessons to discharged Yanks staying on in Paris. But she was always forgetting her appointments. And Manley got fired after five weeks for oversleeping after a rough night at Mamma's on the Rue Tabout. The severance pay and the private account had run out weeks before. Manley hated to do it but he hit Hank for twelve hundred francs. It had been at this nadir that Jere came home with a new eight-hundred-franc hat. An enormous chartreuse hat with peacock feathers. "Wildberg, that is a beautiful hat, but I would like it even better if we could eat it." He was still too much in love with her to be as angry as he should have been. "But Mannie darling, I was feeling *so* depressed. And this makes me feel fabulous and wicked, like Madame Pompadour." Two days later came the check for five hundred dollars from Dorset House. They wanted changes, of course, and they wished he could tone down the satire on the "goings on at the Crillon, especially relating to our own peace commission" but at least they recognized "a new voice." Jere insisted that her hat had changed their luck. The fact that the check had been mailed a week before the purchase of the hat did not disturb her kind of logic. "Oh, I hope we'll make millions on the book."

They didn't make millions, of course. It was twenty-three thousand. They were terribly rich that next year in France with the franc at seven to a dollar. And everywhere they went everybody knew them and adored them. And all the critics said young Halliday was the first American author to reflect the serviceman's real attitude toward the war, after all the fake idealism and the Hun-hating that had been served up to them by journalists and popular novelists after ceremonious "tours to the front." And now all the magazines, not just the few good ones but the high-paying, big-circulation ones, wanted more from Manley Halliday. As fortune would have it, as they say, *Friends and Foes* was not only an impressive first novel but the first work of fiction to be post-war in spirit as well as in time. Manley Halliday was the man of the hour and Jere Halliday was his queen. The story of the hat she had not been able to afford became "typical of Jere," not typical of irresponsibility and emotional instability and neurotic selfishness (as it seemed later), no—of irrepressible vivacity and unconventional impulsiveness and an infectious wildness.

—"Jere—Je-re—don't cry."

Crying, if you close your eyes and listen, makes a horrible sound, cat howling on a midnight fence and gasping and sniffling.

—"Jere—Je-re—*please* don't cry."

But he wasn't as solicitous as he sounded. For a curious little rhyme formed in his head: ah weeping is bleary and weeping is smeary and weeping is very, very dreary. At the same time he remembered his trick for cutting through when she suddenly fell to crying.

—"All right, Lillian, let's have that scene once more, and this time make it gush."

They had heard that when Griffith had invited them to Mamaroneck to discuss filming *Friends and Foes* and they had gone on the set to watch him direct the Gish girls in *Orphans of the Storm*.

It still worked. Jere said, "Look at me, would you, leaking like an old hose."

Manley made the mistake of putting his arm around her. "Oh Mannie, Mannie. I'm sorry but it's—being so goddam alone. God almighty, the nights I haven't been able to sleep thinking about it. The pills I've taken—tracing it back. Where, where was it that it happened? It drives me crazy. How many times I've been at the phone to call you. I just drag along, existing without you. I'm sure my maid thinks I'm a lunatic because once in a while I forget and she hears me talking to you."

He dreaded what was coming next. They had tried it once,

the year before he left for Hollywood and it had been strained when it wasn't listless—no good for either of them. They had nothing left for each other. They were like a couple of runners who pace themselves badly and run themselves out in the first lap. They had tried to make a sprint of what turned out to be a cross-country endurance contest. But it had been a honey of a first lap.

He braced himself. It came. "Man, we're both getting older. We're more sensible now. I don't drink any more—after all, that was the main trouble, wasn't it? And it would be so good for Douglas. Don't you think, if we both worked at it as a . . ."

"Jere—" he did not mean his voice to be so harsh but he felt himself cornered and he had to fight free—"I simply haven't got the time or the strength to go through all this with you again."

"You seem to have plenty of time and strength for that slut I hear you're living with on the Coast."

"Jere, stop it. Right now. Miss Loeb has nothing to do with this."

"Oh, don't think I haven't heard all about your wonderful Miss Loeb. And you dare write me that mularky about having no more personal life. 'My personal life has become my writing life.' *Merde.*"

This time her hysteria only made him calmly superior.

"Jere, believe me, Miss Loeb is getting no bargain. She's just a collector of old relics who went around picking up the pieces of Manley Halliday that nobody seemed to want and brought them home for safe-keeping. It makes no sense to be jealous of her. She came along years after our cause was lost."

"Just the same if that woman were out of the way, if she didn't have such a hold on you . . ."

He took her hand tenderly. "Jere, Jere, what have we done to each other? We can't go back to the dream and we can't go on to anything else."

"Just what I need this afternoon—philosophy."

She had always been too soft or too brittle. Either God had made her without a balance-wheel or the psychiatrists were right about the need for a father.

"Well, Jere, good-bye. I'm sorry I've upset you."

"Good-bye, Manley."

167

"And, oh, I'll send you that money just as soon as I can."

"Thank you."

Silently she led him to the door. In search of a dream, he had found only this carping middle-aged impostor. Well, he had always been too much of a romantic to learn quickly from experience. But what he learned these days he applied. He would never do this again. He would keep Jere Halliday where she belonged—a babe with bounce and beauty on the memory-couch of youth.

Going down in the elevator the let-down hit him hard. When he came out into the cold air he turned once to look up at the window. She was staring down at him. From the angle of the sidewalk, with the curtains shadowing her face, she looked startlingly beautiful again. Hating himself and her and confusion in general, he turned toward First Avenue without waving.

Near the corner of Third Avenue was a bar he recognized as a blind-pig he used to know as Paul and Tony's. Now it had a life preserver in the window and was called the Ship Ahoy. Well, he needed a life preserver. This had been a day. Don't worry, Ann, I know what I'm doing. But I could do with a shot before going back on the job.

"Afternoon."

"Yes, sir."

"Are—are Paul and Tony still around?"

"Who?"

"Paul and Tony—used to run this place."

The bartender looked over toward a small man with glasses studying the Racing Form in one of the booths. "Hey, Al, ever hear of Paul and Tony—useta run this place?"

The man in the booth did not look up. "Never heard of them."

The bartender: "When wuz they here?"

"Oh, Twenty-five, Twenty-six."

"What ya givin' me, ancient history? What'll it be?"

"Scotch and soda. Pinch bottle."

The bartender ignored Manley while setting up his drink.

"Hey, Al, how long you figger it'll go tonight?"

"Aah, the Bomber oughta take him quick."

It was peaceful being the only customer in the Ship Ahoy. Ocean travel always gave him a sense of peace.

"Same thing again. Might as well make it a double."

The second drink raised his hopes. He was really feeling remarkably well, much better than he could have expected after a full day without sleep and an upset diet. He'd go back to the hotel in a little while and block out the college story in half an hour's time. On the third drink the thin red line of confidence was climbing steadily.

12

Four or five drinks (he couldn't be sure how many hours) later Manley came back to the Waldorf. The session at the Ship Ahoy had been just what he needed. He came in singing "I'm on the Crest of a Wave," parodying under his breath the uninhibited bleat with which he had heard Harry Richman render it so often.

Shep hurried to the door. "Jesus, Manley where the hell have you been?"

The violence of the young man's accusation brought Manley's head up stubbornly. His body stiffened, sobered, with a sense of outrage. Who *was* this young snip to talk to him this way? The trouble with him was he was too nice to people.

"Why all the excitement, Stearns?"

"Milgrim is here! Called just a few minutes after you left. He's been phoning every half hour to know where you were. I've been covering for you. Said you had to see a doctor. Then he got on the phone himself. Said he's concerned about your health—your agent promised you were physically fit. So I said you wrenched your foot getting off the plane. God, I've been going nuts!"

"Stearns, I—I 'preciate your efforts in my behalf. But I don't need anyone to cover up for me. I'm—not in the habit of being covered up."

"But look, Manley, I could tell Milgrim was getting sore, and I didn't want him to think . . ."

Manley swayed slightly. If Milgrim fired him now he'd be through. And if he was through in Hollywood . . . damn it these Hollywood jitters. His pride made him sound a good deal surer of himself than he could possibly be.

"Young man, if you want to make screen writing your career—" he closed his eyes and struggled for the lines like an actor in trouble "—let me give you a little advice. What Hollywood needs is a new generation of writers who won't trouble,

170

I mean tremble every time a producer picks up a phone. If screenwriters are ever going to amount to anything they've got to be as independent as we were when we were starting in to write twenny"—he made a conscious effort to articulate— "twenty years ago. We didn't give a damn for the public or the critics or anything. If they didn't like us it just showed us how much behind the times they were. We were cocky. I never saw a good writer yet who wasn't cocky."

"Sure, sure Manley, but *listen*: we've got to go up and see Milgrim right now!"

"Remember something, Shep. Essentially the producer is, I mean the producer is 'sentially our inferior. Because no matter how low they stoop, the executive element is helpless without the creative element. That's why Milgrim treats me with—well, notice the respect? And I'll tell you another thing, he doesn't want me to start truckling to him. That's what he pays me for—so he can look up to me. I know these first- and second-generation tycoons. Inferiority complexes a yard wide."

"Okay. Okay. But do you mind if I call him and tell him we'll condescend to come up and see him this afternoon?"

Manley glared at him. "Tell him I'll be ready to see him in— fifteen minutes."

At the entrance to his bedroom he paused. "And don't let your voice sound as if you're—genuflecting."

Feeling rather pleased with the performance, he went into the bathroom. There his confidence began to falter. He wasn't sure about the dosage. He couldn't even remember if he had had lunch or not. And the caloric content of the whiskey would have to be figured in. Damn it, this lousy trip—for all those months before it he had been so careful. Ann and Dr. Rubin would have a fit if they knew.

In the elevator up to the Towers Manley decided that he was sorry to see the look of annoyance souring Shep's good-natured, conscientious face. As a peace-feeler, Manley produced a smile.

"Sorry I blew my top," Shep said. "I guess no sleep and the damned story on my mind and Milgrim needling me . . ."

"Don't worry, baby, we'll work that touchdown play yet and both win our big block M's."

171

Milgrim's suite in the Tower combined the hectic activity of his office with the full-staffed solicitousness of his home-life. William, Mr. Milgrim's personal valet, opened the door. Mrs. Chenery, the English social secretary, greeted them. Mr. Milgrim was in conference and she hoped they would not mind standing by. They were shown to seats in a wide entrance-way that had been converted into a waiting room. Already there, with the set, bored expressions of those who have waited and are prepared to wait and wait, were a pale young man undoubtedly seeking stardom and a publicity underling from the New York office with the lay-out of a half-page ad on *Live Tonight for Tomorrow,* the World-Wide picture for which a gala opening was being planned upon Milgrim's return from Webster.

The waiting, Shep thought again, the waiting. But this time Manley had no objection. It provided a brief cooling-off period in which to collect himself and perhaps force his mind back to the story.

With her maid carrying a number of large white boxes in front of her, Mrs. Milgrim came in from what she called her shopping spree. She was a real English beauty, faded, but pleasingly so, with a cool grace. Although she had not seen him in years, she recognized Manley Halliday at once. "So nice to see you again, Mr. Halliday. I know Victor is delighted to have you working with him. I hope we'll see something of you while we're all in New York." Her voice was gentle, cultivated, and perhaps just a little more British than it should have been after all these years in America.

Manley was gallant, in a quiet, tired way that appealed to Maud Milgrim as becoming reticence. She wished Victor would hire more writers like him, distinguished and well-mannered. It would help elevate Hollywood social standing. Although Halliday hardly looked distingué in his baggy suit. And he could stand a shave. And his eyes were red-rimmed. The poor man must have been working terribly hard. Victor was such a slave-driver, driving everybody as hard as himself.

"I know Victor won't keep you any longer than he has to. The poor dear always wears himself out so when he comes to New York."

172

They only had to wait twenty minutes. Then they were ushered in by a Peggy Dillon considerably more restrained now that she had to function within earshot of the Great Man. She did manage to mumble for Shep's benefit, "Greetings, Buster. Welcome to our little madhouse," as she led them into the large sitting room where Milgrim reigned. He was wearing a dark silk lounging robe, in excellent taste, and a manicurist was doing his nails while an Eastern magazine writer tried to sell him an original.

Clearly disconcerted by the entrance of Manley and Shep in the middle of his presentation, the writer said, "Of course I don't tell it as well as I could write it . . ." and paused uncertainly, which both Manley and Shep recognized as a fatal opening to give a man like Milgrim.

Milgrim said, "I can see where you're going, Pierson. And I'm afraid it's not my sort of thing—not enough importance."

"I think you'd like the ending," Pierson suggested unhappily.

"Tell you what you do. Write me a letter outlining the whole thing. Thanks for coming up, Pierson."

Pierson rose reluctantly. He wanted to defend his story, but he did not know where to begin. He hesitated, and then suddenly turned to Manley, with a false heartiness meant to cover both his embarrassment and his genuine respect.

"Halliday, you probably don't remember me. We met in Marseilles a helluva long time ago—at that hotel out on Grand Corniche."

"La Reserve?"

"By God, yes. That's what I call a good memory."

"I used to have a better one."

"Well, I-uh-have to dash. But I-uh-want you to know I thought *Shadow Ball* was a honey of a job. My better half thought so too."

"Thank you," Manley said, using only his head for the bow. "And thank the 'better half' too." His voice italicized the phrase with gentle scorn.

"She passed away six years ago," Pierson said, and then he was gone, leaving the compliment in Manley's hand like a faded flower.

"How's your foot, Manley?" Milgrim said suddenly. " I hear you tripped or something getting off the plane."

The *or something* was vaguely accusing.

"Oh, it's—it's coming along. I'll be ready to run against Yale," Manley said.

"If it gives you any trouble, let me know. Dr. Lobell, the best orthopedist in New York, is a great pal of mine."

"A little hot water and a good night's rest," Manley said, uncomfortably.

"Christ, be careful, will you, fella?" Milgrim's warning was still good-natured. "We don't want anything to happen to the star on the eve of the big game."

The manicurist, finished, put her things away with such practiced efficiency as to seem invisible. Milgrim admired the shiny pink surfaces of his nails.

"Well, I suppose you've got the screenplay ready for me to read?"

It was always delivered in the same laughing tone, this tired industrial joke.

"Nize baby, et op all de screenplay."

Shep looked at Manley, trying to warn him with his eyes. But Manley would not look at him.

Milgrim (sharply): "What's that, Manley?"

Manley (mildly): "You make a joke. I make a joke. Score's fifteen all."

Milgrim looked at Shep, asking a wordless question. Shep lowered his head as if in thought. But he could see Milgrim's eyes shifting appraisingly from one to the other.

"Well, gentlemen, if it isn't asking too much—" Milgrim still managed to retain what he believed to be his sense of humor "—I'd like to hear the new attack on the story."

There was a pause. Afraid of what Manley might say, Shep decided to head him off. "Well, we . . ." he began.

But Milgrim wasn't looking at him. Milgrim was waiting for Halliday and Shep's words faded from inattention.

Manley ran his hand back and forth across his forehead. In the silence, Shep tried not to look at Milgrim. It was a little silly to be so frightened, but after that inquisition of the waiter . . .

174

When Manley began, however, he gave a surprisingly able digest of the various story lines they had discussed. There was no cheap attempt to sell, nor to gloss over difficulties. As Manley spoke, Milgrim pushed out his full lower lip, which Shep had come to recognize as a sign of thinking in a deeply troubled way.

"I had hoped you'd be a little further along," he said when Manley had finished.

Manley seemed calm and poised and Shep began to admire him again. His mind was still in the room. Shep had been uneasy about that.

"This is the period of gestation, Victor. In my own work I often think for weeks without getting anywhere. Then one day everything seems to drop into place."

"I suppose regular screen writers are geared a little faster," Milgrim acknowledged. "I know when you do come up with something, it will be a real Milgrim idea. I wouldn't try to rush you at all, Manley"—Shep wasn't there at all for Milgrim—"if it wasn't for this damned second unit at the Mardi Gras. When we get up there we've got to have enough of an outline to know what stock and process backgrounds to go for."

"In other words, you're not rushing us," Manley said with an insolent smile, "just giving us one more day."

"I once rewrote an entire screenplay in nineteen hours," Milgrim said.

"I wrote a short story in a day once that's still being anthologized. But . . ."

"But—?" Milgrim waited.

A puzzled look came over Manley's face. "But what?"

There was a different kind of pause this time, disturbing to Milgrim, confusing to Manley, painful to Shep.

Mrs. Milgrim looked in from the doorway. "Victor, dear, I don't want to rush you but we're dressing—and you know how long it takes you to dress." She smiled at her husband's writers graciously. "Forgive us for letting you in on family secrets."

"All right, Maud. We've gone as far as we can now anyway."

Shep tried to catch Manley's eye to say: Mr. Milgrim may run everybody else but Mrs. Milgrim runs Mr. Milgrim. But Manley was unreceptive. His eyes were not glassy; they merely had seemed to lose interest in what there was to see.

The fine blond head of Mrs. Milgrim popped in again. She was a busy woman.

"Just had an idea, Victor. Maybe Mr. Halliday would like to join us and the Swopes for dinner and the Bea Lillie show—what's the name of it again?"

"Set to Music," Manley mumbled.

Shep was constantly being reminded of Manley's ability to deal in specifics, even when he hardly appeared to be thinking or listening.

"Yes, of course. I'm sure Bea could get us an extra ticket," Milgrim said.

"Thanks, but—didn't even bring evening clothes," Manley said. A brightness came into his eyes. "I'm just the plumber—brought nothing but working clothes—only came in to fix a few leaky pipes."

Milgrim and his wife laughed hollowly. Then he said: "I have a notion Manley wants to work tonight anyway. Say, I have an idea. When I get back from the theater tonight, why don't we huddle again? What do you say I give you a ring around one or two?"

One of the occupational risks of Milgrim writers was this compulsive habit of avoiding sleep.

"You really think that's a good idea, Victor?" Manley said curtly. "With a strenuous week-end coming up?"

"In case you've turned in, leave word at the desk," Milgrim persisted.

Apparently still unaware of Shep's presence, the producer walked Manley to the door. The would-be star and the publicity man and the pale boy were still waiting but Milgrim did not see them either.

"You wouldn't want to come back and have one drink with us and meet the Swopes?"

Manley shook his head. "I'll see you in the morning, Victor."

As the door closed, Miss Dillon was telling the publicity man he could show the lay-out to Mr. Milgrim in the bedroom while

176

the producer was dressing. The beautiful girl and the pale young man would have to try again tomorrow.

On their way down in the elevator Manley said, "I may have to work for Milgrim. But I'll be damned if I let him show me off like a gold key on a watch chain."

"The gold key and the invisible man," Shep said.

"Yes, I feel bad about that. I certainly don't want to hog this thing. When our picture comes out I'll make sure you get equal credit."

"Don't let it worry you," Shep said.

"It's really very funny in a way." They both began to laugh. They had forgotten to give the elevator boy their floor number and had gone all the way to the lobby.

"I'm hungry," Manley said.

"Don't you think we should clean up?"

"Oh, let's just go out and get a bite and then come back and polish off the outline."

"But we can't go out this way—snowing outside—no coats."

"Spur o' the moment."

"What?"

"Always used to do things spur o' the moment. Never make plans, Jere 'n me. Go t'a nightclub, like that. Europe, like that. Bed, like that. Divorce, like that. Suicide, like that."

Shep looked at him and Manley quickly reassured him. "Don't be frightened. I was joke-making."

They were under the marquee, waiting for a cab. Air's supposed to sober people up, Shep thought. Seemed to have just the opposite effect on Halliday.

"Listen, Manley, it's a lousy night. I think we really ought to go back . . ."

"Suppose you think I'm trying to commit suicide by catching my death of pneumonia. Lis-sen. No suicide in my family. We Hallidays 're stronger characters 'n we look."

As the doorman opened the taxi door for the party ahead of them, Manley hurried forward and jumped into it first. There were righteous accusations and angry words. Shep waited uneasily on the perimeter of the tense circle.

"Aw—so's your old man," Manley was saying. He never said these things seriously, but always with a sense of satire.

"Get out of that cab, god damn it, or I'll pull you out," said a man who looked as if he could.

Manley started out to meet the challenge. Shep leapt in and slammed the door. "Let's get away from here fast," he told the back of the head behind the wheel.

"That loudmouth wasn't there first."

"Yes, he was, Manley."

"Well, I didn't see him."

"Manley, do you consider me a friend of yours?"

"Ho, ho, how many people have asked me *that!*"

Shep didn't say anything. He looked out at the soiled slush.

After a few moments of this, Manley said, "Okay. Okay. Be a friend of mine."

"Let's go back to the hotel, sleep till midnight, then get up and work on the story."

"Well, where you wanna go?" a gravelly voice demanded from the front seat.

"Twenty-one," Manley said.

"Haven't you seen enough celebrities?"

"Have to eat somewhere. This'll give me a chance to pay an old bill."

Monty on the door, dour by disposition, affable by profession, knew his business. "Mr. Halliday," he said. "Haven't seen you in a long time."

As they entered the long cellar room with the auburn lights, Jack came over. Manley Halliday had been a good customer in the old, even 49th Street days and such things were not forgotten here. "If you'll send a blank check to the table, I'll pay an old debt," Manley said right away. Having once had pride in his reputation as an easy spender, he was sensitive about his fall from financial grace.

"We've been awfully worried about it," Jack said nicely, with a wink at Shep.

Passing the bar on their way to the tables they saw Dick Watts and Quent Reynolds and at the big table reserved for him in the corner, John O'Hara. Afraid Manley might stop for a drink, Shep took his arm and piloted him on to one of the small tables against the wall.

A big man across the room who must have been quite handsome once, before all the drinking, looked over and nodded. Manley said, as if the name itself had significance, "Larry Bane."

The name was a blank to Shep.

"Larry Bane?" Manley said. "You've heard of *The Grouch? One Million a Year?*"

"Must be BMT," Shep said.

"BMT," Manley caught it. "Before my time? Is that used much?"

"It's one of Sara's," Shep said. "The New Deal influence. Calls her story editor FOB. For fascistic old bitch."

"Well," said Manley. "BYT Bane had two hits running on Broadway at the same time. Even Nathan liked 'em. Popular 'n satirical. Like Barry, only better. The critics kept waiting for him to write that great American play."

"What happened to him?"

"Hollywood."

The captain was ready to take the order. Shep could have used a drink but he decided to pass. More important to get Manley back on the story.

"Let's have a drink," Manley said.

"I thought you were hungry."

"Oh, we'll eat. Let's have a drink first."

"Okay, a drink," Shep said. But he made Manley order dinner at the same time. Manley ordered elaborately, Chateaubriand with Béarnaise sauce, Pommes de terre allumettes, broccoli Hollandaise, tossed green salad . . .

Shep went back to pick up the conversational stitch. "Why does everyone blame it on Hollywood?"

"On Hollywood?" Manley had forgotten.

"This great playwright Bane."

"Oh. Oh, Bane. Bane was brilliant—best we had. Charley Brackett in the *New Yorker,* I think it was, said Bane and Eddie Mayer—you know Eddie Mayer?"

"But, Manley, this Hollywood stuff. Why must Hollywood always take the rap? Why didn't Bane have enough guts to stay with his plays?"

"Temptation," Manley said. "That's writers in America."

"Maybe in your time. But if you mean the new writers, I think you're wrong as hell. They know where they stand. It keeps them moving forward."

"Too easy," Manley said. "Always too easy." His eyes were almost closed and it hardly seemed possible that he could be concentrating. "Your high mortality on writers, that goes on all the time in America. Y'know why?" He was signaling the waiter for another drink. "American idea of success. Nothing fails like success. Write one bestseller here, one hit play, Big Success. Do one thing, get rich 'n famous. Writers get caught up in American system. Ballyhoo. Cocktail parties. Bestseller list. Worship of Success."

He paused. "Gotta find the Johnny. They moved it since I was here last. Whole place turned around. Don't know where I am."

He rose and wandered off. When their next round arrived, Shep sneaked a third of Manley's behind the waiter's back and refilled it from the water glass. Then he watched Manley threading his way back between the tables. He had better remind him to shave and change his clothes before they saw Milgrim again. How long had it been since they left the Burbank airport? Was this only the second night? He could have believed it the twentieth or the two thousandth. Sara, California, normal life seemed remote and unreal. A few tables away Shep saw Manley stop and bow to a lady of uncertain age expensively dressed and still attractive in a fleshy, dissipated way. Shep saw her take Manley's hand and talk up into his face with a great show of animation.

"My God, Mimsey Layton," Manley said when he squeezed in behind the small table again. "Shep, take my advice. Never grow old. Too painful to see the women. Bad enough for the men. Always hate to see an All-American ten years later. But the women. Mimsey. That Mimsey. She was the cutest little hell raiser. Married three times—each one richer. Hadda funny

180

hobby—collecting writers. Ever meet those women who aren't really readers—just made up their silly minds that authors 'd make the most interesting lovers? That was Mimsey." What he was thinking made him snicker. "Good ol' Mims. Pro'lly the greatest living authority on the sex lives of American authors. Wrote a book once, or had it written, *Faithful in My Fashion,* in which all the lovers became 'dear friends.' Some of us thought it was fascinating in a horrible way and some of us thought it was horrible in a fascinating way. Charley MacArthur was the one who said 'Both schools are wrong. It's horrible in a horrible way.'" He was sipping from the watered highball. "Poor ol' Mimsey. Still trying to have a figure. And the Martinis. And you should have heard the gay chatter. Wants me to drop up for cocktails. Doesn't know I don't drop up for cocktails any more. I've put away my childish toys. Jere thought I was in love with her once. Maybe I was, one afternoon at a garden party, for about five minutes."

Shep said, "You can still see a little of what she must have had."

"We had some sexy babies. Or maybe I was just younger. Mimsey was the original flapper. Something new on the face of the globe. Full of merry hell in a way that women had never known how to be before." He smiled vaguely. "Remember one time . . ."

He paused and finished his drink. The Chateaubriand had arrived and Shep was wolfing his. Despite the flourishes of the waiter, Manley was letting his get cold.

"Yes?" Shep prompted.

"What was I talking about? Slipped my mind."

"Something about Mimsey. Something you just remembered."

Manley caught the waiter's eye and held up his glass.

"Another Scotch and soda?" the waiter said.

"Never say *another*. Bad manners. Just say *a* Scotch and soda. Good waiter never rubs a guest's nose in his own lack o' will power."

"Manley, you'd better eat," Shep said.

"Stop nursing me. I'm going to get awfully goddam sick of you if you keep on nursing me."

"Listen, Manley. I'm trying to help you."

"You don't know me. Why should you want to help me? And who the hell told you I needed your help anyway?"

"Forget it, Manley. Take it easy."

"Think I'ma 'fraid of you? Pro'lly got thirty pounds on me and twenty years. But I'll fight you. I'll beat the living—whaddo I care if they hear? Come on. Right now."

He started to rise. What he needed was air. He was very dizzy.

Shep said with authority, "Sit down."

"Bet you're pretty handy with the gloves."

Shep said, "I've done some boxing."

"You look like a boxer. Did I ever tell you how I boxed the ears off Freddy Welsh?"

"Yes."

"I know what you think. You think I'm an old bourgeois windbag. You think I can't write any more because I don't worship labor organizers. You think I drink because I'm aesthetically frustrated and—and decadent, isn't that the word?"

"Manley, I'm telling you. You better eat something."

"What in hell were we talking about again?"

"Mimsey?"

"Oh, stow Mimsey. No, I shouldn't say that. Though it was a mighty sweet little assignment once upon a time."

"Doesn't look so bad right now, if you remember the advice of Ben Franklin."

The thought of Mimsey sobered him, or at least saddened him. "No, she's just a ghost now, a ghost in a tight corset, pan make-up and a Martini mask."

The waiter hovered solicitously. "Are you through with your deener, Meester Halliday?"

Manley waved the dish away with a nod of his head. "As a sign of my solidarity with the working class, I donate this meal to the culinary proletariat."

It got the rise out of Shep that Manley had anticipated; that, in fact, had been his motive for saying it.

"Garçon—" At a certain point in his drinking Manley had a tendency to restaurant French—"deux Ecosses avec soda."

"Manley, what do you say we cut out of here?"

"Have to have a nightcap, how would you say that, *le bonnet de nuit?*"

Again nature called Manley from the room ("Gonna trade these kidneys in for a couple of good sieves") and again Shep worked his sleight-of-hand to dilute the drink. Again Manley stopped at Mimsey's table and again he told Shep this was a girl he used to know.

"My youth tails me like a third-rate private detective too clumsy to keep himself from being seen."

"Come on, Manley, let's take off."

"Shep, what were we talking about when we came in? Something we didn't finish. Something important."

For several minutes neither one could remember.

"It couldn't 've been unimportant," Manley laughed. "Oh—I remember. American writers. Here they come—there they go." He sipped from the watered drink unprotestingly. "That's it— wanted to finish my thought." He closed his eyes, straining to bring the subject back into focus.

" 'Merican writers, full o' promise, tremendous promise; when they die, still promising. Can't seem to keep their promises. Hart Cranes—all Hart Cranes, the best of 'em. Even Ernest. Ernest's a promising writer. Maybe the most promising we ever had."

Suddenly his hand flew up in an ascending line. "European writers, like that—but 'merican writers, like this—" His hand checked its upward flight and nosedived back to the table. "Know why?"

"I think I do," Shep said. "Their unrealistic approach to. . ."

"Oh, I read Granville Hicks too. Trouble with all our writers is they never read Marx. Poe, Melville, Dickinson, all of 'em frustrated 'cause they didn't worship Marx. Booshwah. Banana oil. Baloney. Reason's economic, all right. But more complicated. Writer starts as rebel. Hits out at his own roots. Spoon River. Sauk Center. Pottsville country club—wherever it is. Book's a success—writer's like a race-horse—moves up in class. Gets money —goes away—New York—Europe—starts writing things he doesn't know—shoulda stayed home. Stayed put. Shoulda stood in bed. That's trouble with 'merican writers. Most of 'em. Success uproots 'em. Isolates 'em. Europe, a book is a book, a leaf o' litera-ture. America, a book's a commodity, even the honest book, if it *clicks,* if it *goes over big.* Maybe lucky thing about Faulkner. Never went over big. Just a few thousand to read 'im and know what he is. Bill stays put. Writes people he knows, and his old man knew, and *his* old man. Sense o' past. Sense o' place. Sense o' roots. . ."

Shep found it disconcerting, a little too much like having a corpse suddenly rise and deliver his own funeral oration, or, worse, perform his own autopsy.

"Know what you're thinking," Manley said suddenly.

"What?"

"Said I knew what you're thinking. You're thinking this old windbag's deflated. Uprooted. Ausgespielt. 'Mong my souvenirs. Well, I may fool you, sweetheart, 's Al Harper 'd say. I'm not stewed—I mean I'm not through. Oh, sure, I see it in your eyes, methinks he doth protest too much. But my case's different. I'm doing it, not just talking it. I've got a new book under way that's . . ."

"What's it about?" Shep was anxious to know.

He had almost told. He must be thoroughly potted to have gone so far. In the early days he had told. Kissed and told. Told and written. But he knew better now. Couldn't afford to waste words now. Or emotions, or energy. They were his stock in trade. Sorry, no free samples. Couldn't give anything away any more. Had to keep careful inventory when you worked on narrow margin. Had to marshal his strength, get back on the routine he had started before he came on this damned picture. No drinking, no late hours, no wasted conversations with ex-pendable people. No (it was one of his most important words now) sloth. Keep in training, concentrated, dedicated.

A wreck, Shep was thinking self-righteously, a shell, a skeleton that will not give up the ghost and goes wandering through the capitalist wasteland.

"Marcel!" Manley was holding up his empty glass. "S'il vous plaît."

"Come on, Manley," Shep said firmly. "Let's get some air. I want to get out of here. I'm feeling a little woozy myself."

184

"Okay, keed, let's take off, as you say. As you say, let's cut out. We gotta stick together, baby. We're in this together, baby. We'll travel along singin' a song side by side."

Manley paid the check with a flourish, tipping the waiter, the captains and the headwaiter in an open-handed way that would have interested both Veblen and the family psychiatrist. At the check-room counter there was a bad moment when Manley insisted that he had come in with a topcoat and misplaced his ticket, but Shep managed to ease him out onto the street and hustle him into a cab.

"Where to?" asked the hacky in a guttural, discouraged voice.

Before Shep could say Waldorf, Manley leaned forward. "Eddie Bell's still open in Harlem?"

"Damn 'f I know, don't get up there much any more."

"Well, le's take a look."

"Manley, we can't go up to Harlem tonight."

"We can't? I can."

"Why don't we do it on the way back? After we've been to Webster?"

" 'Member what I told you. Spur o' the moment. Only way to live, t' feel alive. Two o'clock in the morning, go to bed, can't sleep, Jere'd say le's go up to Harlem. Went up in our pajamas once. Nigger cop tried to arrest us. We said we just came from a costume ball dressed as Time to Retire. Then we bought the nigger cop a drink and etcetera and ditto and at seven in the morning he came back to our place for scrambled eggs and started playing the piano and another party started that went on for two days. Luther. That's his name, Luther MacDaniel. A dinge with a Scotch name. Grandmother on my maternal side's named MacDaniel. That's what the party was t' celebrate. Luther got kicked off the Force for being AWOL and made a lot of money bootlegging. Haven't seen him in—Lord—ten years. Almos' half your lifetime. Seems like ten days. Goes so damn fast."

At the Waldorf Shep tried again. "Manley, don't you think you might as well come in with me?"

"No, that's what I don't think."

"We have a hell of a lot to do."

"We'll do it. Promise. Work with you when I get back."

185

"But, Manley, we've had no sleep. We'll fall apart."

"Miss Dillon'll keep us alive with benzedrine. Show mus' go on."

"Honestly, we should be in shape tomorrow."

"Okay. Then honestly close the door. Honestly go up to the room and grapple honestly with *Love on Ice*. It's your story, baby, now grapple with it. I'm goin' up 'n see Eddie. Use'd t' be a wunnerful place. Just wanna see how it looks now. Stay coupla minutes. Hold the fort, baby. And if Victor calls, tell 'im, tell 'im to get some sleep."

Shep shook his head, with a stylized look of resignation, and climbed into the cab. "Okay," he said, in exactly the same tone Manley had used earlier in the evening, "Okay."

13

All the way up to Harlem through the white hush of the park, Manley kept recalling fantasies of shrill Harlem nights in the era when Harlem was the gin-spangled corridor for all good citizens with early-morning itch. Their legendary antics, his and Jere's and their twinkling friends', made him laugh in a way that was new to Shep but old and no longer familiar to Manley. The laughs they had had, the innocent laughter. People didn't laugh any more, just to be laughing; now it was all at the expense of other people and other ideas.

Manley wouldn't let Shep pay for the cab. He pulled out a crushed handful of bills, selected one at random and flung it to the driver. It happened to be a five-dollar bill.

"Manley, you ought to hang on to some of that money."

" 'Fi drove a cab, that's how I'd like to be paid."

From the entrance they could hear a small, sloppy combination racing through a popular riff. "The Dipsy Doodle." Steps led them down to a dark, red cave. There were just two couples in the place. It was a desolate pleasure-dome and the tinny, bogus jazz made it unbearably forlorn. "Place useta be jammed all the time. But Eddie 'd always put a table on the floor for us."

Manley closed his eyes listening to the old time din: *say this stuff isn't half bad* sometimes I'm happy sometimes I'm blue-hoo my disPOsition depends on you-hoo . . .

A dapper, light-skinned Negro, who for some reason affected dark glasses, came up in a hurry and gave Manley not just a big but a warm hello.

"Hello, Pops, you're a sight for sore optics."

He held Manley at arms' length and appraised him fondly. "Here's my boy. Here's a creature I approve mightily."

Shep had the feeling they were making more of it than had ever been really there, because the room was so empty and the glory so long gone.

They clustered around a small table where Eddie bought a round—"Your money's no good here, Pops"—and another round while they talked *remember-the-time* and *what-ever-happened-to?*

Manley felt grateful to Eddie for remaining unchanged. These last ten had been fierce years, not doing anybody any good, an intense erosion eating away flesh and spirit. But here was Eddie Bell with the same smooth figure, face and line, apparently as cheerful a failure as, in more propitious and amoral days, he had been a success.

"Eddie," Manley went with the tide of reminiscence, "will you ever forget that night The Gimp got it? Le's see, he was sitting right over there."

"You can still see the bullet holes," Eddie said proudly.

"The Gimp was a small-timer who tried to hold out on Schultz," Manley explained to Shep, remembering how pleased he and Jere used to be when important mobsters came over to their table. "They're so polite and so much more dignified than respectable people," Jere had insisted.

"We were all here one night when The Gimp came in with a blonde." Manley insisted on telling the whole story.

"Lucinda," Eddie said with the accuracy of acute nostalgia. "Lucinda Edwards. Cute as a flute. She was fingering him for Schultz all the time."

"Let's see—what was the band you had then, Eddie? Oh, Kenny Watts and his Five Kilowatts."

"Man, you've got a good rememory," Eddie said.

"They were playing a song I never could stand, *Ramona,* when something cracked and The Gimp started slipping down under the table. The band was playing a medley and, this you'll never believe, but while the waiters were carrying The Gimp out the dancing went right on. And the tune the band had switched to—Kenny swore it wasn't on purpose—was *And Then My Heart Stood Still."*

Eddie chuckled. "That was phony as Coney. But it happened just like Pops says."

"You wrote a short story around that," Shep said. " 'Midnight Frolic.' You got the whole crazy speakeasy era into that story."

188

"It was one of those things that just drops in your lap," Manley said. "Wrote the whole thing in two hours when I got up that next afternoon."

"It won the O. Henry for the best story of the year," Shep said.

"Yeah man, we had the times," Eddie Bell said. Grinning at Manley, he tried not to see that one of the only two paying couples in the place was drinking nothing but beer. You couldn't even pay this band with what you made in beer. "Come on, Pops, drink up, let us be gay."

Shep was drinking with them, from outside, watching them and wondering how much of this Manley could take. He seemed a little clearer than at 21. Apparently the cool ride through the Park and Eddie Bell's reminiscences, spiraling around them like confetti, had helped to revive him. He was slipping easily into the illuminative atmosphere that had flared up between him and Eddie Bell as if they were two matches struck together.

The band was resting from its fruitless exertions. "Anything you want 'em to play, Pops?"

Why Do I Love You? The words gurgled through his mind with their catchy rhymes that had always pleased him.

"Pops, will you ever forget the night—we had a line of Sepia Sirens then and you and Mrs. H had just come back from some sun-kissed shore and were two shades darker than I was? Mrs. H sneaked off to the dressing room and when the kids came stepping out, there she was . . ."

"Eddie, you talk too much."

It caught Eddie with his guard lowered and brought him down to now.

"Now, Pops, don't snap your wig. I was just trying . . ."

"Aw, shut up."

"Pops, you all right? You're pretty far in the bag."

Manley ignored him. He had remembered something else. That same Arabian night. Some goings-on between Jere and Eddie Bell he had never been sure about. He had always been afraid she had taken Rimbaud's vilification of the white race too much to heart.

He stood up from the table and though he felt positive he had done so quietly, the chair fell over behind him.

"Come on, let's get out of here."

Manley came back to their rooms at the Waldorf shaken and depressed. What a wild-goose chase! He should have known there was no Harlem to run up to any more; it was just a sprawling dark ghetto now.

"What y' say we do a little work?"

If it had been two other people, Shep would have laughed.

"Right now? You know what time it is?"

"What's difference? I always used t' work this time, early i' the morning. Some my best work early i' the morning. Come on, le's get the damn thing over with."

"Manley, don't you think we'll feel more like it after a little shut-eye?"

"Damn you, always telling me what I should be feeling. One thing your time my time have in common—young men lecturing to old men."

"Lecturing, hell. I've had too much myself to be able to keep my mind on our damned story."

"Hell with all this talking. Real writers get sick o' talking. What y' think I am, one of these story-conference streaks? I'm a *writer*, we're both writers. What d'ya say we both sit down 'n start writing?"

"But what are we going to write?"

"*Love on Ice*. Le's just sit down and *write* it."

"You mean both write it at the same time?"

"Sure. Le's each write half. Le's both go in separate rooms 'n *write*. Then in, say, two hours we c'n meet back here and piece it together."

Shep searched the gray, strained face for some sign that Manley meant to be humorous. But no such sign was to be found. At this moment Manley believed quite seriously in their ability to saw a plot in half.

"But Manley . . ." The entire idea was so incredible that Shep couldn't even devise a sensible protest.

"Come on, le's start! Which half you rather take?"

For no other reason than helplessness, Shep said, "Okay, I'll take the first half."

He went into the bedroom with a sheaf of hotel stationery and, somehow falling in with the absurdity of it, began writing whatever came into his head. To his surprise he found this madcap plan a little less senseless than it had sounded. Having to make words on paper forced him to characterize in more detail than he had in all the days of talking the story. Several times he paused to rebuild his highball from the bottle in the living room. Once he went to the threshold of Manley's room and looked in. Manley, using the bed for a desk, was writing furiously.

Dawn was just beginning to filter in when Manley suddenly appeared in the doorway of Shep's room. He had a thick pad of stationery in his hand. If it hadn't been insulin or a shot of something, the work had revived him. He was, obviously, delighted with what he had done.

"Anywhere near through, Shep?"

"Well—I guess so."

"I think mine went pretty well. All we have to do now is splice 'em together."

Shep was not at all sure they were even writing the same story, or the same characters, but, accepting topsy-turvy logic as one does in a dream, he followed along.

"Now first you read yours, then I'll read mine and then we'll drive in a golden spike at the place where they connect," Manley said. "Just the way they joined the first railroad line in *The Iron Horse.*"

Self-consciously, Shep read his section aloud, feeling more and more like a damn fool. But Manley listened seriously, sometimes nodding in agreement. It never seemed to occur to him that what Shep had written was an improvised jumble.

When Shep finished, Manley said, "Well, it needs a little touching up but it's not too bad," mixed himself another drink and began with an air of importance to read his section. It rambled —at times incoherently, and it had practically nothing to do with any college musical they had discussed; and yet, from the first line, evoking a wonderland of evergreens in freshly fallen snow and the reckless laughter of bright-eyed girls, it was much too good for what they needed. But for what they needed, not nearly good enough. When Manley finished, Shep did not know what to say. It had the Halliday touch all right. Apparently the old boy hadn't lost that magical gift of not being able to write a bad line. The only trouble was, it made no sense. As a future item for Halliday collectors it might have some value. But it wasn't exactly what Victor Milgrim was expecting for his $2000 a week.

"There," Manley said. "I told you we were writers, didn't I, baby?"

"It's—it's got some nice feeling." Shep struggled for an out.

"I think we've got a real heroine in Diane." His voice was paced with an ebullience that made him sound youthful. "Couldn't you feel her coming to life? I always was successful with girls who love life, who throw off restraints. Diane's really a second cousin to Julia in *Midnight Frolic*. Your mentioning that tonight gave me the idea."

Shep said nothing but Manley was too pleased with himself, or, more kindly, too pleased with the motions of writing he had gone through, to notice. "I told you we could do it, baby. I told you if we just sat down to the *writing* we'd be all right."

"Yes, you did," Shep said. This was, as Sara would say, a major worry. What did Manley Halliday need, a cup of black coffee, or a whole new life?

"How'd you like that line where Diane sees Toby make his jump, 'a giant bird plunging downward' and so forth, that isn't bad prose, is it, baby?"

That he was supposed to be writing a bare outline for a film seemed entirely forgotten. He had gone home to prose style as an old blind horse finds its way back to its stall. It left Shep with a sense of confusion as to how he felt about Manley now.

The morning light was insistent, unflattering; their beards looked rougher, their clothes seedier. The morning light, taunting Shep with its irritable arithmetic, now added up to forty hours of fruitless wakefulness. The morning light led Manley in a happy daze to the little balcony outside the sitting room. It's a hard job but I'm getting it done, he was thinking. I'm a craftsman, not a bohemian: I get things done.

Shep watched him leaning on the railing in the hazy winter's light. He must be weary to the breaking point after that last try. The bones were sharp in his face and from Shep's point of view there was a terrifying illusion: the fine profile was bony and motionless as a death's head.

For two-and-a-half days—according to Shep's impromptu recapitulation—he had thought about nothing else but Manley Halliday. At first he had thought about how to make himself attractive, *worthwhile* to Halliday. Then he had thought about what he was learning from Halliday, and how to say the things that would bring Halliday out. Then he had begun to wonder about Halliday, and criticize. Now he was worried about him. He had been looking out toward the balcony, thinking he ought to tell Manley to lie down and get some rest, when a streak of independence flared: *the hell with it, nobody appointed me his keeper.* He went on into his own bedroom and closed the door.

Put Manley Halliday out of your mind. Why worry about a ruined man whose mind stopped with the clocks of Twenty-nine? This business of thinking every man was an island. Couldn't they see that just below the waterline they were all connected? Shouldn't every honest writer feel himself inextricably bound to society, to his fellow-men? How could he take off on a ten-year binge like Manley Halliday?

He shifted on the bed and tried to change the subject. This wasn't getting away from Manley Halliday. But the ghost pursued him. What had happened to Manley Halliday? What would become of him?

Closing his eyes, he could not close out Manley Halliday. How long had he known him? Already the worshipful beginning, the awe seemed part of an earlier incarnation. He had known him always, always his intimate and confidant.

All Shep could remember was that he had started out as a healthy, robust, relatively uncomplicated young man. Now he had lost the most luxurious of all youthful accomplishments— the ability to take sleep for granted. He shifted and tossed, felt his nerves hopping under his skin like sand-fleas, and slipped off into brief, disordered dreams only to twitch into wakefulness again.

Slowly Shep began to realize that he must have succumbed to sleep at last, for he was being awakened by a new, strange voice, a voice that sounded as if a man and a girl were using the same vocal cords.

Someone was making a shrill accusation. Shep heard "drunk again" and "you're a damn fake" and "you've been nothing but bad news for me ever since I c'n remember."

"Now, Douglas," Shep heard Manley trying to calm him, "now, Douglas."

"Why the heck should I spare your feelings? When did you ever worry about me?"

Shep couldn't resist putting his eye to the keyhole. He saw a tall, thin, boy who would soon grow into being handsome and who looked as if he had stepped out of Brooks' pre-college display. A cigarette flipped into his mouth with adolescent casualness and Shep noticed that he could talk with it between his lips like an old hand.

Even without seeing Manley, Shep knew how disturbed he was. When he was able to get a word in, his voice was low and strained. From what he had told Shep he was deeply concerned for Douglas, anxious that he become a "useful, integrated human being" and he probably wished this even more keenly than most fathers because of his guilt at having failed Douglas in the formative years.

"What's the use of trying to stay in school?" Douglas was demanding. "What kind of meatball do you take me for? How do you think I feel when the Bursar's office calls me in and asks me if my father knows my tuition is two months overdue? Tells me you haven't even answered their letters! Holy Cow, I'd rather quit and get a job selling cars or something."

"Douglas, there is to be no more talk about leaving school."

"Well—I'm disgusted," Douglas said.

"One of the reasons I'm making such an effort to write for Hollywood is to be sure you finish your education."

"Maybe if you didn't drink so much it wouldn't have to be such an effort."

"Douglas, I—I cannot allow you to talk to me that way."

194

"Aah—look at you—you're drunk right now. You never did anything for me in your whole life."

Listening behind the door, Shep was surprised to discover how closely identified he felt with Manley. This brat couldn't talk to him that way, not to Manley Halliday. One more crack out of Douglas and he was tempted to go out and punch the kid's face in.

Douglas was talking about Mother now. From the way he capitalized and softened the word, one could tell what had happened to Douglas. "God knows you've made Mother's life a holy hell. It makes me sick when I see how she has to worry about money. And all the time you're spending it on flit and some Hollywood floosie. I'll never understand—never understand why you left Mother in the first place."

Manley came within range of the keyhole for the first time. Apparently the pain had sobered him. If only he didn't look so run-down, Shep thought possessively. The shapeless suit, the bristled face, the stupefied look.

"Douglas." Manley shut his eyes a moment in weariness. "Of course I respect you for standing by your mother. It's—gentlemanly of you. In fact, I would be disappointed in you if you didn't."

Douglas waited with his mouth open a little to relieve the tension. It was easier when his father fought back.

" 'Parently your mother has discussed me with you. More sorry than I can tell you that you have to be dragged into adult sit-u-ations." He had to pick his way very carefully not to stammer or slur. "You are remarkably sophis-ticated for sixteen. Nev' theless I suggest there may be certain 'motional problems that are still beyond your—comprehension."

It would have been more impressive if Manley hadn't had a tendency to stagger and to try so hard not to soften the edges of the consonants.

"Aw, if you were a man you'd go back to Mother and take care of her."

"Ah, Douglas, it's not so simple as all that."

"Sure it isn't simple"—suddenly rising hysterically, Douglas' voice sounded even younger than sixteen—"not with that god-damned bitch on the West Coast."

Manley said quietly, "If you were not my son, and you were a few years older, I would have to punch you in the nose for saying that."

"Go on, go on," the young voice screamed, "try it anyway—I'll —I'll—I'll—"

Then Shep heard an unexpected sound. Douglas was sobbing. Manley put his arms around him. He held him like a small boy.

"Why do things have to be so damned lousy?" he sobbed. "If only you and Mother had stayed together."

Families, Shep was thinking behind the door, hating each other without ever having stopped loving each other.

So it all ended with Manley consoling Douglas, telling him not to worry and giving him some extra spending money for the week-end. "I'll pay up that tuition the minute I get next Wednesday's check. Why don't you go in my bathroom and wash your face?"

A soft family ending to a hard family quarrel.

When Shep heard the door to the corridor close behind Douglas, he wondered what he should do. To burst right in on Manley would be too obvious. But he thought—perhaps Manley needs me. Or was that only what he wanted to think?

He was still trying to make up his mind when Manley came in. Manley looked drunk again. He had this strange ability to go in and out of sober focus. It must have been a terrible effort to hold himself in for Douglas; now he was going slack.

"Suppose you heard the whole bloody business?"

Shep nodded.

"Sorry you had to hear that. 'Pologize."

Shep heard himself muttering broken, meaningless assurances. Manley slumped to a bowed sitting position on the bed. "Lad," he said almost inaudibly, "if you'll fetch me a drink I'll give you half my kingdom."

When Shep brought it to him, Manley's hand was shaking so badly that the top of the highball slurped over onto his sleeve. "Not the drinking," he was careful to explain. "Just nerves.

Damned sugar balance all shot." He tried to rise above it. "I'm quivering inside like a Model T."

"That's an awful lot to take."

"My fault. Poor kid's confused. Don't blame 'im. We've led him a merry chase. Jere and I both. He's just bouncing all his resentment off me."

"But, hell, he's old enough to know."

The corners of Manley's mouth began to turn up in an effort to smile that made him look even sadder. "You've probably forgotten already. An adolescent's the most conservative citizen there is. Wants everything to stay just as he finds it. Sixteen-year-old's a moralist. When he says, Mama Love Papa he isn't kidding. Sixteen-year-old doesn't give a damn if Papa's books are translated in fifteen languages. I know what's eating Douglas. An' the hell of it is it's too late to do anything about it."

"I'll swap fathers with him any day," Shep said. "You're—I can't exactly explain what I mean. My old man flies off the handle and thinks with his blood pressure."

It was strange to be considered anybody's father, Manley thought. He never stepped up to a full-length mirror without being a little shocked at the middle-aged image. He could not shake the obsession that middle age had ambushed him unfairly. Nearly all of his life he had been such a very young man, the very model of a very successful very young man. Now suddenly here he was, middle aged, old enough to be a young man's father. But inside he wasn't ready. Inside, he hadn't done enough growing up. Oh, he would have to hurry, hurry to catch up with himself.

"Gee whiz," Shep said, "almost forgot. We have to see Milgrim in fifteen minutes."

Manley shook his head. "This morning I wouldn't keep an appointment with—with Louie B. Mayer."

"Jesus, we can't stand Milgrim up, can we, Manley?"

"If that's a question—yes, we can. Get him on the phone. Tell him we worked all night and—wait a minute, do it myself." It suddenly had become a question of honor with him. He was always having to prove to himself that he was not a timid man. Since when did he have to hide behind a boy? Who did Milgrim think he was, pushing him around as if he were a beginner like Stearns? He would set Milgrim straight, in a quiet, dignified way. "The more you push *them* around, the more respect they have for you—I know how they *think*," Manley said to Shep while he was getting Milgrim on the phone.

But when he talked to Milgrim—Shep noticed and Manley was a little disgusted by it himself—the independence he had meant to assert was diluted by a self-protective sense of caution that was just this side of unctuousness.

"Victor, if you don't mind I'd like to duck the conference this morning . . . You know, to be perfectly frank, conferences aren't my metier. I'm a writing man, Victor, guess you know that . . . Yes, yes, we've been working" (here self-contempt set in as he heard himself sinking into the great mass of screen writers alibiing, fawning, selling) "all night—we've got an outline on paper . . ."

What was meant to be a pause became extended silence. Milgrim was doing the talking. Shep saw Manley close his eyes. Shep could hear the loud, positive voice of Milgrim on the other end. To the young man it was a charade of injustice, that Manley Halliday should have to sit there and take it from Victor Milgrim.

Suddenly he heard Manley say, "Victor, I've always been a man of my word. I'll be on that train this afternoon if you insist. But I wish you'd let me wait here for you. Shep and I are working very well together now. I'm sure he can fill me . . ."

Then Milgrim took over again. Occasionally Manley would attempt to break in and when he did so he sounded half exasperated, half intimidated: "Yes, it's not that, but . . ." "Of course, Victor, of course, but I just thought I could be . . ." Finally he said, "All right, Victor, I'll be on the train. Yes, I'm feeling all right, a little weary of course, but . . ." He was interrupted again, and then he said, trying to pitch his voice smartly again, "Aye, aye sir," and hung up.

He avoided Shep's eyes. He wasn't at all sure how he was going to manage. The trip would be an ordeal and the script a terrifying chore, but there was not the slightest doubt in his mind that he would survive both and go on to the come-back novel. He was glad Shep was along though. In those dark moments when he was in danger of losing himself, Shep's admiration and knowledge of his work helped him become Manley Halliday again.

"Remember, we're in this together, baby. Don't leave me alone up there. I'm going to need plenty of moral support."

"Even a little physical support if you don't lay off the booze." Shep thought it was time to put it to him.

For a moment Shep thought Manley might lose his temper. But all he said was, "All right, I guess you can talk to me like that." He had a way of popping a cigarette up out of the pack that Shep associated with old-fashioned collegiana. God, he was old-fashioned. A fascinating relic.

"I'll tell you the truth, Shep," he said gravely. "I hadn't had a drink for nearly eight months before I took on this job. That's why it sort of knocked me off my trolley when we started on the plane. Soon as I get back I'll put myself in Dr. Rubin's hands and go into my health routine again. Now that I've started, the only way I'll ever get through the week-end is with the help of God and my friends Haig and Haig. For God's sake, stay with me, Shep. Stay with me and I think I'll be all right."

"Sure, I'll stay with you, Manley."

"Le's go over that deathless prose we wrote las' night and see how it stands up in the cold, crass light of day," Manley said. "But first le's have one little drink to two intrepid explorers on the eve of their departure for the frozen North."

They held up their glasses and touched them with the mock formality of two vodka-happy officers of the Czar.

"To us and the frozen North," Shep said. "Mush."

"Tha's what we gotta write," Manley said brightly, as if it were a joke. "Mush."

14

They were rolling northward with a trainload of houseparty girls, girls of sixteen and eighteen; here and there a sleek, smart veteran of twenty-one; girls in bright colors and bright smiles, whose perfume and laughter transformed the Pullman into an Ivy League harem, charged with the special kind of excitement that only a very young woman can feel as she looks forward to the company of a preferred young man. If all brides are beautiful, Shep found himself paraphrasing, so are all houseparty dates.

From behind the lavatory door of their drawing room, Shep heard the miserable sound for which *up-chuck* is mild onomatopoeia. A few moments later Manley appeared.

He took a quick glance out at the aisle and said, in a weak voice, "Ah, the sweet young lambs going forth to slaughter."

"Manley, are you all right?"

Manley made a drunken face of reassurance. "Stay with me, baby, just stay with me."

From the baggy pocket of his shapeless suit, Manley produced a bottle of gin, almost half of which was already consumed. "Have a drink, kiddo."

"Where in hell did you pick *that* up?"

"Old pro'bition training. When in doubt, ask the bellboy."

"But wasn't I with you all the time?"

Manley put his finger to his lips roguishly. "P'fessional secret."

Victor Milgrim appeared in the entrance. He was wearing one of the soft brown tweeds he had bought in London the previous fall. He brought a fine, tangy scent of expensive cologne into the stale little room. As an apparent concession to the collegiate atmosphere he had given up his cigars for a straight richly grained Dunhill. He was all aglow with self-conscious good taste and self-satisfaction. The perfection of his dress and his toilet made Shep feel scaly and dissolute.

"Aren't these girls terrific!" Milgrim said. "Such youth. Such freshness. It's a tonic. Now don't you see, Manley, why I insisted on your coming along?"

Manley looked at him expressionlessly. A few drops of the vomit had stained his lapel. "I've seen prom trotters before. Wrote a story called 'Prom Trotter,' long, long ago. Las' word on the subject. You pro'ly never read it."

Milgrim's eyes went sharp and cold. But his voice was still respectful. "You and I are old codgers, Manley. These girls are a —a new race. No more gin and sex. These girls are healthy, realists, future mothers . . ."

"Crap," Manley said under his breath. Shep did not like the look in Manley's eyes.

"Our picture has to give the audience the same feeling we get as we walk through these aisles, the same lift, the same sense of . . ." Milgrim's eloquence outran his vocabulary.

". . . of cute little tits," Manley said. "Why don't you say what you mean, Victor?"

"You woke up on the wrong side of the bed this morning," Milgrim said. Into his face came a look that was dark and threatening. "Or maybe you didn't wake up on any side."

It was a little pathetic, Shep thought, the way Manley drew himself erect, drew his dignity around him like a tattered coat.

"Victor, we might as well have this out right now. I am not used to being talked to as if I were"—(the pause, a beat too long, weakened the effect Manley was trying for) "some frightened little screenwriter."

"Why, Manley, where's your sense of humor?" Milgrim gave a little ground.

"My sense of humor lives its own life," Manley said. "Right now it's pro'ly on another train, going west."

"Come on," Milgrim said, "walk through the cars with me. It'll do you good. I want you to breathe in the atmosphere—it's terrific atmosphere!"

Manley turned to Shep. "Go with the man. Breathe in some of that terrific atmosphere for me. You've got stronger lungs." He turned to Milgrim cunningly. "You know, Victor, we had trains in my houseparty days too. And the female anatomy hasn't changed appreciably."

"Seems to me a writer—an author—would want to keep up to date."

"Victor, believe me," Manley said persuasively. "Maybe their figures have changed a little. And their clothes. Maybe they call a girl on the make a fast-worker instead of a speed. Or maybe they even have a new word for it I haven't picked up yet. But underneath the new styles and the new expressions, they're still the same little savages they were in my time."

"All right, Manley," Milgrim conceded, "we'll see you later."

"At your service, sir," Manley said. The bow was more mocking now. "And remember, Victor, don't go around pinching their little bottoms. This isn't Hollywood."

Milgrim frowned and went out. As Shep started to follow, Manley said, "Don't let him intimidate you. Stay here and talk to me."

"One of us better keep him happy," Shep said.

"When I want to go through a train brushing up against nice little sixteen-year-olds, I'll do it," Manley said. "But I'll be damned if I call it research."

"Be back in a little while. Now take it easy."

"Don't worry, baby. I won't disgrace us."

In the corridor outside the drawing room, Milgrim looked around carefully and then said suddenly, "Has Manley been drinking?"

Shep fought back an hysterical impulse to laugh. "Oh, we've had a few highballs—nothing to speak of." He kept his eyes away from Milgrim because as a liar he was hopelessly without talent.

"His agent said Manley had given him his word of honor that he was permanently on the wagon."

"We've been pushing pretty hard, Mr. Milgrim. An occasional drink . . ."

"I didn't want to hire him because I was afraid of this damned drinking," Milgrim said. "I suppose you know he's a post-graduate dipso. They say one drink and he's off for months."

Shep thought of Sara's champagne and the way he had urged Manley to that first ceremonial drink. "Hell, someone might have warned me."

"I thought everybody knew," Milgrim said. "For God's sake, don't let him drink any more."

"Christ, I'm not a male nurse."

"But you seem to be hitting it off. I know he resents me. Some sophomoric idea of his—a fix in his mind of the ignoramus producer. I could fire him right now and get Ben Hecht to jump in and save it—but I'd rather not. That would finish him in Hollywood. And I know he needs the money."

"I'll do what I can," Shep said, thinking: This is more than just another location trip for Victor Milgrim. He's moving up into the Ivy League. Maybe he's bucking for an honorary degree. Manley Halliday, one of the few living American authors whose works are recognized by English professors, is the calling card.

"Shortly after we arrive," Milgrim said, "the English Department is giving a reception for Manley. I want you to make it your job to see that he's dressed and shaved and coherent."

"There'll be an extra charge for valet service." Shep was tired enough to speak his mind.

"Save your humor for the script. I know how much work you've done so far. I'd fire you right now if I didn't think you had some influence with Manley."

Shep wanted to talk up—a fighting speech about a man's pride and the degradation of the marketplace. But he thought of Sara, and of his ambition to do *Informers* and *Deeds*. And then there was Manley. On the flight east he had been fascinated by the disorder of Manley's life and mind. But now he had begun to sense the dim outlines of a prolonged struggle. What sense was there in standing up to Victor Milgrim if that only further undermined the cause of Manley Halliday?

So a bitter "Thanks" was all he said.

Milgrim led him down the aisle. "Take a good look at them, listen to them. Get the *feel* of them."

Shep was following him automatically. There were girls stretched out across Pullman seats, girls giggling together, girls playing cards, girls chattering. There was a girl waxing skis, a girl combing and combing her hair, a girl knitting, a girl reading *Screen Romance*. There was even a girl reading Rainer Maria Rilke. There was a sixteen-year-old siren with honey-colored hair who eyed them. There was a tall, dark girl who looked Spanish and had marvelous breasts. But at this moment nothing was vivid but the strained, wretched face of Manley Halliday hanging over the little toilet in the drawing room.

"Look—over there in the brown suit—if she isn't a young Carole Lombard!"

Milgrim went through the Pullman making snap-judgment discoveries.

"Excuse me, miss. Allow me to introduce myself. Victor Milgrim." When the name didn't take as quickly as he had hoped, he added, "Victor Milgrim, of World-Wide."

"Glad to meet you," the youngster said. "I'm Margie Hart of Minsky's."

Milgrim laughed uncomfortably. "We'll be making some shots at the Mardi Gras and I'd like to spot you in a couple. It would be a sort of screen test."

"You mean you want little me for Hollywood?" the girl said.

"If you photograph—and I certainly think you should."

She struck a mock glamour pose. Milgrim had picked himself a sharp one. "Do my eyes sparkle too much for pictures?"

"Seriously, young lady, I wouldn't have taken the trouble to come over if I didn't think you had possibilities."

"Seriously, mister, I'm a freshman at Barnard, my old man's on the faculty there, and he'd kick my derrière from here to Hoboken if I took you seriously."

Milgrim smiled defensively, asked her to call him at Webster Inn if she changed her mind, and, relatively undaunted, went on down the aisle. "See what I mean?" he told Shep. "Fresh personalities. Fresh dialogue. Full of that new spirit."

In the next car Victor Milgrim discovered a young Kay Francis, a young Katharine Hepburn and a young Irene Dunne. There was even a demure child from Miss Wadleigh's who impressed him as a young Janet Gaynor.

Shep passed a nondescript girl who might have been anybody and said, "Look. A young Marie Dressler."

Milgrim looked reproachful. Then he saw a girl who was really startling, with soft yellow hair, peach complexion and enormous blue eyes. "A young—a young Dolores Costello!"

Milgrim gasped. When he introduced himself she was all dim-
ples and Southern accent and "Ah think that would be adoh-
rable." She turned out to be a professional model from Conover's
who had come up from Savannah to go on the stage. Her name
was Savannah Castle. Milgrim told her to look him up at Webster Inn. She would simply *adohre* to. Milgrim felt better when
he moved on. This was more like home. "See what I mean—a
fresh face!" Shep wondered how Milgrim could reconcile his
quest for freshness with his search for younger carbon copies of
established stars. But he went along in silence.

"This is why we should all get out of Hollywood every so
often," Milgrim said. "No matter how creative we are, we need
to meet new people, new ideas—there's nothing like outside
stimulation."

Thus Victor Milgrim walked from one end of the train to the
other, eyeing the girls and feeling better and better.

On the way back he smiled and bowed to Savannah. Her little
pink hand fluttered up to her hard, magnificent mouth in demure recognition.

"There's a great little bet," Milgrim said. "I wonder if our
publicity man could fix it for her to be Queen of the Mardi Gras.
Make a nice tie-in for the picture."

Back at their drawing room at last, Milgrim said, "Shep, you
know a little bit about this business. We'll have a camera crew
waiting for us in the morning. You've got to give them some
idea where the main scenes are going to be played so they can
pick up their backgrounds for the transparencies. You'd better
see to it that Manley gets on the ball. You can use Peggy if you
want to dictate tonight."

"We hired a secretary from the hotel. She's on the train somewhere."

That had been a last-minute whim of Manley's, to bring Miss
Waddell along. Miss Waddell was a large, eager woman in her
late forties who had not been out of New York since she had arrived there, for some reason long since forgotten, from Kansas
City twenty-seven years before. Because she was a home-town
girl and because he sensed that this would be the most exciting
thing that had happened to her since a man followed her

through lower Central Park in the Spring of Twenty-six, Manley had insisted that she accompany them.

"I don't care how you do it, just so long you two geniuses come up with a workable line by the time we get in," Milgrim said.

When he found their drawing room empty, Shep was mildly alarmed. Searching through the adjoining car, he thought he recognized Manley's voice behind the dark-green curtain of the men's room. Inside, surrounded by smoke and a group of natty, good-looking, junior executive types, Webster men, vintage thirty-five, -six and -seven, there he was, passing around the last of the gin.

Shep recognized Gene Hoffman, a big, blond boy who had won his block W in football three successive years without ever making first-string. Gene had been one of those aberrant athletes with a restless, second-rate mind, who begins to have a vague awareness of the intellectual life of the college. In Shep's class, Gene had been elected president of the Socrates Society. As a result Gene had passed from the halls of Webster to his bond salesmanship with a swollen idea of his intellectuality. Four years beyond the academic life, he still took himself seriously.

Shep shook hands with Hoffman, who had put on twenty-five pounds since they had last seen each other at Commencement. After the stylized classmate repartee, Hoffman said, "This joker is trying to tell us he's Manley Halliday."

Hoffman's chums, going back for Mardi Gras in holiday spirits, would have laughed if they had been a little more certain who Manley Halliday was.

Manley glared at Hoffman. "Wha' I have t' do t' convince you I'm Manley Halliday—write you a goddam novel while you wait?"

Hoffman winked to the boys superiorly. "Look, old man, I saw Manley Halliday once. He spoke to the Socrates Society."

"Nnn, nnn, not this baby. Never believed in lecturing. 'specially to college students. Sure it wasn't William Lyon Phelps?"

"No, I don't think so," Hoffman said, but he was less sure now. He had lost touch with these things since going downtown.

206

"I still think it was Halliday," Hoffman said.

"No, Gene, it was John V. A. Weaver," Shep said.

"Weaver, that's right!" Hoffman said. "What got me mixed up was you both used to write for *College Humor*."

One of Halliday's serials and a few of his stories had run in *College Humor,* a lot of quick work to pay the bills.

Manley took the bottle back and tipped it to his lips. "Hoffman, bet I c'n tell you the las' book you finished."

"Mind reader, huh?" Hoffman laughed. "Do you want a blindfold, or are you blind enough without it?"

"The Yearling," Manley said.

"By God, what've you got in that gin—you're right!" Hoffman said.

"And the book you're reading now—" Manley thought a moment "—*Rebecca.*"

"Little man, you win the daily double," Hoffman said.

"I know everything about you—your reading habits, your sex habits, your mental capacities, the extent and the limits of your ambition," Manley said.

"My, my, you should get yourself a job in a 42nd Street Flea Circus telling fortunes."

It bothered Shep that Hoffman confused what Manley was saying with the way he looked. "Come on, Manley, let's go back to our room."

"No kidding, Shep, you mean this is really Manley *The Night's High Noon* Halliday?" Under the surface of Hoffman's contempt was a worn lining of admiration.

"No—'low me t' introduce myself," Manley said. "Zane Grey's the name. An' this is Boola-boola, my Tahitian baitboy."

Hoffman laughed, but not with Manley. "He's like one of the screwball characters in his own books," he said.

"How would you know?" Manley said.

"Come on, Manley, let's go," Shep begged.

"What'sa hurry?" Manley said. "In'eresting case, Hoffman. Gets a liberal arts education t' fit him for business that's as far removed 's possible from liberals an' art."

"Look who's talking, a fugitive from the Twenties," Hoffman sneered. "You jokers went off on one long tear and left us to pay the check. And you don't seem to know yet that the party's over."

"How you've suffered!" Manley said. "Bet the only time you've worked up a sweat since college is when your boss takes you to the Racquet Club to play handball with you—and you let him win. And I bet the boss has a daughter or a niece who goes for good-looking husky blonds who used to play Ivy League football. And one of these days you'll be a junior partner. And you'll be faithful to your wife for a little while . . ."

"Ha ha ha," Hoffman said, not liking it at all. "With a plot like that you ought to be able to buy yourself a clean suit."

"Use t' have fifty suits," Manley said. "Lot o' damn foolishness. Use t' think appearance was important."

"I can see you've reversed yourself on that one, pal," Hoffman said, winking at the chums and directing their laughter at the stained, baggy suit.

"Better'n buying clothes y'can't really afford," Manley said. "I know ya, Hoffman. Y'haven't changed. Pro'ly don't get over five hundred a month."

"So this is the great Halliday. What'd they call you—the spokesman for your generation? Boy, your generation ought to buy you back and keep you under cover."

Hoffman's two hundred and thirty pounds draped in an immaculate pin stripe seemed to be crushing down on Halliday.

"All right, Gene, lay off," Shep said.

"Who the hell are you, his bodyguard?"

Shep would have to spot him fifty pounds but there was a lot of fat on Hoffman. "Yeah," he said. "As of right now I am."

"I've heard about you Hollywood tomboys," Hoffman said, very ready.

"Don't need anybody t' fight my battles," Manley said. "Know how much I make, Hoffman? Two thousan' a week. Three hundred 'an' thirty three dollars a day . . ."

Shep felt painfully embarrassed, but Manley was insulated behind a child's pride. "Even Shep makes twice as much as you do. An' I—did I tell ya how much I make—two thousan' dollars a week."

The prolonged sleeplessness and drinking seemed to have

shrunken him. He looked very small and emaciated as he sat there among the young grads in the men's room holding up his little boasts like half-inflated balloons.

"Oh, sure, you Hollywood bigshots really rake in the jack," Hoffman said. "Tell me, do all great authors go to Hollywood when they die?"

Manley rose, his small hands clenched, his face bloodless and taut. "Why, you young snotnose! Nobody c'n say that to me. Don' care how big he is . . ."

"Put your hands down, Halliday," Hoffman said, "or I'll swat you like a gnat."

There was a terrible expression on Manley's face. "Come on, you sonofabitch. Not afraid o' you. Use 't' hold my own with Freddy Welsh."

"Who the hell was he?"

The insult to Freddy Welsh drove Manley to violence. He threw a wild punch that Hoffman easily avoided. "Don't get me mad," Hoffman warned. Shep felt a nightmare closing in like an ether cone over his face. He forced himself between them and grabbed Hoffman's arms. "Go on, beat it, Gene. Leave him alone, for Chris'sake."

Manley was still struggling to get at Hoffman. "Manley, you take it easy too," Shep said. With his body checking Hoffman, he turned to pin Manley's arms.

"Leggo, I'll box his ears off," Manley insisted.

"The great Manley Halliday," Hoffman sneered. "Stinkin' as a skunk and twice as drunk."

"Disappear, Gene," Shep said.

"All right, I'll leave you two geniuses to earn your hundred dollars a minute," Hoffman said.

Manley sank down against the leather seat. His head was heavy. His chin came to rest on his chest. In the silence they could hear the idiotic rhythm of the spinning wheels and the flirtatious laughter of young men and women passing in the corridor.

"Manley, I'm no Freddy Welsh, but I'm going to start getting tough."

"Don't lash me, baby. I feel lousy enough."

"It's your own goddam fault."

"Don't worry. Not blaming you. Not blaming anybody. All my fault. All the things 'at happened, my fault. Pick people who destroy you—it's second degree self-destruction."

"Manley, listen to me. I've got to score on this job. I can't slide by on a famous name. Keep on like this and we'll both get the heaveroo."

"Heaveroo? Never heard o' that word. You make it up? 'r is it generic?"

"Manley, forget all that. Forget everything but *Love on Ice*. You've got to concentrate. Quit drinking, quit *thinking,* and concentrate."

"All right. All right, Shep. All right. All right, baby. All right . . ."

"How about some coffee?"

"All right."

"A little food with it?"

Manley shook his head. "No food—stomach feel lousy." His head rolled on his chest. "I'll be thinkin' 'bout the story." He shut his eyes and seemed to drift off.

Shep touched his shoulder. "Manley, you can't sleep here. If you want to sleep, let's go back to the . . ."

Manley sat upright. "Sleep? Who wants t' sleep? Let's work. Let's get the damn story straightened out. Where's Miss Waddell? Le's dictate to Miss Waddell."

"Okay, I'll look for her. Will you meet me back at the drawing room?"

"Shsure."

Miss Waddell wasn't in her seat or in the diner and Shep was afraid to search further for fear of leaving Manley alone too long. Manley wasn't in the drawing room when Shep returned. Shep found him still in the men's room, half sitting, half lying on the long leather seat, his eyes closed, his mouth open, breathing heavily. Shep wasn't sure whether to wake him and get him back to the drawing room or to let him enjoy the first nap he had had since leaving Hollywood. He stood over Manley, staring down into his face.

Manley's voice startled him. "All righ', meeting 'll come to order." Manley still hadn't opened his eyes. "You're suppose' t' be a clever young man. Why don' you come up with a brigh' idea?"

"I do have one new notion I thought I might try on you. Manley, are you listening?"

"Shsure, shsure, I'm all ears," Manley said, suddenly smiling.

"It's just a stab in the dark but it might work. What if the boy, Joe, stops near one of those schools where the girls are supposed to go out and get practical training every so often. You know, Antioch, or Bennington. So the waitress in the diner, Gretchen, or Diane, is really the daughter of the President of Webster. Joe goes for her and tells her all about Webster, thinking he's impressing her with being a college man. She plays dumb, laying it on pretty thick—says she's always hoped that some day she'd meet a Webster man, she's heard so much about the Mardi Gras. So Joe winds up asking her to the Mardi Gras and when he gets back to school he tells his fraternity brothers about it. He's playing it strictly for kicks—as a kind of practical joke on the typical upper-class chicks who always show up for Mardi Gras. He even thinks he can fix it to run her in as Queen. Manley, are you listening? I think maybe this'll work. Now, when Gretchen, or Diane, gets to Webster, the first thing she does is . . ."

"Wait. Got a better idea." Manley's eyes were half closed and his head still lay against the back of the seat; the beginnings of a smile pulled at the corners of his mouth. " 'Stead of the President having one beautiful daughter, le's give him twelve. That way Victor can use all the girls he'd like to sign up on the train. The Varsity Eleven gets the romantic idea of marrying all the President's daughters en bloc. The Varsity men can't count so well. They're in on scholarships. When someone, pro'ly a mathematics prof, points out to them that they're one short, they send for the water boy. Mickey Rooney 'd be terrific casting. But terrific. Now, the complication. Can't have a good movie without the complication. Whatta ya call it—the weenie? Okay, here's your weenie. If the Home Team doesn't win the Big Game the President 'll have to cut the players' salaries and they won't be able to afford to marry his daughters. In the last minute of the game, score sixty-nine t' sixty-three against 'em, one of the Eleven 's carried out. Before Mickey Rooney c'n get off the field, play's resumed. When the ball's kicked off it lands right in Mickey's pail. While everyone's hunting for the ball he calmly walks down the field with his pail an' scores the winning touchdown. Now, here's ya topper, an' it's a real topperoo. Webster wins seventy t' sixty-nine an' not only do all the players get bonuses and marry the twelve daughters but the President resigns in favor of Mickey an' we're right into our sequel, Mickey Rooney in *The Sexy Prexy*."

Manley opened his eyes and chuckled. "In the whole, I mean old days Ben Turpin would 've been great for the College President. Or Chester Conklin."

"Who'll play the twelve daughters?"

"Anita Louise," Manley said.

Feeling a little guilty for encouraging him, as with a disobedient child who draws attention from his own misdeeds by being consciously, precociously "cute," Shep had to laugh.

"Maybe we could get Chaplin for the President. Always wanted t' write something for Chaplin. Anita Louise would've made Charlie an ideal dream girl. I mean a dream ideal girl. Edna Purviance. Virginia Cherrill. Know the secret of Charlie? Not a man at all. Sneaks up in attic, puts on father's clothes, pants too big, shoes too big, wears all kinds of different clothes, together, anything he happens to find lying around. Then he pretends he's grown up. But it's all a dream. Girls he falls in love with, 'thereal, too beautiful, 'way little boys fall in love with grown-up women from a distance. Dances with 'em, makes love to 'em, gives 'em won'erful presents, all in a dream. 'Member *City Lights*. An' that face on Charlie. From ridic'lous t' sublime no cliché for Charlie. Real art, real tragedy, only tragedy I ever saw in the movies. That face on Charlie. The pain. I c'n see it right now. All his pictures, same idea, the dream's a beautiful balloon, a kid's balloon an' reality's a sharp point on a fence. The balloon drifts over into the forbidden garden, hits the point 'n bursts—'way all of us wake up right back where we were. Chaplin's the only one saw the movie as the bes' medium in the worl' for dreams, the child being the father, the tramp being the millionaire, the homely little bum being the elegant Don Juan. Jere 'n I were Chaplin fans in Paris right after the war.

Saw he was the mos' serious way back when he was playing slapstick. 'Member one picture little one-reeler, can't even 'member the name of it. Charlie's a drunk being dragged along, grabs a bush as he struggles, finds a daisy in his hand. Daisy changes mood entirely. Becomes a poet, a dreamer, an aesthete. So convincing it looks like impro—improvisation an' when you think of Charlie as a child not even unrealistic, you know the way a little boy sees a toy boat an' becomes a boat captain, picks up a gun an' goes right into character of a soldier. See what I mean? Don't think of Charlie as an adult acting like a child but as a child acting like a grownup. Like *The Gold Rush*. Jere 'n I saw it five times, wrote a 'preciation of it for *Vanity Fair*. If movies didn't die so fast it'd be considered a permanent classic like *Hamlet* or *Cyrano*. Funny as hell on the surface and full of inner meanings an' the idea, the *Gold Rush,* just when the whole country was rushing for gold. Money crazy. One of the signs of an artist is his sense of contemporaneity—didn't say it right, you know what I mean—without going opportunist. Like my books. Lot of writers tried to cap'alize on the era. You know, cheap books about jazz babies n' bootleggers. Some of 'em got serious review in their time. My books were lit up with the light of our time because that wasn't what I was trying to do. I mean not consciously but—how the hell did I get talking about myself? Thought I was talking about Charlie. I'm no analyst, but I could analyze Chaplin from his comedies—that's how true they are. No good work of art I mean there's no good work worthwhile work of art without the artist's exposing himself. You 'n I f'r'instance, *Love on Ice* isn't us, that's why it's so hard to concentrate, easier to write something good than something like that. Only two kinds of writing come easy, when you're a real writer 'xpressing yourself or when you're a natural hack an' haven't got any self to 'xpress." He paused finally. "Damn. Can't stay on the subject. Whatsa matter with me? Charlie Chaplin. Notice how there's always a great big brute of a man pushing little Charlie around—prospector in *Gold Rush*, millionaire in *City Lights,* employer in *Modern Times,* always the same father image, switching suddenly from love to hatred of Charlie like the millionaire picks him up when he's drunk

213

takes him home lovingly tucks him in, then sobers up in the morning an' throws him out. Conflict with the father, whether Charlie sees it or not. All Charlie's pictures full of it. Psychiatrist c'd do a helluva book on Charlie's movies. Thought of it myself. Another of the things I left undone but I was too much of a layman even though I read a lot about it trying to figure out Jere. Read so much about it it was no use being analyzed. Just enough knowledge to make a bum patient an' an'—" he faltered —"what'm I talking about . . . ?"

"The Chaplin movies . . ."

" . . . don't switch from comedy to tragedy. No phony, mechanical change o' pace. The funniest parts, the parts where you laugh the loudest, are tragic. That's where the genius comes in. . ."

"But isn't there more to Chaplin than a comic interpretation of the Oedipus Complex?" Shep interrupted. "Now in *Modern Times*—"

Seeing that Manley was only coherent enough to make his own kind of sense but not equal to the greater effort of listening, Shep stopped abruptly.

And Manley went on talking, like a man hypnotized, in an automatic stream: "Jere and I talked to Charlie when we were out there about writing a story for him. It was an idea Jere had. She wanted me to write it with her. Almost did it. Charlie was interested for a while. Hollywood was—a lot crazier then than it is now—more of a factory town now. But in those days it was —it had the quality of a vulgar fairy land. There were wonderful parties that lasted for days and there was a nice sense of sin that's only found in worlds of true innocence. The girls were —Lord—they were beautiful and the leading men looked the way leading men are supposed to look in a salesgirl's dream. Tall dark and handsome and completely unreal. When you have men playing leads, even becoming stars, who aren't conventionally dreamily handsome, it means the world's becoming more realistic, less romantic. We were romantic as all hell. Even though we thought of ourselves as terribly realistic. Oh, we knew the facts of life. We called a spade a spade. We weren't a-Freud

214

of anything, Jere said once. It was a shameful pun but it made a kind of sense . . ."

Manley rubbed both hands up and down his face from his hairline to his mouth as if he were washing. "Oh, hell, What am I—talking about?"

Shep wasn't sure whether to say Jere or The Twenties or Chaplin or Hollywood or For Christ sake go to bed. Was Manley Halliday (the ominous way Milgrim had said it) a dipsomaniac? Shep had known some heavy drinkers but he realized that dipsomania was still an abstract apprehension. What did dipsomaniacs do? Shep had nervous visions of urinating in public places, of committing rape, of stabbing friends with bread knives, of falling off trains, of challenging a dozen stevedores to suicidal combat; an alcoholic maniac. But Manley, at least now that Hoffman was gone, not only showed no signs of violence, but actually seemed to grow more gentle, and in some ways more sensible, than he had been at the beginning, despite the rambling and the thickening tongue and the heavy lids.

Shep lit his pipe and settled down to listen, resignedly at first, but sympathetically and then with increasing fascination as Manley Halliday, a ghost figure on a phantom train, went back and back and back in restless search of Manley Halliday.

We came out for the opening of *High Noon* at Grauman's. Mona Moray—she played Lenore—let us use that fantastic castle of hers in Beverly Hills. We thought it was going to be awful and that we'd only stay a week, but scads of New York friends had come out and we found a lot of the Hollywood people were fun, in a mad way, like Mickey Neilan and Pringie, Aileen Pringle.

We never thought we'd stay so long. We were really on our way to Hawaii—some friends of ours who had a wonderful house there were expecting us. It was a time when everyone was pressing wonderful houses on us. 'I have a perfectly marvelous house for you to write in,' they'd say. Of course no one needs marvelous houses to write in. I still knew that much. All you needed was one room. But somehow the next house always beckoned.

Everybody was waiting for my next book then. My publishers had announced it two years before, when *High Noon* was still selling. And each time we settled somewhere I found a new excuse for not writing it. A good excuse. There were too many people around. And I wanted to go back and take another look at America, at the Kansas City I was trying to write about (it was one of those books I never finished). And there were magazine stories to write—it was such an easy way to make twenty-five hundred dollars—and we were always short. The year I made sixty thousand, I had to borrow from my publisher. One time when we were very broke and wanted to charter a yacht to cruise the islands of the Mediterranean I locked myself in for a week and wrote four short stories and got ten thousand dollars. They were good stories too. I couldn't do anything badly then. It took me years ot reach the point where I could do things badly.

There were other reasons, of course. There is never a simple reason for not writing a book or not writing your best. It's fear, it's greed, it's sloth—I suppose I suffered from all of these. It was Jere, too. Oh, we were in love, if the word had any shred of meaning left in 1927. In her lean, sharp-boned, restless way she was still more exciting for me than all the Billie Doves, Mary Astors, Corinne Griffiths, and they were lovely women. It wasn't beauty with Jere, though she had some of that. She had a way of saying things, of wearing clothes, of doing things, aquaplaning, gambling, talking French or Spanish or Italian without an accent; she was a marvelous mimic—once she had done Helen Morgan we could never take Helen seriously again; she could walk on her hands, she could fly a plane, until I made her quit, thinking a high-strung girl like her didn't belong in the air; she might have made a first-rate Symbolist poet if she had had any discipline or any confidence. It was strange that a girl as handsome as Jere, who could do so many things, should have such a confidence deficiency.

She could do things and she was fine to look at and I loved her and we had too much money and needed more, and all the time, she was a failure and—though it would have seemed preposterous to me then—I was failing too.

I never knew exactly when Jere began to fail. At first I was afraid it was some flaw in me, but I learned it was earlier and earlier, something to do with motherlessness and paternal neglect.

It was all moonlight and champagne at first, like being on a long date, or like those slick stories of gay crossings and Riviera nights. I wrote some of them myself, God help me. When we were good we were very very peaches-and-creamy head-in-the-clouds castle-in-the-sky good the way our public believed us and wanted us to be. And when we were bad we were horrid to each other, though that was our secret for a long time. Whenever we were out we were those amusing Hallidays; they're so charming, so witty, so perfect together, and they *adore* each other like a couple of kids, and after all their Success—we must ask them for dinner, for the week-end, for the winter. Here we go 'round the prickly pear, the prickly pear, the prickly pear, here we go 'round the prickly pear at five o'clock in the morning . . .

He remembered the afternoon they went to a Dadaist performance, where Tristan Tzara read aloud from a newspaper while an electric bell sounded so clangorously he could not be heard. That same afternoon Picabia had drawn a picture on a blackboard and then, two hours later, erased it, to demonstrate the creative process negated and defied. Manley, who wrote grammatically, with precise syntax and with periods and even semicolons and whose influences were largely Edith Wharton and Henry James, had been appalled at what he called "artistic hooliganism."

Jere had not agreed with all of it—"a good Dadaist shouldn't agree with anything," she had explained. But she did believe in the seriousness of Tzara's motives and in the possibility that they were groping toward a legitimate art form.

Manley had become quite violent about it. Literature was communication. The masters dealt with character and ideas, not with an exhibitionistic play on words.

"But this century is a turmoil," Jere had tried to explain. "It needs a new form to express itself. Maybe bells and reading aloud, maybe something no one has thought of yet." She was quite sure Rimbaud would have been a Dadaist. "He was trying to tear everything down—only he didn't go as far."

"Oh, I'm sick of Rimbaud! Do we have to *live* with Rimbaud?"

In the dark he heard Jere crying.

"Jere. Jere darling. Please."

No answer. The silence was a warm pillow blotting up mysterious tears.

At three-forty-five in the morning, by the luminous clock, he heard her moving near him.

"Jere?"

"Yes, pet."

"What are you doing?"

"This."

"Ah . . . ah . . ."

A long time passed too quickly.

. . . In Nineteen twenty.

He remembered the long white yacht cradling in the moonlight on Alcudia Bay. The sky was paling. Sunrise would be soon. It was that delicate moment just before. It had been a good evening, with champagne and native Majorcan musicians who had rowed out from the island. Their hosts, Freddie and Gilly Patterson, very rich and rather nice, had finally given in to sleep. So had Cholly Prince, the popular composer, and Bootsie, the strange English girl, who had confessed that she was in love with both of them, and had meant it in a way that had frightened them. Sleep had caught up with Whitings, who were such good sports, and with the rest of the motley, amiable crowd. The Pattersons could have been more select, but they liked people with a little added seasoning, writers, theatrical folk, almost any celebrities as long as they were "regular," which, to the Pattersons, meant being just a bit irregular. Anyway, they were all sleeping now. At last the ship lay silent. From her bunk Jere whispered, "Mannie, are you awake?"

"Diane, obey me."

It was their new game, ever since they read, on shipboard, that serious farce *The Sheik*.

"Take your compelling stare away from my bosom heaving under this soft silk," she answered.

"I know. I'm a brute and a beast and a devil."

He slipped out of bed. She was wearing the nightgown with the black lace top that always pleased him. "How much longer are you going to fight? Would it not be wiser after what you have seen today to recognize that I am master?"

"Are all Arabs hard like you? Has love never made you merciful?"

"Shall I make you love me? I can make women love me when I choose."

Laughing together, and warning each other to hush like prepschool roommates, they tiptoed up on deck. The Mediterranean had not yet turned the color for which it was famous; the oncoming sun had filled it with rose-water. Small dark clouds lay curled up asleep on the horizon—"like little cats," Jere had whispered.

"I love you," Manley said, as close to her as he could be. "If you weren't my wife, I'd ask you to marry me."

"Shhh, don't move for a moment," she had whispered. "I want to hear the water."

The ripplets murmured against the hull. Here the world began and here it ended, begins and ends, begins . . .

Later they dove from the bow into the clear water of the harbor. Manley watched as she poised on the edge, enjoying the clean lines of her nudity. The dive was perfect; she swam away from the boat with a strong stroke. He kept up with her for a while, with a sense of exhilaration at their being in the sea alone together at daybreak, feeling deeply involved with love and water, primary forces. But after fifty yards he began to tire. "How about turning back?" She shook her head, humorlessly, he thought, and kept on. A little farther out: "Jere, we better turn back." "You go if you want to," she said. "I'm going to see how far I can go."

"She's so damned extreme about everything," he thought as he slowly paddled his way back to the boat. In his towel robe, he watched the small dark spot moving out toward the open sea. When she was almost out of sight, a sense of panic set in. She wouldn't do that, she wouldn't—would she? A minute later he realized the dark spot was growing larger. Thank goodness she was on her way in. He held the white towel robe for her as she climbed aboard.

"I thought you were on your way back to Monaco."

"When I get started like that I feel like swimming on and on and never coming back."

"But, Jere, you were so happy a little while ago."

"Oh, Mannie, I was—satiated. That's the way I'd like to go."

"You're a crazy minx."

"Look at that fat sun. I'm glad I came back. It's going to be a beautiful day."

They sat on deck together until the sun was up, so happy with each other that they felt sorry for the people who could not be there, could not be them.

The midday heat had sent them down to their cabin for a lazy nap. Dressing for lunch and feeling logy, much worse than on no sleep at all, Manley said, "Darling, I meant to remind you, I'm afraid I wasn't careful this morning." And she said nervously, "Manley, it's a fine time to tell me—I was a little woozy from all the champagne—I didn't even bother to . . ."

"Is it too late for you to—do something?"

"Yes, damn it. Manley, that's lousy of you. You know how afraid I am of being . . ."

"Jere, let's not worry yet. It'll probably turn out all right. Why spoil the trip?"

"But I don't want a baby. I'm too young. I'm not ready. We've been so free, so lucky. A baby would make us so horribly settled. Mannie, honestly, I'd rather die than get too big in front and heavy in the rear and sit in some park knitting and gabbing to other mothers about toilet-training."

"You make it sound like an inferno."

"Well, you wouldn't want me that way either. Oh, damn it, being a woman is a bore sometimes."

When she had found herself a day overdue she had gone to bed and wept. It seemed like such a dirty trick for nature to sneak up on them that morning at the very moment when they had been indulging themselves in the most delicious, romantic fling of irresponsibility.

Two months before "her time" (why were all the terms connected with childbirth so repulsive? Jere complained), they had embarked for America (Jere discovering a patriotic devotion to the obstetrics of Manhattan). But the child had been delivered by a French ship's doctor three days out of New York. If it had been a girl, Manley had joked, they would have called it Oceana. Jere was grateful for one thing: the most ungainly period of her pregnancy had been avoided. After a while she even began to love Douglas, but she never quite forgave him, or Manley either, for pressing on her the dowdy crown of motherhood.

All the Halliday friends and followers felt the same way. The Hallidays weren't ordinary people who bothered about formulas and two-A.M. feedings and jollying infants back to sleep.

Except in rare periods of economy, when Douglas was deposited with Grandma and Grandpa in Kansas City, Douglas was entrusted to a series of French governesses who took elaborate, bilingual care of him, pampering him and practicing the delicate art of platonic seduction that lonely women of middle age know so well how to impose on bewildered and lonely little boys. To her delight Jere found that, quite the opposite from her worst narcissist fears, the existence of Douglas contributed to her perpetuity of youth. "Darling, you aren't the mother of a (3, 4, 5, 6) year-old boy! No, I refuse to believe it! With that waist—why it's positively indecent!" This sort of thing always, and Jere's eyes growing bright with triumph as she said her little joke like a child unaware of its precociousness. "Oh, up in them Kaintucky Hills we're courtin' at seven, lovin' at eight n' nursin' at nine."

But under the half-developed breast under the tight crepe-de-chine there seeped from the half-developed heart a tiny maternal leak. When they had decided to leave the child in Paris while they went to North Africa (Jere's brilliant idea to make a sentimental search for Rimbaud's trading post at Harar) she had asked Douglas if he minded their leaving him for a month or so. "Will Mademoiselle be here, Mommy?" "Yes, Duggy." "Then I don't care how long you stay."

To her surprise, she had cried all the rest of the morning. Manley hadn't taken it very seriously, even when, several times that day, she thought she had changed her mind about going. He knew her tears and her laughter, her conscience and her whims were just a little closer together than most people's. An hour out of Paris, over a second bottle of St. Julien in the dining car, they were hilariously amused by a crotchety old gentleman and his "niece" across the aisle. They improvised indelicate details of the incongruous couple's relationship in a free adaptation of Petronius Arbiter.

One afternoon in nineteen twenty-eight they woke up in Mona Moray's Hollywood-Spanish castle of stucco. Jere (whose sleep had been interrupted by a particularly painful dream: she had seen her mother, clearly, holding her in her arms and when she, the baby, had put her mouth down to nurse, the breasts had been hard and flat like a man's and she had awakened with fitful sobs) came over and sat on the edge of Manley's bed (still looking seventeen in his pajamas). "I have a wonderful idea for a party."

Manley had been lying in bed half awake, vaguely worrying about his novel. Started two years ago, put aside for short stories, started again, put aside for travel, then started a third time, he was no longer sure if it was the book he should be doing, the right follow-up for *High Noon*. Hell, he had never had that trouble in the beginning. *Friends and Foes, The Light Fantastic* and the early stories and *High Noon* had to be written. What happens, what happens? He was wondering. But almost at the same time he was computing how much money he'd have to make in the next six months to stay ahead of the game. At twenty-five hundred a story, one a month would do it, with back royalties and extras coming in—maybe a little help from the Market. His Wall Street classmates were saying Radio might go to 400. With ten grand he might make himself forty. Then a whole year off to write his book. No more of this playing around. There were so many things he wanted to try in writing, so many things he hadn't accomplished. At twenty-nine he was a contemporary success; one critic had called him a "Titan." But it hadn't really turned his head. At least not when he was in bed with himself, half asleep, half thinking, half knowing where he was and what he had to do.

Manley sat up and flipped out of his mood and into hers. "How about an Elinor Glyn party? Everyone has to come in a red fright wig and bring an original novel entitled *This Passion Called Love*."

"No, Mannie, listen—and then tell me you aren't proud you married me. Let's give a party in honor of Rin-tin-tin's stand-in."

Neither of them felt well enough for breakfast, so they got Naga, the Japanese house-boy they had inherited with the place, to bring up a batch of Martinis. Then they sat down together on the bed and planned the party in detail. They both had a way of being completely serious about frivolous things.

"We must ask Tom Mix, he's a dog's best friend," Jere said.

"Do you think we have to ask Rin-tin-tin? He'll be hurt if he isn't invited but he never has anything to say."

"He's a smart dog though. I'll bet he's got the first dollar he's ever made."

"A canny canine."

Jere made a face. "Please, Mannie, be serious. Let's see, we'll need at least one genius; I suppose two is always safer in case one of them turns out to be somebody's kid nephew from Hungary, three producers, five directors, three Germans, maybe a Swede and one American for local color, ten assorted male and female stars, all flavors, a dozen Wampas stars, including one virgin for laughs, three or four screen writers, young and bitter . . ."

Jere's laughter tinkled like the ice in the shaker she stirred. With quick dance movements she hurried to the desk, found pencil and paper and started making out the list: "Now for the odds and ends: one assistant director who thinks he's at another party, a smattering of girls who came from Council Bluffs to break into the movies, one two-thousand-a-week ex-playwright who stands around denouncing Hollywood all night and then goes off with one of the Wampas stars, and, oh yes, two fairies, no three is always more fun, and a call girl who's been given the wrong address and whom we all mistake for the countess who never shows up. Now, anyone else?"

"Don't forget the Capone trigger-man from Chicago—we need at least one underworld celebrity. And a Grand Duke and a Prince or two. We c'n probably get enough real ones but if worse comes to worst we c'n always call in a couple of extras."

"Is the Queen of Rumania in town? She's a good kid."

"That reminds me, should we get a date for the dog-of-honor?"

"Don't worry, they'll be plenty of bitches at the party, Man."

"We should send out some sort of announcement. We're giving a little party for Rin-tin-tin's stand-in—let's see, what'll we call him?"

The best Manley could think of was Sin-gin-fin.

"No, it should be a name with character, with canine *it*," Jere insisted. "Like *Strongpaws*."

"Wonderful! A little surprise party for Strongpaws, a fine artist

224

who's made good in Hollywood and still has his four feet on the ground. Formal dress. Bring your wife or any other dog you know."

Planning a party for three hundred people is like planning a modest-sized socialized state to exist for a single evening. There is the question of supply, in this case Branstatter's to cater, and Rudy, the MGM bootlegger, to provide the principal entertainment. Bartenders must be hired, and musicians, butlers, maids. There had to be two attendants to park the cars of those who came without chauffeurs, and a private detective to see that precious jewels were not removed, or precious skins molested. The days of preparation rushed by in a joyous blur.

The terraced gardens were a wonderland of Japanese lanterns, peopled by a super race of which all the women were unbelievably lovely and all the men, except for the genius, the producers and a director or two, were tall, handsome and marvelously joined with their tuxedos. Manley was proud to see that even surrounded by ladies known for their beauty, Jere held her own. Standing near a bush of flaming hibiscus, the green sequins of her gown flickering in the lantern light, the fascinating planes of her face reflecting the soft glow, looking up wittily (she *could,* he thought) into the collar-ad perfection of Wister La Salle's face (what do girls see in him? He isn't handsome; he's *pretty*), Jere appeared to Manley as a green goddess. There were girls here with the most beautiful faces in America but not even Bebe Daniels had the vitality, or was it vivacity, no, that wasn't exactly what he meant either, the inner spirit, the range from Rimbaud to McKinney's Cotton Pickers. He looked at her now as he had stood looking at her the night he had found her, falling in love again. (Damn those songs, always taking words out of lovers' mouths.) She would always be his necessity.

Everyone was laughing at their sign on a small palm-tree in the Garden: "First tree in Hollywood honored by the attention of Strongpaws." And everyone applauded as the guest of the evening made an entrance on two feet. Like his master at his side, he was in evening clothes. Jere hurried forward, curtsied

225

prettily and took his paw. "Strongpaws, I can't tell you how delighted I am to see you. I thought you were wonderful in *Each Night I Bark*. You stole the picture!"

Everyone crowded around, cocktail in hand, playing the game so well that the panting canine might have been John Gilbert or Don Alvarado.

"Is it true that you're going to sing in your next picture?" a young writer asked.

"I love you when you smile," said either Clara Bow or one of a dozen young hopefuls made up to look like her. "You have such beautiful teeth."

"What's this people are saying about your going to marry that platinum blonde?" Manley asked.

There was a laughing crowd around the outdoor bar. "I've never had so much fun in my life," announced a sixteen-year-old Wampas star in the shortest dress of all, lifting her little glass to her exquisite little mouth. "How did they ever think of anything so cute?"

"This is tame," said her escort, a director who had been around. "You should have seen the one they threw at Deauville last winter."

He whispered some of it.

"Oh!" the child exclaimed. "Why, they're really terrible!"

"*Enfants terribles,*" said the director.

"You said it!"

Mona Moray, the star of *High Noon,* described in the fan mags as the "Sophisticated Lady of the Silver Screen," too exotic to be real in gold lamé, was talking to the husband she was divorcing.

"No, darling, not half the house. The house has always been in my name, darling." She smiled up at him exactly as she had when the cameras had flashed for their celebrated rites the year before, and moved off toward the circle favoring Strongpaws.

"Darling," she cried, throwing her golden arms around the creature's neck in a convincing burlesque of a Hollywood greeting, "I think you're the most virile-looking thing in Hollywood. All that hair on your chest."

226

"Mona should know," at least half a dozen cats whispered to their partners.

Naga had decked out the buffet with true oriental attention to detail. A Hawaiian orchestra moaned softly in the background. Three hundred and fifty guests (for the party was so large that one could crash merely by arriving and going to the bar) clustered around the little rented bridge tables. Manley sat at a table with Mona, Strongpaws and his master. At the next table were Jere, Wister La Salle, Mickey Neilan and Sally O'Neill. Jere was laughing at something Wister had just said. Manley knew that sound, not her own laugh but the one she used in flirtation because she thought it was more musical. All the time he was talking to Mona he seemed to be able to see Jere without ever looking at her. To admit he was jealous was a hangover of provincialism; it disturbed him. But lately, she had been worrying him a little: her absurd notion that people only paid attention to her because she was Mrs. Manley Halliday. Increasingly, she had imagined that people were snubbing her and she was sure, from the way women smiled when they saw him approach, that he was having all kinds of mad affairs.

While Manley chuckled at something Mona was saying to Strongpaws and at the way Strongpaws (the best-behaved guest at the party) turned his head and seemed to listen, he glanced at Jere. She was raising her lovely head and emptying her wine glass. He frowned. She never used to drink champagne like this, not sipping or tasting. Especially in this last year there had been a new urgency in her drinking. He caught her eye—a furtive warning. She smiled at him, challengingly.

The dinner was climaxed with ice cream sculptured to the heroic form of Strongpaws himself, enclosed in a circle of black cherries in wine. There were calls of *speech, speech* for Strongpaws and he obliged, rising with his forefeet on the table to deliver a series of well modulated barks.

"What's Al Jolson got that he hasn't got," Jere was saying at her table, "except knees?"

"He's got better manners than my husband," Mona said.

Everyone was getting drunk. Accents slipped off. Men's hands moved with practiced stealth under gowns hospitably knee-length. Words bumped into each other and coupled like little box-cars. Mild attractions suddenly flamed to irresistible passions; minor irritations flamed to violent hatreds. Couples slipped off into dark corners of the garden. A wife said to her actor-husband "If you talk to that slut once more I'll leave you" and he took the challenge and she kept her word.

This is what Jere and Manley loved about parties; they were a quickening of life's normal pulse; they made dull people bearable and bright people brighter; they put people in a dice cage and shook them up to see what new combinations would appear. A look, a word, a right or wrong move, after the third drink, could make a friend, a career, a lover, an enemy. The sum of a party was so much more than the mere addition of all its parts. The Hallidays loved the sense of mystery, of teasing the fates and tempting the furies, of what's-going-to-happen-*tonight*.

This party was in its ascendancy. It needed only the slightest turn of the swizzle stick to start it bubbling up. The white orchestra (that alternated with the black jazz band) was all soft strings and muted saxophones. There was a spatter of applause and Manley saw that Wister La Salle was on the band stand. His sweet, almost feminine tenor fluttered gently over the garden. "Two by two, they go marching through—the Sweethearts on parade . . ."

—"Look, baby, isn't that Fay Lamphere over there?"
—"Shhhh."

The simple-sweet lyric and the simple-sweet voice crooned on.

—"He's a terrific bet for talkies."
—"I hear he's as queer as a square grape."
—"You should be that queer, honey."

Manley did not miss the way La Salle, turning his head prettily, sang directly to Jere. And he did not miss the way her eyes laughed *yes!* Damn them, he could *hear* it.

—"Listen, chump, Grange never saw the day he could play with Wilson. He just had a better publicity man."
—"Lou, you missed a fight in a million Friday night."

228

—"Don't worry, honey, one more won't hurt you. It'll make you feel better."

". . . Sweethearts on parade." The frail, simpering voice trailed off and Wister La Salle blew kisses to his audience in exchange for their applause.

The band medleyed into *Jeannine* and someone said isn't that Blanche Mehaffey over there and somebody said don't you think Dolores Del Rio is the most beautiful woman in Hollywood and someone said no, Dolores Costello and somebody said the trumpet player is cute and somebody said you and trumpet players and somebody said I heard a cute one in the commissary the other day and somebody said I *had* a cute one in my dressing room the other day and somebody said for the fifth time that evening Won't it be great when we have Smith for President so we can get liquor back and somebody said I wish they'd play *Sweethearts on Parade* and somebody said where were you, dopey, they just did and somebody said I love champagne but it doesn't love me and somebody said look at her talking babytalk why you know what we call her on the lot the human pincushion and somebody said she hasn't got any morals I mean she doesn't even try to *hide* what she does and somebody said Great Just the Greatest Thing Since the Ten Commandments and somebody said which ones God's or DeMille's and of course somebody said you better not let C.B. hear you giving him second billing and somebody said for the sixth time that evening Pardon me while I go into my strange innertube and somebody said for the sixteenth time These are Coolidge stockings They do not choose to run and somebody said how about it and somebody said we'll see and somebody said so I says look Irving and somebody said I think the old songs four or five years ago were a lot better than the ones we have now and somebody said so I speak right up I says lissen Mr. Van Berghoff maybe I'm only a lousy-five-dollar-a-day extra but I and somebody said honestly I don't hate her I'm sorry for her and somebody said O Christ everytime she has three drinks she has to get up and sing I Faw Down an' Go Boom and somebody said I wish she'd just Faw Down an' Go Boom without singing about it and somebody said take my word for it that stock won't stop till it reaches and

229

somebody said I think Manley Halliday is cuter looking than the Prince of Wales and somebody said haven't had so much fun since Marion's masquerade party and somebody said hey kids don't miss this—Jere's doing an imitation of Pavlova doing an imitation of Gilda Gray doing the shimmy on the buffet table.

> Hot ginger and dynamite
> There's nothing but that at night
> Back in Nagasaki
> Where the fellers chew tobaccy
> An' the women wicky wacky woo . . .

Mona came up with a drink for Manley while he was watching and kissed him playfully. "What's this scandalous talk I hear about your being faithful to Jere?"

"Know what I am? Inverted Vic-torian, tha's what I am."

Mona's personality, in the artificial twilight of the colored lanterns, flashed like radium. She was not so much a woman of infinite charm, Manley was thinking, as a brilliant imitation of a woman of infinite charm.

"I wish I had more chance to talk to you. I love intelligent men. I'm so fed up with these Hollywood males—all shop talk and passes."

"Mona, been thinking about you. You're complex. You're an awful little egotist 'n at the same time you're still scared, still searching—in here you know"— the thought was receding from him like the backwash of a wave and he was running down the strand to catch up with it—"you know—you haven't fulfilled yourself."

"Darling," Mona cried in triumph, throwing out her arms as she had learned to do, "you know me! You *know* me!"

> In some pagoda
> She ordered soda
> The earth shakes milk shakes
> Ten cents a piece . . .

Jere and Wister La Salle were doing a burlesque adagio.

"Your wife oughta be in pictures," Sam Loeb, a veteran producer, was telling Manley. "She's a natural little comedienne."

230

"Sir," Manley said, "I'll have you know you are speaking of the woman I love."

The dancers had drifted to the side of the pool illuminated with underwater lights of red and blue and green. A trim little Wampas star from Hollywood High School with marmalade hair who was always taking her clothes off did so again. She posed on the edge of the diving board and for a tantalizing moment Manley enjoyed the unreal sense of beauty of the scene—the fine young body offered so freely to the night, so fearlessly. The sight of her clothed only in moonlight aroused no other emotion in him than a strange pride. When she was old, forty or fifty, she would remember that she had been alive and that her youth had lit up a pool more brightly than all the colored lights.

The child with the marmalade hair, now that everyone had seen her, made her dive—up, up, with mermaid grace, ah now—too bad, a belly flop. He was angry with her, the anti-climax lending a sudden vulgarity to the performance, the mood of fantasy interrupted by the slap of bare breast and belly against the water. Jere would never have spoiled it that way. He had seen Jere diving nude from the bow of a yacht, splendidly silhouetted against the floodlight arching down and knifing through the surface so perfectly that she had seemed not at all a naked woman but some nymph of the sea returning home to the green depths.

Wonder where Jere is. Time he and Jere had a dance together. Time he and Jere . . .

"Watch this, kid, it's gonna be rich." A dapper Middle-Westerner, who passed on the screen for a European sharper, flashed his toothy trademark grin in Manley's face. Manley turned to see a stubby little man impeccably dressed with a red ribbon of honor slashed across his chest approaching the producer J. C. Coles, who had come from Eastern Europe as Jakob Kolinsky a fast twenty-five years before. Coles was fifty, bald, vain, with a hard mind in a soft body, a terror to his employees but clearly inadequate and insecure at parties that were not his own. He would never have come to such a wing-ding as this if his wife of five months, the young star Mary Gay, hadn't insisted. It was

231

a Hollywood joke that Coles adored his little Mary Gay to the point of insanity. He phoned her from the studio every hour of the day and night. He had studio detectives follow her. He adored her.

"Allow me to introduce myself. I am the Count Pierre de Corday de la Corbierre."

"I am delighted to have the honor," Coles announced with a slight accent and a sense of European deference.

The Count whipped out a jeweled cigarette case with his crest on it. He identified himself, modestly, as a cousin of the French Consul-General. Coles, preparing a French Foreign Legion story that required French Government co-operation, became even more attentive.

"Permit me to compliment you," the Count said, "on the extraordinary beauty of your wife."

Coles, tugged one way by pride and another by jealousy, muttered politely.

"Such complexion," the Count went on. "Such elegance. Such hair. Eyes that would turn the meekest of men into Casanovas . . ."

"Yes, yes, thank you," Coles tried to interrupt.

But the Count, apparently swept on by his own romantic momentum, could not be put off. "—with the figure of Diana, Salomé, shoulders as pink and full as . . ."

"Count, excuse me, but I must ask you to . . ."

"And breasts, ah, like white peonies, with their . . ."

Red-faced, dry-throated, Coles began to choke his protest.

"Mr. Coles, I am something of a sculptor," the Count persisted. "Perhaps you know my work. I have done some of the most famous beauties of England and France, in the nude, lovely creatures all—" he kissed his fingers appreciatively "—but none to compare with the charming Mrs. Coles. If I could have the honor of using her for a model—if you would allow her to come to my studio in Carmel for, say, just a few weeks . . ."

Coles let out a terrible sound, between a cry of pain and a warrior's shout, and grabbed the Count by the neck and began to shake him hysterically, while the Count screamed *Help! Help!* and the crowd around them laughed and laughed.

232

Manley, watching the scene in a kind of fascinated horror, broke through the circle and tried to separate them like a referee, somewhat sobered by the unhappy sound of struggle. "I don't know who you are but I'll have to ask you to . . ."

The Count snickered and suddenly switched from his accent to plain American. "F' Chris'sake, Mr. Halliday, I'm Gus Jones."

"Who?"

"Gus Jones."

Something about the bluntness of the name hammered home. Gus Jones. The professional ribber who hired out to parties to needle the guests. He and Jere had talked about him, but he didn't remember engaging him. Maybe Jere had. Anyway it was a joke, just a little gag he was explaining to J. C. Coles and Gus Jones' impromptu audience lifted their voices in laughter as if on cue.

"I see, yes, of course, a joke," Coles repeated, but the blood-pressure complexion, so suddenly risen, had not yet begun to subside.

"Manley, you're a card, you really made it look real," somebody he didn't know chuckled in his face. Manley drifted toward the bar. "Wha'luhave, kiddo?" The bartender grinned. Everybody was drunk. The pool was full of bathers now. Manley noticed that a swimmer who hadn't bothered to remove his tux looked rather indecent. Manley was conscious only of the background babble of water splashing, laughter splashing, music splashing (the colored band *In a Mist*) pierced by the occasional shrieks of frolicking young ladies to whom playful things were being done.

In a Mist—he and Jere were crazy about the Beiderbecke record, he was telling Colleen Moore or somebody who looked an awful lot like her. The girl who except for the cut of her hair didn't look anything like Colleen Moore melted away.

Jere's face floated up big-eyed and expectant.

"Jere, been lookin' all over for you . . ."

"Looking for you too. Didn't think it would be nice if I left without telling you."

Her face seemed to bob back and forth like a balloon in a breeze. He could see that her eyes were unusually large the way they always were when she was excited by anger or happiness. "Hear what they're playin'? They mean well but they aren't Bix or Tram . . ."

"Mannie, I'm leaving with Wister."

A hurried kiss touched his cheek. The sounds of festivity swirled around him. Somebody fell, glass splattered, band tore up *12th Street Rag,* marmalade girl costumed in towels now did a hula on the diving board. There was a terrible cry from somewhere in the garden, Wha'happened? Wassa matter? Manley managed to reach the circle of curious guests jostling for a better view of the little blonde who had been playing the drums. "Sonofabitch bit me," she said, pointing to the dog several men were holding. The owner moved excitedly. "He never bites—he's a good dog—she was teasing him." The victim's escort came nobly to her defense by swatting Strongpaw's owner on the nose. The dog barked hysterically. The little blonde sobbed. It was all over in a moment. Manley, surprised to find he still had a hundred dollars in his pocket, told the owner to take the beast home. "Go on, shake hands with the man and say thank you," the owner insisted. Strongpaws and Manley complied reluctantly. Christ, now he'd probably have to pay for the little blonde's dress, maybe doctor bills. Who's idea was that Strongpaws gag anyway? Jere's. Say, where the hell *was* Jere?

"G'night, 'night, wunnerful time—" The party was thinning out. The hopefuls and the die-hards were still going strong. And the white band was tapping out an old favorite, "Why Do I Love You?"

Look for Jere. No Jere anywhere. No Jere and no Wister. Jere really leave? A word, a kiss, good-bye. Did she say she was going? Was the whole thing in his mind? He wasn't sure. All he knew was he couldn't find her. Fine thing for the hostess. Should always wait 'n say 'night to all your guests before running off with another man.

" 'Night, 'night, glad ya did, see ya soon, lost your *what* in the pool? Oh y'r anklet, look f'r it in the morning, 't's morning now, ha ha ha all right some *other* morning . . ."

Seeing Mona to the gate ("This hour of the morning always

234

frightens me, Manley. Never know what I'll do." "Be a good girl now, Mona. Le's Montmartre later this week") his eyes were distracted to the parking space. Wister's Daimler must be along there some place. They wouldn't just go, wouldn't just— "Manley, I'd adore it if you'd come down to the beach for tea one afternoon." Her lips were cool and tasted more of promise than of passion.

"Love to, Mona, any time." He waved vaguely. No Daimler. No Daimler and no Jere. God damn her. So this is the way the world ends this is the way the world ends this is the way the world ends not with a bang but a Daimler.

The last melodic phrase had drifted out over the garden. The last drunk had been subdued. The last promise was made for lunch or cocktails this week. The last pair of high heels climbed wearily into the last limousine. The last of the bartenders made off with the last of the booze. "Don't bother," Manley heard himself mutter to Naga. "Le's clean it up t'morra." He reached in his pocket to give Naga an extra tip but his pockets were empty now. Must've given it to someone else.

He walked slowly back into the big house, barred the heavy medieval door and stood in the vast stone hallway. It was so quiet he could hear his own heavy breathing. Only in the days of feudal lords or now in Hollywood would anyone think of inhabiting such a house. It was five times too big for two people, a hundred times too large for one. He walked slowly through the cold, formal spaciousness of the living room. *Living* room! Who had ever lived here? This heartless, phony barn of a house. There was only one room fit to live in and that was the little barroom paneled in pine and decorated with Toulouse-Lautrec posters. You could live in the bar. He peered into the icebox under the bar and found a split of champagne. He lifted the glass to himself in the mirror. My God, was that he? He looked forty. St. Bernard eyes. He brought his face closer to the mirror, staring at himself as if the image were a stranger.

When the champagne was gone and he could find no more he settled for half a pint of Golden Wedding. Always Golden

Wedding, the bootleggers' favorite label. After champagne the whiskey tasted awful. To get it down he had to drink it fast. When the bottle was empty, for hell or for spite, he threw it as hard as he could through the archway into the living room. It fell without breaking and slid harmlessly along the carpet. Couldn't do that again, he thought. But then, what can you do again?

He opened the closest bottle on the shelf. It was peach brandy but he didn't care. Jere was gone, out somewhere in the languid Californian dawn with a languid hero whose personality was as synthetic as his name. Where were they now, making for Palm Springs, to some improvised love-nest along the road, or settling down to first-time intimacies in the elegant bachelor bedroom of some luxurious hide-away? And did she have that look in her eyes that no other man was supposed to see? And was she making her own little loving sounds, her monosyllabic incantations that had only the most accidental connection with vulgarity?

He poured out the remnants of the peach brandy into a high-ball glass—the cuckold's cocktail, he thought darkly, new recipe for Harry McElhone, and flung the empty bottle without aiming. It crashed against the far wall and the crash of glass splattering sounded good and violent.

He staggered out from behind the bar, heavy-legged, heavy-brained, up the long winding wrought-iron staircase (over-wrought, he and Jere had joked about it) to the bedroom that wasn't cozy wasn't theirs because they had no home. He stared into the empty room and noticed the lipsticked tips of half a dozen crushed cigarette butts ("Jere, three packs a day, you've got to cut down") crumpled on the floor near the chair, the beige suit she had taken off to dress for the party (never in all their living together had he ever seen her hang anything up), near her bed the murder mysteries she bought and left behind in hotel rooms by the dozen. He picked one up—*The Club of Masks*—wish she wouldn't waste her good mind on this trash—out of the pages dropped a leaf of stationery from the Hotel del Coronado where they had spent the week-end before last. Manley made out the few scratchy pencil lines of an abortive poem:

236

A STUDY FOR THE LEFT HAND NOT KNOWING
WHAT THE RIGHT HAND IS DOING

We are me and me are I
loosened goosened lorelei
if she hollers let her gonium
eeney miney pandemonium

I am what I never could
being what I never should
if she dies before she tries
who'll put pennies on her eyes

She is I and I am wh

Another one of those things she was never finishing. The discarded clothes, the cigarette butts (some crushed out after only two or three drags), the books on the floor, the unfinished poem made him feel as if he were some sort of tourist of the emotions visiting the sentimental monuments erected to the memory of Jere Halliday. Maybe those songs aren't so far off after all, he thought. There's nothing left to me of things that used to be, I live in memory among my souvenirs, even if they are cigarette butts, crumpled slips and bras, broken lines of impulsive verse and other symbols of feminine disorder. Even so, he was moved now in a sentimental way. Salt drops burned in his eyes and he wanted to bawl. He groped to the sleeping porch where he and Jere had lain together a dozen hours before. He looked more closely and found a tiny gold heart; one of her earrings had come off. She had a hole punctured in only one ear because she had started to faint and had been afraid to let the jeweler go on. Strange, she was a daredevil swimmer, diver, flyer, hunter, but the thought of anything sharp drawing blood from her always brought on vertigo. The memory of her one pierced ear, for some reason, was more than he could stand. Flopping down on the day bed he cried hysterically into his hands.

Some time later (an hour, a day, an eon) he must have gotten up, must have gone down to the living room and turned on the radio, for he heard things: Jack Smith whispering *Cecilia* and

I'm in heah-vun when I see you smile, smile for me, my Diane
. . . comes to you from the famous Cocoanut Grove, playground of the stars . . . he's in with a short jab to the mouth,
another jab, and then Young Nationalista . . . Chicago, Pres-
idential Candidate Herbert Hoover said today I foresee the day
and that not far off when every working man in America will
not only own his own . . . and minutes, was it hours, was
it days later, he was crashing another empty bottle against the
stucco walls interrupting the simpering Texas-Guinan-in-Christ
voice of Aimee Semple MacPherson crying out her spiritual
wares like a Panama City crib-girl. Oughta write a novel about
Aimee. He thought he was having an inspiration: female Elmer
Gantry with Hollywood trimmings. "And so I say to all you
good people tonight don't just get out and get under the moon,
get out and get under God!" The bottle in his hand wasn't
empty, but he sent it hurtling against the face of the radio *shut
up SHUT UP,* too stupefied to remember he could turn it off,
too stupefied to tell day from night, gin from brandy, love from
hate.

Beyond drunkenness he lay on the floor and felt himself sliding down as it swung around to serve as wall, ceiling, floor, wall
again. Chri'sakes, wh'sa'matter wi' me? Must've gotten
sick. Couldn't be drunk because just a minute ago I was thinking clear as a bell. "Jere . . . Jere . . ." His voice came to him
as from another room and an unfamiliar throat. "Jere . . ." Too
many people 'round her 'n me, too many people, gets t' be a
habit, bad habit. Only good habit's writing your best. Making
money's a bad habit, needing money's a bad habit, success is
a bad habit, America's fulla bad habits an' you Manley Halliday
you're as American as baked beans and more easily spoiled. Cigarette's gone out. Hadda match in my hand. Where's 'at match
go? Thought I lit it. Can't find it. Where's 'at match? He 'n
Jere . . . the match?

It was warm, not believing, warmer crying over spilt champagne and wasted energy hot crying Jere Jere, there was fire
raging inside him. Damn bootlegger stuff damn trash damn
need for a thousand-a-week, damn Jere damn fire's a word in a

238

song rhymes with desire, pyre. 'f I burned would I be a big talent turning on the spit of success over fagots of cheap fame and cheap stories (at twenty-five hundred berries might as well do one more) (look Honey if I lock myself in for two weeks and knock out four we'll have ten thousand bucks and can go to . . .) big empty house wasn't cold any more red arms of flame reached through a window and gesticulated crazily as if beckoning for help help Jere my talent's on fire it's padded with dollar bills that burn like money help Jere help let the damn barn burn and my fat and my flesh tainted with success but for Chris'sakes Jere anybody don't let the talent burn away to cinder . . .

The house that had always been so cold roared with the heat of a blast furnace. Upstairs in the study with the red leather furniture one hundred and three pages of the novel that Dorset House had expected to publish the year after *The Night's High Noon* was curling to a soft gray ash. At the same time Manley was remembering *O Jesus Burt Seixas had always begged me to make him a carbon.* Forcing himself up out of the crackling stupor, he managed to reach the bottom of the stairway, but as he decided to go up, the stairs were deciding to come down.

—"Mannie darling, it's me! Can you see me? Mannie . . ."

He had seen nothing but whiteness but now a fuzzed impression of dark red hair came down to him. He concentrated on seeing. He was in love with that face. Never knew why. It just pleased him. It had always pleased him. The twinge of a smile moved his lips slightly under the bandage.

"Darling, can you hear me? When I heard what you had done I—I almost died too . . ."

It took him a little time to realize what she meant. Oh, she would love him now. It was one thing to say I can't live without you. It was another to, to actually try to take your own— well, had he? The last thing he remembered was thinking with a terrible, hypertrophic clarity about his life, his shortcomings and the things he did or didn't believe. And he remembered calling Jere. And something about fire.

"Darling, darling, how can I ever make it up to you for

239

being such a—dope? I'm going to buy you a pearl-handled horsewhip."

"Accident," he started to say under the bandages. But then he thought: is that fair to her when her face is lit up with rededication? No, for loss of my girl I tried to take my life and maybe I did, yes, maybe I did . . .

"Mannie, I was a dope," she was saying into the bandages, "a sixteen-cylinder dope."

And then she said, beginning to feel back with him again, "I am not afraid of anything with your arms around me. Ahmed. Monseigneur."

Involuntarily, his shoulders began to shake. "Please, Mrs. Halliday," said the stern-faced nurse, "you mustn't make him laugh."

Sitting on the leather seat of the men's room he felt no leather; bouncing on the spinning metal wheels he remembered a time of peace ("that great beautiful hunk of peace" he had called it) that floated in the turbulent sea of his life like a magnificent iceberg, cool and detached and reaching so far below the surface that waves could not stir it.

He would never completely recover from this irony: in that brief period when he could not walk and when the bandages had not yet been removed from his eyes he had felt more sensibly alive than at any time since the most creative year of his young manhood. He sat on the beach and felt the sun and listened to the sea. At last he had time to think about his own relationship to sun and sea. Timidly, because the experience was still so strange to him, he began to feel himself a part of this natural trinity. Within him was a soothing awareness of wheels that, having spun too violently, were braking gradually to motionlessness. He listened to wind and gulls, to breakers and the whispers of their spray. Within himself it was as if the motor of a furnace had suddenly gone off, eliminating a sound that had throbbed so incessantly that it had come to be accepted as silence; now at last the silence was real, a perfect hush.

For years he had been in the midst of life and now, at this beach bungalow at Santa Barbara with Jere, he had removed himself to the outermost edges; yet sitting there on the beach renewing himself he came to realize that in a deeper sense it was quite the opposite: the social life had been an outer edge and he was coming home to dead-center, returning to himself, just as he and Jere were not merely resuming their marriage but caulking the seams of their joining to check the leakage and waste.

Now they began to hear each other's voices, each other's heart beats again. On the beach and in the cottage after dark Jere would read aloud to him a new translation of Verlaine Yvor

Winter had sent down from Stanford, the *Journals* of Baudelaire, Byron's *Don Juan*, Stendhal *On Love*, fragments from the Old Testament, the letters of Browning and Flaubert, whatever could be found in the local library.

All through these quiet days Jere was as attentive, as devoted as a hospital nun. With her way of dedicating herself to one enthusiasm at a time to the exclusion of all others, his physical and professional recovery was now her only concern; she was convinced that nothing but his welfare had ever occupied her mind. The webs of doubt that had gathered between them dissolved. They had good long talks that carried over from day to night and through sleep to awakening, in which affectionate silences bridged the things worth saying.

At first Jere had shied away from mention of Wister La Salle, but the first time he brought it up in a calm and off-hand way she was relieved and found herself able to talk about it with complete detachment. It had simply been part of the vast confusion they had mistaken for the good life. The mere thought of the fellow now aroused nothing more in her than a great yawn. To reassure her he told her of his brief intrigue with Mona and they laughed together at the dark woods through which they had finally found their way. Again and again (with the unmonotonous repetition of the waves outside) they spoke their gratefulness at having each other. It was not the loving abandon they had celebrated in Paris ten years earlier. But in its place was something they thought to be more durable, that second-wind of love based on understanding, affection and a romantic sense of duality that makes the facing of problems a gratifying experience.

As the bandages were removed and he could walk again, the thrill of the child's first steps and first impressions were filtered through the speculative appreciation of the thoughtful adult. The sheer joy of watching the blue sparkle of the sea was intensified by the *idea* of watching the sea. He could sit for hours meditating upon its fascination. It offered the peace of looking out over a stationary prairie and at the same time the pleasure of rhythmic motion. He thought: in all of us the desires to root and to roam are in contention. The sea, like the best of marriages, was a harmonious interflow of opposites. The sea was that exquisite equilibrium of movement and matter we call serenity.

To his delight and amazement, for he did not think he had that quality of mind, he was discovering the ancient pleasure of meditation, the priceless luxury of inner tranquillity. In the morning before breakfast he and Jere would walk along the beach looking for driftwood, the seashore's own objets d'art. How pleased they were when Jere found a wooden snake that might have drifted in from some celebrated collection of primitive art. Another morning he picked up a water-smoothed abstraction that would not have disgraced Brancusi. Was this accidental piece of driftwood a work of art?

Along the beach they talked for the first time about what they believed in. Until the rust was worn away, the machinery of their minds moved slowly, protestingly. Why had they never stopped to ask themselves and each other the basic questions? Too many things to do, too many radios and phonograph records and party-chatterers to listen to. He had to confess that he did not know enough of the world's wisdom to be ready to believe anything. He just had a few schoolboy prejudices, he admitted.

In their walks along the beach they argued good-naturedly the eternal either-ors. In a restless search for something to believe she had come to the *Pensées*. From the beginning of the decade that was reaching its end, she confessed, she had been rushing madly from one belief to the next—Dadaism, Freudianism, Anarchism (momentarily converted by the teachings and martyrdom of the apostle Vanzetti), hedonism; in Hollywood she had met, at the home of one of the most voluptuous movie stars, a Swami who had almost won her devotion to the Bhagavad Gita. Now, like her noble, disarranged Rimbaud, she was groping her way to the True Church. *It has to make some sense,* she kept saying as they skirted the water's edge and his answer would be *why? Maybe it makes no more sense than that sand flea hopping from hole to hole.*

Like a Rip Van Winkle of the intellect, he felt that he had slept through a lifetime of opportunity. Here he was, he complained, already into his thirties, with nearly all of the world's recorded wisdom still outside his mind. He threw himself into a feverish program of study—he had never read the Bible or Freud or Nietzsche or *The Golden Bough* or the notebooks of Da Vinci or all of Flaubert or the Greek philosophers or Sophocles or Euripides or all of Henry James, not even Conrad or Hawthorne thoroughly. What a dabbler he had been, a trifler, a dandyish dealer in externals.

He began to consider as the most important event in his life the fire that had burned to dust the tawdry merry-go-round that had seemed so dazzling. And that had brought him and Jere, literally, to their senses. It was, he decided, a symbolic fire consuming the highly inflammable, long-condemned, elaborately decorated but essentially flimsy playground in which he and Jere had existed. The burning of the manuscript which had seemed such a tragic loss in those first blistering days, began, in perspective, to assume its proper place, as a warning. He examined himself as an artist now, more thoroughly than he had in the pre-war days when he had carried a green baize book bag across the Yard, and found himself almost hopelessly wanting. Ruthlessly he made a list of all his faults and found them all to be the same fault, an over-supply of vanity, an over-developed concern to hear his name at the end of the cheers. The wish to be publicly admired. To be a Success. Like the others he had sneered at the Babbitts with their ordinary business success, their abysmal bourgeois ignorance that passed for "being a smart operator" and yet inadvertently he had allowed himself to be caught in the great American net.

Like an omen, it seemed as if every book said the same thing, as if each book knew his weakness and spoke for him alone. In the letters of Browning he underlined: *I never pretended to offer such literature as should be a substitute for a cigar or a game of dominoes to an idle man . . . on the whole I get my deserts and something over—not a crowd but a few I value more.* From the letters of Flaubert he learned how that author would labor over a single effect until his bones ached. He took counsel from the reflective struggle of Henry James to purify his themes; from the notebook of Chekov, Aristotle's *Poetics,* the work-habits of Trollope—even Arnold Bennett. He heard the warning of Marcus Aurelius; *cease to be whirled about;* and of Baudelaire: *Pleasure consumes us, work strengthens us. Let us choose.* Men as far apart as the Bible poets, the Elizabethans and the French symbolists all seemed to agree that if there was a single wisdom it was simply *To thine own self be true.*

All he had to do now was decide what was his own self.

How idiotic and disgusting—and remote—from the perspective of convalescence in Santa Barbara their party for that damned dog seemed. As they had with Wister La Salle, they found it an emotional purge to abuse themselves for having stooped to such vulgarity. It had been such an artificial display of merry-making. Here come the madcap Hallidays, they had sensed everyone's saying, I wonder what they're up to next. Like troupers they had gone into their act.

With a solemnity they still found refreshing, they decided on a program of rehabilitation. They would cut away the slough of false friends. They would conserve themselves for inner growth. They would go out to people only for necessary relaxation from creative work. Their motto would be *Contemplate, Concentrate, Consecrate.* Or as Jere suggested, *Datta, dayadhvam, damyata—give, sympathize, control.* And the first test of control was drinking. After a thirty-day period of drying out, they would make an experiment of moderation. *We'll use the stuff, we won't let it use us,* they agreed.

And everything I write will be nothing less than my best, he promised, having written into his notebook his own rough translation of Flaubert's warning: *. . . art is a luxury. It needs clean hands and composure. If you make one little concession, then two, then five . . .*

He even formalized it by drawing up a Declaration of Personal Independence, forcing himself for the first time to answer the artist's catechism: *What is my motive in writing this book? Money? Fame? Social pressure? Moral influence? Personal need . . . ?* He confessed to himself and Jere how much he had enjoyed the wealth and popularity his books had brought. It had taken fire, infidelity, near-suicide to destroy the dragons of Success. *Thank God, it isn't too late,* he told Jere. *Before I com-*

pose another book I will learn to compose myself. Out of his twenties at last, with his century itself facing its Thirties, there was no more time for literary catch-as-catch-can.

One night after dinner they sat on the beach together with their backs against the low stucco wall of their cottage and watched the tiny yellow and red riding lights of passing ships. In the sky the milky cluster of stars could be read as clearly as on an astronomical chart.

I feel clean and calm inside, he said. *I'm ready to go to work.* He had been making notes for the novel that would treat Hollywood as a world of topsy-turvy values where film people were the shadowing two-dimensional reflections of reality and only the figures on the screen were real.

And I'm going to finish Une Saison en Enfer, she promised. *I knew, Mannie! Let's not leave here till we're both finished!*

With the ardor of converts, they immersed themselves in domesticity. For the first time in their married life they stopped relying on room service and Jere tried to do the cooking. She plunged into housewifery with enthusiasm. She became economical, made marketing lists and was childishly pleased when she found ways to pare her budget by a half dollar. She became a budget devotee and worked out an elaborate scheme whereby they could live the ensuing year for just half of what it had cost them in 1928. On liquor alone, she estimated with a flourish of arithmetic, their new austerity program would save them at least five thousand a year.

Only in one respect did their retreat to tranquillity seem anything less than perfect. Their physical relationship subsided to infrequent moments that were almost casual. In the past an equal partner at the very least, Jere seemed to become increasingly passive, responding more from a sense of duty than desire. And yet it was during this period that she spoke of and seemed to feel most deeply her attachment to him. Days when he would be working at a table in the patio and she would bring him a cool drink, she would say—as she never had before—*Manley, I love you so much.* In the days when the beat had been stronger between them, she would have teased him with horrid names and said *I hate you.* At night when he was working now she

246

would bring him coffee she had made—which he didn't have the heart to tell her was invariably bitter—and kiss him with earnest affection, but more like daughter to father than woman to man. None of this seemed serious though, for he was pouring all his energy into his work and his reading. With Jere's housekeeping and the Rimbaud to finish they were always ready for sleep by midnight. If there was a minimum of erotic pleasure, there was a maximum sense of companionship and achievement.

They began to feel, keenly, the absence of Douglas and they had him come on from Kansas City. They found him amazingly "grown up," in that intense stage of development when reason and wonder had begun to exercise his mind and they both enjoyed answering the grave catechism of a seven-year-old. Where does the sun come from? Where do people come from? Why are waves? Who is God?

Out of guilt at having failed him so often those first five years, they lavished too much attention on him. They decided it was unfair to Douglas to leave him as an only child, and Jere, all in her role of homemaker, mother and wife-of-the-artist, decided they must have another. In a rather matter-of-fact way one evening, they attended to this.

All was going smoothly with their work and their lives when the telephone, which hadn't rung a dozen times in a month, pierced the quiet of the afternoon to announce a lady reporter from the local paper. Somewhat hysterical at her own ingenuity in having tracked them down, she was eager to interview them on why they had chosen Santa Barbara. The good, cultured people of Santa Barbara, the phone assured him, were thrilled at the thought that Manley Halliday would honor them by writing his next best-seller here.

He put the lady off. But when she called again and again, and they made the fatal mistake of saying *no* courteously—which, to the worldly, is the same as saying yes—they finally gave way to the old appeasement: maybe it will be less of an interruption to have her in and get it over with.

The coming of the lady reporter (she was the local book reviewer but she was all a-flutter at the prospect that an interview of this importance would start on page one) meant locating a bootlegger to supply them with gin and perhaps some Scotch. And to prepare themselves for the ordeal, he and Jere thought they'd better have a drink or two before she descended upon them.

Mrs. Lucinda Hunt Hitchcock (who quickly identified herself as a grand-niece of the author of *Ramona* and the discussion leader of the local Bookworms Club, "which gives us lots in common") was thrilled to meet the Hallidays, thrilled to find them such a young, charming, attractive and sensible couple, thrilled to have one teeney-weeney little cocktail with them ("we oldsters have to keep up with this younger generation"), thrilled to hear (by putting most of the words into their mouths) that they were seriously considering permanent residence in "this lovely bit of Old Spain by the Pacific we call Santa Barbara." Having forced him to the half-promise that he would address the Bookworms ("The B.W.'s simply won't take no for an answer") she hurried off to write her rosy and totally erroneous impression of the young love birds gaily creating works of art (that sell for fabulous sums to magazines and Hollywood) in their cozy (but exotically redecorated) bungalow by the sea.

The departure of Mrs. Hitchcock was as if a sudden gale had blown through and left them wind-tossed in its wake. In a drinking mood for the first time since they had come, they finished another batch of cocktails. He had planned to go on working that evening, but the alcohol had eaten away his will and he took refuge in the decision to relax tonight and get a fresh start in the morning. That night he wanted Jere more insistently than usual but she complained of a headache—"can't seem to take the pain-killer any more"—and for the first time since they had come he brought into the open his fears that she no longer had that kind of love for him. She gave in, to put an end to such foolishness, she said. But when it was over he felt even more letdown. What had dulled the fine, shining blade of their passion? Alone he wandered out onto the beach with a bottle in his hand, less sensitive to the elements than he had been a month before, to find an easy peace in solitary drinking.

The next day he was full of remorse and sour humors. When

Jere reminded him of their pious resolutions, he accused her of being surly and unsympathetic. So it just happened that he was especially vulnerable when who-of-all-people-but-Bertie-Heinemann should call—"had no idea you rascals were in Santa B. till I read the big write-up in the local Bugle." Bertie was staying with the Marstons who were "our sort of people" and were "simply panting to have you two booze-hounds in for cocktails." He and Jere could hardly say no. The last time they had seen Bertie they had had an outrageously good time drinking wine together in the Blue Grotto and the coincidence of their all turning up together in Santa Barbara-of-all-places was an event that called for at least a token celebration.

From the Marstons', where they had a much better time than they expected, they came home (as they now called the hotel bungalow) pleasantly pie-eyed and it was Jere's suggestion that they make up, though there had been more ennui than disagreement between them. That night recalled earlier times when they had been too impatient to wait for darkness.

After that they decided it wouldn't hurt to have a cocktail or two before dinner. Nothing after dinner was the new rule. Since he was working fairly well, there was no sense in being too rigid.

But their appearance at the Marstons' led to a rash of new invitations. By holding them off to week-ends, they still managed to accomplish a good deal. Jere, the better linguist of the two, was studying Greek. Forever crossing a dozen bridges before she reached the first, she thought it would be fun for them to try a modern translation of *Iphigenia in Tauris*. The Rimbaud had been put aside again. Unable to catch the rhythm of the poems in the *Delirium* section, she was quickly sure she had gone stale.

At first their week-ends began at Saturday noon; then, without their quite noticing it, the social drinking began Friday evening. When Bertie insisted his heart would be broken if they didn't come along with him on a yachting party that was to get under way late Thursday afternoon, they thought it'll be an exception this one time and we'll make up for it next week. What to do with Douglas was a problem for a while, but Bertie solved that by getting the Marstons to take him in with their little boy.

They had a peach of a time cruising down the coast to Laguna. Bertie, whose role in life was to know everybody everywhere, had some friends who had a marvelous house down there. They stayed over for a party that turned out to be a beaut. They couldn't get back until Tuesday. By the time he finessed his hangover, Wednesday was all used up. Another week down the drain of secondary pleasures. They would have to be firmer, they warned each other. He went back to reread that document he had drawn up for Personal Independence. But they had to make an exception when Bertie was leaving for Honolulu. The bon-voyage party for him would be their last stab at whoopee in Santa Barbara. "After Saturday night we'll retire with the championship," he laughed with Jere.

It was a good party, no better or no worse than a hundred others, with the normal proportions of genuine release, harmful and harmless flirtation, moments of beauty, ugliness, boredom and titillation, happy and unhappy drinking, breakage, cigarette burns, fits of laughter, tears and several calls from the management to cut out the noise. A few minutes after four o'clock Douglas ran in crying from his bed and drove most of the guests away with his determined hysteria.

At five-thirty, all quiet at last, they held a troubled postmortem while they watched the dawn roll in. What had the party accomplished? How could they have wandered so far from their course? What was this compulsion to please other people? Bertie Heinemann was a playboy pure and simple with good taste, money, nice manners and a cultivated sense of humor and his generosity had made things comfortable for them in some very nice parts of the world. But he had nothing to say to them they hadn't heard a hundred times. "He's exactly the sort of nice guy I should start cutting out of my life if I ever want it to have any meaning," he had decided.

It was at Santa Barbara that he had begun to think of his talent as if it had an objective existence separate from himself, as something precious that had been entrusted to his care. As he said to Jere, "I feel like a bellboy who is given a thoroughbred poodle to walk in the park, lets it get off its leash and has to chase it desperately through the streets."

The day after the party brought a vicious awakening to the dream of serenity in Santa Barbara. A little after three, when he was finally beginning to pick up the thread of his narrative, he rose from his work-table in the patio to find a cigarette and happened to glance into the bathroom window. After he saw what Jere was doing it was impossible to keep his mind on his work. When Douglas had been put to bed that evening, he told her what he had seen. She came over and sat on his lap and like a little girl began to cry. "Man, I'm glad you caught me. I'm miserable when I hide things from you. I've been dying to talk to you about it. Something's the matter with me. This drinking. I hate it. I don't know what it is. It makes me feel"—she nestled her face into his neck as if she would have liked to crawl inside him—"oh I don't know, I don't know, it frightens me. Help me, Mannie, help me."

A tenderness for her that had always been there welled up in a moment of love that was exquisitely painful and that he would always remember (was now remembering). For better or worse, it was through sunlight and the dark, and the worse it was the more loving he had to give. And he remembered thinking what a rare and complex growth a love-marriage is—this effort to cross sexual attraction with common sense and binding partnership. Yes, he and Jere had come close, with the *help me, Mannie, help me* kind of closeness. Except of course that it had never been a marriage; at its best a love affair as bewitched as those that live in myth, at its worst a nerve-racking contest.

While he held her in his arms and loved her in his mind, the telephone intruded again. He went to it reluctantly. He was appalled by the manic ebullience that swept across the wires to him. It was an Ellie Slocum. ("Man, just wanted to tell you that party of yours was a knockout. Haven't enjoyed getting a hangover so much in y'ars. Kitty's so fulla wood alcohol she left splinters in my lip when she kissed me this a.m.") He had only the vaguest idea as to who Kitty was, or Ellie Slocum either, though this voice obviously assumed the right to address him in terms of intimate and hilarious camaraderie. "Well, I just wanted to check on tonight, Hally." He winced. He had always loathed this liberty with his proper name. Tonight? What could he and Jere possibly have told this overwrought stranger about tonight? "Yeah, remember you wanted us to show you that little joint we were telling you about—the Chatterbox? 'Taint elegant but it's a barrel o' laughs. What time you kids be ready?"

"We kids," he took pride in hearing himself say, "are leaving town tonight. Have to go East right away. Uh, serious illness in the family. G'Bye."

He went back to Jere and said, "We've worn out Santa Barbara. Too many people know us. These last two weeks we've been about as private as a couple of flag-pole sitters."

Four weeks before, they had leased the bungalow for six months, which would have been the longest they had ever stayed anywhere. To force themselves to some kind of permanency they had thought it was a good idea to pay six months' rent in advance. "We've been living too much of our lives on margin—let's buy six months outright," he had said, and she had agreed that it was a brilliant idea. Their landlord thought so too, for he wouldn't come up with a refund. Even so they considered it a good bargain.

He: "We'll find peace and quiet if we have to go to the North Pole."

She: "I wonder if Eskimos like frozen Daiquiris."

With a stab of regret they glanced back at their white stucco cottage, its border of cheerful geraniums and its vast front yard of sand and sea.

"We had a nice time there," Jere said.

"It was getting kind of hot," he answered.

When they had followed the hot dry coastline for twenty miles she had suddenly remembered the things she had forgotten to pack, the red alligator shoes, the douche bag and a Greek grammar. He had been dipping into *The Psychopathology of Everyday Life* and he puzzled over the key to this combination.

—"Manley, Manley," Shep nudged him, "don't you think you'd sleep better in the drawing room?"

—"Jere, awful sleepy, wake me up when we get to L. A."

—"Manley, hey Manley, listen to me, it's Shep, Shep. You've got to—"

The train rolled on through the bitter New England night with the body of Manley Halliday. But the memory of Manley Halliday, fully awake behind the mask of sleep traveled another track toward another destination, following a time-table ten years old.

A year may crawl like a turtle or zigzag madly like a fox in panting fury to outdistance the pack. That year would always seem like one long terrible fox hunt with the pack yelping at their heels. They had started out so grandly to lead the chase, but somehow it was they who had become the driven and the hunted.

Douglas, adored and abandoned, according to whim and need, was once more deposited in Kansas City with his grandparents. Then a friend loaned them a farm in Connecticut, but there were mosquitoes and neighbors and the nights were heckled by the senseless groan of the bullfrogs. They tried to fall back on the metropolitan anonymity of Manhattan and for two memorable weeks they saw the city with fresh eyes, but then people began to discover them and the phone started ringing and there were week-ends on Long Island when it was more difficult not to drink than not to breathe and Jere said *help me help me Mannie* and he spoke to her in a voice he had never used before and she cried and they made up and swore that everything was going to be all right again.

They tried an apartment in the Village but it wasn't the Village any more, just a precious slum for poseurs. One Sunday afternoon when they awoke for breakfast to find the place full of lesbians, shattered minor poets and self-pity, they looked at each other across the debris and knew, lease or no lease, the time had come to move on again.

Someone of the thousands always talking of places to go—was it Covarrubias up at Small's Paradise?—had mentioned Mexico and for no more reason than that and the desperate desire to get away from themselves and the feverish stupidity of Boomland they headed south through Texas. As soon as their train had crossed the border they became immediately convinced that they loved Mexico, its sense of age and simplicity without the smell of

253

decay that hung over the great cities and pleasure towns of Europe. On the train was a bull-necked mestizo whose one expression was a menacing frown; he was pointed to with starched-collar pride by the steward as the man who shot Pancho Villa. Passing through the surrealist-like monotony of Durango they heard much talk of railroad bandits who liked to rob the male passengers and molest the female. People said, no doubt mistakenly, that the assassin of Pancho Villa was there to protect them from such trials.

Across the table from them in the dining car were an aristocratic Mexican lady and her daughter who were white-skinned and spoke Castilian Spanish and alluded darkly to the Catholic counter-revolution that would boil up in Mexico and wipe out the atheists who had seized power in the Revolution. Asked whether the atheists hadn't brought some long-needed social reforms to her country, the lady politely withdrew behind a shield of small talk. "Dolores Del Rio," she would say sweetly, "yes. Lupe Velez, no." And her daughter would nod in righteous agreement. Each time they met in the dining car after that, the Mexican lady would immediately reiterate what apparently was a firm moral judgment, "Dolores Del Rio, yes. Lupe Velez, no." By the time they had reached the old world city of Mexico it had passed into their collection of stock remarks.

Once they reached Cuernavaca, where they found a lovely pink house for fifty dollars a month including a cook (and her entire family who ate and apparently lived in the kitchen), they felt they had left forever the world of I'ma-friend-of-Joe's, hot tips, installment buying and *Ding Dong Daddy from Dumas*. The fervid Mexican sun darkened the yellow pigment of Jere's skin until, in her native skirt and white embroidered blouse, she could have passed for a girl from Tehuantepec. Rivera did her portrait with the emphasis on high cheekbones and dark-eyed intensity. There were rumors that she and Rivera—but of course gossip in Mexico is cheaper than pulque. More nearly husband and wife than they had ever been, they climbed the pyramids of Teotihuacan and lost themselves in the ancient Toltec mysteries. They read together and were captivated by the *True History* of Bernal Diaz, they studied Spanish and Mexican history and felt

254

themselves drawn to the dignified brown people who still managed to hold out in their pastel villages against the invasions of the gringos and the vulgarities of the rising mestizos in their brown business suits.

In a month Jere was getting by in Spanish and everybody was saying she must have Mexican blood she was so *simpático*. A new life was on its way, but they no longer had any use for it and a nervous Mexican doctor who smelled of cheap cigars and stale disinfectant approached her with his sleeves rolled up to dirty cuffs and put an end to what had seemed such a happy idea back in the false dawn of Santa Barbara.

She developed a great thirst for tequila after that and for dashing up to Mexico City while he was working. He was so preoccupied with trying to make his book amount to something that he didn't pay much attention to Juan Fortunas, the Indian boy with the waist of a ballet dancer and the flattened nose of a boxer who had just received his *alternativa* in the Mexican bullring. Never very real was the day of Fortunas' triumph when, in addition to his own bulls, he handled with fantastic courage and integrity the bulls of the *torero* caught in the first *corrida*. For all the women who watched the lean figure go in over the horns for a true killing with the long steel blade it was a moment of almost painful sexuality and perhaps that night at the ranch of General Ferrero, the rich ex-Revolutionary, where a victory celebration for Fortunas became a contest of endurance between tequila and the guests, Jere could not be blamed.

The next afternoon at breakfast it was the chief amusement of the day. The General, despite Latin regard for courtesy, could not conceal his anti-gringo pride that one of his own had demonstrated the superiority of Mexican manhood to the effete *yanqui* variety. Even so it might have remained an inter-family affair if a wealthy young friend of Fortunas in the General's bar that evening had not drunkenly executed a mock veronica as Manley approached. He had been in Mexico long enough to take offense. He swung on the offender and knocked him down. A moment later he had been crushed to the floor in a swarm of outraged Mexicans.

Three days later he and Jere were back in El Paso. This time they had four months to go on the pink house in Cuernavaca. On the train Jere cried nervously and wondered what the evil was in her that spoiled all the places that promised so much.

After Cuernavaca New York was an inferno. The speaks were full of gangsters who looked like businessmen and showgirls who looked or would like to have looked like Jean Ackerman and young men of the Class of '24 and '25 with alcoholic complexions who had made twenty-five thousand dollars between the one o'clock and five o'clock cocktails. Wally Betz, a classmate of his who made his first million on the Exchange before he was twenty-eight, said, "Give me ten G's to play with and I'll run it up to forty for you in less than a year. Friends on the inside of Radio," he winked. "If they don't split that baby it'll go to a thousand." John J. Raskob had just said that if a man invested only $15 a week in good sound stocks, at the end of twenty years he'd have a life income of four or five hundred a month.

He and Jere had always been a little scornful of all the sure-thing talk, but now they saw themselves settling down in their middle age at St. Michele or some place on a life pension, free to age gracefully in some literary pasture. But their favorite character wasn't Wally Betz whose brain was stuffed with ticker-tape; it was Garry Vanderhof, the young, willowy New York socialite who had been given an eighty-foot schooner for a graduation present and who was using it to run rum from the Bahamas. "And the beauty of it is I'm not breaking any laws because I sail under the British flag and the boats meet me twelve miles out," he was telling them at Jack and Charlie's. "I came in last night with twelve cases of honest-to-God Johnny Walker. Going back Thursday. You kids should come along. Might give you an idea for a story, Man."

Garry Vanderhof, a modern pirate in clean linen, appealed to him and he knocked out a serial about a Social Register boot-legger that was snapped up by Hollywood for the absurd price of $50,000. He gave half to Wally Betz, who was going to run it up to a quarter of a million for him, and hurried away from America again. They crossed with Benny Field and Blossom Seeley, George Bancroft and Young Stribling and his Ma and Pa and brother Buddy who confided that they were going over to fight an overgrown freak by the name of Primo Carnera. One day at the rail George Bancroft, who had made such a hit in *Underworld* the year before, said to him, "I want you to write a Bancroft story for me," and went on to explain that he was going to Europe "to tour their underworlds," a phrase which immediately took first rank in their collection of cute sayings by adults.

It was a little depressing to go all the way to London to exchange insults with Aleck Woollcott at Claridge's. Paris was somewhat better because nobody could quite spoil Paris even if the bars seemed to be full of the same people they thought they had left behind in New York. It was the year everybody was in Paris, the writers, the Wall Streeters, the movie actors, the college boys and Mr. and Mrs. Haddock.

One afternoon Hank Osborne showed up at the Crillon, defiantly Left Bank, with his beret, an uncanny Parisian cast to his face and a tendency to lapse into French to express himself more clearly, almost succeeding in blocking out his New England heritage. Hank had hardly sat down before he was lashing him for his surrender to Mammon and mediocrity. "For Christ's sake, Man, you were our one best hope. When I read the *College Humor* crap I get so mad I want to crown you with a chair."

A bottle of brandy turned an honest argument into an emotional collision. Because in his heart he felt guilty, he said Hank was just being a sorehead on account of the unpublished novel Hank had shown him. He said Hank's sniping at his artistic lapses was the lowest kind of professional jealousy and that a real artist (which Hank would never be) can separate the chaff of money-making from the harvest of his real work. What began as healthy discussion deteriorated into splenetic confusion, even to the silly old charge of his drunken pass at Mignon. When it seemed as if the next answer must be a punch in the nose, Jere forced her way between them and told Hank to go. Hank went off proudly carrying the flag of the *avant garde* and his unpublished ("because it's too damn honest") novel. Jere said, "Man, what *is* the matter? We used to have so much fun."

He wouldn't stop drinking the brandy, furious with his old

friend Hank for having said so much that was true. But when Jere said exactly the same thing *You know, Man, there's a lot in what Hank says. You keep doing all these pot-boiling things,* all the guilt and confusion and self-hatred that had been storing up in him burst loose against her. There was a scene that shook them both with its violence.

When the reconciliation came it was violent too and they decided the flaw was Paris' and not their own and that all they needed was a second honeymoon, or was it their third, their fifth, their tenth? So they hired a Renault (with a dark brute of a chauffeur who most of the time would ride in back) and places and people flew past in a blur, like the scenery at 80 kilometers: Grasse, Biarritz, Juan-les-Pins, Nice, Monte Carlo, San Remo, Lake Lugano, Florence, Rome and Taormina, the next place always the hope and the postponement—refuge in flight. *I must move to keep the wind in my face,* Jere had written, *the moment I stop I am consumed in my own fires.*

They had to believe that nothing could spoil the seagreen depths beyond the raft at Juan-les-Pins or the maturing radiance of Jere in the most backless of all the one-piece bathing suits. Nothing could quite spoil the enchantment of gliding across the marble floor of the Provençal Hotel among the dark pines to the sweet foolishness of *Avalon. I like dancing with you, Lieutenant Hallenstein.* They had to believe that nothing could quite spoil the twisting twinkling drive to the Pre Catalan where not even an American jazz band could succeed in shattering the lavender quiet of the Mediterranean, all changed and changing and not so much fun any more, but not quite spoiling the sense of resurrection as they dove into the cool magic of the tideless sea and not quite spoiling the still-loving taction of their tanned and homeless bodies. No, nothing ever could quite spoil the succession of honeymoons except the fear, the crawling fear, that something beyond their control was stalking them. Something evil and outside their love was closing in on them with nightmare inevitability from which one runs and runs without being able to move, as on the night that Jere was carried beyond the bar of gaiety to drugged surrender, not even to a fine animal like Fortunas (alas killed in Madrid by a bull who had not heard how great he was in

Mexico), but to the ugly pock-marked dark brute of a chauffeur and the bottomless helplessness of *I don't know. It isn't enjoyment. Don't know why. Feeling of falling, of falling down into darkness* and out of delirium the last lines of *Saison en Enfer* she had been working on *Ah, the stinking rags, the bread soaked with rain, the drunkenness, the thousand loves that have crucified me. Will she never let me be, the Ghoul Queen of a million dead souls and bodies that will be judged? I see myself again, the skin eaten with filth and pestilence, with worms in my armpits and in my hair and worms even larger in my heart, lying among strangers without age, without feeling . . .*

And after the reality of the stomach pump the precise French physician who had his own ideas of these intemperate Americans ("A race is not civilized until it gains a sense of moderation," he would tell his mistress later that evening) asking him how she happened to obtain so much Elixir of Terpene Hydrate. She was bothered by a cough before she left the States and took a supply along. A supply, the physician smiles. She has had at least two pints today, that is, 40% alcohol, you understand, in addition to the codeine and she has taken a number of codeine pills besides. I have reason to believe she is an *addict.* The physician had pronounced the word harshly, with a cynical emphasis that made it all the more painful to hear. *Addict.* And she had looked particularly lovely and like her old self that afternoon with her powder-blue scarf and her firm brown shoulders.

Someone who had been through it pointed the way to Dr. Simmel and his Schloss Tegel in Berlin and like de-luxe pilgrims (with Radio zooming to five times what they had paid for it) they journeyed to the Adlon to await the miracle. Jere took up residence in the Schloss. After three weeks, during which he developed a healthy antagonism for the arrogant modernity of Berlin, he had one of those talks with Dr. Simmel that left him in a state of revelation.

Alcohol, Dr. Simmel explained (in the tone of an orthopedist explaining a compound fracture) defends the ego against the patient's inner unconscious conflicts. In Jere's case there was the hunger for parental love lost through the death of the mother

259

and withheld by the father. "In search of a father to replace the one who has failed her, Jere has been trying for a long time to transfer you from a husband into that father. That is why she began to flinch from you as a sexual partner at the same time that she turns to other men. You hold a position of authority and prominence much as her father did and that is why, also, she has shown such a tendency to compete with you and to belittle you. Also," Dr. Simmel continued, "drinking is a substitute for the repressed wish to enjoy auto-erotic pleasures. This is where your solitary drinking comes in. Notice the similarities of infantilism—the symbol of the bottle itself and the regression it induces. The patient drinks until she staggers like a tot, until she can no longer articulate words like an adult. The patient becomes as helpless as the infant she wishes to be. Her face must be washed; she must be undressed and put to bed. The important thing for you to understand is that when your wife drinks herself into a stupor or finds release with other men it does not mean at all that she wants to leave you. On the contrary, young man, more than ever she wants you to protect her and care for her."

He had nibbled at the meanings of Freud, but only now did it come to him as a flash of understanding that here is a new morality based on what *is* rather than on what should be. To believe that anyone was *unfaithful* was as archaic as believing that unbalanced people had stones in their heads. As Dr. Simmel, another redeemer in the great line, went on with his precise explanation of what he called the post-war disease of dipsomania, it occurred to him that the Christian advocacy of forgiveness and understanding had, after nearly two millennia, been given a scientific rationale. It was in Dr. Simmel's office in the Schloss Tegel, pondering the teachings of Christ, of Freud and of their apostle Simmel, that he remembered shaking off the first scale of the skin of prejudice he had worn without question from his youth.

"Doctor, this helps me very much. But what is the cure? *Is* there a cure?"

"Dipsomania." The doctor put his hands together and looked into them as if the answer were something he had palmed.

"Yes, of course it is possible. Ours is a science of possibilities. But it is not merely a cure. It is a kind of engineering of the soul. We must rebuild the ego. Psychotherapy, occupational therapy, a year, maybe two years, if you both have the will, the patience— I think we can develop a mature ego that will replace the infantile narcissistic pleasure principle with the reality principle."

The reality principle. Maybe he could use some of that medicine himself, he was thinking. Maybe this was what they all needed—the entire generation—a rebuilding of the group ego. Jere's was just an advanced and somewhat more spectacular case of a terrible plague. He wandered down the steps into the daylight of a bright late summer afternoon.

By willfully avoiding the amiable company of correspondents who waved to him from the bar, he found a new kind of lonely peace at the Adlon with Jere gone. He found himself working unusually well. In another six or seven weeks he was going to have a completed draft of the book he had begun in Santa Barbara, dabbled at in Connecticut, pushed ahead in Mexico and worked at in fits and starts in a score of hotel rooms from the Savoy in London to the Viaigiea Grand in Sicily.

Then the door swung open and there was Jere.

"Darling, darling, I ran away. Keep me with you. I've stopped drinking. I'll never drink any more. I'll never do anything to hurt you. I promise, I promise, only take me away, please take me away."

Schloss Tegel was a medieval chamber of horrors, she told him. The attendants were unbelievable villains. Dr. Simmel was not as bad as the others but he was never there when she needed him. One of the male nurses kept trying to take obscene liberties. There was no beauty there, there was only beauty when she was close to him. He was all the cure she needed. And on and on in a torrent so convincing that he had gone to see Dr. Simmel who smiled at the charges and said but of course you understand this hostile reaction is symptomatic and such delusions of persecution are to be expected.

But Jere would not go back, promising over and over that she would behave herself. She looked so adorable as she begged with her full lips in a kind of pout that was at once childlike and seducible. Wasn't there some way of retracing their steps and picking up the golden thread? He softened and fell in with her and they ran away to Salzburg, where they could escape together into the post-card unreality. Then in an open Pierce-Arrow (just how that had come to Salzburg he could no longer remember) on to Lake Constance, where they got mellow on sidecars on the balcony of the hotel looking out on the lake and then on again through the grandest country in the world to Kitzbühel, a story-book town made of pure gingerbread, where Jere wore peasant skirts as no Tyrolese peasant ever could have worn them, where in a few weeks they were "Die Schöne Amerikanische," where he began to think of working again.

They found a Tyrolean lodge on the Schwarze See that had belonged to one of those madmen of the old nobility ("made the countess wait on the maid he slept with in the master-bedroom" so ran the local scandal-legend) and they said Kitzbühel was just right, just the right size, just far enough away. They would drink nothing but the local yellow wine and he'd finish the book in a month or two and in such peace as this she'd finish the Rimbaud job at last. Meanwhile she picked up piano again, practicing intensely for an hour every afternoon. They made friends with a German poet and his wife on the other side of the lake. Now at last they had found a life where temptations were balanced by compensations. Just to offset the danger of vegetating, they'd have a semi-annual spree in Paris to see the plays and the opera and the people on the boulevards and the friends passing through; then home to the Schwarze See, with the incredible Alps for a fortress against reality.

The sound of the tracks, the inner weakness, the uneasy sleep, the pressure of something that had to be done. But why be anxious on the Wagon-lit (wasn't Jere better, Radio passing 100 again and the book near done?) with Paris to meet them in the morning like an old friend? (What was it he had to finish by the time they arrived?) No, after Kitzbühel it was never clear, more like a Fourth of July pinwheel burning itself out as it whirls into darkness. *Cease to be whirled about.* He and Jere whirling and whirling as on an amusement park turntable. (How *do* you get out of this amusement park?) The wonderful memory that could bring back every word and look and gesture going out of commission after Kitzbühel, except for the things he'd rather forget. These survived erasure like indelible ink: the transatlantic call from Wally Betz to their fifty-dollar-a-day suite at the Crillon which went off in the middle of their Paris vacation like dynamite. *Hello, hello, is this Wally?* It didn't sound like Wally who always started with some sort of a rib. But anyway here was Wally with a voice like a man confessing a murder. *Manley this has been the God-damnedest day the God-damnedest day! I've just come from the Floor. This is tough to tell you but you need thirty thousand to cover your margin. I'd cover for you in a flash. Didn't even bother telling you about it last month. Looked like a little leveling that'd take care of itself. Christ, Charley Mitchell himself said there was nothing to worry about but I lost two hundred thousand today, maybe more. The goddam ticker is still three hours behind. Feel like somebody just whopped me in the belly with a sledge hammer.* "But I haven't got thirty thousand in cash, Wally." *Well, borrow on whatever you can, insurance, go into hock. Hell, you'll be in good company. If we c'n all come through with our margin maybe we c'n hold this thing together. Charley Mitchell says . . .*

Next morning's Paris *Trib* was a footnote to debacle and he hurried over to the customers' room of Halle Steiglitz, already jammed with American investors on whose faces the fatal numbers were written as clearly as on the big board on the wall. On the board and over the cables disaster came ticking. He sat there among the other victims fascinated by the terrible little numbers on the board, the fascination a man must have who having slashed his wrists in the bathtub now watches the blood flowing softly from his veins. He looked around at the others and their faces were gray with physical illness. There was a distinguished old man with white hair parted in the middle like a young man's who took a cigarette from a beautiful gold case, lit it and crushed it out without smoking and lit another. When the *Trib* reported his death from heart-attack, the involuntary suicide, it said he had sold an independent steel company to Big Steel and had come to France to retire. His losses were reported as $480,000 in two days. There was a fat man from Biloxi (whom they had seen gay-blading around the nightspots) who held his puffy cheeks in his hands and sobbed. A genteel lady in her late forties, upon hearing that 5 now stood for 25 rather than 55 cried out in her suffering the foulest oath in the language.

Once he had accustomed himself to the idea of being wiped out, he began to appreciate how his $55,000 had bought him a ringside seat for the knockout in the tenth year of Young Jazz Age, otherwise known as Big Bull Market. And he wondered what he who had thought he was fleeing the American money-machine was doing here in Halle Steiglitz with the coupon clippers and the heavy plungers. Until the year before he had always said the market was a game for Yale Club men and chambermaids and he had handled it in *High Noon* as the bog in which his hero is almost lost. Now it seemed even with his own instinct for prophecy that he had written his own defeat into Ted Bentley's. What was it Hank had said? *Man, the trouble with you is you never learned how to keep your distance. You can't decide whether you're the photographer or the one being photographed.*

Maybe that's what drew them to Maxims that night where they knew all the recently rich Americans would be holding a wake for themselves. Through the desperate gaiety the waiters moved with a cynical obsequiousness, as if to say, "Let this batch have their last little fling. By the time they pay for the champagne we'll be richer than they are."

President Hoover was clearing his throat bravely, but the party was over. With no more dollars to cash in for francs, the expatriates were folding their manuscripts and quietly going home. It turned out even Hank had been drawing a modest income from some family investments; now he came in a little sheepishly to say he was going home. Everything was going to pieces. The word *home* had a strange sound on his Gallicized tongue. Hank had found a real home in Paris. Just as so much American writing had. Perhaps in the quick fever of the Twenties it had had no other. Yet, saying good-bye to Hank, he realized that he had never belonged to the literary Americans-in-Paris. He hadn't belonged to anything.

Defeated soldiers falling back to shorten their lines, they withdrew from the Crillon to a pension near Hank's studio on the Rue de l'Université. It was all a pinwheel jumble flashing into darkness. Bits and pieces were flying off into space. Jere with whom he was increasingly out of sorts came home with a Rose Rescat creation that had cost 750 francs. "But, Man, I felt so blue. And" (remembering that fabulous hat in '19) "I thought maybe this would change our luck." His only answer had been to look at her dully, knowing there was no way to tell her that luck had nothing to do with them, that luck was a schoolgirl's dream, that luck was only the bulb that shone when the current was on, a result and never a cause, and now the powerhouse that had illuminated their world had gone dead.

But of course Jere would not understand, so she turned to brandy instead of breakfast and was off for three days with the stragglers of a *Surrealiste* group who in his opinion mistook their own foulness for the infections of society. When finally he came to fetch her he was sick with what he saw, unable even to summon up jealousy against such a circus of the flesh. Jere, homelessly home with him in the rooms with the scaly wallpaper and the so-called plumbing, remembered less of what had happened than if suddenly she had been awakened from a dark dream. The bits and pieces flew about as he dreamt of arms, legs, eyes, birthmarks, toes and tufts of hair, all jigsawed into scattered twisty parts. As he reached out to put them together, a piece dropped off the window-ledge and then another. When he rushed into the street to rescue them, the pieces had been swept into the gutter and washed down the sewer. He would wake in a sweat with a dry sob and Jere would be lying there with him and he would wonder if she was the part that had slipped off the ledge.

When he tried now on the train to bring back into focus the how and why of separation, the pinwheel had almost burned itself away and the crazy circles of light were dimmer and dimmer. The cable from Jere's sister with the clear cold words *Papa died this morning you are needed here for the settling of the estate*—They agreed it might be better or at least cheaper for him to stay on and finish the book. It was no good without her or with her, but he worked and worked to make this the book.

When it was finished he came back to the new America of soup kitchens and apple vendors and Communists, to the professional cheerleaders pointing to prosperity around the corner, beating out the musical assurance that Happy Days Are Here Again and following Jimmy Walker's advice to avoid depressing movies. The big joke was the hotel clerk asking the man if he wanted the room for sleeping or jumping, which was hard to laugh at with Wally Betz doing a swan dive from his penthouse facing the Park and not even succeeding in doing away with himself but merely in twisting up his spine.

He had cabled Jere to meet him, for they weren't really separated though she hadn't answered a letter in months. But she had always been an erratic correspondent. On the pier he kept hoping until an executor for the Wilder estate came along and told him where she was.

At a luxurious sanitarium in upper New York he found her on a croquet lawn as smooth as a putting green playing intently with an ex-senator, a steel magnate's soft son who had drunk his way through five wives, and a depleted Follies girl who had once been a front-page scandal. A guard whose function was not concealed by his sportclothes had led him to the group. When she saw him she went on playing her ball and missed the wicket.

She came over and said, "See what you did? You made me miss my shot." When he apologized, feeling like a latecomer to the garden party of the White Queen, she became almost the Jere he used to know. "It doesn't matter. I hate this silly O.T. stuff anyway. You should see us all trying to sew and play bridge in the salon after supper. I think it'd make a hilarious play. My doctor thinks I should try it."

It seemed that she had been furious with him for deserting her and not leaving Europe sooner. Apparently she had forgotten all about their decision that she should come back and join him when she was ready. "Oh, well, it doesn't matter. I guess nobody cares whether I live or die any more," she insisted on ending the argument.

His talk with Dr. Stedman was no more satisfactory. He had discounted Jere's charge that Stedman was a phony, but somehow the man was a little too suave for a scientist. His answers to the hard questions were diplomatic. With a great many high-sounding phrases he knew how to say nothing at all in such a way as to reassure the average visitor. The impression he left was that at $40 a day he was in no hurry to let go of a good thing.

The book came out to mixed notices and a disappointing advance sale. The ephemeral quality of the subject matter made him seem wordy and decadent. Most of the reviewers buried him respectfully. Some of the critics actually blamed him for "the social irresponsibility of the Twenties" as if the entire spirit of the decade had been his own private idea.

The reaction, or rather the lack of reaction, made him feel as if in entering this new decade he was entering a strange house to which he had not been invited. It seemed almost too damned easy to think of himself and the Twenties as going smash together, as if he were unconsciously acting out the Twenties in some ghastly charade, and yet here he was in the first year of the Depression with his money gone, his wife nearly gone, his reputation going. What had Hank said? He didn't know how to keep his distance.

Hank came in to see him at the Harvard Club one day, an American radical now with vague plans for organizing a new left-wing book club. "Man, one thing the Crash has done, it's killed the illusion of a middle class. We have to take our stand with the workers or go over to the ruling class." They argued as they always seemed to now, and Hank made the grim prediction that he'd never write another first-rate book until he faced the economic realities (seemed as if people were always shaking fingers in his face and warning him to Get Reality like a new religion). But when they parted Hank still said, "Now, for Chris'-sake, if you need me for anything, a little dough or something, holler" and "Remember for my money you still start where the others leave off. Write the story of our generation from a social point of view and you've got the first important book of the Depression."

Old Man Wilder had written Jere out of the will and only one of the sisters helped at all (though she was thoroughly ashamed of Jere like the others). So forty dollars a day was soon too much and he had to move her into town to a place on Central Park West for a hundred a week (still too much but what could he do?). There people wandered up and down the corridors all day and all night and lived on little black capsules of bella donna (and God knows what else) that Jere began to crave almost as much as the Terpene Hydrate. But one night she called from an obscure hotel on the West Side—*Man, I couldn't stand it any longer. I've just taken two dozen sleeping pills and I want to say good-bye.* "Jere, for God's sake, I thought you were at Coomb's." He found her lying across the bed breathing hideously. Up through a city that didn't care screamed the ambulance. Then three days under the oxygen tent, with Hank and Burt Seixas there with the money for the private room. Watching her breathe and holding his breath with her, loving her still. Yet when the tent was removed and she could talk enough to say *Man, let's try it again* and promise all the old promises, he knew he had to say, "First you go back to Coomb's and stop drinking and then let's try another analyst and then we'll see." She turned her head to the wall and cried and he put his hand over his eyes to hide his own helpless tears.

The ordeal with Jere, the frustration of money-needs, loneliness, disorientation and the first real writing block of his career made drinking a necessity. Alcohol had always loosened his wits and his sense of festival, but now it only dragged him down into despondency and evil temper. For the first time in his life he was thrown out of a speak for insulting a guest; another time when he started a fight he would have been booked for disorderly conduct if Burt Seixas hadn't come to his rescue and pulled some strings.

An old friend from Amherst got Douglas into Eagle School near Greenfield, Mass., and that cost money. So he squeezed Burt Seixas for advances and because it was cheap and still had a few memories he holed up at the Murray Hill to crank out formula for the magazines. He had to do five before even, with his name, they would take one. Somehow he managed the tuition and Jere's bills at Coomb's. He would have sold his eyes right out of their sockets to keep her out of a state institution. And his own drinking was mean and double-desperate, murderous and suicidal. One day, one day, where was he? Could you tell me where I am? I mean what hotel? What town? Greenwich Arms in Stamford? Oh. An' an' what day is it? Friday, June tenth. Date means something. Hasta mean something. Lord, Douglas' graduation. Ready for Lawrenceville. Musn't let Douglas down. Trying to hold himself together among the oh-so-proper parents of the boys at Eagle School and the stares the who-in-the-world-is-*that* looks and the hurt of hearing the outraged parents from Brookline saying *He looks like something from Skid Row* and the answer that half killed him, *They say he's the author of something or other*. Christ, what a humbug this whole educational system was, he was telling them, not just thinking but actually *telling* them and people were laughing and the headmaster hovered over the scene like a buzzard ready to snatch his rotten presence from the midst of all this respectability. Then into this nightmare thrusts the face of Douglas crying, "God damn you, you're stinking drunk. All the guys're laughing at me, they're *laughing*." The child's pain came through sharply to him and he slunk away. On the B & M going back to New York he churned in an agony of self-disgust.

He remembered walking up the steps of the fine old Fifth Avenue mansion that housed the publishers who used to make a celebration of his every appearance. He remembered having to wait twenty minutes while Burt Seixas finished reading a new outline with Caulfield Kdaly, the new twenty-two-year-old flash, then listening to Burt, his old close friend, talking from behind his big curved pipe, "Man, we simply can't see our way to any further advances. You know how the book business has been hit. Frankly, Man, it would be easier if I could show them upstairs that you were actually at work on something. But, Man, if a few dollars will help you in a personal way . . ." "No, no, thanks anyway, Burt. So after all I've done for Dorset House, I'm not even a good professional risk." "Now, Manley, be reasonable, you know it isn't that exactly . . ."

And getting back to his two-dollar room in the Hotel Excelsior (after all those palatial Excelsiors on the European circuit) to find a hundred-dollar bill in his overcoat pocket pinned to a note that said only *I believe in you. B. S.* Lying low in a cubby-hole room in this Hotel Excelsior was like not being in New York at all; that night he bought a box of fig-newtons for supper and sat down at the desk to make an inventory of the cluttered disorder of his mind. On one page of stationery he added up his debts, $32,475. On another, the money he had loaned to friends through the years when he was flush, $11,500. Paring to the bone he budgeted his living expenses and family responsibilities for $12,000. He made a list of all his literary assets, the stories that might be resold for radio programs or movies and the ones he had in mind but had never written. There were ideas for at least three more novels he was going to write. The mere listing of these things started a feeble current. Finally he listed the names not only of those who owed him money but some moral indebtedness or mere wealthy friends from the past who had once made that nice little speech about feeling free to call on them.

They all came up with the same answer, as if they had rehearsed it together; wished they could, but times 've changed, maybe if things improve with the new Administration . . . The run-around, the stall, leaving him to wonder just how many friends he had of all those masquerading as friends, made up to look like friends, *I know what—I'll go as a friend,* but now the costume party's over and they've all gone home.

When the last phone call to the last name on the list led no-where but back into himself, a heavy hammer went thud against a leaden bell and he said, Well, worse has come to worst and I'll wire Phil Coyne. For years he had been conscientiously ig-noring the fabulous offers from Coyne in behalf of producers looking for polish jobs to give their scripts the Halliday touch. Well—his telegram tried to sound light-hearted—the Halliday touch was on the market at last.

Two days later his answer was one of those exuberant Holly-wood responses—tickled to death know I can get you fifteen hundred a week quicker than you can say Spyros Skouras buzz me what plane to meet.

He couldn't tell Coyne he was coming by bus. All he had was the C-note from Burt, fifty dollars from Hank and another sev-enty-five for a first edition of *Bleak House* in its original monthly installments he had paid $785 for in 1927 when he had thought of becoming a collector. ("Rare books are always a good investment," he remembered explaining to Jere.) He also had a complete leather-bound edition of Cabell, twenty-two handsome volumes, which he had once thought of passing down to his son and heir as an invaluable possession. When he asked fifty dollars for the set, the dealer just showed his bad teeth in a mirthless laugh.

He traveled across the continent with his head back against the seat rest, a part of the gray crumpled mass crowded into the bus, a piece of human cargo in a cross-country truck with seats.

Like the others he moved dully West with the listless dream of *maybe it's a little better farther on.* He looked out through un-focusing eyes at the monotonous American landscape. He hardly listened to the drone of complaints that took the form of idle argument about the course of the depression, Roosevelt, Com-munism, the bonus, the eviction strikes. And through it all, through twenty-three sovereign states, a young man in a shabby suit with a thin face discolored with impetigo sang in a tireless drone: I guess I'll have to change my plan . . .

When he climbed out of the bus and called Coyne, his agent said, *Sweetheart I'm tickled to death,* and he observed morosely,

"People have been tickled to death. I understand it's a form of torture among certain African tribes."

"Are you an expert on Africa?" Coyne said, right on the ball. "There's something at Universal called *The Gorilla Woman*. About a beautiful white girl raised by gorillas. She can't talk, kind of a female Tarzan, until this white hunter finds her. She attacks him like a gorilla and he captures her and keeps her in a cage until he tames her. Ends in a helluva chase with all the gorillas after them. They want to make it as big as the elephant stampede in *Chang*. But I hear they're having script trouble."

He heard himself saying with admirable restraint that he did not think he'd be ideal for *Gorilla Woman*.

"To tell you the truth, I've never been even formally introduced to a gorilla woman."

"Well, hundreds of you writers are out of work," Coyne said reprovingly. "We're beginning to feel the pinch out here too. But don't worry, sweetheart, I'll have something for you by the end of the week."

Meanwhile Coyne had made reservations for him at the Beverly-Wilshire. "Mr. Coyne, you might as well know, if I were in a position to maintain myself at the Beverly-Wilshire, I wouldn't have bothered coming out here at all."

"Don't worry about it, sweetheart. After all, you're a famous author, aren't you? You've got to keep up a front. You don't have to pay the bill till you get a job—the manager's a pal of mine. And you're a cinch, even if things are a little tighter at the moment and you aren't quite as hot now as you were last time out. You'll hear from me, Hally."

Up on Yucca above Hollywood Boulevard he found a room in a boarding house for ten dollars a week. It was a run-down wooden mansion built in that fussy hybrid architecture of twenty years before, full of run-down movie people. A blonde who had been something of a name only a few years back, somewhat bloated with drink but still attractive enough to lead a busy life, showed him her scrap book and he liked the way she tossed off the good years without a fleck of self-pity—"What the hell, I had a lot of laughs." A stunt man who had broken his back doing a comic fall down a flight of stairs and would never be able to straighten up again said he was going to write a book to solve the depression. There was a wrestler who thought he had an operatic voice and made the rounds of the studios each day to convince them he was a second Lawrence Tibbett. There was an old couple who used to make fifty dollars a day playing bits but now "the directors we knew are nearly all gone" and a hundred a month was doing well. There was quite a pretty young girl from Hazelton, Pa., who had been picked as a star by her high-school dramatic coach and who wrote her mother every day. She had a terrible time with the operatic wrestler and Manley couldn't help feeling a little sorry when she finally succumbed.

He found himself surprisingly at home among all these people, the has-beens and the never-will-bes. Here in this flea-bitten rooming house were the pain and the false hope and the terrible day-to-day waiting that was more Hollywood than all the fanfare of Grauman's Chinese.

Once he had written the story of an extra, *The Telephone Slave,* and he had not done badly with his imagining, but now he *was* an extra and his constant calls to Coyne followed a cheerless pattern in which both parties pretend to be friendly and light-hearted. "Hello, Hally . . . just going to call you . . . nothing new at the moment, sweetheart . . . Joe Siskind may have something for you when he gets back from New York . . . I'll be in touch with you, Hally . . ."

But less and less in touch as the months dragged on. No, Mr. Coyne hasn't come in yet, no, Mr. Coyne has just gone out—the technique of the snub which the business world has done so much to develop. With a sense of outrage he worked himself up to calling Coyne at his home while Coyne was giving a crucial dinner party for J. C. Coles. The brush-off incited him to the point of telling Coyne off, which left him not only jobless but agentless, a kind of Hollywood *untouchable.*

Summer came on in a wave of enervating heat that all the natives assured one another was pleasantly dry. He walked the steaming Middle-Western streets of Hollywood—Kansas City with prettier girls and pistachio architecture. Friends of his were receiving two thousand dollars a week here every Wednesday, but he was careful to avoid them. He would liked to have looked into Stanley Rose's Book Shop but he had no desire to be introduced to the young men of promise who were said to hang out there, and he was wary of Stanley's reputation for generosity.

He had taken the precaution of registering as Joseph Manley and it gave him an inexplicable satisfaction to be addressed as Joe. Not that the chances were very great of anyone's quickening to the name of Manley Halliday. But this Joe business gave him a gratifying sense of a new identity. The idea of moving to another country with a new name, perhaps even a new occupation, beginning again as someone else, appealed to him enormously, became an insistent day-dream.

With an unexpected check for $803.17 for reprint royalties, he bought an old Lincoln roadster, an impractical purchase which he recognized as a hangover from his habits of the Boom. He had always been the slave of elegant machines. He had worshiped Stutz, Pierce-Arrow, Rolls-Royce, Daimler, Renault, Hispano-Suiza, Duesenberg. The big Lincoln was a steal.

On a Monday morning (is there anything that makes a man feel so adrift and unemployed in America as going nowhere in particular on a Monday morning?) he drove up the coastal highway, past the hotel-size beach house of Marion Davies where he had once been a guest of honor. Although the day promised to be warm it was still early and the beaches were almost deserted. He enjoyed the way the giant sea stretched lazily along the sand. He enjoyed the typical Southern Californian flourishes, the hamburg stand built to resemble a feudal castle, the arrestingly developed young girl whose yellow dab of sunsuit allowed nearly all of her to darken to golden brown.

This was the passive journey of a tumbleweed at the mercy of winds carrying north. At Topanga Canyon the radiator boiled over. He walked along the row of ramshackle cottages on stilts above the water. There was one that attracted his attention, first because of its name *San Simian* (between *C-Breeze* and *Dive Inn*) and then because of the small for-rent sign on the door. Forty minutes later *San Simian* was his: $50 for the summer months, $25 after the season. It was just beaver-board inside, a room, a small bath and a kitchenette. Each time the waves

274

pounded up beneath him *San Simian* would shudder like a small ship in a heavy sea. But the room had a good wide window, where he could sit for hours and watch the ocean. He liked the idea that this room was a one-man cave where he could hibernate to lick his wounds. He made a game of seeing how modestly he could live and, depending largely on fig-newtons and crackers, was especially pleased with himself the week his food bill cut under six dollars.

He would sit at his window watching the waves or the birds forming up for flight and think how good and peaceful it was that not a person in the world knew where he was. No phone, no address, no neighbors. He sat at his window and watched the sandpipers chase the foamy line of the surf back into the sea.

On rickety supports that somehow managed to be more secure than they looked, like those of his shaky retreat, bothering no one and only asking not to be bothered in return, he lived through the crowded summer into the fall, when only the hardy ones trusted themselves to the sea; then on into the winter, when the beach was abandoned to the desolate and the foolhardy.

Now, with one exception, he had the beach colony all to himself. A young woman whose regular dips at seven each morning had become, without his noticing it, part of the pattern of his day, like the rise and fall of the sun and the tide, the passing of the fishing boats and the movement of the birds. Each morning he watched her from his window, running a hundred yards up and down the narrow beach, then neatly putting her towel down and plunging out beyond the breakers to swim perhaps a dozen strokes in one direction, then a dozen in the other. He grew fond of watching her ride the last wave in, remove her yellow bathing cap and shake out her thick black hair. With a nice sense of physical disinterest, he grew accustomed to her tall, sturdy, full rather than plump and not at all unhandsome body. He found himself looking forward each morning to her ritual.

One winter's morning he was especially pleased when she appeared and went through her program despite a driving rain and a gray, roiled surf. On several occasions they were the only people on the beach and there seemed an obligation to nod or mumble good morning as they passed, but he felt no desire to break out of the pattern of solitude he had established. She seemed perfectly willing to accept this arrangement.

As winter drew on he took a mild pride in their relationship. They had a mutual respect for each other's privacy while maintaining a pleasant seashore civility. One cool morning in March, unable to sleep, he had risen to stroll the beach. When she appeared they said their usual good morning but this time he was closer and he stopped just beyond the water-line to watch her take the waves.

"Pretty cold?" he felt he ought to say when she ran over to pick up the towel lying near him.

"About fifty," she said.

She dried herself vigorously and unself-consciously. She had a fine reassuring face. It was not one of the beautiful faces in his life, but it was interesting. The nose was classically high-bridged, graceful in an ancient Semitic way. The eyes were dark blue and unusually direct.

"You stay down here all winter?" he asked, so he wouldn't seem to be staring.

"Yes, I like winters here. Well, I have to hurry. Good-bye."

She walked rapidly up the beach to her cottage and went in without looking back.

The following week-end brought one of those warm spring days that reward year-round beach-dwellers for all the grayness and gloom. He was sitting on the beach when she came out, smiled at him matter-of-factly, and began to read. When, after half an hour or so she put the book down to take a dip, he couldn't resist wandering by, as if by accident, to see what book it was. It was *Shadow Ball*. He would have thought himself beyond such things but the unlikelihood of this coincidence seemed to arouse his sleeping vanity. On his way back to his cottage for a bite of lunch he paused for small talk of weather and swimming and then asked in a casual way what she was reading and how she liked it. "Nice job," she said. "He's caught something true about Hollywood. The extravagance and the fear."

"Oh, I think he's pretty half-baked and second-rate," he had said, enjoying himself immensely.

She said, "That's ridiculous. He makes some silly technical

276

mistakes about Hollywood, but it's thoughtful and it's damn literate."

She seemed so interested in the works of Halliday that he couldn't resist saying, "I wonder where he is now."

"Haven't heard of him in years," she said. "My father used to know him when he was in Hollywood."

This called for introductions. She was Ann Loeb. Loeb. Loeb. Name's familiar. "Not the daughter of old Sam Loeb?" His powers of deduction almost gave him away. "Yes, how did you know?"

"Oh, after all it was a big name. Is he still producing?"

"Died last year. Poor guy, pretty much broken. When he was on top our house Christmas Day was Grand Central. Christmas before last the phone didn't ring once. Mean town."

Uh, Jack Delaney he said his name was. First one that came to him. He had seen Delaney put up a sensational fight against Paul Berlenbach in the Garden years ago. Delaney had been one of his heroes too, before Jack hit the skids.

He had stood talking to her so long that it seemed easy to accept her invitation to sit down. After all the months alone it was good to talk to someone again. Miss Loeb had a calm, accurate way of going at things that was stimulating without being too disquieting. She seemed very sure of what she knew, but more in a scientific than in a defiant way and when she said, as she often did, *That's ridiculous,* she had a way of making whatever she was passing judgment on seem indeed the most ridiculous thing in the world.

All that next week she was away and though he desired no more than to have little conversations with her the beach seemed desolate without her. On the beach the following Saturday she mentioned casually that she was making spaghetti and perhaps he'd like to drop in for a bite. "Nothing formal, just come if you feel like." Despite all resolves he was still a social animal and, though very much on his guard, he even showed up with a clean shirt. To avoid laundering, he had stripped his wardrobe to beach-combing essentials.

Her cottage was four rooms, built more substantially than his, furnished with rough-and-ready good taste. There was a surprisingly good library for a beach shack and a record player with a lot of chamber music, Bach and some Ravel and Stravinsky. She made a batch of Martinis and they listened to the *Chaconne* from the Violin Sonata and sipped a fair local red wine with the spaghetti. The moon threw a ghostly road across the sea. It was the first civilized eating since he had come to Topanga and the wine and then the brandy on top of the Martinis brought him a sense of well-being that began to blur into dizziness. He remembered her saying she was a film cutter and his drawing her out with a conventional attack on the movies and her beginning to explain a number of technical phases of the art he had never thought of before. He remembered sliding off into space with her face and her words farther and farther in the distance. But after a vague struggle of *where am I?* he remembered nothing until late the next morning when with a shaky feeling of self-reproach he realized the answer was: on her daybed in the front room.

She brought him a glass of orange juice. She already had been swimming. She said it was a nice day.

"This proves exactly what I feared," he said. "My days as a social human being are definitely behind me."

"That's ridiculous. All it proves is that you have a very low tolerance to alcohol."

But he insisted on the tragic view. He was sorry he had spoiled what promised to be a pleasant acquaintanceship. "If I have any genius," he said, "it's for making an unholy mess of everything I do."

"You're too intelligent for self-pity," she said. "Now go home and shave and stop worrying about yourself. And come for supper next Saturday night if you feel like it."

Before he could realize its true significance, the Saturday-night supper had become the hook on which his whole week hung. They had a running argument about movies which they both seemed to enjoy. He insisted that any art which was not dependent on the skill and taste and integrity of a single person was doomed to everlasting mediocrity. But she said, "That's ridiculous. You're judging from the Hollywood pictures and nearly all of them are mediocre. But they're mediocre for business reasons, not for the ones you give. Building pyramids was a group art. There must have been a producer in the person of the Pharaoh who had the money and the general idea, an architect, a sculptor, and master masons to carry out the design, skilled workmen under them and so forth. Or the totem poles. Of course there can be a valid group art. We've seen it in the movies with Griffith and Eisenstein and Chaplin. It needs a guiding genius or at least a knowing hand like Vidor's or Ford's. But when you start with something good enough and everyone does his job, the director, writer, cameraman, cutter, composer and sound mixer—for some reason I always leave out the actors —it's an art all right."

They talked about Thalberg—funny how after all the blank years his memory could fill in everything that had been said —and he wondered whether he was the great genius that Hollywood believed.

"Well—it's a worn-out word," she had said. "Maybe in its original sense Irving was a genius. A kind of inspirational god. Genius has its practical side too. The man who gets there first when he's most needed. A man who manages to dig a well in the dryest part of the Sahara is a genius even though there may be a hundred who dig much better wells in town. Irving is that kind of genius. He's come to the desert and he's struck water. It may not be a very deep well but it'll do for a start."

"In other words God was the first genius," he said. "And you have to be at least a little god in a little pool to qualify."

"Are you doing any writing at all now?" she asked suddenly.

He began to answer and then he remembered he was *Jack Delaney* and caught himself. "What makes you think I'm a writer?"

"Maybe I shouldn't have told you. I've known for weeks. Since the day I was reading *Shadow Ball* on the beach. When I went in I looked at the picture on the back. You haven't changed that much."

"That picture was taken a thousand years ago when I was still a young man and still a writer."

"S. P." she said.

"S. P.?"

"Self-pity. It doesn't become you. You're better than that."

After that he found he could talk quite frankly about his predicament. It was not a nervous or a mental breakdown, he said, just a feeling that too much had happened. And he told her his image of the boat that could not be steered or propelled for ever needing to be bailed. "I used to be pretty good at bailing when Sam had a boat at Laguna," she said. "Madame, I shall be delighted to hand you the pail," he said with an echo of his old charm.

The following Saturday night she asked him again if he was writing and he said just remaining alive seemed to require all his energy and creative power now and she said, "That's ridiculous. Why don't you try writing your life? Just a kind of summing up of what you've done and thought and become. Write it for yourself so you won't have to compete with anything. A lot cheaper than going to an analyst. Now start right away."

To his surprise, he did, and just the sound of the typewriter's clicking was tonic for him. It felt good even to be going through the empty exercise of writing and he began to think that getting it all down, the too-early triumphs, the reckless celebration, the soaring success, the plunging to earth of his dreams and twenties, the wreckage and the attempt to salvage, would give him a blue-print at last on which to build for middle-age. He was like a crustacean, he had written, that sheds its first bright shell and then fails to find the larger, duller, more substantial one it needs for protection through maturity.

He read some of this to Ann, including the confession that at first he had wanted the applause of his friends and then the rewards of his own society and now he saw through temporal success to the life-after-death of being read by future generations. "Like Stendhal, I'd settle for a hundred years," he said. "But if you don't get that, you're just like any sandpiper chasing crabs along the beach, living for the moment."

"You have a chance if you think of yourself as just beginning. If you think of the writing and the living so far as just a preparation."

He knew what she was trying to do, pull him up out of the past, but he said, "Ruth's home-run record didn't prepare him for hitting more home runs. He had just so many home runs in him and he got rid of most of them before he was thirty."

"That's the most ridiculous thing I've ever heard," she had said. "For a gifted, intelligent man you are full of the most juvenile nonsense. Forget these silly sports heroes. An athlete's career is just the opposite of an artist's. The athlete matures faster, loses his reflexes through his twenties and is washed up in his thirties. But an artist should build slowly through his twenties, start maturing in his thirties and reach his peak in his fifties or sixties. Maybe that's the trouble with you American writers, you think of yourselves as athletic stars."

"I always had a crazy ambition to be a backfield star—I'll never know why," he confessed. "To break out into the open with one of those dazzling exhibitions like Red Grange or Chris Cagle."

"I think you're the second author I know who wanted to be a football player. And two others who are frustrated pitchers and one would-be Jimmy McLarnin. In Europe the authors would like to have been composers or painters or mathematicians."

"We're a more muscular race. And I suppose since writers are fairly sensitive registers of national consciousness, they naturally reflect the hero-worship of their times. After all who else had any grandeur in American life except a Ruth, a Dempsey or a Bobby Jones?"

"You go home and start your novel and leave the touchdowns to Orv Mohler," she said.

He had begun dropping in for supper Sundays as well as Saturdays and without either of them thinking anything about it they began to say, "If you're going up to the store we need some ketchup and a can of coffee." There was no danger of his falling in love with her, for his heart was hidden away securely in the vault with Jere's, but he had the fondness for her that a crumbling wall might have for the post that shores it.

One night talking about the writing that was starting to trickle into a flow again (he had finished a short story that seemed as good as ever he had done) he wondered how it would affect his work to be so withdrawn, not just from the world but from himself. "My only real experience comes when

I'm writing now. I woke up this morning thinking I'm not a man at all, just a man-like machine for writing fiction."

"That's ridiculous. Of course you're a man. Sounds like S. P. to me."

("Every time I catch you in an S. P. you have to go to the store for the groceries," she had said, beginning a cure remarkable for its simplicity. Every time he caught himself in a soft attitude he'd find himself thinking *S. P.* and after a while it became automatic and the self-pity began to dry up like a sore exposed to ultra-violet.)

But this time he said, "No, Ann, there's a difference; this is S. A. and it doesn't stand for sex-appeal but self-analysis. For instance, if this had been ten years ago I'm sure I would have thought about wanting you. That's probably as far as it would have gone, but once or twice at least I'd have thought about it, wondered about it."

"And you don't think about it now?"

He shook his head.

"That's ridiculous."

It was like urging him to write, or to exorcise self-pity. It was all part of her effort to convince him that he was a better man than he gave himself credit for being. By the time summer came on again it seemed unnecessary to keep *San Simian* when her cottage was more than large enough.

"You understand, I'm completely incapable of loving you, but much to my surprise I like being with you," he had felt obliged to say.

"Let's leave it this way," she said. "Any time it gets too much for you just feel free to go, the same way you came."

Perhaps because this enabled him to have a relationship without being weighed down with its responsibilities the bond grew stronger. By the end of summer he had sold two stories that were not pot-boilers. He had been thinking about the new novel since the previous spring and by autumn was ready to begin. But after a few pages he tired exasperatingly. At times nausea left him unable to work for days and by mid-afternoon his brain would be dull with the need for sleep.

He despised himself for his inertia and told Ann he was determined not to succumb to symptoms he was sure were psychic —his unwillingness to face the challenge of a new book. Said Ann, consistent pragmatist, "Don't be too sure everything's neurotic. There's a danger of swinging too far the other way. Before you give yourself up as a subconscious malingerer, I want you to see my doctor. Dr. Rubin's a diagnostician with enough psychoanalytic knowledge to advise you if that's your trouble."

Dr. Rubin said: diabetes. It was a final blow to vanity to realize he carried an incurable physical flaw. On the other hand, it was reassuring to learn that his routine could be stabilized by careful diet, rest and drugs rather than by the more uncertain correctives of the mind. There was more energy to draw on after that, and the manuscript began to grow. But the medical treatment had added to his expenses. Jere was trying a new analyst, Douglas was in prep school, and in addition to these burdens there was the embarrassment of slipping into a dependent's status in a household supported by Ann. So the sugar balance was restored but not the financial, and this began to prey so insistently on his mind that he kept interrupting his work to write short stories again. It was like groping through a maze of underground tunnels from which he could find no exit. But if he could ever work his way out into the light, he'd be all right. He was sure of that now. With Ann, he was absolutely sure. Only these story sales would never heal the wound. You didn't apply a band-aid when a man has a six-inch gash in his side.

That's how the idea of a movie job was resurrected. A job of fifteen weeks at two thousand a week would square him with the world. With that behind him he could stay with the new writing program until he was as old as G. B. S. Fifteen weeks— it wouldn't be easy to put the book aside—but he rationalized the delay as the debt he owed for past transgressions. Ann was willing to loan him the money to see the book through but when he insisted she told him about the *Love on Ice* job. She knew Milgrim was looking for a new writer. And he was partial to literary reputations. She'd talk to Al Harper, the agent, about seeing Milgrim.

So there it was, full circle, from Hollywood when it wanted him to Hollywood when he wanted it, or rather, needed it. A college musical—the chore appealed to him about as much as if he had been asked to write the text for a Sears Roebuck catalogue.

But there was that ten weeks' minimum of two thousand a week—ten weeks' minimum of two thousand a week—ten weeks' minimum of two thousand a week the tracks seemed to be saying.

If only he could keep his mind on the story, *keep your mind on the story—keep your mind on the story,* the tracks kept saying, *what story—what was the story—what story—what was the story.*

Ann was asking him, *Manley, are you all right?*

No, it wasn't Ann. Where the hell was Ann? Pro'ly not back from the studio yet. My God, his head. Must've forgotten to take his shot. Must've fallen asleep waiting for Ann. *Ann's 'it you?*

"Manley this is Shep, *Shep."*

Shep? Oh. Oh. "Got my part finished. Think we got it now, Shep."

The train suddenly screamed its warning into the night.

"Shep? Shep. Where are we Shep?"

"Not sure. Think we're coming in to Springdale."

"Coming in . . . ?"

He felt the unfamiliar leather, slowly remembering, the men's room—what was he doing in the men's room of a train coming into Springdale? He lay back experimentally and tried to open his eyes again in the familiar darkness of his room in the cottage. No good, he was on the train all right, he was writing that damned movie all right, he was on his way to Webster all right, *and suddenly as he went down for the last time his whole life passed before his eyes.* Good Lord, maybe the slicks had something there after all, he was always going down for the last time, his life was always passing before his eyes, at least one of his eyes was always watching his life pass before him, only what he had told, what he had dreamt, what he had thought, was all a horrible tangle.

"'F I said anything I shouldn't . . ."

"Forget it," Shep said. It had begun as if he were going to spill his guts but then it had wandered off into a meaningless jumble that finally reached an end in restless sleep. "Manley, are you sure you're all right? Not sick or anything?"

Manley said, "Gotta keep our promise. Gotta work out this story."

Looking at the spent face with the dark shadows under the eyes, Shep said, "Manley, you better lie down and get some more sleep. I'll see what I can do alone and wake you up an hour before we get in to talk it over."

"No. Feel like I was deserting. 'F I could just get a cup of coffee. Stayed up three days and nights once to finish a job on nothing but coffee. Gonna lick this thing with you."

He staggered to his feet, sick inside with a tremendous effort to hold together. "Let's go the diner get some coffee."

"Know what time it is—nearly two."

"Gotta have coffee."

The train was slowing down for Springdale. Shep asked the sleepy porter how much time they had. Ten minutes. He peered out beyond the squat dark shadow of the little station to the fuzzy red neon of an all-night diner across the street.

"Maybe we c'n make that diner if we run for it."

"Gotta have coffee," Manley said. "Be a new man 'f I have a cupa coffee."

15

Raw wind drove the wild-falling snow into their faces as they hurried across the street. The all-night diner was a bright chromium refuge. There was a sense of timelessness about the brassy riff of the disc-jockey program from the tinny radio, the expressionless face of the swarthy short-order cook doped with monotony, the skinny, fortyish waitress with too much make-up carrying on a weary tradition of idle flirtation with a truck driver.

"Wottle it be, boys?" the waitress said.

"Two cups of Joe but fast," Shep said.

"Suppose I ought to eat something," Manley Halliday said. "Did we eat dinner tonight? Or lunch? Funny, I can't remember."

"Let's see. Can't remember dinner. Damned if I know if we had lunch either."

"Didn't we order lunch in the room. The German waiter—?"

"No, wasn't that yesterday? We're in great shape."

"'S funny, three days ago I'd be upset if I missed a mealtime by five minutes. Rubin and Ann had me working like a clock. It's this drinking's got me all mixed up."

"Manley, if you want to eat something you'd better order fast. We've only got seven minutes."

"Let me think—oughta get back to my diet—need to get back in shape so I can help you. I guess soft-boiled eggs."

"Manley, we haven't got time for that now," Shep said crossly.

"If you're in a hurry, better fry 'em honey."

"All right, one egg."

"Turned over, honey?"

"No."

"And it's no gag about the rush—we're off that train." Shep added.

"A sunny one, toot sweet," the waitress called to the cook.

"That's why you hafta listen all the time," Manley Halliday

said. "You could think for days an' never write a line like that, a sunny one, toot sweet."

"Yeah," said Shep. "Better start drinking your coffee, Manley. That clock isn't waiting for us."

From the radio came the incorrigible cheerfulness of the all-night jockey: "And now for Sue and Earl, a couple of night-owls in Brattleboro, and for Johnny and Edna of 331 Canal Road and for Rose and Morris and for Margaret at Vic's diner in Springdale . . ."

The dark, sullen face of the short-order cook grinned. Margaret their waitress laughed, embarrassed, and the truck driver took it big.

"Hey, Margaret, c'n I have your autograph?"

"Gee, I been waitin' for three weeks. I thought I missed it."

"The boss oughta give you a raise, all that free advertisin'," the cook said.

"I wonder if Frank heard it," the waitress said.

Their check was under the glass and Shep with a "we've got to cut out of here" reached for it, but Manley Halliday, as if this were Voisin's, said no, it was his party, the stop-off had been his idea and he insisted.

"All right, all right, then pay the lady," Shep said. "But for Christ sake *hurry*. If we miss that train we might as well settle down here in Springdale."

"All right," Manley Halliday said, pushing the egg away with childish pique. "I can't eat when you're riding me every minute."

"Go ahead and finish it. We've got four minutes."

"Wasn't really hungry anyway. Just thought I ought to try and eat something. Oh, Miss—" He was reaching for his wallet to pay the check.

"Haven't got change? Here I've got change," Shep said impatiently, on his feet and ready to run.

"'T's all right, need some change anyway," Manley Halliday said.

"Look, Manley, why don't you start for the train? I'll pay it and catch up with you."

Manley Halliday opened his wallet slowly and, Shep thought, with exasperating deliberation. He looked into it, then he looked up for a moment and then he looked into it again. A small "oh" formed in his mouth but never quite came out.

"Whatsa matter?"

"The check?"

"It's right here," Shep said, his voice rising as he grabbed the tab from the counter.

"No, my check from the studio. The advance for the first week."

"What the hell were you carrying that around for?"

"I took it East to deposit in my bank in New York. I thought it'd be faster."

"Well, look for it—you must have it—here gimme your wallet."

While Manley Halliday waited helplessly, Shep ran his fingers through the wallet. "Look in your pockets, the coat pockets, maybe the inside pocket of your jacket."

Manley Halliday groped through his pockets. "Don' understan' it. Haven't taken it out since we . . ."

A warning whistle from the train made Shep say, "Forget the damned check. Let's run."

"Just a minute, mister," the cook said in a tone meant to inform them he was on to such shenanigans. "All I hear so far's a lotta talk. Let's have the money."

"A couple of smart guys got away with this two weeks ago," the waitress said. "Ran out just in time to jump the train."

"Here," Shep flung a dollar toward the counter and ran toward the door. It was one of those sliding kind but he had forgotten and tried to push it open.

"Damn thing's stuck," he cried.

"Slide it, slide it," the cook said, shaking his head to the truck driver with a look that said unmistakably *the morons we get in here*.

Shep finally slammed it to one side and threw himself out into the dark night of whirling snow.

"Train's still there," he yelled. "Come on!"

Manley Halliday ran as fast as he could but the footing was uncertain. It was easier to believe he was in the Topanga cottage or the Garden bungalow running through an anxious dream than that he was running for a train in a Godforsaken

288

New England whistle-stop at some awful hour before dawn.

"Are you coming? Are you coming?" Shep shouted. *"Run,* the train's still here."

When Shep reached the train there was not a light anywhere. He ran along the car to the steps from which they had descended, but the platform was down and the door was closed. No, maybe he had made a mistake, easy to do in the dark, all the cars looking the same; he raced down to the next. But it was closed too. He reached up and shook the handle. It was locked. Manley Halliday came up behind him breathing heavily. The train lurched forward a few inches and stopped. Shep cupped his hands to his mouth and shouted. Nothing stirred within the dark train. He pounded on the door. He yelled as loud as he thought it was humanly possible for him to yell and then a little louder than that and the train just stood there deaf and impenetrable.

Manley Halliday stood by, becalmed, as if watching something made less terrible through the perspective of passing time.

"Help! Help! Stop the train!" Shep was yelling, for it was moving now, creeping tantalizingly into motion. They stood there stupidly while it gathered speed. This incredible thing that couldn't really be happening was happening: the train chugged off into the night. The little red tail-light winked at them mockingly and, in less time than would have seemed possible from the cumbersome start, was gone from sight.

Shep's voice wavered as if in piteous prayer. "I'll be a son of a bitch."

Shep looked at Manley Halliday. He thought he was coughing but it turned out to be what Shep least expected, chuckling.

"I wish you'd let me in on the goddam joke," Shep said. "We're marooned in East Jesus. It's cold enough to freeze the balls off a brass monkey. This is probably the last train out of this hole till morning. And when Milgrim finds out we're gone—him with his heart set on arriving with the great Manley Halliday—he'll kick our tails right off the payroll."

"Don't you think I know it? When I think of Victor getting off that train without me, how he'll try to explain, when appearances mean so much to him . . ." He began to laugh again, a kind of hard inside chuckle that became more of a cough.

"Damn it, you're drunk," Shep said.

"Uh uh, too cold to be drunk. Feel a little giddy but afraid it's more the sugar balance outa control."

"Well, if you're not drunk, you've a damn strange sense of humor."

"Lis-sen, baby, no law against having a sense o' humor same time you're miserable, is there? I'm an old hand at being miserable."

"Yeah. Come on, let's get in out of the cold."

They picked their way slowly through the snow to the diner. Shep slid the door back as if he were going to drive it all the way to the end of the diner and barged in ahead of Halliday.

"Miss your train?" the waitress asked.

"No, we just like it here so much we thought we'd stay," Shep said.

"Where you guys trying to go?" the cook wanted to know.

"Middleboro—Webster."

"What you fellas do, play in a band or something?"

"Ever hear of Gene Goldkette's orchestra?" Manley Halliday said.

"Yeah, seems to me somewhere I did."

"Well, this is Gene Goldkette," Manley Halliday said. "My name is Trumbauer."

"We get a lot of you musicians in here. Paul Whiteman was in here once. No kidding. Sat right over there."

"On that little stool?" Manley Halliday said.

"No kidding. I got his autograph on a menu. Know who else was in here one time?"

"Mad Dog Coll?"

"Jessica Dragonette. And you wanna know something, she acts just like anybody else."

"Him and Jessica Dragonette," the waitress said.

"Listen, we're in a real jam. How can we get out of here?" Shep said.

"Next train's five-oh-five."

"What's the next stop for the train we were on?" Manley Halliday asked suddenly.

290

"Le'see, South Harmon, ain't it?"

"What time's it due there?" Manley Halliday asked.

"Le'see, around four o'clock.

"How far is it?"

"Le'see, thirty-five maybe forty miles."

Manley Halliday had taken over. A hectic travel history that included missing and chasing trains across several continents had taught him how to face these emergencies.

"Can you find us a cab that'll put us back on that train?"

"Jesus, at this hour?" The cook looked doubtfully at the waitress. "Think Freddie 'd be willing to get up?"

"Try," Manley Halliday said to Shep. "Call Freddie."

But Freddie said he wouldn't take his car out on a night like this for Christ Almighty himself.

"Le'see," said the cook, getting interested in the problem. "Think Alva would try it?"

"In that wreck of his?" the waitress said. "You'd have to want to go awful bad."

"Call Alva," Manley Halliday told Shep. "Tell him . . ." He turned to the cook. "How much will it take to make Alva happy?"

"Oh, I'd say twenty-five bucks. It's a tough night."

For twenty-five bucks Alva was afraid he'd get stuck; he heard the road was none too good around Stangford. "Tell 'im fifty," Manley Halliday said. For fifty Alva said he guess he could try, maybe the snowplow had gone through since he last heard. "Ain't got no heater, though," he added. "Went kerflooey on me yesterday."

"Ask him if he's got any liquid heat?" Manley Halliday said.

Yes, they'd need something, if they were going to pull through this ride, Shep agreed. "Alva says he's got some applejack. Five dollars a bottle."

"Tell 'im to bring two bottles and get down here right away. Oh, and tell 'im to bring a couple of blankets."

Hurrying to the diner from the train they hadn't even bothered to go back to the drawing room for overcoats.

"Alva says the blankets 'ill be a dollar a piece extra."

"Tell 'im okay and God bless New England."

"He'll be down in ten minutes," Shep said. "How you feeling?"

"You must wanna go awful bad to go with Alva," the waitress said again as she brought more coffee.

"Margaret," Manley Halliday said, "the older you get the more you learn that you spend nine hundred and ninety-nine one-thousands of your time doing what you have to do in order to enjoy that one-in-a-thousand chance at what you want to do."

"Brother, you can say that again," the waitress said.

"I doubt it, Margaret, I doubt it," Manley Halliday said.

"Go on, drink your coffee," said Shep.

Alva's cab was a Model A Ford Sedan with all the felt covering torn away from the floor boards and the stuffing pushing out through holes in the upholstery, so that after a few miles it felt as if they were sitting directly on the springs. Alva had been promised a bonus if he got them on the train and his Yankee acquisitiveness had routed his caution if not his common sense. The squeaky old Model A threatened to shake itself loose from its axle as it bounced along the icy road. Once it skidded into a snowbank but Alva was able to rock it out. "Good girl" were the first words Alva uttered since the start of the journey and it was obvious that Alva had been raised with live transportation and that this car had become more horse than machine.

Shep and Manley Halliday huddled under the thin blankets that could not keep the cold from piercing to the bone. The applejack did what it could, but after a few miles their feet were numb. They could stamp them without being able to feel the movement.

Their faces were so cold that they pulled the blankets over their heads and passed the applejack between them under the improvised tent. Manley Halliday felt light-headed and disembodied. The lapses into memory were the vivid part and this rushing on through the frozen New England darkness in a rattletrap with his head (like the top of a tent-pole) pushed up against the inside of a damp blanket was a nightmare improbability.

"Reminds me of a hilarious trip we took to San Sebastian in a taxi at three o'clock in the morning," he was telling Shep under the blanket passing the applejack. "This fella who was with us oh what *was* his name he was a writer who couldn't write that we liked for a while that winter and then there was a fairy designer an amazing guy who was a pretty good amateur bull fighter haven't even thought of his name in years Sylvester Michaels we called him Silly and the funny part was he actually went crazy later anyway this trip was a riot . . ."

Abruptly he stopped, hurled forward by his own momentum, out of the bright chaos of the past into the grim chaos of the present.—"Oh God, I wrote checks in Hollywood against that advance I meant to deposit in New York and now—oh, what a mess—they're going to bounce."

Cold and stiff and worrying if it was really going to be possible to get back on that train, Shep didn't bother to answer. Christ, he was fed to the teeth with Manley Halliday. Was that all those people thought about, their fun, their parties, their self-indulgences? Wasn't he just a screwball, a congenital ne'er-do-well, a foul-up artist? Christ, people had to grow up. You couldn't go through life in a dream. No wonder most of these characters petered out when life caught up with them and they found it wasn't one continuous New Year's Eve.

Cold and anxious and desperately tired he grew inwardly furious at the idea of Halliday's treating this latest ordeal as a joke, as just another in an endless series of hilarious escapades. In his bitterness he wondered how he ever could have admired Manley Halliday. He began to blame the entire Twenties for this ride in what could only be a vibrating machine crossed with a frigidaire. Goddam the Twenties. He was turning in his suit. He had had enough of Manley Halliday and his goddam Twenties. Well, he just hoped to God he could drag Halliday through this assignment to some sort of credit and not let the old bum drag him down instead. Christ, we drink, he thought self-righteously, but we don't drink ourselves into oblivion or the grave.

In the darkness of this night and the more profound darkness of his own confusion, Manley Halliday sensed the young man's mood and lapsed into silence. So the young man was sore. Well, let the young man be sore. If he was at fault at all it was in having begun this wild-goose chase in the first place, against his better judgment.

After a while when the air was too close and Shep pulled the blanket down, Manley Halliday was sleeping against him with his mouth open, breathing with difficulty. In spite of the harsh things Shep had been thinking and still believed, the plight of the older man softened him to a more sympathetic attitude: after all he had been up there and now he was down here and whether it was his own fault or the blame of faulty times, it isn't easy or nice to see. In the mood of one who checks his temper at the entrance to the burial ground and goes tender inside regardless of previous resolution, he looked down at the exhausted Manley Halliday's sleeping face and wondered where this would end.

From a distance he heard the peculiar moan of an engine's whistle.

"That's yer train," Alva said.

"How far's South Harmon?"

" 'bout sixteen miles."

"Think we c'n make it?"

"If the road up ahead wants us to."

The train let out its distant wail again, a mocking sound coming to them down the dark, treacherous road.

"Stay with it, Alva. Drive like hell."

"Understan', young fella, if I get us all killed I'll hold you personally responsible."

In such a flat voice.

With a tail-wind now, they careened down the icy road.

Twenty minutes of this and there was another skid that almost carried them into a tree. Shep shouted something frightened and fierce that made Manley Halliday sit up and try to see what was happening. He felt cold all over, even colder than before. The cat-nap had completely taken care of the jag.

"How far to South Harmon now?"

Shep looked over in surprise at the clear, quiet way he had asked it.

" 'Bout five miles."

"And the train?"

"It's behind us now, I'd say a good three miles."

294

"Always something nice about going back to your college, isn't there?"

"Mmm."

Alva turned sharply, drew up to the station and said, "Well, we did it. She oughta be comin' along in about five minutes."

In the dark on the desolate wooden platform they stood shivering in the silence gradually penetrated by the sound of the oncoming train, a distant *whoosh-whoosh-whoosh-whoosh* that swelled with audible increase until at last the headlight was shining into their faces and the platform shook with the roar and Shep was ready to hand it to Manley Halliday for thinking so quickly of the taxi-chase. On in a terrible rush without slackening speed the train bore down, the light of the engine illuminating the platform and then leaving them in darkness and new confusion as the train rumbled past. Again they were standing in the cold and the darkness watching the red tail-light winking and mocking the left-behinds.

"Now ain't that a howdy-do?" said Alva, scratching his head.

"Now what?" Shep said, this time too tired and forlorn even to relieve himself with profanity.

"Maybe this train's like Melville's whale," Manley Halliday said. "Maybe it isn't a train at all. Maybe it's the unattainable, the . . ."

"Aw, shove it," Shep said. "It's so cold my eye-balls are beginning to ache. Whatta we do now—find a hotel—wire Milgrim we're writing the goddam story in South Harmon?"

"And all for the show," Manley Halliday said. "This nonsense of having to see the Mardi Gras. All of a sudden Hollywood's so worried about authenticity."

"Mebbe we c'n still flag her at Davidston."

"How far is that?"

"Thirteen miles. The road's good'n straight. I c'n beat her there easy."

"Well, you wanna try Davidston?"

"I suppose we might as well freeze to death in Davidston as South Harmon."

"That'll be ten dollars extry," Alva said.

"Alva, my good man," Shep said, "if we don't flag that train at Davidston we're going to make you stand us to a round of coffee."

Back into their frozen blankets, their eyes fascinated by the slippery road cut between the deep snow banks they raced on to Davidston, not talking now, tired and shaken and bone-cold, with ears, noses, eyes, hands and feet numb and yet able to feel the painful gnawing burning. Passing in and out of consciousness of movement and cold, Manley Halliday thought of death and drove it from him as a vision of panic.

Then just as unreally as they had been separated from the train at Springdale they were joined with it again at Davidston. The details would never be clear to either of them, but there was a tiny platform with a red wooden arm that could be raised, which Alva did, and once more the train came on in a flood of light roaring *whoosh-whoosh-whoosh-whoosh*. They stood there dumbly waiting, ready to be not at all surprised to see it swoosh by them again, at least half-reconciled to that taunting tail-light's winking. Instead the sound of braking, of a slackening of the enormous rhythm, and a conductor, alert now, threw open the door to the platform steps. Then the train was moving under them and the little red light was winking at Alva who could wink back with seventy-five dollars in his pants, a good night's work. He'd 've done it for half that, but it seemed only justice for these city fellers to spread a little of their easy money out here in the country where it was needed like rain in July.

16

"Know what the trouble with this drawing room is?"

Shep didn't bother to look up. "Don't tell me. We've got enough troubles."

"Trouble with this drawing room is we gotta leave it in a couple of hours."

Manley Halliday was sitting on the long side seat with his head bent almost to his knees.

"You better stretch out, unbutton your shirt, Manley."

Shep was worried about the pallor. It wasn't a dead-white any more, but discolored as if by jaundice. And there seemed to be no color left in the eyes at all.

"They'll be serving breakfast soon. I'd better take my shot. Wish I could remember when I took the last one."

He had to use the rim of the upper berth to pull himself to his feet. The few steps to the washroom were precarious. Once the lurch of the train almost pulled him off balance and Shep jumped up to break his fall. Manley Halliday tried a sallow smile and said, "I'm all right."

Shep said, "Well, you don't look all right. If there's anything I can do . . ."

"There is one thing," Halliday admitted. "If that happens again—like on the plane—you might sort of keep an eye on me." Again, without smiling, his voice used the tone that goes with smiling. "I been a good ol' wagon, but baby how I done broke down."

When Manley Halliday emerged from the washroom his eyes appeared brighter and he could stand more erect.

"How much time 'fore we get in?"

Shep looked up hopefully. Behind the crumpled clothing, the stubble of beard and the bilious complexion his man sounded a little more pulled-together.

" 'Bout two 'n a half hours."

"I've thought up lots of plots in two 'n a half hours."

"Well, brother, we could use one now. That camera crew's gonna be on us like wolves the moment we come down the platform. I can hear Hutchinson now, all full of p. and v. saying, 'We're ready like Freddie—where d'we line up first?' Manley, are you listening to me? This is our last chance. Absolutely our last. We've got to do it now or get off the pot."

"All right." Manley Halliday made it sound like a turning point. "Le's each have another inspiration tablet." He passed the benzedrine. "We'll sleep when we get back to New York. Now le's rise to the occasion. All ready—one, two, three—rise——"

"Maybe you think it's funny, but I want to keep this job."

"Young man, you have the word of an old clown, I don't think it's a bit funny."

"Okay, then what do you say we cut out the comedy? You know, you haven't come up with an idea since we started this damn thing."

"All right. All right." He assumed an expression of intense conscientiousness. He was thinking and at the same time trying not to think. "Now let me see. Let me *think*. Let me stick in my thumb and pull out a plum and say what a good hack am I."

Shep watched him shut his eyes, reaching in, making himself think *Love on Ice*.

"My God, I see it!"

"Okay, let's hear it."

When Manley Halliday began to speak, it did not sound at all like the presentation of a fresh idea. It seemed a kind of self-hypnosis, an uncanny playback of something recorded long ago.

"I see it. I see a white fairyland in the Green Mountains. The steep white hillside falls away into a broad valley, as in a skier's dream. In the distance on high a tiny dark figure appears and starts sweeping down toward our camera. Faster and faster he flies over the freshly fallen snow that forms the perfect carpet for the sheer ice beneath. He is the Lone Skier, Youth charging down into the virgin field of trackless snow."

Shep listened in fascination.

"Along the lower edge of the skier's field runs a winding road. Rounding the corner into view is a handsome touring car

—driven by a uniformed chauffeur and carrying a single passenger, a young woman whose face is aglow with the cold of the air and the warmth of being alive. The way only a girl aware of her own youth and beauty can ever feel alive. She is a Princess Solitaire and her blond curls originally molded into an elegant coiffeur that rode her beauty like a golden crown are slightly windblown now. She is snugly bundled in a luxurious fur carrobe and her head is thrown back the better to enjoy the glories of this winter day. As her bright young eyes lift to take in everything, *everything,* she sees our skier, a breath-taking masculine blur of green against the snow-white slope . . ."

"Yes . . . ?" Shep murmured, already half-convinced of *here it was.*

"At the same time a sudden, graceful *Geländesprung* offers our skier first sight of the Girl. In a flash, he sees the pride, the readiness, the lovely out-of-doors flush, the golden curls. Arrested by this vision on the road below, in the very moment of headlong flight, he throws his body in a sudden *christiana* that checks his speed from a breathless fifty miles an hour to a breathless zero. His skis throw up behind him a dazzling white fan of flying crystals. Leaning on his ski-poles he stares boldly to see what he has seen.

"On the road the sport touring car has come abreast of him now. Slowly, with her eyes drawn to the figure on the hill, the girl removes a hand from the chinchilla muff under the robe, leans forward and taps the chauffeur gently on the shoulder. The car comes to a stop. She looks up unashamedly, call it even flirtatiously, but the flirtation of a princess allowing herself to be amused by one of her subjects. The passionate whim of a Goddess of Winding Roads Through Winter Mountains.

"For a moment as pure and still as the trackless snow they look questioningly into each other's eyes across the field of white. In their thoughts they meet, love, marry, age together, die, are buried together on this very hillside, side by side."

Manley Halliday paused and Shep waited as the sound of the train rushing them on came in like the dramatic emphasis of an orchestra in the pit.

"This moment is only a lifetime. This lifetime is only a moment. Lowering her eyes at last, the Girl reaches forward with poised reluctance and signals the chauffeur that she is ready. In the opposite direction from that of the skier the car creeps into motion.

"With a shrug, a shrug of inevitability, the skier pushes off and begins slowly stemming across the hill toward the road she's left behind. When he approaches a knoll that will carry him out of sight of love no sooner glimpsed than forever lost, he steals a last look over his shoulder. And as the touring car rounds its turn, the Girl, who is really the Goddess of So-Near-and-Yet-So-Far, a lovely Miss-as-Good-as-a-Mile, this golden creature flings her head for a last half-defiant, half-regretful view of her lost skier.

"Then she drives on into the bright morning, into the future, and he skis on toward other virgin fields beyond, into her past. Boy and Girl forever losing, finding and not keeping, even in Fairyland . . ."

Shep thought Manley Halliday had merely paused, but when perhaps twenty seconds had passed in silence he looked up inquisitively. It would make a good scene all right, a nice silent opening, and he was eager for the rest.

"Mmm-hmmm, mmm-hmmm," he said encouraged. "And then what happens?"

"Happens?" Manley Halliday said incredulously. "What *could* happen? They never see each other again."

"And that's the whole thing?"

"Yes. Yes. Naturally." Manley Halliday's whole manner cried Eureka. "Well, how you like it? Told you we'd get it, didn' I, baby?"

Shep wasn't sure what to say. Was this just another gag projection like the farce of the twelve daughters of the college prexy? But on the plane when they had laughed it through, the amusing idea had shone in Manley's eyes. But this time, Shep thought, those eyes were serious; they were bright with a sense of achievement that disconcerted Shep.

"Tell me the truth, I surprised ya, didn' I?" Manley Halliday insisted. "I told you, I have a *talent,* baby. 'S long as I hang on to it I'll never go under."

"You mean that's it, what you just told me, the *whole* thing?"

"Sure. Sure! Know what Ann says. Average picture has too much story. Director's so busy getting rid of a plot he hasn't time for mood 'n composition."

"Who's Ann?"

Manley Halliday looked up in surprise. Hadn't he told Shep about Ann Loeb? He had done so much talking. Better not bring up Ann any more. That was his secret. Good old reliable secret of Ann.

With an unsteadiness more than compensated for by his new rush of enthusiasm, Manley Halliday stood up and waved Shep to his feet. "Come on, let's go in and tell Victor."

"Tell him what?"

"That we've licked his old story for him."

"Manley, know what time it is?"

Outside their window it was no longer night but a transition landscape of pale blue.

"Doesn't matter. Why not relieve Victor's mind soon as we can?"

"Manley, I really think we ought to wait. Try to work it out a little more."

"Details. We c'n always fill in the details." Through a haze, Manley Halliday smiled at Shep. "Come on, let's go wake Victor up—tell 'im the idea while the bloom's still on it."

"Manley, I—I say no. I don't think it's such a hot idea."

Manley Halliday stared at Shep with astonishment, with indignation. "I thought we were in this together," he said, striking an attitude that might have seemed funny to Shep under less manic circumstances. "Thought you were going to stand by me." Shep grabbed his arms. "Manley, you can't go now. Wait a couple of hours."

Manley Halliday wrenched free, "All right, summer soldier, I'll go see him alone."

He threw open the door and started out.

Yes, it was funny, only it wasn't at all funny and Shep, after weighing for a moment the idea of letting Manley go alone, sighed and trudged after him into the aisle.

Pushing Milgrim's buzzer at 5:45 in the morning to tell him the fragment of an idea did not seem to Shep the surest way of

301

gaining the Great Man's confidence, especially considering the worse-for-wear condition of their clothing and their minds. But Manley Halliday pressed the buzzer with positive exuberance and even winked at Shep to signal what had become in his mind the end of an ordeal.

After the buzzer had been sounded repeatedly, Shep had just finished saying, "Why don't we come back around eight?" when the sudden opening of the door brought them terribly close to the sleep-dulled face of Victor Milgrim. Intensifying all this for Shep was the fact that this face at the door staring out at them from the dark confines of the sleeping room bore so little resemblance to the alert and dapper face of the official Milgrim with whom they had been dealing. This face was softer around the mouth, perhaps from the removal of bridge work, and in need of a shave and a wash, a combing and a powdering, it retained little to suggest the polish and assurance, the attraction of forcefulness that distinguished its public appearance.

"Ye-es?" he said uncertainly and then, "Well, to what do I owe this—" undoubtedly meant for some elaborate sarcasm he was too near sleep to develop.

"Victor, we've been working all night. We've come up with something we'd like to try out on you."

A faint, ambiguous smile began to animate Milgrim's face. Well, it's an outrageous hour to rouse a man from his bed, it seemed to say, but maybe this is the way genius operates; it's the hacks who rent me their brains from ten to five; takes genius to strike like lightning at five o'clock in the morning.

"All right, come in Manley, let's hear the brainstorm."

Shep followed Manley Halliday into the drawing room. Milgrim turned on the overhead light. He moved some scripts aside and a contemporary novel his story department wanted him to buy (carefully underlined for him to save precious time by reading only the vital parts) and made a place for them to sit down. He buttoned his pajamas modestly to hide the fat on his belly his tailored suits hid so cleverly and, like a judge getting ready for the bench, seemed to take on authority with the silk lounging robe he drew on. "So you really think you've licked it?" he said. He was sure this is how genius works now. He was feeling better.

"I think it has everything you were looking for, Victor," Manley Halliday said.

Unable to look at either of them Shep stared through his legs at the floor.

"Good—just what I've been hoping to hear—" Milgrim looked at his watch "—even if it has to be at six o'clock in the morning."

Then, there was an unexpected pause. Victor Milgrim and Manley Halliday looked at each other with less warmth than their voices had indicated. Shep glanced up reluctantly to see what was wrong. It seemed as if suddenly and without warning the crazy flush of enthusiasm had drained from Manley Halliday. Perhaps it was the sitting down that caused this false vitality, ebbing and flowing in a berserk tide, to run out again.

"All right, go ahead, I'm listening," Victor Milgrim said. "Shoot."

Manley Halliday opened his mouth, said nothing, and then turned to Shep. "Why don't you tell it?"

Shep blushed and began to stammer. "Well—I—I guess I—"

Victor Milgrim frowned. "Go on, Manley," he ordered. "Let's have it."

Shep put his face into his hands and breathed into them so quietly he was almost holding his breath.

Inhaling deeply through his mouth, Manley Halliday said it all again, even more elaborately than before, with a number of new details brilliantly improvised, all of it told with such conviction as to persuade almost any listener that this sow's ear lined like a silk purse was the whole hog.

Hearing it again, Shep was surprised—even a little alarmed— to find how completely he had begun to identify himself with this man—a kind of super-sensitive alter-ego able to suffer the humiliation Manley Halliday should have been feeling. That Manley Halliday should go on beating his head against this dull post of a story, lavishing so much on an effort that only grew more ludicrous as the embellishments grew more filigreed, was almost more than he could bear. While Manley Halliday went

303

on *building it up* in what seemed to Shep both a parody and a refinement on story-conference technique he wondered whether this was a sign of the persistence of Manley Halliday's narrative genius despite the most forbidding circumstances or merely a sign of Manley Halliday's permanent deterioration. Was it the live light of the darting firefly or just the afterglow of the lightning bug dead in a bottle? And listening to the inspired, pointless presentation, he wondered how they would survive the traps that seemed to lie in wait all along their path today.

Yet he couldn't help marveling at the way Manley Halliday could endow this inconsequential bit of fluff with the impressive qualities of his own artistic attitude. It did evoke a scene, a mood, an emotion. Once he had said it, the Girl, luxuriously bundled under her fur car-robe on the rear seat of the sport touring car, was alive for them. And the Lone Skier was an eternal force challenging the elements and making his own path through the winter vastness.

"And so, true to their own divergent destinies," Manley Halliday was saying, "as they must inevitably, they go their separate ways. And though they may wonder and want and wish for that second chance to do it differently, of course it cannot be. This last stolen look is forever their last. Since they are a pair of lovers in Never-Never land, how fitting that they should never never meet again."

Just as he had with Shep, Manley Halliday stopped and waited for his applause like a concert singer.

"Well," he said exuberantly, "was that worth being awakened for?"

Shep turned his head for a quick study of Milgrim's face. He saw perplexity there, uncertainty, and yet, and yet it sounded good but with the implausibility, the sense of *what's-wrong-with-this-picture* one has in dreams. The truth was, Shep suspected, Victor Milgrim didn't have the story mind to risk a final judgment. He was the kind of producer who sent the same script to a dozen friends and canvassed them for a verdict.

"Well, how do you like it?" in all innocence Manley Halliday asked.

"Mmm—it's—well, it's a start," Milgrim said. And then as if

304

suddenly realizing that they had intruded on his sleep and privacy to tell him something that wasn't fully assembled, wasn't ready to be driven off the floor, he became a little testy. "I'll sleep on it—I think we'd *all* better sleep on it. God knows you look like something the—" he blocked a cliché in self-conscious deference to Halliday's literary reputation "—like you'd been dragged behind the train."

"Well, as a matter of fact, I *have*."

Milgrim gave a hollow laugh. "Let's see how this—inspiration —of yours strikes us in the morning."

He rose and with what in the daytime of his charm would have been a friendly pat practically pushed them out into the aisle.

When the door had closed them out Manley Halliday clapped his hands together like a happy child and then tried to hug Shep in his glee.

"What did I tell you! He went for it! He went for it! Our troubles are over, baby. Let's go back to the room and write it down!"

17

From the crowded Webster platform came exuberant whistles, wolf cries, shouts of "Over here" "Yoo hoo!" "Hey, Jocelyn" and "Peggy, it's Fred!" Pouring out of the Pullman cars in a riot of color, ready with their young faces and young bodies for the time of their lives, came the bright company fifteen hundred young men had been carefully choosing, saving weekly allowances for and devoting a disproportionate amount of thought to for the past four weeks. But now all of these grave indecisions were at an end. The Moment had arrived. Committed to their choices for three carefree days, they were all prepared quite literally and quite exhaustively to make the most of them.

Manley Halliday and Shep watched apathetically from their drawing-room window. They had decided to wait until the crowd thinned. To be pushed along in a mob of semi-hysterical adolescents, Manley had said, was more than his old nerves could bear this morning. The insulin shot had been wasted again. They hadn't had breakfast after all. A score of girls ahead of them at the second call had helped to make up their minds to eat when they reached the Inn. Now he was having to munch sugar to compensate once more. His nerves felt as if the protecting skin had been pulled away.

Shep could imagine how Manley Halliday must be feeling. For even with half his years and much less than half his anxiety, even with his youthful strength to absorb the shock of fatigue and alcoholic drag, he still felt toxic, nerved-up, *hateful*. He positively hated, for instance, the glowing young men and women in their colorful ski suits and sports clothes greeting one another with smiling kisses and promising embraces on the platform just outside the window.

"God damn them all to hell," he said unreasonably, aloud.

"Amen, baby," Manley Halliday said.

Shep said: "Funny, ever since they sprung me out of here I've had daydreams of how I'd come back. Walter Mitty stuff about arriving in style. Showing up with someone like you. And now it turns out to be just something to go through, to get over with as painlessly as possible."

"That isn't funny," Manley Halliday said. "That's the big practical joke of growing up."

Shep looked thoughtfully at the holiday throng. Christ, he thought, to be as young as the faces festively two-by-two on the platform, and then to be as old as Manley Halliday; to have the Girl and the Name and the Means and then to have nothing; and then, having nothing, to go on hoping and struggling—I wonder if I could do it, if I have that kind of strength. Suddenly, sitting between the oblivious Mardi Gras couples and the ailing Manley Halliday, he felt a new emotion, neither the fatuous hero-worship of the first days nor the impulsive contempt of the night before; now he saw neither all strength nor all weakness, but the weakness for the strength and the strength for the weakness.

"Come on, Manley, we go to the Mardi Gras."

On the platform the official cameraman was photographing for the *Alumni Magazine* the visiting celebrities from Hollywood. Victor Milgrim, in a tailored polo coat and a Tyrolean hat (but with a conservative feather) bore only the slightest resemblance to the slack-faced, unimpressive figure they had surprised in the drawing room. Man of the world who had raised himself at least a notch above the popular conception of a film magnate, Victor Milgrim accommodated the camera with gracious splendor. He made an excellent public figure and could have passed for an international banker or a trusted emissary of the State Department, just below the rank of Ambassador.

Now that the platform was empty, Shep and Manley Halliday climbed down. The younger man was conscious of the contrast of their crumpled, haggard look to the sweet-sixteen freshness and fresh-nineteen enthusiasm that gave such vitality to the atmosphere of festival. To make it worse, for them, it was a crisp, clear day, what Webster knew as perfect Mardi Gras weather and young complexions exposed to all this fresh air produced cheeks so red and eyes so bright that Manley Halliday realized he had forgotten how downright young and healthy the healthy and young could be.

"There they are!" Hearing that loud, familiar voice, they turned to see Hutchinson bearing down on them. He had gotten himself up in a bright red ski-suit, his balding head was concealed in a Russian-style fur hat and his face was ruddy with quick movement and cold. Sure enough he started pounding them on the back, this man of inexhaustible energy.

"Boy, oh boy, are we glad to see *you!* We've been up here for four days going nuts waiting for you two geniuses" (he had picked this up from the Boss) "to tell us what to do."

Hutch put a confidential hand on Manley Halliday's stooped shoulder. "Now just between us, we're gonna work together like this. To hell with the Boss; he's up here to have some fun. Boy oh boy, is this town loaded with St. Quentin quail!" He made an appropriate face and whistled. "If I didn't have so damn much work to do I'd show these young bucks what an old one can do!" His wink was wasted on Manley Halliday, who was neither listening nor watching and seemed barely there at all. It drew only a polite smile from Shep, who was figuring what to say. Hutch went right on:

"Now you know how I like to work. I like to work fast and no bull. I don't go for all these fancy conferences and I don't kiss anybody's tochis. If the Boss gets all screwed-up we'll tell him off together. You just let Hutch know what you want and I'll work my crew in snow up to their tails to get it." He threw a quick glance down the platform toward Milgrim—to make sure the Boss wasn't hearing any of this, Shep imagined. "Okay, now what's our first set-up? My boys haven't earned a dime since they left the lot. I wanna put 'em to work before they start chasing some of this young stuff you boys brought with you."

Manley Halliday flinched from Hutchinson's lascivious grin.

"Shep, I'd better sit down. Can't we talk later, in the room?"

"Hutch, we're all in," Shep said. "Give us an hour to catch our breath."

"This fresh air 'll take care o' that," Hutchinson assured them. "Boy oh boy, I feel like a kid!" He let go with a wolf-call, un-

308

dergraduate style, and a Webster boy turned around and laughed. "Atsa spirit, Pop."

Manley Halliday turned away. In an hour, maybe; yes in an hour he might be ready to endure Hutchinson.

The assistant (in charge of public relations) to the Secretary of the College looked doubtfully at them, then made up his mind that it was his duty to approach. "Mr. Halliday, welcome to Webster. Shep" (he had never been so cordial before) "nice to see you back. We're taking a few shots with Mr. Milgrim. Perhaps you'd like . . ."

He waved them toward Milgrim. But when Milgrim saw them, when he looked closely at Manley Halliday, he frowned and said, "Er, Manley's been working awfully hard—better give him time to get to the Inn and, er, freshen up."

He looked hard at Manley as if to say *that is what you are to do at once.* But Manley was too wretched to worry about the disapproval of Victor Milgrim. As Shep helped Manley into a cab—the gesture was involuntary—he was quick enough to catch a look intended for private exchange between the Secretary of the College and his assistant. In fifteen minutes, Shep could bet on it, it would be all over the campus that Manley Halliday and Shep Stearns had to be poured off the train.

It was an impressive view up the long winding road through snow-covered College Park to the plateau from which the white Georgian buildings overlooked the river. But these scenic staples were lost on them as they lay back with their eyes half shut, less like Hollywood screenwriters than victims of the Terror riding a tumbril. On the hill, taking a needless chance, a roadster swerved out and passed them, carrying five week-end couples, all on each other's laps. Shep and Manley Halliday seemed to rock in the wake of their wild young laughter.

A historical landmark between the campus and the small college town, the Webster Inn was a remodeled eighteenth-century hostel proud of its original beams and woodwork and the clutter of long rifles, powder horns, pewter teapots, oil lamps, primitive cradles and a thousand other commonplace items of Colonial times that made the Inn top-heavily picturesque. A large, darkened-with-age painting of the original boniface, John Treadwill, hung over the great fireplace in the lobby.

"Reservation for Mr. Halliday and Mr. Stearns?"

The clerk shuffled through a stack of reservation cards. Two-thirds through, his lip began to push out in an expression of doubt. He paused on one card and looked up hopefully: "Holifield?"

Manley Halliday shook his head. "Halliday." He spelled it out.

"Manley Halliday," Shep emphasized.

The clerk shook his head. "Nothing here for that name."

"We're with the *Love on Ice* party," Manley Halliday said.

The clerk became more respectful. "Oh, you're with Mr. Milgrim?"

"Yeah, we're a couple of Milgrim's boys," Manley Halliday said.

"What did you say your names were again?" the clerk said.

"Halliday and Stearns. You'd probably recognize us if you saw us in our stage make-ups," Halliday said.

The clerk wasn't sure. Old grads get drunk early and pull some funny tricks, he remembered. "I'll call Mr. Milgrim's suite and see if they can straighten this out."

"Let me speak to Miss Dillon," Shep said.

While they waited, several young married couples came in, laughing and stamping out the cold as they asked for their reservations and went on upstairs. When Manley Halliday felt he could stand no longer he sank down into one of the chairs in the lobby. A good-looking undergraduate and a cute-looking lemon-haired girl glanced at him as they hurried by in step arm-in-arm. "Boy, *he* started early."

On the phone Shep was saying, "Listen, Peggy, this really stinks. Who the hell made the reservations? I could always find a place to flop, but how the hell could they forget Halliday?"

"Got me there, kiddo. Transportation in New York had all the names. Supposed to take care of it."

"Listen, Peggy, we're riding on the rim this morning. Go tell the Boss either he gets us fixed up with a room or we head back for New York."

310

"The Great Man is in his bawth, dear."

"I don't care where he is. You go tell 'im."

"Hold your water, buster. I'll be down see what I can do."

Manley Halliday joined Shep at the house-phone.

"No room at the Inn?"

"How do you like that?"

Manley Halliday shrugged. "Symbol," he said.

"What?"

"Sure. Symbol of th' writers' status in Hollywood. Forgotten man."

"You ain't kiddin'," Shep said, sore. He turned back to the clerk, who, with the defensiveness of his kind, had begun to resent them as trouble-makers.

"You realize who this is? *Manley Halliday*. Sure you can't find something, a single room . . . ?"

The clerk frowned. "Well, if you don't mind the attic—it's—more or less an unused servants' quarters. Not the most comfortable accommodations."

Manley Halliday laughed harshly. "Unused servants—not too comfortable—that's us, isn't it, Shep?"

They were waiting for the elevator when Peggy Dillon came down. "Mr. Halliday, I can't imMAGine how this happened. Mr. Milgrim is going to be terribly upset."

"Miss—Miss Dillon—" it was like reaching into a card file "—don't trouble your pretty head. As we used to say. And tell Mr. Milgrim not to trouble *his* pretty head. We have just been given the—penthouse. Come up and see us later. We'll be having a little attic-warming."

Miss Dillon looked at Shep.

"Now, now," Manley Halliday said, seeing everything. "Don't look at him about me that way."

"I—I wasn't," Miss Dillon started to say, and Shep was thinking it was the first time he had ever seen her with her poise down.

"No, of course you wasn't," Manley Halliday said with a nasty edge.

Peggy Dillon glared. As if amused, Manley Halliday said to Shep, "Y'see, ladies don't like me any more. I assure you, ladies used to like me, Miss Dillon. If I had died the year Rudy died I'd 've had a full chorus of women in black following my coffin."

Peggy Dillon was very glad to be let out at the second floor.

" 'Tractive," Manley Halliday muttered. "Knows how to dress. Small-town girl gone sophisticated."

"Uh-huh." Shep was worried. Manley seemed to be off on a new jag now. Not exactly drunken, and yet . . .

"This way," the townie bellboy had said, and they were following him down a long dark passageway.

"Don't," Manley Halliday said under his breath.

"Don't what?"

"Don't worry so much about me."

"Well—"

"I'm not really in the bag. I'm just—just trying to talk my way through this, talking off the top of my head, helps me keep going. Don't forget I'm tough inside, baby. Tougher 'n I look."

At the end of the hall a narrow staircase led up into a tower room under the eaves. Manley Halliday tripped on the first step.

"Take it easy, Manley."

"Wasn't a drunkard's slip. Just a plain happen-to-anybody slip. Don't get so damn—well, if I need a male nurse I'll hire one."

"Keep your shirt on, Manley."

"And how! Same shirt I've had on since I left Hollywood. Good Lord, how long ago was that?"

The bellboy led them into a room Shep would never have expected to find in the Inn. Long and narrow, with a low ceiling, it could have been a studio version of a medieval dungeon if it hadn't been for the single dormer that offered an excellent view of the snow-laden campus bordered by the nice old buildings. Directly across the commons was the library with its graceful white bell tower. In the middle of the campus was an imposing snowman of Michelangelesque proportions wearing a Webster freshman cap and holding a pair of skis.

As they looked around this strange tunnel of a room the chimes were punching out a melody that bore some slight resemblance to "God Rest You Merry Gentlemen."

"Playing a melody with chimes always makes me think of an

312

armless man picking out a tune on the piano with his stumps," Manley Halliday said.

He stood in the middle of the room and surveyed its desolation. The only furniture was a double-deck metal bed without any bedclothes and a cheap, beaver-board portable closet. Not even a rug on the floor. In the corner under the eaves a small sink, and that was all.

"Ah, how quaint," Manley Halliday said. "Such simplicity. This really has atmosphere." He pretended to admire the bare double-deck bed. "Look at that! Not a nail in it. What craftsmanship! Ah, what stories this old bed could tell if it could only talk." He felt the springs tenderly.

Abruptly he stopped and pulled from the pocket of the overcoat he hadn't taken off the half empty bottle of applejack from the almost forgotten night before.

"Manley, for Christ sake."

"Shep, don't. I've got to keep drinking now. Need it for fuel. Fuel's courage. All *right,* a terrible joke, baby. The joke's on me, baby. Lord, and it's just beginning . . ." He started to say something else, interrupted himself with a long swallow of the applejack and handed the bottle to Shep.

"Mmm. Feels good. Feel better. Ever seen anybody drink himself sober, Shep? I did once, over at the Lido, ever tell you how I . . ."

Shep had been swigging as much of the bottle as he could, partly from his own need, partly to limit Manley.

"Yes," Shep said, "I'm sure you did. I think you must've told me every goddam thing you've done since you were three."

"Now—now, that isn't true, kid." Manley Halliday was really hurt this time. "I keep some things to myself. I know I do. The good things. Things you keep in a little strong-box locked away in your mind and only take out when you're alone and lonely in a special way. Like Jere. I haven't told you about Jere. All I could say was Jere this or Jere that but that wouldn't be Jere. You had to see Jere. You had to—well, that's getting to the part in the strong-box . . ."

Shep saw that his eyes were wet.

"Manley, lie down."

"Why?"

"Maybe a little nap."

"Naaap." He drew the vowel out to ridicule the idea. "How the hell c'n I nap? Think I'm so far gone I don't know what's happening? All we need is a simple little story. That's the trouble, it's too simple. See? I'm not so damn gassed I don't know that stuff I dreamed up this morning is banana oil. Wasn't any good, was it? You weren't buying it for bird-seed were you? 'S funny I c'd always judge people's reactions—in the daylight 'specially—dawn's when I c'd always kid myself—make myself think I was madly in love with someone who actually bored me in broad daylight like an actress I knew once. Silent star before your time. Mona Moray. . ."

"Yes, I know."

"Oh. Told you that too?"

Shep nodded. "Listen, Manley, you keep saying stick with me, we're in this together. Well, same goes for me. Every time you get talking you start slipping away, off to something you did, someone you knew and pretty soon you aren't here at all. It's beginning to drive me nuts."

The intensity of Shep's charge chastened Manley. He sat down on the edge of the bed and said, "I know. I have to stop this. I have to think from Ann on. Next time I start slipping back, grab me, Shep, snap me up the way Ann does."

He had taken from Shep the bottle of applejack and gulped a drink so quickly that it must have gone down his windpipe, for he began to cough and was coughing very hard with Shep slapping him on the back when Hutchinson burst in on them without knocking.

"What you guys doing, getting fried?" He tried to make it sound robust and casual. "Jesus, they really gave you the suite deluxy." He shook his head in exaggerated sympathy. "You should see how the Boss got himself fixed up. The bridal suite. When I see the big double bed I tell him he can't kid me he isn't all set up for a little of this Mardi Gras gash. I get a bang out of riding the Old Man."

Behind the buddy-buddy congeniality, Shep thought he saw

Hutchinson looking sharply at them once or twice and Shep made a mental note to be careful. With all that talk of independence and telling the Boss off, he strongly suspected Hutchinson of being a front-office long-nose and all-around suck.

"How about letting a pal in on some of your bug-juice?" Hutchinson said. Taking the bottle from Manley Halliday for a token drink, he handed it across to Shep. His simulated casualness was so broad that Manley pointedly asked for the bottle again.

"Now let's get with it," Hutchinson began. "How about our process backgrounds? You boys got a list of what you want? We wanta get barreling on this thing."

Manley Halliday looked at Shep and Shep said, without looking back at Manley, "The damn notes are in a suitcase that got mislaid at the station, Hutch, but got a pencil? I c'n pretty much tell you what they were."

"Fire away," Hutchinson said, with his gold pencil—a gift from Victor Milgrim—efficiently poised over a pocket notebook.

Without hesitation, and without much shame, Shep rattled off half a dozen settings which he described as locales for key scenes in the continuity outline. "Oh, yes, and the Skating Club balcony," he added. "That's our first love scene."

"Okay, we'll give ourselves plenty of protection on the balcony, backgrounds from every possible angle," Hutchinson said. "And wait'll you see the quality. This boy Gannon would've made first cameraman long ago if he could only stay off the sauce."

At the door Hutchinson turned back. "Oh, by the way, the Boss wants you down in the lobby for the reception in about fifteen-twenny minutes. Got some sort of luncheon lined up with the faculty. I think I'll duck it an' say I'm working. I'm liable to say ain't and scare everybody to death."

"If you see Mr. Milgrim you might tell him I do not intend to leave my room," Manley Halliday said. A good deal of effort went into getting all the words right.

"Are you kidding? You're the piece de resistance or how the hell you say it. You should've heard the Boss building you up

315

to the welcoming committee driving up from the station. Weren't your ears burning?"

"Not burning—ringing," Manley Halliday said.

"Hell, you know I'm the last guy in the world to tell you to jump every time the Boss whistles," Hutchinson went on, "but no kidding, Hally, if I was you I'd get down there."

Hutchinson went briskly down the steps, whistling "Let's Roll It Up for Webster."

"I don't trust that joker. He's too happy," Shep said.

Manley Halliday didn't answer. He was sitting on the metal rim of the bed. His eyes were open but he didn't seem to be looking at anything. He sat that way for three or four minutes. Then his eyes began to blink and the timing of the blinking slowed down until at last his eyes had been shut for perhaps thirty seconds.

"Manley."

Manley Halliday opened his eyes slowly and shut them again. Then Shep remembered they had skipped another meal, breakfast, although Manley had taken the anticipatory shot and then had had nothing but liquor and now it was nearly noon. Moving quickly he found the sugar in Manley's pocket and pushed some into the slack mouth. It was eerie to watch Manley's eyes fluttering open again so quickly. An uncertain smile pulled feebly at the corners of his mouth, which began to move as if in continuation of something he had been thinking and imagining himself saying.

"—just the manners change, that's all."

"Manners?"

Manley took a deep breath, a very deep breath, as if he were fighting to live, as if nothing was going to stop him from living. Then he said:

"Yes, the manners. Maybe they buttoned all their buttons or the pants hung differently or now they say babe where they used to say girlie, but it's still the same college, same's it was when I was here for Mardi Gras before we joined the R.C.A.F. Same boys from substantial hardly first-rank families having their fun learning a little and making their contacts. Oh, I know them, I

316

know them. One in five hundred'd amount to anything if he didn't have Papa's business waiting for him. Maybe five in five hundred deserve an education and three of those spend the rest of their lives trying to forget it, so it won't get in their way. Yah, now you grin, think I'm a radical. Slip me the grip, comrade, well not so fast, baby, I'm scared to death of any authority. But I've lost my faith in the rich . . ."

His words went wandering off into their own cloudy, unintelligible world. The dead pause was interrupted by a groping mutter of disgust. "Oh, what am I talking about!"

"Shh—just relax," Shep said quietly.

Manley saw white circles inside of white circles inside of white circles flowing out of the blackness into his eyes and for some reason he was trying to think of the title of the Gershwin song from *Treasure Girl* that for some reason never caught on.

A knock at the door brought Peggy in. "Listen, Shep, the Boss is beginning to burn. Wants to show off his writers to the heavy thinkers in the lobby. What's the matter with you two? Need some bennies?"

"Come on, have a drink. Quit looking so official."

"Thanks, Mr. Halliday, but—well, you really must come down. Didn't you hear a loud crash a minute ago? That was our Führer hitting the ceiling when Hutch gave him your message."

"My dear young lady," Manley Halliday wound up slowly, "kindly inform your Mr. Milgrim that I hired out as a screenwriter. I am ready to fulfill my ob—ligation. The contract says nothing about personal appearances. I am not on public exhib'-tion like a two-headed calf."

"All right, Mr. Halliday, I'll try. But he isn't used to this. He's a man who likes you to think things over carefully and then do 'em his way."

"Tell 'em we're working. Tell 'em we'll see him when we're darn good 'n ready."

"Okay. Anything you want particularly for your last meal?"

At the door Peggy said in what she thought was an undertone to Shep, "Well, your little playmate is feeling no pain."

But Manley Halliday, as his ordinary senses ebbed, seemed to develop a new compensatory super-sense, for somehow he over-heard. "Ah, my dear self-assured Miss Dillon, tha's where you're wrong."

The smile was a slight twitch of facial muscles behind the sallow skin.

Manley Halliday spread his coat on the springs, stretched out on his back and closed his eyes. Then he opened them again because he could sense Shep staring at him. "In this together, baby," he murmured, and then he made a really brain-racking effort to think of a fresh approach to *Love on Ice* that would dispose of the matter once and for all. But instead (this was the damnedest thing) he said aloud, "The complete history of everyone."

"What are you talking about?"

"The fundamental character of everyone, the bottom nature in them, the mixture in them, the strength and weakness of everything they have inside them, the flavor of them, the meaning of them, the whole history of each one . . ."

He put his hand to his head as if suddenly there was an ache there. ". . . the living loving eating pleasing smoking drinking thinking scolding working dancing walking talking laughing dreaming worrying potential and fulfillment of them . . ."

"What the hell are you doing?"

"What we oughta try to be doing every time we sit down, every time we start, making Americans . . ."

"Hey, Manley—more sugar?"

"No. *No.* I'm not raving. Just understan'. Mean you. Complete understanding. Know what I mean?"

"Oh, sure, *sure*," Shep said heavily. "It's as clear as torsan on the parfluroy."

The door opened suddenly and Victor Milgrim himself was there, in soft brown tweed, in starched white linen, fresh from the bathroom with the odor of Caswell Massey radiating from his powder-smooth, indignant face.

"What goes on up here?"

Manley Halliday sat up and with his uncanny ability to brave through the most humiliating scenes with a deeply rooted dig-

318

nity, said, "Victor, these are our personal quarters—such as they are—and there is no 'ception to the rule that no one should enter without knocking."

"Manley, you're jeopardizing everything I'm trying to do up here. I must ask you to stop drinking. I beg of you."

"Not drunk."

"Manley, for God's sake, I'm trying to be patient with you. But this is so damned embarrassing. We need the co-operation, the respect of the College. That's why I didn't choose to bring just any Tom-Dick to Webster. To the College your coming here is an event. You should see the main vestibule of the Library. Big picture of you, all your books on display, even dug up old articles by you and about you. And now they're all downstairs waiting to meet you. The Administration, the entire English Department, reporters for the school paper, picked undergraduates. Good God, aside from what you're doing to me I should think you'd have more respect for your own reputation . . ."

"Ah," Manley Halliday sighed.

"I came up to urge you to put in an appearance," Victor Milgrim said, "but I've changed my mind. I'd rather you didn't disgrace me—disgrace yourself. I'll have some hot coffee sent up and for Christ sake shave, pull yourself together." He moved angrily to the door. "I'll send for you right after lunch. Whatever you've got on the story, I'll want to hear it then. And if you're still floundering around you can both—well, no, I suppose it wouldn't look very well for you to leave Webster before the end of the Mardi Gras."

"Victor, I might remind you I have a contract."

"And it's you guys who're always crying how producers mistreat you." Milgrim said this partly for Shep's benefit. "If I only had a little more time in my day I'd write this damn thing myself."

The door slammed behind him. It left Manley Halliday trembling, not just his hands but his whole body, as if he had a chill.

Shep went over and in a gesture he didn't even think about put his arm around Halliday's shoulder.

" 'S'll right, Man, 's all right."

"Copey used to define Greek tragedy," Manley Halliday said softly. "Said we must all pay for our sins on this earth and the gods determine the kind and amount of payment, but that when a man's punished beyond the limit determined by the gods, that's Greek tragedy." He looked up at Shep but from far away. "Suppose Ann'd say self-pity. Hones'ly don't think so. So I have it coming to me? Well, let it come. I don't want anything for nothing."

He stood up abruptly. "Le's go downstairs."

"But you just told Milgrim . . ."

"You mean after he told me. Well, I'm sick of these walls, this ridiculous cave. You heard what he said. My books 're on exhibition. Well, I'll be on exhibition too." He raised his head defiantly, his tone sharply malevolent. "Give those stuff-shirt p'fessors something to talk about. Come on, Shep my ol' collab'rator, le's collaborate on killing this bottle and then le's collaborate ourselves down to the reception. They can't laugh at me any more 'n I'll be laughing at them."

18

At both ends of the long table in the inner lounge were large cut-glass bowls filled with a timid concoction popularly known as Faculty Punch, an unsuccessful compromise between teetotal beverage and alcoholic fillip. Although at least a hundred academicians had gathered to welcome these strange birds descended on them from Hollywood, there was such an emphasis on decorum that it did not sound like a social gathering at all but more like an assembly of lip readers standing around murmuring to themselves.

The entrance of Manley Halliday was a sly joke, passing swiftly from one end of the gathering to the other. These cool, clean, sober, respectable people were duly shocked, but in a way that pleased them. They began to share the delectable piece of gossip, *Halliday is positively plastered,* that murmured and snickered discreetly through the lounge.

The humor of it did not escape Manley Halliday as he stood on the landing looking in at this gathering of the courteous and proper. He had a reasonably clear appreciation of the spectacle he was making of himself but he was neither embarrassed nor otherwise disturbed. There was his basic independence, his old enjoyment of shocking staid gatherings and, working just below the level of consciousness, his superiority to all those who had lived less fully and with far less accomplishment. What also carried him into the room was a dim but overwhelming sense of inevitability, a sense of being borne on through darkness, through strange corridors, unfamiliar rooms, as on one of those boats gliding through an amusement pier's tunnel-of-love, except that those had a clearly identified beginning and end and offered a journey for the light-headed who had parted with a specific amount of small change to immerse themselves in a routine experience with darkness, while this journey was through a tunnel whose end no one could foretell, that grew darker and darker and for which he had not had to pay anything in the beginning (on the contrary they were paying *him*) but for which a terrible price might be exacted before he could exit.

Shep was helplessly aware of the grotesque figure slumped beside him, a bloodless face behind a three-day beard, a crumpled body in a stained and crumpled suit that had become so baggy as to suggest the soiled declassé elegance of Charlie Chaplin. The comparison, thought Shep, was more than casual, for Manley Halliday in his humiliating contrast to the orderly people gathered to honor him had something of Charlie's innate dignity, his laugh-provoking, absurd, yet somehow impressive superiority to the self-possessed assembly.

When Victor Milgrim saw them his face lost its assurance. For a moment it actually could not seem to find any expression at all and remained blank. Then, when the Secretary to the President said, "Ah, Mr. Halliday," and came forward to intercept him, Milgrim muttered something about "how hard he's been working, hasn't even had time to clean up" and decided on the desperate measure of passing Halliday off as a colorful eccentric—the traditional mad genius of the arts.

Manley Halliday started forward and—perhaps through accident, perhaps through buckling of the knees—stumbled and might have fallen if Shep had not in quick reflex caught his elbow.

The Dean, who had made excellent grades for an athlete at Webster, made a remark Shep couldn't quite hear, yet got the pith of it—something about this beginning to look like a real Hollywood cocktail party, complete with drunks who got two thousand a week. Shep sensed the hostility this outlandish income aroused in educated people having their troubles being middle class on three to six thousand dollars a year.

The Secretary threaded them smoothly through the assembly, introducing them to the more important of the campus hierarchy who acknowledged Halliday with conscious good manners. "Well, you must be having quite an *adventure,* Stearns," said Prof. Blodgett, an owlish, apple-cheeked bachelor of fifty known for the catty quality of his wit. Loyally, Shep felt he had to say,

322

"Yes, I'm learning a lot from Mr. Halliday." "I'm sure you are," said Prof. Blodgett with an emphasis that stung. "Now tell me, is this going to be one of those super-colossal productions, or merely colossal?"

Another English professor, Bridgman, a young man who had never known youth, said to Manley Halliday with unconscious cruelty, "I had occasion to reread *Friends and Foes* last summer. It holds up surprisingly well."

"Well, don't we all?" Manley Halliday said.

Farther down the table they met Prof. Crofts, the Emersonian who had had such hopes for Shep as an undergraduate and who could not pretend to be pleased that Shep was "doing movies." With the characteristic directness that bordered on rudeness, Crofts asked, "Will you be able to get anything of your own into this film?" Shep answered uncomfortably, "Not this one. Maybe eventually—I hope." Then Prof. Crofts had turned to Halliday. "Did Shep tell you he chose your work for his final paper in my course? He admired you very much. Although he saw you as the classic decline of the middle-class artist."

Manley Halliday lowered the punch glass someone had handed him. "Well, I admire him as the clashic decline of the young Marxist critic, so we're even. Maybe the reashon we admire each other so mush is becaush we've been declining together so mush."

"He's a total wreck, isn't he?" Prof. Crofts managed to say to Shep in an undertone as the Secretary steered Halliday along. Shep said, "Well, he does have another book he's working on." "Then what is he doing up here on the movie?" Prof. Crofts wanted to know. "Needs money," Shep said. "Huh!" snorted Prof. Crofts, transcendental as Emerson.

At last they reached Milgrim who was cornered by Prof. Connolly, the head of the Drama Department, a worldly monk of a man. Prof. Connolly was springing on Victor Milgrim a cherished idea. Ever since he had been brought to Hollywood as technical adviser for *Twelfth Night* and had had pictures taken with Bette Davis, Paul Muni and George Arliss (the one with his arm around Joan Crawford he had decided not to hang with the others in his office), he had been movie struck. It long had been his plan to establish a movie course with a library of actual scenarios and perhaps with Hollywood notables as guest lecturers. "I thought perhaps we might have a special wing in the library," Prof. Connolly was saying. "With your permission, the 'Victor Milgrim Room', with bound movie scripts and a collection of all the books and magazines on the films."

"If a thousand dollars will start the ball rolling," Milgrim replied. "I'm sure I can get Academy co-operation on old scripts."

"Most gratifying," Prof. Connolly purred. "And perhaps—I know how busy you are—you could deliver the opening lecture on The Art of the Cinema."

"I'm delighted you recognize that it is an art," Milgrim said modestly.

"Oh, my, yes. Before you leave perhaps you'll have time to look over an article I'm doing. I call it 'The Eighth and Liveliest Art.'"

"This summer you should come out as my guest and study film production at first-hand," Milgrim said, confident he was picking up the scent of his honorary degree. "You can use one of our executive offices. I'll be glad to loan you a secretary."

"That would be elegant," Prof. Connolly beamed.

All through this buttery exchange, Manley Halliday had been standing by with his eyes practically closed, his head bent forward as if too heavy for his neck, his legs strategically apart to afford better balance for his swaying. Milgrim and the professor had been ignoring him politely when suddenly he interrupted with a blurt:

"Scrip's no good."

The two men looked up warily. Like a man talking in his sleep, Manley Halliday continued.

"'S'like reading a book about plumbing. On'y way t' learn how to fit th' pipes t'gether is t' get some pipes 'n try it. Let 'im send you the pipes, movie camera, sound equipment, a movieola, study a picture on y'r movieola, take it apart 'n put it t'gether again. Learn more that way 'n memorizing Eisenstein."

"Yes, yes, I quite see your point, Mr. Halliday," Prof. Connolly promptly agreed. "Of course if Mr. Milgrim could spare us some movie equipment . . ." He did everything but rub his palms together.

324

People were coming up and wanting to be introduced to Halliday, a few with genuine admiration, the rest merely sightseers eager to get back to their friends with a vivid story of Manley Halliday's debacle.—"I saw him at a party in New York years and years ago," Shep heard someone saying behind him. "God, what a beautiful man! He's gone completely to pieces."

Then Shep knew what it was that had been angering him. Manley *was* drunk and he was a spectacle. But they seemed *glad* this had happened to him. That is what galled.

"Shep!"

"Hello, Hank."

Shep had been strong for Prof. Osborne from the time they had worked together in the League Against War and Fascism, in the years when most of the faculty hesitated even to sign a petition against the Nazis for fear of forfeiting their precious and precarious objectivity. But at this particular moment, knowing Osborne's friendship for Halliday, Shep welcomed him like a fellow-countryman in a strange land.

"Shep, I think we ought to get Manley upstairs."

"Have you seen him yet?"

"I'm afraid so. But I don't think he's seen me. Or maybe he doesn't want to see me."

"He's—he's in pretty tough shape."

"How long has he been drinking?"

"Let's see—'bout three days."

"Damn. I read somewhere, I thought he was all through with his drinking."

"He was. Hank, it was my fault. I started him drinking on the plane. I didn't know."

"Aw he's been doing it for years. I love him but damn it makes me mad, a man like that, well, anyway, the big talent of our crowd, deliberately destroying himself."

Near them Manley Halliday was fortifying himself with punch while holding off a group that could best be described as fawning tormentors. "What makes you think you know enough to cri'size *Shadow Ball*? Bet you anything you don' even understan' *Shadow Ball*. C'n see it in y'r face. Jus' because

325

you grew up without a sense o' humor—prol'ly a Presbyterian minister's son—you mistook it for intelligence."

"Man can still see in the dark," Osborne said. "Bridgie is a small-town New England minister's son. But we better get him out of here before he swings on the Dean. I know the symptoms."

"Come on, Man, let's go up to your room. I haven't had a chance to talk to you," Osborne said, taking Halliday's arm firmly.

Manley Halliday thought he heard, imagined he saw Hank Osborne as one of the phantom figures looming up in this dark labyrinth where the past twisted with terrible confusion into the present. Remembering the arm of Hank Osborne as having guided him many times along the edge of the precipice, he went along peacefully. He didn't even bother with *hellos,* for this was not a meeting in time and place but more like the resumption of a memory.

This was how they led him back to the attic room where Hank said, "Now lie down, Man, and try to get some sleep," which reminded Manley Halliday of where he was. "Where the hell you come from?" he said to Hank. "Who in-vited you? Always telling me what to do. Why didn' *you* write *High Noon,* if you were so goddam good? Yes and don' think I've forgotten that letter you wrote me about *Shadow Ball.* '. . . the style has the faint beauty of a rose picked a week before an' beginning to decompose . . . ' "

"Jesus, how he remembers, how he remembers everything," Osborne muttered to Shep.

"Well, lis'en, your style didn' have any smell at all, just the smell of typewriter ribbon an' Hammermill Bond, you jealous hypercri'cal bashtard."

Osborne said quietly, "Manley, I told you a long time ago you can never make me mad again. Minnie and I have made up our minds to go on liking you no matter what you do to us—or to yourself."

"Aah—ish-kabibble," Manley Halliday said.

"I'd better go," Osborne said. "Damn, I've been looking forward for years to seeing you again, but . . ."

" . . . Says I made a pass at Minnie," Manley Halliday muttered. "Christ, we were all swacked and maybe I said I think I said Minnie's the kind of girl who makes every man think of going to bed with her—but, hell it was jus' talk an' if you don' like it you sonuvabish you know I'm not afraid of you . . ."

Manley Halliday lunged forward with his fists clenched. Carefully backing out of his way, Osborne said, "I'm your friend, Manley. Remember that. Come to see us if you're feeling better."

"Yeah, so I'm starting to decompose. Well, I'll decompose you, you smart smug sonuva . . ."

Outside the door Osborne said to Shep, "God Almighty, it's a terrible thing to see."

"Three nights without sleep," Shep said.

"Three nights," Osborne said. "A thousand and one nights."

"He still sees everything. I don't know how the hell his mind keeps working."

"A tremendous talent," Osborne said. "You don't lose that. You just lose the way of putting it to work."

"And how old is he, forty-three?"

"He lived twice as fast as anybody else. That makes him 86. When he came in to that reception he *looked* 86."

"I don't understand it, Hank. The Twenties was your time too. But you got over it. You kept up. You'll be as much at home in the Forties."

"Partly, it's because I wasn't a success," Osborne said. "Being a failure—if it doesn't ruin you—can teach you something. Trouble with Man was he had his youth and he had his success and he thought the two were the same thing and that both could last forever. Well, you better go back. If you need any help, call me. I used to be able to handle him sometimes." He smiled fleetingly and a look of unexpected sadness came into his face. "I don't envy the poor bastard from here in."

When Shep went back into the room Manley Halliday was sitting on the edge of the bed with his head in his hands.

"Baby, we're wasting time," he said accusingly. "Victor's gonna call us any minute—remember? Shep, we've got to think of something. Wasn't going to tell you this but I—I need this job. If I c'n just once get out of debt, buy six months of writing time. Shep, I've loused up so many chances I don't want to muff this one. Just get us started, start talking story and don' let me get off the point. So go ahead, Shep. *Please* start talking story."

"Well, we've made about five different starts but we never seem to be able to stay with one to the finish," Shep plunged in. He had gone so stale on this that he could hardly remember the various formulas they had tried.

"Tha's right tha's right le's go back to the very first one you had, isn't that usually wh'happens? 'Riginal one turns out to be the best? Now, remind me of it again."

"The waitress, Sally, I called her, is elected Queen instead of Miss Rich Bitch, Lorna, so Lorna tells Hugh . . ."

"Isn't it just Girl Meets Webster, Girl Loses Webster, Girl Gets Webster? All we need is some cute business an' a few little mishunderstandings . . ."

He shut his eyes as if in intense concentration and when Shep spoke and he did not answer except with a swallowed groan, Shep realized he had slipped off into some private limbo.

"Manley, you can't go to sleep now." The shaking startled him. He looked up accusingly. "Where'd you go?"

"Manley, for Christ's sweet sake."

"The girl," Manley Halliday picked it up dormouse fashion. "Shtill can't see the girl. Gotta be able to reach out 'n touch my people when I write. 'Member Laura-Lee? So much in love with her Jere was actually jealous."

His eyes opened wide, suddenly, and he strained forward, staring fixedly at something only visible to him.

"I heard her. Laughing."

"Heard who?"

"Jere."

Shep looked at him hard. Outside, on the pavement below, a couple of undergraduates were throwing flirtatious snowballs at their dates. "Jack *Jack* eeeeeeeeek," came the girlish protest, followed by a soft laugh that rose musically.

"Outside. Somebody's date," Shep said.

"It's—amazing. Sounded like Jere. Sounded exactly like Jere."

As quickly as that it was all over. The shock of what he had thought seemed to have jolted him out of his partial coma. Now he was simply embarrassed.

"Now where are we?" he persisted. "Ann I mean Fran meets her rival at the fraternity house . . ."

The knock on the door was ominous. It was Hutchinson with a big forced grin. "Well, we got the Boss out of the clutches of those long-hairs. Jesus, is that Prof. Connolly a super-salesman. The Boss kills me the way he falls for that crap." The grin was carefully maintained. "You boys ready for the big moment?"

Shep looked up warily. "We already had our big moment."

"No—the story conference. You're on. The Great Man's ready to hear all. He's got the joint filled downstairs. Even Professor Connolly and the Dean and Mrs. Dean."

"The Dean'll be a big help," Shep said. "What the hell is this, a story conference or a public exhibition?"

"Listen, guys, don't let the Boss get you down. Just between you, me and the outhouse he goes a little nuts when he's around these campus characters. You shoulda heard him and the Dean and the Prof. All you gotta do is go in and lay your story on the line so a simple schnook like me c'n understand it and to hell with those big shots. We'll get together on this and make a hell-uva picture if the Boss'll just leave us alone. I'd like to talk him into letting me direct the whole thing. Us three'd work right together with none of this Hollywood crap."

Neither Shep nor Manley Halliday was paying the slightest attention. Each of them had withdrawn into his own hive of anxiety.

"Say, I'm anxious to hear this yarn myself," Hutchinson said.

"So am I," said Shep.

"Ha ha, you mean Hally's gonna tell it?"

"Hutch, before we go down, haven't got a shot on you?" Manley Halliday asked suddenly.

Hutchinson became wary. "Well—you've been hitting it pretty heavy, haven't you, Hally?"

"Hutch, believe me, a drink'll steady me. Steady my nerves."

"We-ell . . ." They were seeing Hutchinson shrink to his true identity of timid employee. "Now fer Christ sake, don't let the Boss know where ya got it." He slipped a flask out of his pocket. Manley Halliday grabbed for it in his eagerness. "God help us all," he said and poured it down.

"I could use a little of that myself," Shep said.

"Well, here's to your story, boys," Hutchinson cheered them. "And remember what your pal Hutch tells you—talk right up to the son-of-a-bitch same way I do."

19

The suite they entered was so large and lavish it seemed to Shep that Victor Milgrim must have brought it with him. It was of a piece with his rooms at the Waldorf Towers, his office, the accommodations he had on the *Normandie*—anywhere he happened to be. A great bay window provided a magnificent view —a swell angle, Hutch had said—of the heroic-sized ice sculpture that dominated the campus.

Victor Milgrim sat in the center of a half-circle of chairs that had been arranged by Peggy and Hutch. On his left sat Prof. Connolly and Mrs. Connolly, a pretty woman with gray-blue hair who had once played a few parts with minor road companies and who gradually had come to be identified as a former Broadway leading lady. "Never quite a star," Theresa Connolly would acknowledge with appealing modesty. On Milgrim's left was the Dean and the Secretary in charge of public relations. Definitely making a production of it, Shep thought.

In addition to the V.I.P.s there were Peggy, Hutch, Gannon, the cameraman, and Prinz, the production manager, who looked sickly, perhaps because he worried so much about production costs.

Milgrim could not hide his misgivings when he saw that the appearance of his writers had been in no way improved. But he would do his best to charm his way through. "You understand, of course, our story is just in its uh experimental stage," he explained to his guests. "But I thought you might be interested in seeing how we develop what we call *the line*. It's pretty much a trial-and-error process, not so different from your physics professors in the lab; sometimes when we pour the contents of one test tube into another we even find the whole thing blows up in our face."

Hutchinson was still laughing when the polite laughter of the college guests had trailed away. "Boss, I gotta remember that one," he said.

Milgrim frowned at him. Hutchinson was a good second-unit man but he laid the yessing on a little thick. Or did the sycophancy only seem more pronounced in this Ivy League setting? This idea of bringing Manley Halliday had seemed so *right,* such good thinking. And now, *look* at him. What were these College people thinking? How desperately he wanted that honorary degree! Victor Milgrim, Doctor of Humanities, for his outstanding contribution to inter-American and international understanding in the field of the cinema, something like that. He would have had one of his writers prepare him a simple, dignified acceptance speech, Hollywood's Growing up to Its Responsibilities, that sort of thing. Ned Glassman, his publicity man, could probably place it as a front-page feature for the New York *Times* drama section . . . He stopped frowning at Halliday and forced a professional smile.

"Well, Manley, I knew you've been—er—awfully rushed—not even time to clean up—but why don't you just give us what you have, not in too much detail, just the main characters and the continuity?"

"Victor, I know thish isn't a very 'riginal way to begin . . ." Manley Halliday started to say.

"Go ahead, Manley, after all, how many plots are there supposed to be—" he looked around at Prof. Connolly for approval "—in the entire history of the drama? Isn't it nine?"

". . . but I c'd use a li'l drink."

There was Scotch and soda on a small table near the window. Milgrim hesitated, pushing his lower lip out in suppressed disapproval. When he said "Hutch" and nodded toward the table, Hutchinson sprang to mix the highball. "We don't usually drink at story conferences, gentlemen," Milgrim felt he had to explain, "but this has been a pretty strenuous trip, working on the train all night and. . ."

Prof. Connolly just smiled, as if he too were a man of the world. The Dean waited stolidly. The Secretary stared at Halliday as if he were some out-of-the-way animal brought back alive. He was being careful to conceal his feelings, however, in the hope that Mr. Milgrim might be induced to make a consider-able contribution to the college funds.

"How 'bout a drink for Shep?" Manley Halliday said when Hutchinson placed a glass in his hands.

Shep would have said no, but this reflex loyalty to his companion warned him that Manley would seem too conspicuous drinking alone.

"I'll have a short one," Shep said.

Milgrim was forced to offer drinks all around. Prof. Connolly thought he might have one "very much on the mild side." The Dean and the Secretary said thank you, no. Milgrim was being meticulously careful of his own behavior. Joe Gannon, the cameraman, said, "You can hit me with a shot," but Hutchinson was in charge there and he said, "Listen, Joe, you got a camera to focus this P.M., so don't start going out of focus on me now." It was said in a dry workmanlike voice that made everyone laugh because of tension.

Milgrim looked at his elaborate gold watch. "We all have to be out at the ski jump at two o'clock. Why don't you get started, Manley?"

At this moment Shep, without even knowing he was going to do it, rose to his feet and, in a way he had never been able to do before, took command of the room. Liquor, exhaustion, benze-drine, nerves, fear and a boy-scout determination to pull Manley Halliday through had lent him a feverish verve.

"We open with what we think is a cute little scene in a diner," Shep began, dispensing with all the *maybe's* and *what-ifs* and *how-abouts* that had been bogging them down for days. In a rapid and convincing voice he followed the waitress to the Mardi Gras, at the same time (somehow tying together all the random threads they had tried) using Manley's meeting of the Lone Skier and the Girl in the Open Touring Car to introduce Florine and Joe. In the same way that water adheres to the bottom of a pail if the pail is swung around rapidly enough, somehow this story hung together as Shep found himself turning into one of those glib elocutionists who electrify story conferences with their artificial lightning.

"When Joe takes first place in the slalom, Florine moves in,

333

because the ski champion is to have the honor of choosing the Queen of the Mardi Gras."

Shep paused to look around. They actually seemed interested. He went on with his show of confidence. Wildly ad-libbing, he could feel the relief of Milgrim, the admiration of Peggy Dillon, the interest of the college officials, the grinning approval of Hutchinson and the adding-machine affirmation of pale Mr. Prinz. When Shep paused to catch his breath there was a hush all over the room and he knew he had them and hurried on.

"In love with Joe now, and feeling she's made a botch of her last Mardi Gras, Sally goes out skiing alone and follows an abandoned trail through the Green Mountains. Suddenly this trail falls away to a steep incline and she finds herself plunging downward, faster and faster, fifty, sixty miles an hour, through the tall pines that race by her, threatening to smash her to pulp . . ."

"I can get that effect for you," Hutchinson broke in.

"Now we cut back to Joe," Shep went on. "It's growing dark. Time for the Mardi Gras Icecapade over which he and Florine are to preside as King and Queen. But he hears that nobody has seen Sally for hours, that she's gone off on skis. He says he can't go through with his part of the show until he finds out for himself what's happened to Sally. The entire ski team backs him up and they all go to the rescue.

"Now we finish with a tremendous chase on skis, Sally racing down the mountain side toward a treacherous ravine, Joe and the Webster team racing after her. They pick up her ski tracks, realize what she's heading for—and oh by the way they all carry the torches they were to use in the skiing exhibition . . ."

"Nice touch," Milgrim murmured.

"We'll get that for you," Hutchinson said.

"With their torches lighting the way, they start down. They know a short cut to head Sally off. She's closer and closer to the precipice. She'll be dashed to pieces. Joe is gaining on her. The short cut may be fatally littered with boulders but he leans forward into the night wind. She's only fifty feet from the edge, thirty, ten, five, when suddenly he comes swooping in from nowhere, grabs her and they plunge into a tree.

334

"For a tag we pick Joe up in the infirmary. His head is bandaged. Sally comes in, bringing him a hamburger, just as she did at the diner at the opening. 'I'm getting kinda used to having you wait on me,' he says. 'Maybe we oughta get married.' "

Shep took a deep breath. "Well, of course, it's still a little rough, but . . ."

But everyone was talking at once.

"By God, you've licked it!" Milgrim said. "Sounds terrific. Really terrific."

"I must say it held me right to the end of your little epilogue," Prof. Connolly added.

"I'm glad you made all the Webster men good fellows," the Dean put in. "We were a little afraid you might . . ."

"As you see, the real hero of our picture is the Webster Ski Team." Milgrim was beginning to expand. "Or should I say, the Webster Spirit?"

"It's going to be tough stuff to get, that ski chase, but, damn it, when we do get it we'll really have something," Hutchinson said. "Okay Joe, let's start lining up at the ski jump."

"I'll see you out there," Milgrim said. "I'm driving over with President Sellmer." He turned to his writers with a bright smile. "Looks like you came through, just when I was afraid it *was you* who might go over that precipice."

He patted Manley Halliday's shoulder condescendingly. "Now go up and change your clothes. And remember, no more drinking." He started toward the door, then returned and picked up the bottle of Scotch. "Better put this away," he told Peggy Dillon.

"Lissen, Victor, don' patronize me. Too old to be patronized."

"Now, for Christ sake, Manley. *Behave.*"

"Victor, be senshible. You don' really need me out there at the ski jump."

"This is what you're up here for. To get the color, the feel of it. And a little air won't do you any harm."

"But I've seen ski jumping. Right here. In Fifteen. Stu Anderson from Dartmouth won it. Remember? I'm the man with the memory. If Stu hadn't been killed in the war . . ." He caught himself. "Victor, believe me I've seen all this. Do I have to swallow a whole ocean to describe salt water?"

335

"Manley, I'm in a hurry. Be out there. It's what I'm paying you for."

He turned away and quickly left them. Manley Halliday started to grin at Shep and then he threw his arms around him and hugged him. "Baby, you were inspired. You saved our lives."

"I didn't even know what I was saying," Shep confessed. "All of a sudden I just went crazy."

"Well, it was inshpired, inshpired. We've got 'em right here." Manley Halliday extended the palm of his hand.

"Only trouble is, what've we really got? Same crap we had before, just dressed up a little. Let's not kid ourselves. It only sounded good because for once I told it like an old pro."

"Hell with it. Least we're not fired. Takes a little pressure off us for a few hours anyway. How the hell'd you do it? Shep, I'm proud of you. I could've kissed you."

"Well, let's push on to the ski jump."

"Not sure I c'n make it. Tell you a little secret, Shep. I hate snow. An' my feet still feel frozen from last night."

"He'll be looking for us, Manley. I think we'd better try."

Back in their attic room, Shep brought out his galoshes. All Manley Halliday had were rubbers. And a worn overcoat. And a shapeless gray hat that had once been a fashionable Stetson.

Coming out of the elevator into the lobby, Manley Halliday said "Oh, forgot something, be right down," and disappeared for a few minutes.

Driving out to the point nearest the ski jump he slipped a bottle from his overcoat pocket. It was the Scotch from Milgrim's room.

"How the hell'd you get that?"

"Got the bellboy to let me in. Said I left my script in his room. Important lesson in life, Shep. With the possible 'ception of murder, almos' nothing a bellboy won't do for a buck. Comes in very handy sometimes."

He took a long swig from the bottle. It felt so good inside that he laughed out loud. "Mmm, warms you up. I'd've died up here without this." He handed the bottle to Shep. "Drink hearty, my young silver-tongued collab'rator. Ah. I'm feeling better. Say, I

336

may live through this yet!" It struck him funny. He raised the bottle to his lips again.

When they got out of the cab, Manley Halliday insisted on offering the driver a drink from the bottle. Then they had to walk at least a quarter of a mile through the snow to the crowd gathered in an enormous U around the lip of the jump. In his gray coat and battered hat, with the cold biting into his face, Manley Halliday looked more like a discouraged ghost than a holiday spectator at one of the highlight events of the Mardi Gras. He walked slowly, his footing uncertain, feeling club-footed from the numbing cold. A group of young people came up behind and a youth who showed his indifference to the elements by wearing only his letter sweater above his ski pants went *beep-beep* like an auto horn and shoved Manley Halliday aside to hurry on with his laughing friends.

"That roommate of mine's a real screwball," the letterman said.

"You mean a meat-ball," said his girl and everyone guffawed.

Manley Halliday sank down into the snow-bank. "Secret o' laughter," he said.

"Huh?"

"Didn' I ever tell you about the secret o' laughter?"

"No."

"Secret o' laughter's—poise. 'ats why they laugh, those kids, they're running over with poise. Me, I useta have it but I lost it at the Astor. Poise I mean. 'ts like hair, when you have it you pay no 'tention to it. Only when you lose it. Ain't gonna have poise no more no more, all I got is this jug."

"Get up, Manley, you'll catch cold."

"*Catch* cold. I'll need an ice pick to take my shoes off."

As Shep reached down and started pulling him to his feet, another youthful foursome came by.

"Don't give up the battle, Pop," one of the young men called and the girls giggled.

Manley Halliday trudged after them, his mind shuttling un-clearly between a tragic and a comic view. The show must go on, the mail must get through, the script must be finished, the ski jump must be seen, the vanity of Victor Milgrim must be

337

satisfied, the destiny of Manley Halliday must be fulfilled. Finally reaching the youthful spectators assembled to watch their teams he was aware of bright colors of ski and stocking caps and scarfs and lips. *Oh Lord to be young again to be able to laugh that way as if every remark were unbearably witty.* Swoosh the jumper bending forward from his skis stood in the air with his arms working like wings sailing down down—ooh how graceful —until *slap* his skis came down to meet the steep runway and he went gliding on along the flat while the next contestant appeared as an incredible dot away up there on the take-off platform.

"Boy, what a jump!" Enthusiastic applause was muffled by heavy mittens. Shep was telling him about it, the tremendous leap of Webster's young Norwegian star, and he realized he hadn't been watching, not because his eyes hadn't been looking in the right direction but because his mind hadn't been there to record what was seen. A few minutes later it was announced that Rolaag's winning jump set a new Webster record; the event was over. The large, good-natured crowd started moving in the direction of Red Robin Pond where the skating events had already begun.

Manley Halliday sneezed with a force that seemed to weaken him to the very joints of his knees. He felt as if he were sinking down into snow drifts. "Shep, now I'm really catching cold. My feet. But I think I'll be all right if I c'n get back to the hotel."

Just then Victor Milgrim caught sight of them and took command. "Wasn't Rolaag terrific? We're going to use that record jump for Joe, and Rolaag's going to work as a double for us. See what I mean now, Manley? You couldn't write *that* without seeing it. And the *color,* the *girls.* Glad I found you. We're all going over to the Skating Club balcony. Jean Tozzer's giving an exhibition. I'd like to spot that somewhere. They say she's sensational."

It was no easy hike to the Club from the ski jump. Manley Halliday trudged along in constant dread of losing consciousness. "All right?" Shep asked once. "A little woozy but—all right," he had answered. Secret nips from the bottle would temporarily revive him though he stood through the exhibition and the skat-

338

ing races without really seeing them. Then they all went on to the slalom hill.

By this time the snow was turning blue in the twilight and Manley Halliday could barely drag one benumbed foot after the other. The unflagging energy and enthusiasm of Victor Milgrim tore at his nerves like the uninterrupted blowing of a stuck automobile horn. Something inside him wanted to scream *oh for God's sake shut up leave me alone let me lie down* but he held on.

Somehow he got through to the end of the sports program. Milgrim reminded him that the evening torchlight skiing and crowning of the Queen would begin at 7:30. Of course Manley would have to see that. The President had asked them all to his house for dinner but Milgrim thought Manley would do better to go back to the Inn and rest. "And, Manley, for the fifth time, will you *please* try to clean up and shave, pull yourself together?"

There was a traffic jam of both pedestrians and autos going back to town. All the taxis were taken by the time they reached the road. They tried to hitch, but every car that passed was already overcrowded. By the time they had walked a half mile the darkness was almost complete. It was four above, they heard someone say. Several times Manley Halliday had to stop to catch his breath and when Shep saw his face in the glare of a street lamp it looked less ghostly than cadaverous. He began to go limp against the post and Shep supported him. This time Shep took out the bottle of Scotch, three-fourths empty now, and held it to Manley's lips. Then he picked up some snow and rubbed it over his forehead.

Manley Halliday opened his eyes. "Hank Osborne," he whispered.

"What?"

"Frena mine. Hank Osborne. Teaches up here. Oughta see him. Le's go see him."

"You saw him, Manley."

"Bes' fren I had, Hank Osborne. Le's go see him."

"All right. He doesn't live far down this road. Maybe he'll drive us in."

The Osbornes lived in a small white cottage on a knoll over-

339

looking the road. When finally Shep managed to lead Manley to it and the door opened, the warmth and coziness of the interior, the sense of comfortable domesticity had such an effect on the young man that his eyes began to dampen in an unexpected overflow of emotion. Why, he wasn't sure—possibly just the contrast of Manley's sickly pallor and sagging figure to the ruddy complexion and well-fed waistline of Hank Osborne, who came to the door with a hot buttered rum in his hand. There was a crackling blaze in the fireplace behind him.

"Well, come on in, you two, come on over and get warm."

Osborne's voice was like the fire, warm and reassuring and good to be close to. "Just in time for hot buttered rum."

With practiced discretion he overlooked Manley's condition. But Shep said, "Thanks, Hank, but I'm afraid another drink's in the hole-in-the-head department. That goes for both of us."

"Not foolin' me," Manley accused Shep. "Don' be so goddam noble. Take a drink if you wan' it. I'm gonna have one anyway, Hank."

"Coming up in a jiff," Hank Osborne said, and going to the kitchen door he called, "Minnie—surprise—come and see who's here."

Mignon, no longer petite, with a face so French as to seem almost a caricature of the handsome Gallic housewife, came in with an apron around her plump waist. "Oh, goood, goood," she said when she saw who it was and she hugged Manley energetically. "Well, Monley, thees is such a wonnerfool surprise." She and Hank spoke French together and since she was not one of those faculty wives who visited other faculty wives, her heavy French accent never improved.

"Minnie, Minnie, my old girl," Manley Halliday said.

Mignon saw that he was very drunk and that she would have to use her basic wisdom on him.

"Here, sit down." She led him to the biggest, most comfortable chair. "You morst be veree tired—all that hiking in the snow."

"Shixty three days across a continent of ice. Shtrong men cried when we hadda eat the lead dog."

She laughed. "Ah, Monley, I see you are not so change-ed."

340

"Who said I changed?"

Mignon saw she had said the wrong thing. She groped quickly for something more cheerful. "So what, everybodee change-ed. Look at my nice little waist. It eees gone with the weend."

"Gone with the Wind. 't'sall people c'n talk about any more. Rather read Mrs. Humphry Ward m'self."

"Monley, you funnee boy, the book I did not mean . . ."

" 'Book I did not mean.' 'F we talk French like that you laugh at us, jump down our throats. Yeah, I heard you kidding my French to Hank that Sunday driving back from Tessencourt. Made me damn sore."

"Silly boy, that was—oh how awfool—sixteen years ago."

Back with a tray of hot rums, Hank Osborne said, "Well, remember our old toast, 'here's to us and what's usn's.' "

"Oh, so many goood times," Mignon said.

Manley Halliday rose abruptly. "Well, I wanted to see you. Long time since Thirty-three. But I didn' think this'd happen."

The Osbornes looked at each other understandingly. "Think what'd happen, Man?"

"Aah, skip it skip it," Manley Halliday muttered. "Hell with ya. Never did like Jere, did ya? Jealous of her, jealous of both of us. Well, now I suppose it's turned out how you wanted. Jere in the flit academy an' me going off the ski jump with no skis."

Osborne's voice was low and very kind. "Manley, try to hear this. No matter what you say to us, or what you think, we're your friends."

"You c'n go ta hell."

He lurched toward the door.

Mignon said, "Ah, Monley, we laav you—please please be nice."

"Hell with it. I don' hafta stan' here 'n be insulted." He threw open the door and stumbled out.

Hank Osborne said, "He thinks it's us but it's really himself—that's what he's fighting."

"Well, don't talk about heem. Go help heem," Mignon said.

They found him wandering down toward the road.

"I'll drive you back to the Inn," Hank said.

They got him into the car without a word. He was passive and pliant now, resigned to stupor. He had given up trying to talk.

They had reached the Inn. "I'll take you to the side entrance," Hank said. "No use giving everybody in the lobby a chance to gawk." He helped Shep ease Manley Halliday from the car. "If you need me again, holler. I'll do anything I can. Not so much for what he is, for what he was."

"Aah, balls," Manley Halliday said. He knew what he wanted to say, but he couldn't say it.

"I think I'd better go down to the Coffee Shop and bring up a bite for us. What do you feel like eating?"

It was Shep's voice, and they were back in the attic, though Manley Halliday could not remember how they got there. It had seemed to him that they were standing in the snow watching the ski jump.

"Oh, anything. Anything."

"And if you're going to eat, you'd better take your shot. Want me to help you?"

"No. I'll do it. You go ahead."

In the bathroom his hand was trembling so that he had to try to steady it with his other hand. Every time he hesitated he had to fight back an impulse to let go and cry. *Ann Ann help me,* and the thought actually did control him until at last he plunged the needle.

The hamburgers were only lukewarm by the time Shep brought them up.

"Manley, you've got to eat something."

"I'm trying."

"You haven't eaten in days."

"Don' feel too bad," he said stubbornly.

Shep stared at him. "Look—the torchlight procession should be starting now. Why don't I go while you take it easy? I'll come back here right after it's over."

"No. I'll finish. I'll see it all."

"Manley, you look like . . ."

"I know what I look like. I also know what Victor'll say if he finds I'm not there. Hell, I've come through this far—I don' wanta be fired now."

"Maybe if I talked to him. Now that he likes our line."

"He'll come up an' find me here an' say I'm drunk. Makes me furious, checking up on me like a Fifth Former."

Manley slung his coat over his shoulder. "Lead the way, my young friend. On to the next installment of 'Manley Halliday, Script-Writer in the Frozen North.'"

20

Five hundred couples followed the band and the torch-lit skiers out past the lake to the slalom course. Making a lark of the weather, the marchers sang their college songs, their faces flushed with cold, houseparty cocktails and the titillating possibilities of Mardi Gras night. Suddenly, inexplicably confident, Shep found himself enjoying it again.

"How you feeling, Manley?" he asked as they marched along with the stragglers.

"I could climb Mt. Blanc, if a St. Bernard'd just follow me along with a brandy bottle."

"Here—help yourself."

It was a classmate of Shep's, Bill Bonner, with a pert, pretty girl on his arm.

"Try some of our anti-freeze." They all passed the bottle around during introductions and went on together.

"You're not *the* Manley Halliday," said the girl.

"No—T. Manley Halliday. T stands for Torrio, Johnny Torrio, my godfather. I dropped it when they rubbed him out."

The impromptu zero-weather flirtation made him feel a little better. The brandy bottle went from hand to hand, all the way to the hill.

"How'd you like to be in our movie?" Manley Halliday asked the girl.

"With *my* pug-nose, I'd look a fright."

"Well Shep 'n I'll write in a part for a fright. Parts written in while you wait's our motto."

Everybody laughed, thanks to brandy. Manley was more like his old self, or at least the self of the flight East, Shep was glad to see. Maybe everything was going to be all right.

At the bottom of the hill had been erected a papier-mâché Bavarian village. Swooping down on it with torches in their hands were members of the various ski teams in Bavarian costumes. A ski clown kept taking outlandish falls and then would struggle ludicrously to get to his feet.

"Reminds me of us trying to write our story," Manley Halliday said. He had the bottle in his hand, having more or less appropriated it from Shep's classmate.

To a platform in the middle of the village, pages escorted the twelve most beautiful girls who had passed through the gate. At the top of the hill appeared the ski champion, wearing a suit of silver and a silver crown to personify King Winter. Followed by six torch-bearing courtiers he flashed down the hill in a series of graceful turns to glide into the village, where he mounted the stage to select from among the twelve aspirants his Winter Queen.

"You wouldn't mind if we had one little drink from our jug, old man?" Bill Bonner said. Manley Halliday had been drinking the brandy in great gulps.

"No'tall," he said, handing it over with a magnanimous flourish. "Jus' don' forget where you got it. I borrowed it from a frena mine—a St. Bernard—an' he's liable t' bite me if I don't give it back."

"Take it easy," Shep said.

"Shep thishis really a beau'ful sheremony. Thishould make a beau'ful shequence."

"You'll make a beautiful corpse if you don't lay off that stuff."

"Shep, tha's cruel. Shows how young you are. When y'get to be my age you won' joke about death. Death's too close, death's . . ."

At this moment a giant spotlight was bathing the new Queen in a silvery, momentary glory.

"Why, looks like—it *is*—Savannah!"

The almost too perfect blonde model they had met on the train was looking up at the cheering crowd with a triumphant, professional smile.

Over the loudspeaker system came the forced cheerfulness of a mechanical voice: "And now—for the crowning of Queen Winter. The world-famous author Manley Halliday who has honored us with his presence this week-end was to have officiated at the coronation. Unfortunately, Mr. Halliday has been taken ill . . ."

Loud, rude laughter rose from the crowd and it was several moments before the loudspeaker could regain its attention. "Mr. Halliday's place will be taken by the eminent motion-picture producer Mr. Victor Milgrim, who will feature our Queen, Savannah Castle, in his forthcoming picturization of this Mardi Gras, *Love on Ice."*

But the last words of the announcer were lost in the mounting laughter of the crowd as it saw the miserably bedraggled figure start forward in a hesitant, shaky, opera-bouffe approach to the platform. Several times he almost lost his balance and the youthful onlookers, quickly entering into the spirit of the impromptu performance, shouted *whoops* and then laughed and cheered when he regained his footing again.

"Manley! Manley!" Shep screamed and ran after him into the illuminated village. The audience was enjoying an unexpected comedy act. Manley Halliday had almost reached the steps to the platform. Then he raised his foot too soon, lost his balance, went reeling backwards and flopped Leon Errol fashion into a snow-bank. The young spectators rocked and shrieked with laughter.

Shep reached him a few moments later. With the help of someone he got him back on his feet and off to the sidelines. Somehow they got him through the crowd to a car. In the car Manley Halliday lay his head back on the seat and breathed heavily with his mouth open. "Shouldna tried to come out again," he whispered. "I've seen all this. Baby, I've seen everything before."

The bellboy helped Shep get him up to the room. Shep laid him on the lower bed of the double-decker, loosened his collar and his belt, unbuttoned his shirt and started removing his shoes. "Ooo, that foot," Manley Halliday groaned. Then, with his eyes closed, he suddenly began to speak:

"Bet you're getting a bang outa this—having t' take care of Manley Halliday. Somethin' t' tellya friends, huh?"

The tone was bitter, nasty, resentful, and it made Shep mad. It was part of something Shep did not understand and he was sick and tired of it, tired and sick of this man, this lodestone—no he didn't mean that, though he was that too—this millstone, he meant, whatever it is that, tied around your neck, won't let you run or even straighten up.

"Well, the hell with you," he heard himself saying. "Who asked you to rise from the dead anyway? Why couldn't you stay dead? You're a bum, just a goddam bum—just another hopeless derelict from the Twenties, staggering into snowbanks, a laughing stock. Take off your own goddam shoes—solve your own goddam life—from here on in I don't give one good goddam what happens to you."

Manley Halliday's eyes opened to trembling slits. "Don't talk to me like that. I'm sick. Can't y'see? Not just the booze. I'm sick."

"Oh, balls. I'm sick too. I'm sick of paying for your fun."

Manley Halliday closed his eyes again and began to make a peculiar moaning sound that startled Shep when he realized what it was—not moaning at all but the sound of quiet chuckling.

While Shep stared, shaken, the chuckle spread to laughter. "This whole day's really funny. The face on the President's stooge when he was frightened by how I looked an' trying to be p'lite at the same time. An' that Abercrombie 'n Fitch outfit Victor had on. Y'know 'till today I couldn't figure out why he was such an ass. It's because he's such a tyrant with us an' such a toady with people he thinks outrank him socially." He was laughing again, but out of a face that did not look as if it were laughing. "An' these kids, the way they talk so cocksure, the way they handle the slang, sort of possessively, arrogantly, 'sif they made it up. Most of it's the same old stuff brought up to date a little bit combined with Negro jive talk. Heard one little number with a Boston *a* telling her boy friend to 'relax in your slacks before you collapse in your chaps.' Almost worth coming up for, notice I say *almost* . . ."

Shep, flabbergasted: "How the hell you could see that much in your condition . . ."

" 'Member, wrote it all twenny years ago. Baby, no one 'll ever do it any better. Had a talent once, baby. Got enough left for one more book. Two or three if I pace myself . . ."

347

His grin had the chilling effect of a death's head. His eyes were shining up at Shep's but they saw nothing but their own tortured dreams. Suddenly he screamed out, half-rising on his elbows as again a girl's voice from the busy corner below rose to them, "Yoo hoo, here I am!" and Manley whispered, "Hear that? She's here, she's here! They've let her out for the week-end . . ."

"Manley—you're at Webster—Webster, remember?"

"Then I'm going to her. I know where she is now. She's at Sloan's. The place near Katonah. I'll get her. I'll take her away. We'll go somewhere. Some—some island. A cottage on the beach. We'll swim in the moonlight."

This goddam romanticizing of everything, Shep thought, as Manley Halliday, in this strange and agonized sleep, began to rise from the bed. It could never be a real home any place, always a cottage small, a villa at Sorrento, a beach in the moonlight.

Manley weaving but insisting, "I'm going—gonna get Jere," and actually starting forward to the door one step and then another, swaying to catch his balance and then groping for the door knob where Shep was grabbing him, shoving him back toward the bed while he kept stubbornly pushing forward: "Damn it, lemme go! What you got against Jere? All my frien's against Jere. Well, hell with you all, I'm going, gotta find Jere. . ."

He lurched for the door and almost fell, his knees giving like the joints of a break-away chair. He had started down when Shep caught him. He was limp in Shep's arms now and Shep carried him back to the berth with disturbing ease, for there was so little weight to him, a mere bag of memories and bones. His eyes were closed at last and from his mouth came no longer the frightful voice that had been so mysteriously clear as to seem disembodied, came no sound at all but that of exhausted breathing.

Shep waited for ten minutes, until he was sure it was real sleep. Then he felt an irrepressible urge to put some measure of time and distance between himself and Manley Halliday. For days and days—he had lost all sense of how many—he had been

348

closed in with this man and his terrible afflictions, in offices, airplanes, hotel rooms, Pullman compartments, diners, back-seats, men's rooms and finally here in this incredible attic. Desperately he needed to get away, talk to ordinary people, have a cheerful drink, maybe dance with a pretty girl—anything to escape from this wreck of a man with his racking obsessions, his malignant dreams.

He tiptoed out, shut the door noiselessly behind him and felt an absurd elation when he realized he had made it and that he was outside by himself, on his way to the Phi Delt house where he might find old friends, Pat Jackson, Roy Moorhead and the rest of the gang. He hurried past fond couples walking in step, ready to give himself to the party atmosphere of the fraternity house, the drunks being walked outside by patient friends, the riotous crowd in the hallway, the same old jokes of the stags, the house snake, the girl who plays so innocent, the knowing male laughter, the dim lights, the undergraduate band with the bespectacled drummer coming in on the vocal *jeepers creepers where'd ya get those peepers* and the babes in their smooth evening gowns with the eyes in their young faces closed in practiced ecstasy.

Feeling better, Shep went downstairs to the bar, crowded and smoky and "drunk out tonight" he heard a smart-looking brunette announce. With a glass in his hand, feeling better all the time "'Lo, Gene," he said, seeing Hoffman down the bar. "Where's your little friend?" Hoffman asked, carrying a load now. "Getting a little rest?" He didn't even want to think about it.

"If you ask me he needs a permanent rest."

"Nobody's asking you."

"Can't you fellas make a good movie once in a while? I saw *Gunga Din* last week. Gong." He made the sound of that's all on the Major Bowes program. Everybody along the bar laughed. "You sul-lay me," said a really good-looking straight-haired blonde. The way she said it, it sounded obscene. She was with someone else who was beginning not to like the attention she was giving Hoffman. Hoffman went stag to the Mardi Gras every year just for this sort of thing. Upstairs they were playing—and the tall blonde sang along with them—This Can't Be Love Because I Feel So Well . . .

Shep caught sight of his old roommate Pat Jackson. Pat had been captain of the swimming team and vice president of the class.

"Pat!"

"Shep, you old bastard!"

They punched each other fondly. The harassed bartender finally got around to their empty glasses. "Well, here's lead in your pencil," Pat said.

Hasn't changed a bit, Shep thought happily, with a young man's exaggerated sense of what two years could do. Pat was still a great guy. Hard to explain but it always made you feel good having him around. A happy-go-lucky and yet with something to him underneath. "First one since the last one," Shep said, feeling at once the psychological effect of the drink, able for the first time in days to feel his nerves slacking off. He lowered his glass, beginning to look around and see the sights, beginning to join the party and it was then that he felt the hand on his shoulder.

Somehow he knew without looking around that it was all over with his little outing. He accepted this so completely that he didn't even wonder by what drunken miracle, what quicker-than-eye sorcery, poor old Manley had risen from the dead and followed him. It was as if Manley Halliday merely had to reach out to pull him back into the nightmare again. Watching him standing there blood-shot, heavy-bearded and unkempt among all these immaculate young shirt fronts, Shep thought you couldn't dream it up worse than this, couldn't imagine anything more unfortunate than what happened when Manley Halliday called the bartender and Gene Hoffman looked up and said, "Well, if it isn't Mr. Two-Thousand-a-Week."

"Yesh, an' worsh it too, what you thinka thash?" Manley demanded, trying desperately to hold himself in one place.

"I think you must've left your false teeth in your room," Hoffman said.

Behind him Shep could hear the Greek chorus building: You mean *that's* Manley Halliday? *Manley Halliday,* the famous

350

writer, that drunken bum. Sure, didn't you see 'im at the Coronation? God, he was funny when he went on his keester out there. . . .

Sometimes a test-tube blows up in your face, does it? Well, Shep was ready to blow. Ready to cry out, Listen, you dressed-up dummies, this drunken bum will be remembered and respected when you're nothing but a lot of forgotten names on neglected tombstones. Something really dramatic, a big tell-off scene that only seems to happen in plays. Maybe it might even have happened here, but Shep never had a chance to find out because something else had actually begun to happen. Ultra-formal, almost as if he were about to bow and suggest a drink, stiffly formal and wobbly drunk at the same time, Manley Halliday was addressing himself to Hoffman:

"Thash a remark that c'd only be made by a callow mind too shtupid to—lowest type o' *Sturm Abteilung* humor."

They glared at each other across the barricade of time.

"At two thousand a week your dialogue oughta be brighter than that," Hoffman said.

"I useta do a little boxing, Hoffman."

This effort at menace made Hoffman laugh. He said to the tall blonde girl, loudly, "Listen to the little man. A champion—lush."

It was painful to see Manley Halliday, leading from weakness, try to reach the strong young mocking face of Hoffman with a feeble roundhouse that Hoffman laughed away from. It was such a mismatch that Hoffman, embarrassed as to what to do next, swung on Shep who was trying to pull Manley back out of danger, while Manley brave in a crazy sick way was screaming "I'll kill 'im! I'll kill 'im!" and straining to get at Hoffman while young men from everywhere pinned his arms to his side and drew him out of danger.

It seemed to Shep not at all coincidental or melodramatic but simply according to the plan of this dark journey that Victor Milgrim suddenly should materialize with Queen Savannah to watch the wretched scuffling at the bar. In his Bond Street evening clothes, a model in tailored black-and-white, with the unreal beauty of Savannah Castle at his side it was all too much

351

like a bad dream or a bad plot for Milgrim to say, "What are you fellows trying to do, get us laughed off the campus? I want you to go to your rooms at once and stay there until I send for you."

"Hear that, baby, r'stricted to quarters," Manley Halliday said. "What we got here, martial law? Heil Hitler!" He raised his arm in a mock salute. The bar crowd loved it.

Milgrim colored. "Immediately," he said. "I'm very serious."

" 'raus mit uns," Manley Halliday said. He insisted on putting his arm around Shep's shoulder, which couldn't have presented more blatantly the stereotype of two drunks. Conscious of this, Shep had an impulse to draw away, but his resentment of the house-party crowd for their mockery of Halliday carried him through. There was a touch of martyrdom in his walking out through the ridiculing laughter with Manley.

Along the cleared path between the snow-banks under the ice-stiffened black branches of the maples, still arm-in-arm in school-boy alliance, they tried to keep in step together. The air was numbing cold and Manley Halliday in only his rumpled suit, too hurried in pursuit of Shep to bother with an overcoat, should have been frozen, but he was beyond reach of the elements now. The only sound was the rhythmic crunch of the hard snow under their feet. The sharp corners of the moon cut cleanly into the gray-blue winter sky, lighting the campus with a pale Christmas-card glow.

" 'S really a beau'ful night. Wonnerful night."

"It is?"

Manley Halliday looked at Shep in hurt surprise. "Come on, Baby, le's not worry about that sonuvabish. Le's have a li'l fun. We oughta get a li'l fun outa this expedition. We worked. Day 'n night. I don' feel guilty. Be damned if I'm gonna feel guilty. Be damned if I'm gonna feel beholden to Mister Victor Milgrim."

"Come on," Shep said, taking his arm. "It's too damn cold to stand still."

"I like you," Manley Halliday was saying. "You're gonna be my young man o' the Thirties. 'Sfunny, I haven't known a young man in the Thirties. Maybe some day I'll write a book about a young man in the Thirties."

352

What the hell would you know about young men in the Thirties, Shep thought.

"—I was sitting with his girl."

"Whose girl?"

"Jack Thomas' girl."

"Jack Thomas?"

"The writer. Damn good writer. Could've been. She an' Jack hadda fight. It was down in the old Stork an' I was tryin' to tell her it wasn't anything—just a two-sided hangover an' t' wait there while I got him t' come down. An' when I called . . ."

"Yes?"

"When I called they had just found him, an' I hadda tell the girl."

"Tea for Two," Shep said.

"Tha's right. When I wrote it I made it a tea dance. I'm a son of a bitch."

"Why?"

"Because here he was, a frena mine, dead, a talent finished off 'fore it ever got started an' there I was tellin' his girl an' alla time I'm thinkin' of how it c'n be 'mproved, the li'l changes I'll make when I write it—like a cannibal eatin' their flesh while they're dyin'."

"But you can't help that, that's—" he hesitated "—your job. Your art."

"Sure. Sure. Tell me more, baby. Tell me what big eyes I got. All the better to see through you, my dear. To see through Webster."

Manley began to laugh again. "Lord, that scene at the bar. Victor with neon lights across his dress shirt flashing *How c'n you do this to me?* Poor Victor's dancing bear won't dance pretty for the people when the impresario cracks the whip! Oh, God, it's really funny, it's funny . . ."

He faltered and put his hand to his face. Shep wondered about the crack in his voice. He looked down—was Halliday always that short or was he shrinking?—to affirm his fear that the man was crying. No, by Christ, he was revved up like a madman. He began to sing:

> "Heigh ho heigh ho,
> To the morrow's work we'll go,
> But tonight our fun
> Has just begun,
> Heigh ho heigh ho . . ."

They marched along in step, Manley completely (Shep trying his best to be) forgetful of the shadow stalking them to the Inn. When Manley Halliday tired of improvising neat little rhymes he started in on the ribald Webster Mardi Gras Song:

> "Oh, if all the babes at Mardi Gras were laid end to end
> I wouldn't be a bit surprised.
> They come from Smith and Well-es-ley their honor to defend
> But the first day they're compromised.
> The second day deflowered . . ."

"Didn't think I'd 'member it any more," Manley Halliday cried happily. "Okay le's try it again. You sing the harmony. Ooooh—no, that's too high. Oooh—that's it!—Oh, if all the babes at Mardi Gras . . ."

They were approaching the lights of the Inn. Manley Halliday was singing uninhibitedly. A couple passing in a sleigh recognized the song and looked at each other in laughing embarrassment. "Peace, it's wonderful. Thank you, Father," the boy called out.

"Better stash the song," Shep said. "People."

"Oh, nuts t' them," Manley Halliday said. "Le's sex it up a little bit. Knew a funny fella used t' say that at parties, 'c'mon kids, le's sex it up a little bit.' Randy Sears. Christ, he's gone too. Why is, so many of the gay fellas were in such a hurry t' get down they couldn't wait for the elevators. Oh—come on, 'If all the babes at Mardi Gras . . .'"

He sang it with the desperate joy of second childhood.

"Say, baby, did y' notice the smooth li'l babe at the end o' the bar? Li'l finishing-school miss, I betcha, with yellow eyes saying *Oh look lookit me I'm here I'm on my way*. One in the gold lamé dress—looked exac'ly like a li'l yellow kitten."

354

He began to chant:

> "Li'l yellow kittens
> With pink li'l noses
> Loving to be petted
> Dancing on their toe-ses.
> Li'l yellow kittens
> With pink li'l ears
> Waiting to be divested
> Of their pink li'l fears."

Shep couldn't help laughing, at the same time wondering: Maybe that's how he always lived. Always aware of and always trying to laugh off disaster.

Manley Halliday hadn't forgotten where but when he was. This was a party with honey-eyed girls and crooning saxophones, plenty of booze and a campus to roll up and push to one side for the dancers.

"Le's go get a drink at the Psi U's. They prol'ly have the smoothest women."

At the entrance to the Inn, Shep tried to steer him up the steps. "Come on. Here we are at Psi U House."

But Manley Halliday caught it instantly. Far gone but not *that* far, he gave Shep such a look as he would never be able to forget, pulled his arm away and started running across the street. Shep just had time to notice how Manley was limping before an undergraduate car making a reckless turn bore down on him. Car and runner swerved from each other in a haphazard frenzy and Manley Halliday kept on in a jogging, limping stagger toward the Psi U House. He hadn't forgotten where it was. Shep was chasing him. Oh, Lord, his foot—it was numb, asleep—if he could only outrun him. But Shep was overtaking him, grabbing him with strong hands against which he was squirming.

"Lemme go. *Lemme go!*"

Shep didn't say anything. He was pulling him back to the Inn. Halfway across the street Manley made a desperate try at escape. When Shep turned to regain and tighten his hold, Manley Halliday struck him in the face. In the reflex of anger, Shep struck back. Manley Halliday sagged. Shep caught him and half-carried, half-dragged him toward the steps of the Inn. It made two young couples on the corner laugh.

"Sweet dreams, Grandpa!"

A quick shot in a crazy dream montage, Shep was thinking. Lugging across the street at the height of the Mardi Gras one of the all-time big ones, and nobody pays the slightest attention. Just another Mardi Gras drunk.

Outside the Inn Manley Halliday said suddenly, "Unhand me, offisher. 'M'all right now."

Shep, taking a chance, loosened his hold.

"Let's both hit the hay."

Manley Halliday hesitated. He had to spread his feet to keep from falling and even then his body bent forward at a precarious angle.

"Cupa coffee. Maybe a san'wich. Kindadizzy. Prol'ly needa eat something."

The Coffee Shop was just a few doors down and Shep suddenly realized that he was weak with hunger himself. So he said all right, but no funny business, from the Coffee Shop straight up to bed. Maybe if they got a good clean start in the morning, pulled themselves together, brought Milgrim something on paper, this day could be erased.

But now it all seemed to be happening like the line of an old joke—accidentally on purpose—for who should be coming out of the Coffee Shop, in ski clothes, her lips made up, her cheeks becomingly rosy, so transfigured as hardly to be recognizable— Miss—Miss—Shep struggled to recall the name of the matronly stenographer they had hired in New York and entirely forgotten.

"Miss Waddell!" Manley Halliday managed to remember.

"Oh, Mr. Holloway! Mr. Stearn!" She was overjoyed—"I want you to meet my friend Mr. Gilhooley."

"Hello, boys," said Gilhooley, a plump, short, out-door-complexioned, middle-aged figure in ski clothes.

"Mr. Gilhooley is the trainer of the Norwood College winter sports team," Miss Waddell exuded new-found happiness. "He's been showing me *everything*. We went for the most *heavenly* sleigh ride. Oh, really, Mr. Holloway, I think this is the most wonderful time I've ever had. Just to get out of the city—it—

it . . ." There were simply no words for the metamorphosis of Miss Waddell. "It *does* something for you. Gee, Mr. Holloway, how can I ever thank you enough? It—" she looked at the self-possessed Mr. Gilhooley and actually blushed. "—why, I think it's going to change my entire life."

"Good," Manley Halliday said. "Good. Haven't changed anybody's entire life in months." Then he became abruptly businesslike. "Miss Waddell, we've been looking all over for you. Got some work t' do. We didn' come up here for an outing, y' know. Have a lotta dictation."

Miss Waddell quieted a little. "Why—why surely, Mr. Holloway. You—you mean right now?"

" 'F you don' mind."

"I'd—I'd have to get my book."

"All right—get it."

She looked appealingly at Mr. Gilhooley, who manfully stepped into the breach. "How long would you say she'll be, Mr. Holloway?"

"Oh, halfa nour," Manley Halliday said offhand.

"Well—I'll wait for you at the Skating Club. How'll that be, Kitty?"

"All right, Monk." Miss Waddell reluctantly surrendered him.

"Le's go in hava cupa coffee 'n then we'll get started," Manley Halliday said. "No—tell ya what y'do. Bring your book in there. We c'n dictate while we eat."

The Coffee Shop was crowded with animated couples attractive in their evening clothes, fortifying themselves with coffee, getting ready to make a night of it. It wasn't twelve o'clock yet. The big time was just getting under way.

Self-consciously Shep felt all these bright glowing faces made mock of his and Manley's condition. Quite a few did laugh, especially when Manley Halliday lurched to an empty table and almost fell.

"Waitress—ma'moiselle," Manley Halliday called, and snapped his fingers for service. This irritated the young lady and she took her time coming over. She was singularly unattractive.

"We're from Hollywood—this is Mr. Stearns, the well-known screen writer and we're very busy working on a movie," Manley

Halliday began, while Shep wished himself at the top of the ski-jump, or the farthest reaches of Alaska, anywhere but here. "We've got a screenplay t' write t'night so we'll need fast service, toot sweet, n'est-ce pas? So let the others wait—they got nothing t' do but go back n' get plastered."

"Are you ready to order?" the girl said.

Manley Halliday looked up at her. "Saay—you've got beau'ful eyes. Shep, why don' we put her in our picture? You'll be *our* discov'ry, our Savannah Castle."

The waitress snapped her book shut and B-lined to another table.

"Manley, let's forget the coffee. I think we better go right up."

"Shhh. Don' worry 'bout me. 'M'all right. I won' dis—disgrace you." He looked up slowly. "Ah, Miss Waddell. Well, anyway we 'complished something on this trip. Fairy godfathers, 'at's what we are. Her Mr. Monk, I mean Mr. Dooley, he's Prince Charming."

He tried to rise for Miss Waddell but fell back into his chair.

"All righ' le's go," he said. "C'mon, Shep, *think*. We gotta write our movie righ' now this ver' minute." He hung his head in thought and then came up with a sickly smile and an idea:

"This'll be called Campus Capers by S. Manley Hallenstearns the fearless surrealist . . ."

"You want me to take this down?" Miss Waddell asked.

"'Course take it down. Whattya think I'm dictating for—my own amusement? Well, I am."

Troubled, Miss Waddell lowered her head to her dictation book.

"We fade in," he began, "on the slick, bright ice-shiny surface of the ski jump. Dissolve through to the slick, bright shiny surface of an undergraduate mind . . ."

Shep laughed and Manley Halliday turned toward him, pleased. "Like that? Okay, Comrade C'lab'rator, take the wheel."

"The undergraduate's mind is divided into a series of watertight whiskey-tight compartments," Shep ventured. "Camera moves up to a medium close shot of one of these compartments.

358

It's a compartment on the B & M, taking the boys up to Quebec for a dirty week-end."

Manley Halliday nodded and resumed. "Now, close up of upper berth, containing upperclassman. He leans down toward the lower berth t' talk to the lower classman. He says 'Mach'—this boy is really Niccolo Machiavelli, an exchange student from Italy—'I just been thinkin' about college. You on'y put into it what you take out of it.' Young Machiavelli '41 looks up. He has very bright eyes an' a cynical smile. 'One must learn to balance one professor against another if one wishes to maintain his position of pre-eminence as a B.M.O.C.' he says. Have you got that, Miss Waddell?"

Poor Miss Waddell, her mind divided between the glamour of Mr. Gilhooley and the glamour of finding herself involved with Hollywood madcaps, shook her head in bewilderment. "I'm only up to 'one professor.'"

"Miss Waddell, don't let Mr. Dooley hear you say that," Manley Halliday said broadly.

"Who we going to get to play Machiavelli?" Shep asked.

"Don Ameche, who else?" Manley Halliday said. "Don Ameche playing Nick Machiavelli, the designing captain of the ski team who wins for Florence by playing one rival team against the other."

"Who'll play Florence?"

Whether it was really this funny or merely a sign of cracking nerves, they were hilarious.

"Florence," Manley Halliday considered a moment. "Florence Rice? Oh, I know—Toby Wing. We owe it to the readers of *Film Fun* t' see to it that Toby Wing actually gets into a movie."

"Good idea. Cheese-cake with winter icing. But won't Toby Wing look kinda out of place at a winter sports meet in those little panties she always wears?"

"Can't have ya cheese cake an' freeze it too? Well, take it from an ol' *Film Fun* man, Toby Wing won't catch cold, she's a hot number."

"Mr. Holloway, am I supposed to be taking this down?" Miss Waddell wanted to know.

"Almos' finished," Manley Halliday said. "Shequence one. Gotta end shequence one on a high note, Shep. How 'bout this? We see a skier in the distance moving slowly along the beau'ful sloping hill of snowy white dissolve through to the freshly manicured hand of Victor Milgrim moving slowly around the snowy white contours of Savannah. The hand moves down down to the white smoothness of the thigh that becomes a smooth white field that carries the skier Nick Machiavelli to the edge of a lovely woods. Leading into this luxuriation is a dark passageway and as Nick boldly glides in we slowly fade out while the music crescendos to an orgiastic crash."

"In two words," Shep said, "Tuh riffic."

"If Don Ameche's too busy we'll get Fred Astaire t' play Mach, turn the skier into a skater an' he'll do a tap dance on the ice."

"Holloway, you're on the front burner."

"My feet feel as if they're still in the icebox." He looked at Miss Waddell. "'S 'everything perfec'ly clear?"

Miss Waddell's face was a study in frustration. "Well, I wasn't sure . . ."

Manley Halliday interrupted her. "'S all right. 'F you're confused, so're we, so just make it up yourself. Always takes a bunch o' people t' write a movie anyway." He became businesslike. "Have that ready first thing in the morning. Original 'n five. You may go now, Miss Waddell."

The woman rose uncertainly. "I'm not sure—is this all a joke? Or do you really . . ."

"You're right," Manley Halliday said. "'S 'all a joke. They laughed when I sat down t' write *Love on Ice.*"

Miss Waddell hurried off as if she were slightly afraid of them. The waitress returned and stood over them righteously.

"Lissen, folks're waitin' for this table."

"Now, miss, don't get impatient. You don' wanna be a waitress all your life, do ya? Smile at me 'n I might give ya a screen test. Make ya a star. You come upstairs with me 'n you'll get a screen test."

"Lis-sen—fresh—"

360

"When you get off go t' the desk 'n ask for Victor Milgrim. I'll be waitin' for ya, girlie."

"Go on, beat it."

"Now, honey, don' get sore. Y'know y'gotta live before y'c'n act. . ."

"I'm gonna call the manager."

"Come on, Manley, let's go."

"I mean it, the manager. You c'd be arrested."

"Don't bother, miss, we're going anyway," Shep said.

He half-lifted Manley Halliday from his seat and hustled him out.

Everybody in the Coffee Shop had a laugh on their sorry exit. But Manley Halliday wasn't seeing people any more and Shep was too preoccupied to care.

Outside on the pavement Manley Halliday no longer knew how frozen, how miserable, how near the edge he really was because exhilaration—an early stage of delirium—protected him.

"Don' you think our script has posh'bilities?"

"Manley, the only possibility I'm interested in is flopping into bed before something else happens. I don't even know if I'm drunk or sober. I'm beginning to meet myself coming back."

"Don' look so dour, comrade. Us masses gotta come out on top."

"But we can't wait that long. I mean Milgrim can't wait that long. He wants something tomorrow."

"T'morrow we'll dictate that brainstorm you had this morning. Lord, was that on'y this morning? Today I feel as if I lived a whole life, died 'n was buried."

He put his arm around Shep, who wasn't playing any more. "All right, killjoy, back to the penthouse." Staggering, he almost pulled Shep down with him into the snow. "Ooop—s'pose you think I'm drunk. Not drunk, just—my feet feel funny. Too much walking. Toes 're asleep." He tried to stamp them on the snow. Then he hobbled along at Shep's side. He was snickering again. "Won' it be a scream if the waitress really goes up 'n asks for Victor! That was a'ninspiration. That's what put me where I am today. An' where am I today? Up to my arse in snow, as Hutchinson 'd say, covered all over in sweet violets."

As they turned the corner, laughing together, Victor Milgrim was approaching the Inn with the Dean and his wife. In his top-hat, his dress overcoat and his indignation, Milgrim seemed perfectly cast as a morality-play actor representing Outraged Respectability.

"Excuse me a moment," he said to the Dean and quickened his steps to intercept Manley and Shep, as if the closer this drunken, dissolute, disgraceful pair came to sober, responsible, uncontaminated people, the worse would be their crime.

Even when Shep heard Victor Milgrim say, "The two of you are going to get into that cab, go down to the station and wait there for the next train back to New York," it wasn't real enough to have impact. Shep couldn't adjust himself to the theatricality.

For Manley Halliday, who barely deciphered the meaning through the distortion of pain, exhaustion, alcoholism and a crisis of nerves, the theatricality—even to the corny device of the potentate in the topper confronting a battered drunk fallen from grace—was somehow inevitable, part of the dark pattern of deterioration out of which he had been trying to break away, as the drunkard breaks away from one bar to stumble into another. Yes, suddenly he could have foretold—damn it, he almost had foretold, only to let himself slip back and be illusioned—that his employment by Victor Milgrim on such a job of shoddy as *Love on Ice* would have to end with Milgrim in a top-hat and his own head bloody and bowed, at cross-words, cross-roads, cross-purposes on this cold, dark, unlikely corner of the world. The chimes were actually chiming and Manley's thoughts struck with them, gong gong going going goingngngngn going-ngngngend dend deadend deadendnnn

Shep: "That cab? Right now? But our clothes? Our bags?"

Milgrim: "I'll have Hutch send them down after you. I want you two" (lowering voice so the Dean couldn't hear) "bastards out of town, right now, this minute."

Manley Halliday heard this and, with considerable effort, raised his head. "Victor, thish is out-rageous. I won' be spoken to ashif I'm jusht . . ."

"You'll be spoken to for what you are—a drunken bum. I'm going to write every studio head in town and tell them what happened. You'll never get another writing job again. Now get into that cab and out of my sight before I lose my temper."

From the depths, Manley Halliday managed to summon a last-ditch dignity. "F' goodness sake, Shep, le's get outa this town 'fore I lose *my* temper."

He turned, and taking Shep's arm like a habitual invalid, dragged himself toward the waiting cab. From the running board he half-turned and called back:

" 'Farewell, you broad-backed hippopotamus.' "

Shep pulled him into the cab.

21

Rolling down the hill to the station through the falling snow, Manley Halliday crumpled against the seat said faintly, "Well, kid, I did it. Really loused it up for you. Christ, what luck! What luck! If only we hadn't met Milgrim."

"If." Shep looked out the window at the dark pines heavy with snow. A gay sight, from the point of view of a window-seat in a fire-warmed fraternity house, cuddled up with your best girl. But a desolate landscape now as you drove away from the scene of the crime with a man too brave for suicide but unable to prevent the murder of himself.

Manley Halliday rolled his head against the back of the seat as if delirious. "Dizzy—I feel—oh . . ." His body started to shake with a dry laugh that was like a dry sob. "Brought me up to dignify his silly trip—prestige—a living classic—me . . ."

The laugh was a kind of gasp.

" 'S his fault, you know. Hadda be such a damn in'ellectual show-off. If he'da listened t' me an' left me home t' work on his damn story, neither one of us woulda been disgraced."

"Hell, my fault too," Shep said. "I'm no better than Milgrim. I wanted you to come. I urged you to. I wanted Webster to see me as a big-shot working with Manley Halliday. And that damn champagne. Oh, that goddam champagne."

"Shoulda told you," Manley Halliday mumbled. "Think I started to tell ya. But I felt so lousy, so tired, I thought—Lord, my foot. Like in a cast. Oh. Oh. God . . ."

There would be a train through in about an hour. There was only one other person in the waiting room, an elderly salesman sleeping beside his sample cases. The only sound was the occasional clicking of the telegraph key. The seats were hard; after half an hour even harder. Manley Halliday sat hunched over, half asleep, finding consciousness more bearable than the broken mosaic of his dreams.

Shep rose, sat, rose and paced the floor with an inexhaustible restlessness. He watched Manley Halliday anxiously and finally went over and said, "Manley, you okay? You asleep?"

"Still play our songs . . ." The weak smile was a show of strength for a man who could no longer remember where or when he was.

They heard the engine pound in.

"Manley, *Manley,* our train's here!"

"Hafta—get—back—on—the—train—" Manley Halliday murmured "—'fore Victor finds out."

The porter helped Shep pull him up the steps. The whistle screamed; the train moved on through the cold New England night.

Manley Halliday lay silent a long time on the lower berth, his eyes half closed. But each time Shep was sure he had given in to sleep, restless thoughts would break through.

"Really owe 'im that two thousand. Victor. Pay 'im back some time . . ." Whatever he went on muttering, Shep couldn't be sure.

Shep said, "Shhhh. Try to sleep. Don't think about it."

He didn't know what else to say. He was worried, worried and fidgety-nerved. It was good-bye job. Maybe good-bye, career. Back to his old man's car-rental business? Some collaborator! Some foul-up artist!

Silence. Heavy breathing. What a damn racket the tracks made! Lousy B & M. Listen to him groan. Why the hell hadn't he called a doctor to the Inn when Manley came up with that going-to-Jere routine? He wasn't drunk; he was sick. With those shots all bollixed up. Hadn't there been another shot before that crazy meal at the Coffee Shop? Oh, brother, what a rat-race. Maybe the sugar. Guess he'd better do the sugar.

He reached into Manley's coat pocket. There were a few lumps left. He pushed them into Manley's mouth. Manley began sucking on them automatically. The sweat was uncomfortable on Shep's forehead. Jesus, everybody was so helpless. Too easy to push buttons, call doctors, have it done for you. Maybe he was killing Manley. Maybe with his silly pride and the champagne

365

and the urging him on he had been murdering him by inches all week-end.

Manley Halliday looked up at him and talked quite distinctly. Maybe it was the sugar. Maybe it was—Shep still had a romantic notion about dying words.

"Don' look at me that way, baby."

"What way?"

"As if I'm all through. You think I'm all through."

"No . . . no . . ."

The shadow of a smile drifted across the ashen face and was gone. "I c'n read your face. Oh, I know faces, baby. Well, lissen kiddo. My work's ahead of me . . . I'm growing up. I know where I'm going, kiddo."

"Sure. Sure, Manley. Now try and get some shut-eye."

Manley Halliday stirred in anger.

"Damn it don' say *sure* to me like that. Don' patronize me, you young young . . ." It was epithet enough and with effort he went on:

"Don' believe me do ya, kiddo?" Anger was a kind of insulin, reviving him. "You kids with your cubbyholes. The ruined writer of the Twenties. Oh, don't think I can't see it."

Shep was too startled to say anything.

"Okay, you think I'm raving, poor old Manley Halliday. Well, just read—read the first three chapters—then tell me if I'm ruined."

He struggled to sit up. "There—there—my inside pocket."

"Thought I'd have li'l time to go over it with all this traveling. Still needs work. Still rough. Wasn't going to show it to anyone . . ."

Shep reached in for the crumpled manuscript. Manley Halliday touched it lovingly. "Read this 'n see if I'm ruined. This is *Halliday,* kiddo." He used the name like a talisman.

He held the manuscript to him slyly. "Let you read it if you buy me a drink."

"A drink. I haven't got a . . ."

"Don' kid a kidder, baby. You sneaked that bottle of brandy out of my overcoat pocket into yours. Saw you back in the room."

Well, the harm was done, the bridge was burned and could it be any worse? Shep handed him the bottle that still contained a couple of fingers of brandy.

"I'm cold. I'm still cold all over. My feet feel . . . Guess I caught a chill."

He drank and went hhhhhhh, enjoying it. He sank back into the pillow. "Available," he muttered. "Tell 'em—I'm available . . ." His mouth remained open in sleep.

In the upper berth, Shep smoothed out the manuscript. Folded between the fourth and fifth pages was the check Manley thought he had lost on the way up. Shep tucked it into his wallet and began to read the first eighty-three pages of *Folly and Farewell,* subtitled *A Tragedy of Errors,* though Manley Halliday must have thought better of this, for it had been lightly penciled out. On a page by itself was a list of Books by Manley Halliday, which struck Shep as strangely unprofessional and vain, for, after all, such flourishes are actually added by the editor just before sending the typescript to the printer. There was also a dedication: To A. L. My Seeing-Eye Dog; but again all but the initials had been scratched out.

Shep read the first page with skepticism. It wasn't easy to shed his preconceptions. There was grace and a mature sweep to the opening, though. It was obviously the story of Jere, disguised as Jenny, and Manley, called Lee. Before he had finished the first chapter, Shep was admiring the style, the craftsmanship, surprised to find so much of the old Halliday. Jenny and Lee had begun to live a life of their own behind the words. This was not only a love story of exquisite delicacy, Shep was discovering (wondering for the first time in his life why the love story had gone out of fashion for serious novels), but an incisive picture of an era.

He hurried on through the second chapter into the third, amazed by the sharpness of the imagery, the fresh impact of the words. But the best Halliday had always had that. This had something more, Shep was beginning to see. A maturity, a wisdom about people and the fabric of their lives. A capacity not merely for feeling pain but for interpreting pain. Even the best of the old Halliday had been marred at times by a certain callow-

367

ness, a naïveté that seemed to confuse misbehavior with sophistication, a blurring of perspective. But this was the work of a sure hand, with the insight of the rare author who can appraise what he loves and love what he condemns.

By the time he had finished the last page, Shep was stunned. There was no cubbyhole in Shep's convictions for this sign of growth over Halliday's previous work. Methodically he went back to the beginning and read carefully, taking sentences apart, tapping passages of description and characterization to make sure they weren't hollow, talking the dialogue out loud to hear if it was true. But once more the whole of it gripped him, these crazy beautiful mythical collapsible people of the moon carrying him on to the end of—only chapter three.

He looked down at the author motionless in sick-sleep. He *had* to finish this, not just another good novel, the promise of a milestone job. Then it hit him hard: how was it possible for Manley Halliday to write this well in 1939?

After all, Shep knew why Manley Halliday hadn't published in nearly a decade: because he was defeatist, an escapist, cut off from "vital issues," from "The People," a disillusioned amanuensis of a dying order——oh, Shep hadn't read his *New Masses* for nothing! Yet here were these eighty-three pages. My God, this was *alive,* while the writers who were not defeatist, not escapist, not bourgeois apologists and not "cut off from the main stream of humanity" were wooden and lifeless. Was it possible— and here heresy really struck deep—for an irresponsible individualist, hopelessly *confused,* to write a moving, maybe even profound, revelation of social breakdown? If poor old Halliday, aware of himself and of his own friends in their own neurotic little world, could do what he promised to do in this new work, wouldn't Shep have to re-examine his own standards? Maybe ideology wasn't the literary shibboleth he had believed in so dogmatically.

Terribly awake, he lay there retracing the reasoning that was leading him into these strange, uncharted waters.

What had Manley Halliday said, the process of growing up is that of continual disenchantment, of continually shedding the old enchantment for the new?

Lying awake through the night, with nerves that would not sleep, Shep was hardly ready to go this far. But that now he should be so impatient for Manley Halliday to finish a work that a few hours before he had *known* Manley Halliday could never write—this was a severe lesson in humility.

Shep's long, wide-awake, nerve-twitching, mind-restless night was one of exhausted, open-mouthed sleep for Manley Halliday. He lay heavy with his legs apart, occasionally wetting his lips, a faint frown on his face, as if with some deep pain of subconsciousness that unconsciousness ignored. A number of times he spoke out indistinctly in the dark. Once Shep turned on the light to see if Manley had been awakened by his own cries. No, he was in deep sleep, far, far away on some snowy height of his own, for Shep heard him call out, "Jere—Jere—out of the way—I'm coming down . . ."

22

Cutting through Shep's finally exhausted sleep: the insistent buzzer and the porter's drawl. New York in half an hour. Shep eased himself over the edge of the upper, knew his own weariness as he dropped to the floor and took a quick, anxious reckoning of Manley Halliday's condition.

Manley had not moved. He still lay on his back in his rumpled suit with his legs sprawled and his mouth open with a need for air. Fish out of water, Shep thought. Give him five more minutes. Shep hurriedly drew on his wrinkled clothing. We'll tumble into bed at the hotel and pull ourselves together when we wake up. *If* we wake up, he thought cruelly, fascinated by Manley's drugged oblivion.

"Manley. *Manley*." The crushed figure on the bed did not respond. Well, give him five *more* minutes. Shep went out into the aisle and watched the suburbs thickening toward the metropolis.

"F'teen more minutes," said the old voice of the porter.

"Guess you wanna start getting our bags out."

The porter looked at him. He had carried folks back from Mardi Gras before. "Didn' see you bring no bags aboard, son."

No bags. It came back dimly. Milgrim with his top hat. End of a perfect debacle. The chilling laughter of Manley's chattering teeth. Of course no bags.

"Oh. That's right. Listen. Tell you what you do. Go in and gettim up. My friend up. Tellim he's gotta get off."

The porter looked at him with resigned perseverance. An old man, used to everything that happens on trains. "Yessuh."

The last of the suburbs had given way to outskirts. Shep bent his head to look out at the Sunday-morning quiet of the Bronx. Peaceful people leading peaceful Sunday-morning family lives. That was an automatic reaction. There he went generalizing again. If Manley Halliday was a hive of bad habits, he had been a hive of stock responses.

The porter was back, interrupting. "Par' me, mister. You better come in have a look at your friend. He's not hearin' nothin'."

The porter followed Shep back to the berth. He knew it wasn't going to be a one-man job.

Shep nudged Manley Halliday's elbow, shouted in his ear, sponged a wet towel on his face, shook him hard by both shoulders. But Manley Halliday lay buried under layer on layer of sleep.

"Gottah get him off," the porter said gently.

"How much time now?"

" 'bout seb'n minutes."

"Well. Help me. Lift him up. Together. There. Now lift."

Together they maneuvered him out into the aisle and down to the platform. Shep wasn't too clear about any of it: they were in the tunnel, holding the limp body between them and then Shep had Manley Halliday in his arms while the porter was opening the door—"Yes*suh*—hope you be all right now"—and then they were on the station platform, Shep still managing to hold up the sagging body of his friend.

They made their way to the taxi landing. "No bags?" asked the driver. "Hell, no," Shep said. Why in hell must they all ask silly questions? They worked Manley Halliday onto the rear seat. "Waldorf, and we're in a hurry."

"Everybody's in a hurry," said the driver whose name—Shep always studied their I. D. cards automatically—was Louis Conselino. "Twenny-one years uv hacking and never had a fare yet that wasn't in a hurry."

Shep bowed his head in a silent plea—get us out of this, to the Waldorf, a warm bath, sleep.

"What's the matter with your chum, too bigga night?" The driver had to laugh.

"Just get us to the Waldorf," Shep said.

At the entrance to the hotel he took a kinder view of Conselino. There was something to be said for the way he moved in. "Want me to give ya a hand?"

371

"Guess you better."

At the desk the clerk looked at them from behind cool eyes and a smooth, unbending manner.

"Yes, sir?"

"701, please."

The clerk observed Shep with faint distaste. "You may call on the house phone."

"No, I mean the key. That's our room."

"*Your* room?" The clerk frowned. Since when would the Waldorf stoop to such clientele? "Name, please."

Shep gave it. He glanced behind him anxiously. Louis Conselino had a good grip on Manley.

The clerk worked deliberately. "Halliday and Stearns? Why, you were checked out last Friday."

"Checked out! The hell we checked out. We said we wanted to keep that suite."

"I'm sorry, but your office left instructions . . ."

"All right, all right, give us the same rooms, we'll register again."

Expressionlessly, the clerk sized up Shep and his disabled companion. "I'm sorry, that suite is occupied."

"Well, okay, we'll take something else. Anything. One room."

The training of the desk clerk had immunized him against this sort of thing.

"I'm sorry we don't have a thing available at the moment."

"You mean not a single room in this whole goddam hotel?"

The clerk looked wearily over Shep's shoulder, perhaps in the direction of the lobby detective.

"Nothing at all. I suggest you try elsewhere."

"All right damn it, we'll try the Ambassador. But don't think the studio won't hear about this."

"I'm very sorry," said the clerk with the same bland meaninglessness of "very truly yours."

Not until they were back in the cab did Shep appreciate the emptiness of his threat. At the Ambassador the obliging Conselino again helped Shep support Manley to the desk.

"Double room and bath?"

372

The clerk—hell, was it the same clerk?—looked them over with a noncommittal face.

"Yes, sir—do you have a reservation?"

"No, but this is Mr. Manley Halliday and we just came in from . . ."

The clerk smiled coldly. "I'm very sorry. All our rooms are held for reservations."

Maybe the Park Lane. Manley Halliday was more and more of a dead weight as they dragged him into the lobby.

—"Do you have a reservation?"

That same clerk; he was following them. Determined to keep them out in the cold, on their feet.

—"I'm very sorry, but if you have no reservation . . ."

Outside the New Weston, Louis Conselino said to Shep, "Look, bud, why don't you first go in alone this time?"

Shep tried that. He recognized the clerk, but this time their enemy seemed to have forgotten him. "Double room and bath? I may be able to accommodate you. Are your bags outside?"

Shep stammered through an explanation of the inexplicable. Their bags were still up at Webster. Hadda leave suddenly. 'Mergency.

And then the mechanical voice of hotel authority: "Sorry, I thought you had a reservation. We're completely full."

Good God, did the same inhospitable hack write all their dialogue?

The Warwick. The Ritz Towers. The Chatham.

—"Sorry, unless you have a reservation . . ."

"Look, I've got the money. I c'n pay," Shep pleaded at the Roosevelt.

And the clerk, that same bloodless automaton: "Sorry, unless you have a reservation . . ."

"Oh, reservation my ass," Shep heard himself sob. Wasn't this the way psychologists drove guinea pigs to nervous breakdown? They had been on this unmerry-go-round for almost an hour. Seven dollars and forty cents of Mr. Conselino's measured time. Shep's fingers wanted to choke that clerk with his starched white collar and his stiff, colorless smile.

373

Manley Halliday, collapsed into the back of the cab, was wondering why it was taking so long. Why all this in and out? What was happening? Didn't they know he should be lying down? Why was it that no one could ever do anything right any more?

As they drove up to the Lexington, Louis Conselino gave Shep some corner-of-the-mouth advice. "This time leave me go in first. See what I c'n do."

"An' tell 'im our bags 're coming," Shep called after him.

Manley Halliday opened his eyes. "There yet?"

"We're between hotels." It didn't click. "We're trying the Lexington."

"Mmm, wanna lie down." He settled deeper into the seat.

Shep got out and paced the sidewalk. This was too much on top of too much. He looked at Manley's face against the glass, staring at him with his eyes open. What was he thinking about, *with his eyes open?* Think he could stare with his eyes closed? Maybe *he* could. This must be what it's like to go crazy. Here he comes our friend Conselino and he's grinning. Good ole Conselino, good-ole Lexington. Ah, that bed, that hot bath, those clean sheets . . .

"Well, I think I got ya fixed up. Le's bring 'im in."

They were lugging him in again. Another hotel lobby. Another try at that hotel clerk. Same cool eyes. Same cool appraisal. He saw Shep, what *that one* looked like; he took a good look at the one they were holding up.

—"Do you gentlemen have a reservation?"

—"Why, no, we—"

—"Then I'm sorry. When I told your driver we had a room I was under the impression . . ."

Okay, okay, Shep knew the impression he was under . . .

In the cab Shep said maybe we should try one of the big transient places, the Lincoln, the Commodore.

Louis Conselino ($8.65, $8.70) said, "Look, fella, I'll be glad t' drive ya around all day, but why doncha go down to Gran' Central, shave, clean up or a Turkish Bath maybe?" He really wanted to help.

374

Manley Halliday's eyes were open again. He had been listening. All of a sudden he understood.

"No use hotels," he mumbled.

"Manley?" Shep meant: are you functioning? "Know what's been happening?"

Manley nodded. "Call Burt Seixas. Burt Seixas." Burt'll help. Burt might disapprove. Might not be able to hide his disappointment. But he could stay at Burt's house. Till Ann came for him. Burt never failed him. Not Burt. Good old Burt was always there.

"Hello, is this the Seixas residence?" Shep was saying in the hotel phone booth. "Let me speak to Mr. Burt Seixas, please."

This was Mrs. Seixas. Who was calling? A friend of Mr. *Halliday's*. But surely he knew that Mr. Seixas had passed away almost a year ago.

Shep went back and reported this to Manley. Burt Seixas—dead. Oh Lord, of course. Poor Burt. Heart attack. Always told him he worked too hard. Worried too much. Even back in the early days when he himself could find nothing more serious to worry about than the reliability of the new bootlegger. Now Burt Seixas was dead. Damn, nearly everybody was dead. Harry Crosby and Jeanne Eagels and Marilyn Miller and Hart Crane and, Christ, let's not call *that* roll. But Burt Seixas; *that* was hard to take.

" . . . says Mr. Seixas is dead, Manley."

All right, stop saying that, stop using that word. Does he think everybody over forty years old is deaf?

Manley didn't appear to be listening. He seemed only to be staring blankly at Shep and Shep was about to repeat what he had said about Seixas when Manley finally spoke.

"All right. Then call Dr. Wittenberg. Paul Wittenberg." Funny, even the number came back to him. Cathedral 8-9970. Dr. Wittenberg, the model for the blunt, intuitive physician in *High Noon,* who had pulled Jere through when she had all that trouble after Douglas. Should have thought about Wittenberg before.

The Cathedral exchange was no longer in use, but Shep got the number through Information.

"Dr. Wittenberg's residence. Well, just a minute I'll see if he's in."

"Take the name and say I've gone out," said Dr. Wittenberg's son. He was a fashionable middle-aged man who probably would not have become a doctor if there had not been the tradition and a Park Avenue practice to inherit.

"Calling for—just a minute I'll write it down—Manley Halliday, and it's an emergency."

Manley Halliday. That famous old patient of his father's. Was *he* still around? The old man had taken quite an interest in him. Part of his weakness for odd characters. All right, maybe he'd better find out what it was.

"Dr. Wittenberg," said Dr. Wittenberg's son.

Shep described Manley's condition. Dr. Wittenberg listened. Yes, he remembered the alcoholic background, and now there was a diabetic condition out of control? Well, nothing much to do but put him under care and follow the book.

"All right, I'll call Mount Sinai to arrange a room. Yes, I'll meet you there in a few minutes."

Oh, Mount Sinai. Familiar place. Dr. Wittenberg had tapered him off here after some bad ones years before. It was all a circle, a vicious circle, growing smaller, pressing in.

A nurse was just beginning to undress him when Dr. Wittenberg hurried in. There was a quick examination, stethoscope, eyes, a tap here and there. "Semi-coma due to inadequate insulin," Dr. Wittenberg told Shep on the way out. "In addition there's the alcoholism and physical exhaustion."

"But you think he'll be all right, Doctor?"

"Oh, my, yes. He'll come around soon as his sugar balance is restored. He won't be feeling too frisky for a while. And of course he's got to stay on the wagon."

"But, Doctor, he hasn't been drinking, I mean before this. He's . . ." Shep didn't like Wittenberg's over-simplification.

"I'm acquainted with the history of the case." Dr. Wittenberg glanced at his watch. "I'll check on him again in the morning. Meanwhile, not a thing to worry about."

376

23

It was the nurse, Miss Gillam, who first noticed his toes when she stripped off his socks.

As soon as she had him in bed she called the intern, Dr. Lewis, the new one who looked at least five years younger than the twenty-six he was.

Dr. Lewis glanced at the chart, took a quick look at the blackening toes and said, "Well, you've got yourself quite a frostbite." He frowned and turned to Miss Gillam. "Call Dr. Resnick immediately, nurse."

Dr. Resnick, the resident, whose premature baldness gave him the look of a much older man, confirmed Dr. Lewis's suspicion. "It's gangrene all right. Diabetics are particularly susceptible. Get an electro-cardiogram on him right away. And . . ."

"Emergency liver and kidney function tests?"

"Correct. Call me as soon as you know the results."

Manley Halliday lay comfortably in the white bed, fully restored to consciousness. With an overwhelming sense of relief, he was giving in to his exhaustion. At least he was rid of *Love on Ice*. What would he do now? Shhh, like his own physician he warned himself against undue anxiety. Don't press now. Just lie back. Rest. Knit. Sleep. An irrational confidence sustained him. Every man had a destiny to fulfil. A Manley Halliday couldn't leave off in the middle this way. Not with *Folly and Farewell* merely begun . . .

Dr. Lewis was calling Dr. Resnick from the cardiograph room. "You can come down and look at the wet tracings, doctor."

Dr. Resnick read the evidence. "Mmm. Considerable myocardial damage."

"You're not kidding."

"I'm afraid this complicates things."

"What's the story—digitalis right away?"

"Yes, a rapid and full digitalization. Call me as soon as you have those tests."

When Dr. Resnick returned to his office he tried to get in touch with Dr. Wittenberg again. Dr. Wittenberg would not be home until evening. It had been old man Wittenberg's reputation not to have been out of communication with the hospital in thirty years.

Meanwhile Manley Halliday was coasting on in a delicious half-sleep. In his drowse he was describing sleep in some elaborate new work: *sleep is deeeep releeeeece is peeeeece* he kept dreaming his little random poems and dozingly drifted on.

A few hours later Dr. Lewis had the results of the other tests. "N.P.N.'s 110. You suppose that's all renal, Doctor?"

Dr. Resnick shook his head. "Unquestionably part of it is hypatic. Because, look, his cholesterol is only 104 and the free cholesterol is 52 percent."

"What you think his chances are?"

"Well, analyze it. Bad heart. Liver and kidney damage. Diabetes which can't be adequately controlled in the presence of the gangrene and the toxemia. And with that he's facing surgery within twenty-four hours."

Dr. Lewis whistled. "I'd lay twenty to one against."

Dr. Resnick frowned at him. "That's a little extreme, Lewis. An infusion set immediately. Glucose in saline solution, insulin added to cover the sugar, of course. After 2000 cc's add 500 cc's of whole blood. And start giving him sulfa," Dr. Resnick said over his shoulder as he hurried back to a dozen other urgencies.

Manley Halliday was a little surprised when he saw the infusion set rigged up, but he didn't say anything until he noticed those 500 cc's of whole blood.

"Blood transfusion?" he asked the adolescent in the white uniform. Could *this* be his doctor? Where in hell was old Dr. Wittenberg?

"Right," said Dr. Lewis.

"For diabetes?"

"For your foot."

378

"My *foot?*"

"Right."

Oh, he had almost forgotten. "You mean the frost-bite. Transfusion for frost-bite?"

"It's more than that, fella. You have a" (Lewis remembered how Dr. Resnick would say it) "a serious condition."

"Don't give me generalities, damn it. What is it? Tell me exactly."

He struggled to draw his foot up to see for himself.

"All right. You have gangrene, right foot, first three toes."

Gangrene. The ugliest word in the language. The crazy chasing after the train in the unheated cab. The useless trudge to the ski-jump. The numbness. From *Love on Ice* to frost-bite to gangrene—what was it made the word so horrible?

He made an effort to phrase his question as much like shop talk as possible, something he always took pride in doing with professional men. "So the blood's to get me in condition for amputation? That what Dr. Wittenberg recommended?"

"We haven't been able to get in touch with Dr. Wittenberg since he left the hospital."

Strange. Wittenberg practically lived in her room when Jere had her post-natal repairs. That's what he always had admired about Wittenberg, the conscientiousness, the reliability.

"Then who ordered the operation?"

"The resident, Dr. Resnick. He'll get Dr. Wittenberg in as soon as he can reach him."

"Get me Dr. Resnick."

He waited angrily. What were they trying to do, see how much he could take? God damn them. From the start he had tried to tell them. He was angry with all of them. Gangrene. God, he hated that word. Three of his toes turned black with death.

Dr. Resnick was looking down at him, with eyes that showed a fine intelligence, inspired confidence. He liked Dr. Resnick's face. Dr. Resnick wasn't the sort of man who cut your toes off just for the hell of it. Only where was old Doc Wittenberg? He'd feel even safer with good old Dr. W.

"So how soon will it be, Doctor?"

"Not for twenty-four hours."

"What's the delay?"

After all it was just dead tissue to cut away. Like cutting away dead tissue in a manuscript, leaving what lived intact.

"Liver and kidney aren't functioning too well. Have to stimulate your heart."

Manley Halliday looked up at Dr. Resnick. "What kind of—operative risk am I?"

Dr. Resnick withdrew behind the fuzzy curtain of medical diplomacy. "In twenty-four hours time a much better one than you are now."

"Even chance of—not dying?"

"Oh, we'll do a good deal better than that for you. You can do a lot, these days, in twenty-four hours."

Twenty-four hours. They were gambling on twenty-four hours. How recklessly he had gambled away these last twenty-four years!

Shep was in the room. Shaved at last.

Manley Halliday smiled when he was sure it was Shep. An old friend.

When Shep looked down at the vulnerable figure with one arm attached to the infusion set, he felt that he had never known anyone so well.

From where Manley Halliday lay, Shep loomed bulky and overpowering in his youthful camel-hair wrap-around.

"Well, I really fouled it up this time, baby."

"Manley, listen, I haven't had a chance to tell you, but I finished those chapters on the train last night. They knocked me for a loop. Nobody writing today can touch it. Nobody. It's the old Halliday—but no, it isn't, it's new, sounder . . ."

Ah, pour it in, pour it in, better than insulin, better than blood and glucose.

"Christ, baby, I've got to live." He wasn't sure whether he was saying or thinking. "Give me ten years. That isn't much to ask. Ten years of nothing but work. Never, never let it come second again."

Manley Halliday fell silent.

"But you've got to finish this book." Shep was close to him.

380

"This time you see it all, not just what happened and how it happened but *why*. You never knew *why* before."

If only the light behind his eyes didn't flicker out. In such panic as he had never known before, he said, "Shep, please, I want you to call Ann."

"Ann?"

"Yes. I must've told you. Ann Loeb."

"Ann Loeb, the cutter?"

"Yes, yes. Still get her at the studio. Tell her I said: come."

So that was *Ann*. He couldn't imagine them together. Ann *Loeb*. He had never heard of them even seen them together. He wouldn't have thought her Halliday's kind at all.

Shep called her from the booth in the waiting room. When he had told her the worst of it, she said: "I see. I think I can make the six-o'clock plane. If I don't call you back by eight-thirty your time, tell him I'm on the six o'clock."

Shep tried to tell her a little more of what had happened but she made him feel garrulous the way she cut him short with, "Thank you for calling. I should be at the hospital just before noon."

In the morning when the first visitor was allowed, the nurse told Shep, "He had a very fitful night. He kept calling and calling for somebody named Jerry. Would you have any idea who that could be?"

When he went in to see him, Shep asked, "Manley, they say you kept calling for Jere. Should I phone her? Do you want her to come up?"

Manley Halliday shook his head. "I don't want to see her. Ever again. I want to see Dr. Wittenberg."

When Dr. Wittenberg came in, Manley stared suspiciously. "Dr. Wittenberg? You're not Dr. Wittenberg."

Dr. Wittenberg smiled. "I'm Dr. Wittenberg all right. You must be thinking of my father."

"Oh, isn't he taking care of me?"

"Dad passed away nearly five years ago."

What was this, was *everybody dead*? It shook him badly;

381

Burt Seixas, and now Dr. Wittenberg. He closed his eyes to concentrate. People let go into death when their will wasn't strong enough, didn't they? It was like falling asleep. People could stay up for weeks if they willed it strongly enough. Like marathon dancers. Remember the time he and Jere for a lark—Jere. "Jere."

"There he goes again." The nurse. "Do you think we ought to call her?"

"I don't know. He says he won't see her," Shep whispered.

Manley Halliday didn't think he was going to like this Dr. Wittenberg. This Dr. Wittenberg was telling him, "The moment we undressed you we recognized the gangrene. But there's nothing to worry about. There isn't a better surgeon in the city than Dr. A. A. He's had enormous success with these cases."

He would have felt so much safer with old Dr. Wittenberg. That was silly, of course. Nothing much he could have done from this point on. It was up to surgery now.

A Miss Loeb was outside. So soon? Hadn't he just asked Shep to phone her? O Lord, he was losing track of time. And he needed every one of those twenty-four hours. That doctor had warned him. He couldn't afford to lose any. He had to be a miser of time and keep counting the hours to be sure he didn't lose a single one or give any away; he had given so many away.

"Ann?"

"Yes, Manley."

"Ann, I—took a drink."

"Yes, I know."

"I tried to think about his silly story."

"That's behind you now. Just think ahead to getting well."

"Ann, Shep read my opening chapters. He likes them."

"He should."

"But I took a drink, Ann. I had to. I was so tired, and worried."

"Should you be talking so much? I think they want you to rest."

"But you can stay here, can't you, Ann?"

"Yes, I'll be here. But rest, rest. I want you to get well."

In the waiting room Dr. Wittenberg decided to tell them the truth. The operation was a calculated risk. "He's toxic, feverish.

I wish his heart were better. But he's in the best possible hands. I don't mean to sound too pessimistic."

"Christ, if anything happens I'll feel it's my fault." Shep wanted to confide in Ann. "That champagne on the plane. And not thinking of frost-bite."

"I shouldn't have let him go unless I went with him," Ann said. "And of course I should have warned you about him. But he didn't want anybody to know about us. He's surprisingly old-fashioned about some things." Her strong sense of self-discipline reasserted itself. "But there's no point to all this. I don't think Manley would approve of it either. He knows himself well enough to assume full responsibility."

Miss Gillam, the nurse, came up to Shep. "He's calling for Jere again. Begging us to find her. Don't you think . . ."

Shep: "But every time I asked him . . ."

Ann: "I think she ought to be here."

Her positiveness decided it. Miss Gillam took the number and went to make the call. Shep slipped in to see Manley again. He was groggy with the pre-operative medication.

"Manley."

"Mmmm."

"We're sending for Jere. She should be here soon."

"Who?"

"Jere."

He shook his head again. "No. Won't see. Don' wan' her t' come."

"But the nurse keeps saying . . ."

"Ann. Ann here?"

"Yes, of course."

"When—did—she—come?"

"You talked to her. Remember? You saw her."

"Ann? Ann here?"

The nurse came in with more nembutal.

For Shep it was something of a shock and a disappointment, after all his imagination had done with Manley's description, to see Jere. It was impossible to picture how this dumpy-figured woman with the anachronistic bangs and the obviously touched-up hair ever could have served as the model for Manley's vision, the belle of the ball that had lasted a decade. Her dress was a ridiculous length that had been out of fashion for years. It was weird, seeing this Jere, as if she had been aging in an old wardrobe trunk that hadn't been opened since the Hoover days. Even her gestures and her emotions were out of style, the way she entered with her arms flung out—"Where is he, where is he, my poor baby?"—like the performance of an old melodrama by a third-rate road company.

Fighting for a future, Manley Halliday was plummeting deeper and deeper into the past. He was losing all sense of north from down or why he was going where. *Cease to be whirled about.*

"Jere, Jere," it came out. "Why can't you find her? *Find her.* Jere, Jere, where are you?"

She was bending over him, smeary with tears, her face coming down to his searching.

"Mannie. Mannie. I'm here. I'm right here, darling."

"Jere, Jere." He pitched his voice up into the void. "For God's sake, can't you find her? Can't you find her?"

"Mannie, *Mannie,* look, it's me, your Jere."

He peered upward, hoping to see once more the fabled radiance of Jere Wilder. But all he saw was a strange middle-aged woman whose face was too close to his, pressing down against his mouth, cutting off his breath.

He needed that breath: it was all he had. "Get away. Get away. I want Jere, Jere. Find her for me, someone. Jere, Jere . . ."

Jere withdrew from him her tear-stained, worn-out flapper's face.

"It's no use," she said heavily. "He's too delirious. He doesn't even recognize me."

384

24

It was the waiting, Shep was thinking, always the waiting. They had been waiting for hours. In the cramped corridor of tension intensified by Jere's shrill resentment of Ann Loeb, it seemed like days.

The cold shadows of winter's early twilight were lengthening rapidly when the doctors came down. Everyone stood up. It was unexpectedly formal. All three tried to read the faces of the doctors. Dr. A. A. had thrown a white coat over his operating uniform. His mask still dangled from his neck.

Dr. Wittenberg said, "We hope everything will be all right. I thought you should hear from Dr. A. A. himself as to just how it went."

This was the part the surgeon did not like. They were races apart, Wittenberg and the bedside-manner boys, and the ones like himself who did it with their hands and let others explain. Dr. A. A.'s little talk was a harsh camouflage of his true feelings.

"The surgery went fine. But he suffered a pulmonary embolism immediately afterwards."

Jere began to whimper. Ann bit her lower lip and said, "I see." Shep had to ask: "Will he pull through?"

The surgeon answered, "That has nothing to do with surgery. Depends on how many other—uh—loose clots there are."

Jere cried out, in a way that made Shep and Ann wince, "Tell me the truth, he's going to die, he's going to die!"

Dr. Wittenberg would not look at her directly. "It's hard to say. If another one of those clots breaks off . . ."

Jere's scream was a horrible intrusion on the hospital silence. "Manieeeeee. I can't bear it I can't bear it I can't bear it I can't *bear* it." She wept into her nervous fingers. Her head moved from side to side in a primitive show of grief.

Dr. A. A. turned away. In fifteen minutes he had a gall bladder to remove.

Dr. Wittenberg said to Jere, "He'll be brought down in a little while. You'll have a chance to see him for a moment. There's hope, remember that."

Under the cute bangs, Jere's face was old with grief and confusion.

"Oh, why did everything have to happen to us? Why doesn't anything ever go right any more?"

On those inappropriately trim legs the bloated figure swayed.

Shep hurried to support her. She withdrew with a vacant smile and moved off into some half-lit chamber of her own.

Ann was standing by the window, hard-eyed and as sharply complex as a prism.

Shep came up to her and said, "Ann, some time I'd like to see you and . . ."

"Yes. Some time. Come and talk to me. Tell me everything that happened. Not too soon though. For a while I want to think about it all to myself."

She turned back to the window, to keep it that way.

Shep went wandering around the room, around and around. If only he could make some final sense of this. Was Manley Halliday the playboy of the Western world played out and dragged down in the collapse of a generation? Halliday's Twenties had begun with a wonderful blowing of horns, New Year's Eve, year in year out, getting pleasantly stinko and going home—or to somebody else's home—with somebody else's girl. Waste, of course, a round of empty pleasures (soon *Waste Land* was their label for it), a palace of silver that turns out to be only papier mâché covered with tin foil that peels off in the first real storm. Just the same, just the same. To think even for a moment that your house was built of silver. To be able to romanticize, even for a moment, about the wool you pulled even over your own eyes, while at the same time knowing exactly what you were doing and what it was doing to you, to hold it up to the fluoroscope, diagnose it, find it suffering from high stock pressure, hardening of the material arteries, cirrhosis of the spirit—and predict its death. And then to mourn at the bedside like the doctor who has also been the lover, himself fatally infected. Or was it too simple to blame it on the times? Was Manley

Halliday just a lost soul or was he really a symbol of that feverish age he had glorified and gloried in? A child of his times, more vulnerable to epidemic than other, stronger children? Less cautious about crowds, more careless of infection?

Shaken and upset and somehow driven to find some order in the chaos of these last few, terrible days, Shep was questioning not only his answers but even his questions now. What *were* these eighty-three pages of die-hard talent? Was Manley Halliday to have another chance? And if he managed to fight through, would this be a meaningful victory or just another happy accident? Was failure inevitable and tragic? Or merely the biggest and last of the bad breaks? Would death, like the unfinished manuscript—another broken promise—be the final symbol?

O Christ, maybe he should die and get it over with, Shep's thoughts twisted in a sudden fit of bitterness. Die all at once, before another failure, another fiasco. Die now, so as not to submit himself to further humiliation of the spirit and the flesh. Die now, Shep thought hysterically. Let him be lowered into his grave so that disciples may begin to worship, so that readers may savor the pleasure of rediscovery. Let us bury the remains. Let the Halliday revival begin.

They carried Manley Halliday down to his own bed. It had become his bed, this bed. He stared up into feverish confusion. White lines pinwheeling outward from dark centers. Wider and wider circles flashing and a roaring in his ears, a tri-motor roar, oh he was flying East *Shep let's think THINK we've got to get it before we land* a waitress a waitress but what was he thinking about? Jere wasn't a waitress Jere was that's what he meant an heiress a disinherited heiress well weren't they all? disinherited by choice and taking no for an answer but what a beautiful answer what a beautiful moment never again the grace or the poetry of evasion never again would the myth of the immediate pass for eternal truth O Lord O Jere O genius he called down the endless corridor of time and the echo that came back to him was only the sound of his own breathing and as he listened it sounded familiar yes where had he heard it before *shantih shantih shantih* on the plane recalling it had he known the meaning of *These fragments I have shored against my ruins* mere fragments of might-have-been with too much of the wrong kind of *Datta* and damn little *damyata* suck air *shantih* suck air *shantih* suck air *shantih* then and RED funny he didn't remember *that* in the poem *no* that was life, his brief taste of life, the taste of blood as he spewed it forth and then he thought *wait a minute* (oh time hold still) diabetics don't cough blood not even diabetics with gangrene (ugh!) *this is something else*

a Something choking him that he must FIGHT he jerked convulsively trying to sit up if he could sit up he could stop this thing opening his mouth wide to breathe *breathe* (sucker) of life's sweet air. This couldn't be it not *this* oh you talked about it philosophized about it worried about it even joked and lived with it but it was always *it,* nothing real, nothing that could happen to you, not *you* Manley Halliday half done and half undone, and then O choking on pain and fear This *was* to be all, Be All and End All of human achievement human waste human dreams human failure human being a joke a joke a blood-spitting joke and then remembering everything (*we have exhausted the future all the realities, what will they be tomorrow in comparison with the mirage we have just lived? ring down the curtain I'm certain at present my future just passed*) just as clear as on a screen but even brighter he saw it, like a deadly subtitle they once had offered him fabulous sums to write (oh why do you never see it in time?):

A second chance. That's the delusion. There
never was but one.
                                        SLOW DISSOLVE

But one but one but one but *take it from me, baby, in America nothing fails like success*—(pause)—and then when he thought he could almost laugh he thought he'd die: this is one pause that won't refresh, Mannie old boy—

For one convulsive moment ("Doctor Doctor Wittenberg come at once!") he sat straight up and suddenly, with the power of final sight, he could look forward a lifetime into the future and backward a lifetime into the past. What he saw brought a final stab of pain and when he fell back, at last, he had ceased to be whirled about.

388